A
CONGENIAL
CONSCRIPT

Fergus Doyle

*From its perch on the hinge of fate, our bird of destiny takes
flight and swoops down upon us. We must obey.*

Published by eprint limited

ISBN: 978-1-910179-74-1

A CIP catalogue for this book is available from the National Library

Printed and Bound in Ireland by eprint.ie

Misery acquaints a man with strange bedfellows

(The Tempest)

CONTENTS

*With heartfelt thanks to editor
Eugene Hogan for his steadfast patience.*

A
Congenial
Conscript

THE PROLOGUE

Dawn. The hour of the fox. The four volunteers of the outlawed Irish Republican Army stood, facing the whitewashed farmhouse gable stupefied beyond fear. The eighteen soldiers of Her Majesties Parachute Regiment huddled in groups. Some smoked, others exercised to ward off the bitter nor'easter. The remainder trained their weapons on the four prisoners.

The muffled staccato pumping of helicopter blades pounded the silence of the morning, scattering a murder of crows trashing into the overcast heavens. The craft powered down, rested, and through the sliding side door appeared eight of The British Army's Special Air Services, who trudged across the rising dew; silent...sinister... the business of death cloaked in their movements.

Captain Charles Nicholson was a seasoned career soldier and sometime assassin. He had never encountered any of the four prisoners personally, but immediately identified each of the group. Drawing heavily on a cigarette, he examined the captured cache of Armalite Ar-180 .233 calibre assault rifles with the tip of a polished boot. A sideward shrug beckoned the sergeant in charge of the capture.

"OK Sergeant. Sign them over.....we'll be airlifting to HQ Interrogation." With a stroke of a pen the SAS relieved the regular British army who, some minutes later, bounced down the gravel laneway in the three laden Landrovers and disappeared. Nicholson then cupped one of the captured Russian grenades and ordered his men to move backwards to safety. With a nod, the burst of machine gun fire ripped through flesh and bone like a gravel grinder. Nicholson then lobbed the grenade underhand as one might toss a ball to a child. The explosion belched into a mushroom of inky choking explosive which folded in and out of itself until the wind streaked it away to emptiness.

The morning settles to silence but for the last sounds of the dying and the final constrictions of the limbs which stirred the loose gravel to a mesh of steaming blood and human carnage; a grim and terrifying scene, the background through which weaves eight hundred years of turbulent Irish history.

Three days later, a bitter arctic wind rips down from the hills, ruffling the wreaths which rest on the four hearses that crawl with slow menace up the Falls Road in Belfast. The many thousands of mourners line the pavements. There is omnipresent silence, but for the sweeping rain, the footsteps of the cortège and the slick of the hearses on the wet surface, which amplifies the solemnity of this, the ritual of the martyrs, a protocol of eminent significance within the republican movement.

Martyrs, martyrdom, and the cult of the martyr are as old as taxes and the burning bush. The static nature of mankind's reason is rooted within the seven corners of the deadly sins, thus it follows the powerful oppress the powerless, resulting in conflict, great suffering, wars and death. The cult of martyr exists only within the rituals of the oppressed, heroes being the claimed sacrifice of the oppressor. The martyr, in death, takes precedence over all else such as family grief, and becomes exclusively emblematic of his 'brothers in arms' and their ideology. This takes the form of a quasi 'habeas corpus' which bears testimony to the penultimate sacrifice the movement is prepared to endure. The coffin is draped in the flag he espouses. The martyr will then be laid alongside other same martyrs in a special plot as a display of the movement's solidarity in life and in death. The funeral and the laying to rest are traditional rituals of eminent significance which are used by the movement to yet again express their unyielding defiance, and the implacable certainty of the continuation of the struggle until total victory has been achieved. Thus the cycle of death and more death continues, and seldom ends as can be evidenced by the re-occurrences of history repeating itself over and over again for the same reasons. Many philosophers and theologians alike would say this is the cycle of pain and suffering to which mankind burdens himself, as long as evil prevails over good and the oppressor over the oppressed.

To the other side of the crowded cemetery, British Army observers scrutinize the funeral through high-powered field glasses. The ceremony ends with an oration from an IRA political leader who says that the struggle will continue with greater resolve and that blood will fertilize the soil of a New Ireland. He quotes Patrick Pearse, one of the leaders of the 1916 Rebellion in Dublin, subsequently executed by a British firing squad, who said, referring to another generation of Irish martyrs: "While Ireland holds these graves, Ireland unfree will never be at peace! The crowds of mourners filter out quietly along the narrow curbed pathways of the cemetery. Children gripping the hands of parents, the widows return to fatherless homes and blank futures. The youth and men gaze to the ground, their hearts crushed in loss, their spirits locked in revenge.

There are no mourning politicians or powerful industrialists in this gathering; just the betrayed and impoverished souls of a totalitarian state unique in modern Europe. In the minds of the British Government and the Loyalists of the North of Ireland, the laying to rest of the four was to be a temporary solution to a permanent problem. Instead, it marked the beginning of a series of events which would in time catapult the Irish Republican Movement to the pinnacle of its political and military power in Irish affairs since its very foundation.

ONE YEAR LATER.

The creamy dawn sunshine searched a dour terrain as Brigadier Andrew Cartwright surveyed the morning from his quarters at Aldergrove Airport, Belfast. A gale wind ripped down from the North Sea, swirling 'to and fro' the uncut meadows between the runways. This was the kind of day he knew he would need to be particularly harsh on his men in order to hold their concentration. Outside, the hoarse roars of commands, the stomp of boots and the clash of arms rang in crescendo through the daybreak. The Brigadier continued to primp himself for this Guard of Honour which would in one hour welcome the unpublicized arrival of Royal Air Force One.

Some moments later, as the band of the Royal Grenadiers struck up "Hail Britannia," the Brigadier mock-saluted his image to the full-length mirror so to remember the pose for his first up-close with a Royal. Stepping outside, he was greeted in singular salute by eight of his officers standing rigid to the sides of the idling Landrovers. The convoy sped in the direction of the main terminal and came to a halt to an area in front of the six Lynx helicopters.

On the parade grounds, the six hundred soldiers of H.M.'s Parachute Regiment stood to attention in formations of one hundred men each, their symmetry broken only by the random discharge of steaming exhaling breath along the lines of still profiles. They were young men, mid to late twenties, who for the most part had joined the British Army out of the notion of a career, the perfect sanctuary for the masses of unemployed youths to embark on a blind mission for Queen and country. Beyond this ritual of blind obedience, out there somewhere; ever patient; ever vigilant and infinitely more dedicated, cunning and deadly than any army of occupation, lay in wait The Irish Republican Army.

As Cartwright inspected the last of his men, he noticed a Lynx disappear into the clouds and requested information from his second in command.

"Crossmaglen Sir; suspected IRA small arms fire on the RUC, nothing too serious, sir!'

The Brigadier nodded his head in vague agreement and continued the important agenda of the morning which would be exceptionally thorough. Cartwright liked guard of honour inspections simply because, being a simple soul it was one of the very few duties he could manage without suffocating attacks of inertia. Cartwright was always at least half an hour and sometimes a full hour early. The earlier his arrival, the more unnecessary torture he could perpetrate on his soldiers, and therefore being inwardly a weak man looked forward to these psychotic exertions with unbridled pleasure. The Brigadier snail paced along each line of one hundred fifty men, gloved hands clasped to his fore, commanding officers to his sides and rear. First the momentary stare to the eyes, then the line of examination to the footwear, the leathers, badges, hardware and then the dreaded maroon beret of the regiment. Cartwright was hysterical about the de-pursing and folding of the beret against the forehead and sheared hairline at the back of the neck. The regiment's insignia 'Untrinque Paratus' ('Ready for anything') had to be perfectly placed to the dead centre of the flat folded front of the beret. Then the intimidating stare. Nothing would be said at that moment but each soldier would know the penalty if Cartwright's snail pace changed to that of the dead man's march. He was known numerous times to have finished very large inspections and then from sheer memory to have returned to three, four or whatever number of delinquents, and stared them down with appropriate penances to follow.

Within minutes the helicopter was hovering over the area infamously known as "bandit country" - Crossmaglen in the County Armagh, some sixty miles south of Belfast. The eight Paras sat in readiness as the order to prepare to disembark crackled over the intercom A rattle of magazines and safety catches filled the cramped chopper. The sporadic gunfire below became louder. There were nine very young souls aboard the doomed aircraft.

One and a half miles away, the tube of a shoulder-launched FIM 92 Stinger surface-to-air missile peered out of the lush hedging, the targeting processor scanning and then locking on to the heat emissions of the helicopter's scorching Rolls Royce engine. A hooked finger tightened against a crescent trigger, punching the missile through the protective cover at the forward end of the barrel. The rocket of the thirty pound projectile ignited at a distance of thirty feet, wobbling drunkenly for some moments, straightened and then screamed directly for the aircraft.

A thunderous crack filled the heavens as the warhead sheared through the undercarriage plunging the aircraft of roaring flames into a tilled field, nose down and crumpled into a skeleton of tangled metal except for the tail rudder, which somehow remained intact. Royal Air Force One touched down on runway number two at Aldergrove Airport minutes later.

At 8:35 a.m., The Belfast Telegraph, Northern Ireland's largest newspaper were informed that the Provisional IRA claimed responsibility for the downing of the Lynx and for the future would be concentrating their attention on 'other' military aircraft..

John Thompson was one of the first pressmen on the scene. The narrow road leading to the site of the stricken aircraft was blocked with dozens of official vehicles and British Army. The journalist heard the words "NO PRESS" being shouted in anger. He dumped his car at the nearest spot, and stood on the bonnet from where had a full view of the carnage in the distance. He spotted a break in the thick overgrown ditch and forced himself through.

The field was littered with shards of metal and debris. Becoming more concentrated as he approached nearer, Thompson began scouring the scene through his zoom lens. His stomach heaved as the viewfinder revealed large charred lumps of dying flame inside and about the craft. There was a frenzy of activity as military and forensic personnel began setting up a security barrier of two hundred meters radius. Concentrating on the last portion of the engine nearest the fuselage, he snapped the camera as a dozen soldiers covered the unit with a large black polyethylene sheet. He was ordered to move back at gunpoint and complied immediately. As he picked his path between the furrows a sheared cylindrical object caught his eye. He glanced around, working the camera as fast as he could. Thompson rushed to his car and drove furiously to the tiny city of Armagh. Within the hour, at the newspaper's regional office, he was perusing over the ten by eight inch black and white photos. It was the last series of prints that took precedence. The letters FIM 92 were clearly visible, and underneath in smaller, more official lettering, the word "STINGER" was centred above an etched serial number.

Within moments, Thompson was speaking to Mark Heally, London correspondent of Arms and Ammunition, the Swiss-based catalogue of ARMS AND AMMUNITION. Heally confirmed that the STINGER "is an American shoulder-launched heat-seeking missile, utilizing an electronic tracking processing unit and accurate at distances of up to four miles and altitudes up to 10000 feet"

STINGER missiles got their first true test in battle when they had been supplied by the CIA to the Mujahedeen in Afghanistan, who used them against Russian helicopters and fighter jets. Within six months, the weapon had been directly responsible for tilting the war in favour of the rebel Afghan tribes, eventually causing the Soviets to withdraw in defeat. Later that day, The British Army held a press conference at the Ulster Arms Hotel in the tiny city of Armagh. The statement read thus: "The Lynx helicopter which crashed this morning at approximately 7:40 a.m. in the vicinity of Crossmaglen, Co. Armagh, tragically taking the lives of 9 British soldiers, suffered an explosion in the fuselage just before landing. The Army wishes to take this opportunity to convey its deepest sympathy to the relatives and loved ones of the deceased." John Thompson did not attend that press conference, but instead was busy speaking to every news editor from Fleet Street to Dublin. During the day and into the night, rotary presses churned out the sensational news.

People in high places lock-jammed the security lines of communication between London, Dublin, and Belfast. The Irish Army and the Special Branch combed the border area and rounded up every known IRA sympathizer within hours as did the forces of law and order in Northern Ireland. As bundles of newspapers were hurled from early morning delivery trucks around the British Isles, the Security Forces were conducting a welter of interrogations which some forty eight hours later would reveal absolutely nothing.

The headlines as usual varied in style and sensationalism, the gutter press showing full front page close-ups of the metal plate with the headings:

"IRA Definitely in Possession of Surface to Air Missiles!

"9 Soldiers Die as Missile Blows Out Lynx Army Helicopter!

The London Times and Daily Telegraph were less alarmed:

"IRA Believed to be in Possession of Anti-Aircraft Missiles"

"Lynx Helicopter Crashes, Taking 9 Lives - Speculation About Guided Missile!

Chapter One
A STATE OF AFFAIRS

S ean McCahan drained off his pint of bitter at the Rose and Crown Tavern in Camden Town, North London. The bar was jam packed with the hardy nomads of the construction industry, the hum of conversation and laughter drowning out the evening news on the BBC. The Irishman was bone tired having begun his day's labour at 6:30 that morning erecting concrete shuttering on one of north London's newest sewage pipelines. There exists, no matter what anyone says, a few very special few hours in the week for most working folk the world over which is called Friday. Even the worst of news in some way, no matter how small, is not quite so bad on a Friday.

The Provisional was a native of the County Tyrone in the North of Ireland and one of six children, not unusual for a traditional Catholic family. Like so many volunteers of the Provisional IRA, his initial involvement in the movement was fused out of a hatred of the Unionist and British Army's regime in Ulster, rather than that of any particular political ideology. As with most fanatics, he was a person of extremes. On one hand being possessed of a passionate sympathy for the suffering of the oppressed and on the other a recklessness fired by a consummate loathing of injustice. Now, at 43 years of age, and bent from his years in construction, his face ruddied from exposure to the seasons, his hands leathered from contact with concrete and steel, Sean McCahan was resolved to a declining life of hard work bordering on destitution. He concentrated on the BBC News, which was reporting on the deaths of the four IRA volunteers the previous morning. A British Army spokesman explained that the arrest was under control until one of the prisoners, feigning surrender, produced a hand grenade. There was no choice but to open fire. The usual sequence of predictable statements followed: the Nationalists condemning the incident as cold blooded murder; the Unionists, British Army and British Government proclaiming a victory for law and order and intangible evidence that they were winning the battle with terrorism. McCahan checked himself before his face turned full scowl.

McCahan had been summoned to attend a squad meeting that evening to address the very subject. Within the hour, he was negotiating the aging Ford Escort westward out through the crawling London traffic, the driving rain blurring the windscreen, the onward glaring headlights making driving difficult. It took a full seventy minutes to reach his destination, a small inconspicuous semi-detached house on a quiet tree lined suburban avenue in the suburb of Ealing, West London.

He pulled into the driveway and was greeted at the front door by a small bespectacled man, his features indistinguishable in the dull glare of the yellow porch light. The men made their way in silence up the deep carpeted stairs to a large room which glowed with an open fire and a fine burly set of Victorian tables and chairs. The shadows of the firelight dancing about the dark walls and ceiling concealing the faces of the group.

The bespectacled man sat at the head of the table. Men like Colm McNiff were typical of the IRA's leadership. Middle-aged and jail-hardened, for decades they had felt the scorn of their own people and the failures of their efforts against the British Government. Prior to the escalation of serious violence in the North of Ireland, the IRA for the most part existed only in name, a spent force deserted by a shattering indifference. And then suddenly these forsaken visionaries found themselves at the head of an army of working class youths larger than anything they had ever dreamed of through their years of isolation. The bitterness of the old, of those who had sacrificed everything, leading the recklessness and wrath of the youth created a force with a terrifying potential for destruction.

Now twenty five years into "The Struggle," Colm McNiff had to choose self-delusion over reality. The obstacles of financing 'The Struggle' coupled with the aged methods of securing working capital in the circumstances of a radically changing world were looting the movement of its most trusted volunteers and emissaries. The once gung-ho battles of the rural valleys and the fields, the border roads and the Catholic enclaves of the cities had upgraded to a war fought with hi-tech bombs planted in the North and the cities of England, on targets patronized by British soldiers and politicians.

To McNiff's left sat a younger man, Niall O'Toole. He was one of the many of the working class poor of Belfast, who, like McCahan, had rallied to the movement in the aftermath of the 1969 riots. O'Toole did not come from a distinctly Republican background and had shown little or no interest in Irish affairs till that bloody time in Irish history.

That generation which formed the first volunteers of the Provisionals were typical of young Niall O'Toole. Their leaders, however, in many ways, reflected the rural Catholic conservatism of the movement, in spite of their urban background. O'Toole was a nondescript young man, with a full head of chestnut brown hair. The sunken sinister eyes were still and arresting. His initial involvement in the movement was created out of raging thirst for vengeance, having witnessed the brutality of the British Army during the riots. He had seen his father, a hardworking, simple man, dragged out of his house in the dead of night and beaten mercilessly. O'Toole to his fellow volunteers was affectionately referred to as "the square root" a terminology he used regularly. "Don't worry, that's square rooted, or "I'll square root that" or "Has such and such been square rooted". It was an apt term as his life was almost exclusively made up of a welter of even equations. Following in his father's footsteps O'Toole trained as a motor mechanic. He loved the precision of mechanical engineering but hated the cold damp work pits and the sapping "tugging and dragging" filthy physical work. This was not for young O'Toole. Nearing the end of his training he specialized in carburetion design and within 2 years was well on his way to a very bright future in the research and development of racing carburetion systems. That was that problem "square rooted." O'Toole mostly listened, did not have to "move" often or for anyone, but when he did, he moved with distilled focus and square root finality. The IRA in Belfast chose as a symbol for their organization the mythical phoenix arising out of its ashes. The slogan underneath: "Out of the Ashes of '69 Arose the Provisionals" as if to set them apart from the previous organizations of Irish freedom seekers. There were many reasons why they did so. The appeal of the new movement was strongest in those areas most vulnerable to sectarian attack in the isolated enclaves of North and East Belfast. The Provo's original function was that of a local police and defence force which, as the crises deepened through 1970 and 1971, recruited many members from these groups, eventually absorbing them. And yet, at that time, this would have seemed impossible, for the IRA was tiny, disorganized, discredited; a beleaguered force who in reality existed only in Irish folklore. But then their growth was rapid, the momentum of their violence relentless. The Unionist backlash against a defenceless Catholic minority in the body of the Civil Rights Association together with the intransigence of the British Government who, in their astonishing lack of foresight transposed innocents like Niall O'Toole into walking time-bombs capable of the most terrifying mayhem.

The third person attending that meeting was one Bobby Millar. He was thirty eight years old, well-educated and highly intelligent. Since his early teens Millar was a committed socialist whose politics were by now somewhere to the left of Mao. Born in north Antrim, he was reared in London from the age of twelve, his occupation as a math schoolteacher in Croydon maintained his deep cover for some 10 years without the remotest attention from the security forces. At his own insistence the teacher had not on one single occasion been observed in public association with a subversive. He had never attended a public meeting, protest, parade, funeral, nothing. His real identity was known only to Colm McNiff whom he revered dearly. Millar was 'the' irreplaceable cog in the movements most covert hierarchy, procurement; because....from day one, that's what he was always going to be.

The agenda for this meeting consisted of several topics. General Headquarters in Belfast required to be advised of information regarding a forthcoming assassination on a leading British cabinet minister. The second matter was less simple. In the wake following the murders of four of their leading members the previous morning, Belfast was demanding immediate proposals to escalate the struggle to a new level of ferocity on the British mainland from each of its cells. The arrangements for the assassination were not yet complete. Sean McCahan spent the following twenty minutes outlining his surveillance report in exacting detail. The situation would be relayed verbally to a Belfast businessman, attending an Earls Court trade exhibition the following day. The PIRA (Provisional Irish Republican Army) are not British Telecom's most trusting subscribers.

Bobby Millar was next to address the meeting. He was an articulate person, deliberately slow in his speaking, succinct and purposeful in his submissions and conclusions. He would not speak often, but when he did, he always commanded uninterrupted silence from his listeners. Topics of complexity always seemed trifle when explained by Millar. He was one of those few people gifted with a computer memory and a superior intellect compounded by his mathematical background.

In the genius of his simplicity, he was by far the most far-seeing of the group. The teacher's track record was unblemished in his capacity as a foreign liaison director, responsible for arms purchases from Eastern Europe, the Middle East and the United States. He stood erect and placed both hands to either side of his notepad. He would continue to speak for an hour. The opening statement was conducted in Gaelic, the contents of which dealt at length with the execution of the four volunteers. The identity of the informant had now been established and would be dealt with the following week Miller came to his most important topic of the evening.

The Teacher reached behind his pad and produced photocopies of an article from The New York Times, handing a photo copy to each of the volunteers. The heading read: "U.S. Intensifies Bid to Reclaim Stinger Missiles." The newspaper article was dated July 24, 1993. Pictured was a moustachioed, turbaned man squinting into the sighting aperture of a bazooka-like weapon.

"What's the big revelation?' Colm McNiff grumbled. "We've been trying to get these things for years and every time a complete failure."

"But not from the Afghans! This is no FBI sting operation like the Florida Four- the Mujahedeen are strapped for cash; they need to rebuild after ten years of war with the Soviets and their alienation with the regime in Kabul. I have direct access. The Mujahedeen, these "holy warriors," were given tremendous amounts of material from the CIA, Egypt, Pakistan, and Saudi Arabia. Their war with the Soviets is over for four years now and the CIA want these Stingers returned. The CIA offered multi millions for their return, which was met with silence. This weapon levels the playing field for the one man to hoist it to his shoulder and take down any aircraft or heat omitting machine from miles away with absolute accuracy. For once we could put awesome pressure on the British without necessarily any loss of life and force some serious settlement negotiations. I can tell you this about the Mujahedeen with surety: that it is not so much the money, but to whom they are willing to sell. The preference is for fellow holy warriors. They say the enemy of my enemy is my friend, and who qualifies to the Mujahedeen any more than ourselves?'

The meeting erupted in a welter of questions. How... when... who?'

Millar raised his hands to command attention. "There is only one answer, gentlemen, and one answer only- money, money, and more money. Money, gentlemen, speaks all languages - but it never makes a sound!

Chapter Two

An afternoon fog descended over west London as Howard Bennett pulled a sheet from the delivery end of a six-colour litho press in Browne's Printing Works, located at Bothwell on the city's outskirts. He placed the large sheet of Her Majesty's Insurance Stamps on the light table and proceeded to examine the image for quality. His final day on the job did not in any way deter his concentration.

Why an erstwhile stable, talented person like Bennett should have elected to alter radically the direction of his life was known only to his family and very few close friends.

Bennett completed his apprenticeship having secured a City and Guilds with distinction, and then a H. Dip. in Packaging Science and Paper production. Lucrative job offers came his way through the graphic industry's grapevine. He opted to take up a position with Heidleberg of Germany, the industry's leading press manufacturers. The position involved constant travel throughout Europe and the Middle East, overseeing the installation and quality testing of multi-coloured litho presses. After three years, the novelty had worn off and the travel became just too inconvenient. At that time Bennett was completing the installation and quality control contract for who would become his present employers; Browne's of Bothwell, Government Security Printers. During this installation, he had solved a maze of plant productivity flaws. One month later, Bennett was introduced to the staff of Browne's as the new pressroom manager. That was nine years ago and now Howard Bennett was deflated, bored and tired of that alarm clock ringing in his brain at the crack of dawn day in day out. He would no longer have to endure the expressionless stares of silver spooned directors, and nepotistic management, as he observed them outstrip him year after year in financial merit and corporate stature.

He was drained of the sapping weekly management meetings, of the meaningless cross-examinations and demands for utterly unattainable targets, and most of all their arrogance at the presumption that he would be at their service for the duration of his life in remainder. His eight year marriage was now for the most part an old bag of bones; a full-time juggling act to reserve the time for his moderate drinking and gambling habits.

Like most men, in many ways Dusty Bennett was still very much a boy. A rugby football fanatic, he still played on each Saturday morning with the over thirty team at his second home, the Bothwell Rugby Club. The game was always followed by a clatter of pints of dark ale and an afternoon spent studying the nags in the clubhouse bar with his friends of similar persuasion.

Bennett's weekends all but ended on Saturday evening when stumbling from the taxi around 9pm. The mandatory Sunday visit to his in-laws, an elderly legal couple from St. Albans who had viewed the marriage with clouded reservations in the first place was anything but a labour of love. A boring afternoon of "social tripe and inconsequential nonsense" is how he once described the weekly pilgrimage in one of his futile protestations at his wife's suggestion that he had a duty to be there. His in-laws were ultra conservative, very much in the Spirit of Dunkirk and typical of that 'social class' who placed Margaret Thatcher as the last Lord Protector of all that is 'the great and the good' though she was now long gone and replaced by John Major.

Howard Bennett simply was not a professional, thus in the minds of her parents, positively not suitable marriage material for their only daughter.

"He is destitute of everything that we stand for," her mother would argue on end. "He has absolutely nothing, neither the family nor the education nor the stuff of which the backbone of England is made of- he's a factory worker... a bloody factory worker," she would scream and collapse like some mortally wounded animal.

But true love knows no boundaries and the marriage went ahead almost out of spite on a freezing winter's day at the local Presbyterian Church in St. Albans. His only relatives were comprised of his father and a small group of his life-long friends. Bennett's mother had passed away. The reception was a static affair at the Bothwell Rugby Club, into which Bennett was later coerced to join at the request of Debbie's brother, Charles Hailsham, the club's vice president and one of London's budding socialite divorce lawyers.

At that time, Bennett was supremely fit and one of the better outside centres in the Southern Counties. He was a player's player, a superb all-around athlete fired by the heart of a lion, battlefield cunning and an immovable presumption of success. The players saw in Bennett a freshness of attitude, ability and confidence much the envy of the upper bastions of power in the club.

Training was lifted from one to three sessions per week, which lasted long after the club's mentors had departed for warm firesides. Bothwell won the Southern Cup that year for the first time in their forty year history. But for all his effort, Howard Bennett was frowned upon by the club's hierarchy, a mixed bag of accountants, solicitors and businessmen. His gestures of friendship and were coolly shunned. His inner resentment festered for some three years and exploded when he was refused a seat on the board of team selectors. After the meeting, Charles Hailsham offered Bennett his shallow condolences.

"Tough luck, old boy. Perhaps when you are more accepted in the club. So, going to play with your printing machines again tomorrow, are you?"

Bennett snapped.

"Play with my printing machines- how would you like it if I twisted your head off and played with it like a fucking football, you jerk! The Printer ripped a wicked right hand to Hailsham's solar plexus and followed with a left cross. Two punches, pop - pop, fast as greased lightning, left Hailsham buckled on the floor grasping for his breath, murmuring the words "no more." For the first time in his association with the Hailsham family, his wife and Bothwell Rugby Club, Bennett had now thrown down the gauntlet.

"You listen to me Hailsham and listen good- if you or any of your family or any of your prick cronies here at this club ever trespass on my dignity again I swear to Christ I will leave you in bits and pieces"

That was the end of Bennett's pretentious relationship with both the Hailsham family, the Bothwell Rugby Club and to some extent his wife, who to his surprise sided vigorously with her family in demonstrating disgust at her husband's behaviour. In purely pragmatic terms the only soul to whom he could relate was his father, George Bennett, who was now in the very final stages of terminal cancer.

Bennett stepped into St. James Hospital to see the old man for the last time, anguished in the certainty of losing his link to the only truth in which he found solace. Moments later as he entered the cubicle, an inexplicable force encapsulated him in a place he once was before adulthood forced him to grapple with life's 'so-called realities'. At the bedside, he held his father's hand, the protruding knuckles and joints now hardly supporting the drape of the lifeless draping pallor skin. George Bennett spoke, the purple lips hardly moving across the skeleton teeth. "How are you, son...," the limp hand twitching around Howard's finger. Bennett's father had by way of his wisdom succeeded in preserving his own marriage and his unshakable devotion to his only son, Howard. As the years passed, Bennett could feel himself in increments aligning to the thinking of his father. By now, life's torments had come to full exposed undeniable fruition; the job, the marriage, the bullshit.

Bennett's throat tightened as he felt his father's hand weaken, the eyes now closing, drifting to another place. Bennett knew his father had recognized in him desperation for direction, a truth, a reality in life which he could capture, serve and employ.

George Bennett explained that the tonic of distance was blessedness, the savoir of all things good. His choice to become a fitter in the Merchant Seamen and spend half his life at sea had in its own peculiar way enabled him to cherish and support his loved ones without the sometimes 'trying grind' of daily familiarity. Although an only child, Howard blended well with his schoolmates, especially in that he was able to report weekly on the telephone conversations he would have with his father from some far off port or other, before another departure to the high seas. The young boy would then plot his father's position on the world map pinned to his bedroom wall.

The regular knock on the door with parcels containing stamps, coins, banknotes and other boyhood goodies from all over the world was as regular as clockwork. The quarterly homecoming was an occasion the subject of frantic excitement by both wife and child. And for those few weeks, his mother disrobed her disciplinary gown to see her man. And then the train ride on the old steam puffer, to Southampton or Bristol, where they would wait by the dockside with the kin of other seamen.

It was as he left the hospital that evening, crippled in profound sorrow, and stepped into London's rain, he began to charter his departure from England, the Hailsham family, and the profession and company he had once served so loyally.

Debbie Hailsham Bennett, a former schoolteacher, was plain yet not at all unattractive. Often, over the years, she had longed for the euphoria of the brilliant summer evenings as she strolled along the banks of the River Thames with her tall blonde acquaintance.

Along its banks, the couples strolled as always on summer nights - slowly, hand in hand. Slowly, as if drinking in the bliss of love and blind optimism that will never, however hard one tries, be quite the same again. The open-fronted pubs along the Thames were clattering with chatter and boisterous laughter. The magic of London on an August evening now lost forever; the present a shameful apology to those truly wondrous moments.

She had been so impressed with the ease with which her man flung himself around the cities of Europe and the Far East, commanding a salary much the envy of her fellow graduates. The eccentricity of his capricious sense of humour, the graphic and spontaneous impersonations and the innocence of his boyish appetite for the game of rugby football and the fanaticism with his collection of rare currency notes and bonds.

Most of all, she craved the understanding, the patience and the tenderness which oozed so easily from this wayward schoolboy, qualities which were absent from her shadowed upbringing. She had often sat in his empty flat in Hampstead, pining for his return from some far-off country or other, desperate to suffocate herself in the warmth of his embrace; to feel the strength of his arms cradle her head and upper torso to the expanse of his breast. She would deliberately place her ear to the gentle rhythm of his heartbeat. The lovemaking was voracious then.

Time, familiarity, and the grind of daily life passed on to the pulse of its own inevitable rhythm, like a phantom in the night, invisible, untouchable, tearing away at that which was once the sacredness of man and woman and life... ever patient... pricking and teasing and stabbing at the human weaknesses of the mind and the body and the soul. The phantom awaits its moment of truth, and those moments first come to pass slowly, like the gathering clouds that blot out the sun on a warm summer's morning, full of peace and hope and sanctity.

Bennett longed for those summers also, but as the events of his marriage would pass through his mind, the fleeting joy would turn to resentment and then anger and then to an internal rage. Rage at them all, her and that family of hers.

He had become tired, drained by the daily drudge to satisfy the whims of those who controlled his life; Debbie now distant and cold and calculating. The board of directors at Browne's had succeeded in de-unionising the company, thereby galvanizing its staff in daily fear of the unknown, and the family into which he had

21

inadvertently married, ever aloof, faceless, absent. Life had come to a point where his every action seemed to be for the purpose of winning the acceptance of those around him, or the avoidance of the unpleasant. It was time for a change, a change of life and maybe a change of wife.

The dream of a new life had tormented him over the last few years, a life where he could claim some measurable membership within his own destiny, There was neither logic nor purpose why he should continue to delude himself he would ever transcend his niche in the English caste system. Bennett had fallen in love with the south of Spain since on holidays as a teenager and into his twenties. To combat stress he would allow his mind to wander back over the years to his favourite sanctuary, the Costa Del Sol. He craved the turquoise vastness of the Mediterranean; the tiny snow-speckled villages of the mountains; the fire of the music; the hysteria of the bullfights and the soccer football. But the overriding reason lay in the shredding of his 'master and slave' lifestyle to be replaced with the pursuance of peace and self-determination he believed his birth right. The notion of moving over the last years had festered from wishful thinking to an immovable obsession. But then there was his wife.

During the month of October, Bennett discussed the matter calmly and often with Debbie, who was at all times firmly against any move from the home base or the disruption of her comfortable agenda. Finally, she agreed, albeit on the calculation that the marriage was doomed to failure anyway should things continue status quo. The Managing Director of Browne's, Gordon Fraser, an ex-army man of few words, was indifferent at Bennett handing in his two month notice on the first of November. By the second day of January, Bennett's company car had been returned, and all matters relating to his period of some nine years at Browne's had been finalized. The Printer received his gratuity of twenty thousand Pounds Sterling, which was lodged directly to his bank.

He inspected the last sheet in the same way as he did the first, with his usual standard of care, taking time to make a hairline adjustment on the feed end of the press. Handing over to the night foreman, the Englishman removed his shop coat for the last time and made his way to the board room where he had his final appointment with Fraser. He had taken this route many times before to attend meetings on production strategy, precaution on standards, and least important in his memory, taking instructions on company policy in relation to staff discipline. He could not recall once over the last years returning from the boardroom feeling better or worse. Being a professional on the floor and taking the responsibility where it counted, he was given to swallowing incongruous management waffle with indifference.

Fraser sat one place down from the head of the boardroom table. Bennett, through experience, knew his boss favoured this position for unofficial meetings, but failed to understand the significance. Little was known about Gordon Fraser, although Bennett heard through the grapevine that he had been an army man, responsible for the setting up and running of Her Majesty's Stationery Office in Nairobi before the Mau Mau. Fraser was certainly a print craftsman from a bygone age, probably a letter press operator, printing security material of one sort or another. During Bennett's nine years of association with Fraser, he had detected in the managing director a distinct lack of modern technical expertise. Fraser was prudent enough to recognize the weakness did not escape Bennett's attention from time to time.

Their relationship had been at all times courteous and purely business like. Gordon Fraser was in the classic mould of British Army, his broad shoulders now conceding to the years, his huge gooseberry nose bearing testimony to his love of scotch. Fraser always wore tweeds which complimented his ginger sideburns and full drooping moustache. But behind the jolly exterior gregarious image he peddled, Bennett knew there lay a powerhouse of callous ruthlessness and an insatiable appetite for power which had taken him to the Managing Director's chair eighteen years earlier.

The Printer had on occasion over the last five and a half years felt deep and bitter resentment towards Fraser during a number of internal conflicts, where he could so easily have painfully exposed the Managing Director's lack of modern production knowledge in the company of board members. Dusty Bennett was not disposed to verbal confrontation and had at all times opted to soak up the abuse and get on with the job. He was often to wonder, however, how Fraser could have manipulated such an important position in view of his unimpressive background.

"Ah, Bennett, please sit down," waving the Printer to a chair. "This is indeed a sad day for us all, Bennett. Clearly there is no need to convey to you how distressed the board are at your departure. Unfortunately, as you have been made aware, we are not at liberty to re-employ you due to the security nature of our business. I trust all financial settlements are in order?' Fraser opened his bloated hands momentarily in query.

"Yes, Mr. Fraser, thank you very much." Bennett replied in his usual courteous tone.

Fraser continued, "I have, as I promised you made certain inquiries from retired friends of mine living in Spain. Sadly, they were unable to let me have an objective judgment on commercial prospects down there. They're not in that flow of things, you understand. I am given to understand that the owner of an apartment block where my friend Ron Parkinson resides would be able to guide you on the matter. I understand he is a highly successful operator down there and he is British ex-army. His name is Peter Harris and is due to visit London on this Friday. I have arranged for you to meet him at the Ariel Hotel at Heathrow on Saturday, at about noon. I take it you will attend," the Managing Director stated without any hint of question.

Bennett's boss of nine years stood and offered his hand, his final words untouched by any hint of emotion. "Now, Howard, I must bid you a fond farewell. You do appreciate that I shall not be attending your farewell party at The Brewers."

"I understand," replied Bennett.

Fraser was a man of few and carefully chosen words, and was even more selective with his company. They parted as they had met some nine years ago- courteous, brief, and perhaps a little less frosty on this occasion. Bennett made his way out through the front offices, now empty, and stepped briskly across the empty floodlit car park. For a moment he had forgotten that he no longer had a company car. Suddenly he stopped, and swivelled on his heels to contemplate on the building that he had served so loyally for so long. The passage of events of the last nine years churned through his mind in rapid succession; the corporate games, the favouritism, the self-destructive guilt at his blind obedience to the entire life sapping charade. Now it was over. He became overcome with relief. He felt like a gladiator of the universe who had rid himself of some ever looming predator. But for one brief moment in that rain drenched car park he knew that for the first time in his life he was truly alone. The euphoria of relief was replaced with a blot of uncertainty which disappeared as quickly as it had come. The world was now his oyster and he was going to prise it open. After a brief walk along the High Street he stepped into the warmth of The Brewers Pub, to the applause of his staff.

The sight of Bennett's friends and co-workers, the people with whom he had spent most of his waking hours in the past nine years was a touching, regretful, necessary ritual. Hopefully it might be the best thing that ever happened.

Chapter Three

A RECIPE FOR DISASTER

Peter Harris shook hands with Dusty Bennett in the lounge bar of the Ariel Hotel at Heathrow Airport some three days later. Harris had the appearance of a sun worshiper, the Mediterranean complexion a stark contrast to the London's overcast skies, winter gusts and abundant rain. Harris explained that he had served in the Army in Nairobi in the late Fifties, confessing that he only had a vague recollection of a Gordon Fraser... something to do with security at H.M. Stationery Office. He had been honourably discharged in early 1962, then taking up a job with "Overseas Property Limited" selling Spanish properties in the halcyon days that followed. Harris had never since looked back.

Through a series of lucrative property deals, Harris acquired his first night club in 1970 in Marbella, when property was relatively cheap. He invested the substantial cash flow into land and development, specializing in long term rental and outright purchase to retired ex-British Army. By the middle seventies, Peter Harris, at the age of forty, was well on his way to being a self-made millionaire. He was of blocky build, with a star quality dolphin smile, the dark hairline sharply parted and perfectly trimmed. The fingers were stubby, the nails manicured to pearls. A charcoal double breasted suit clung to the pigeon torso, the broad lapels hand stitched, the base of the arm length exposing the quarter inch of starched white French cuff. Harris was hygenised to surgical standard or 'squeaky clean' as the Americans would phrase it.

Harris struck the Printer as a man of quiet disposition, calm almost to the point of being carefree. He was a highly successful professional in his chosen field and was certainly a man in control of his life, characteristics to which Howard Bennett aspired. The subsequent two hours were spent in explorative cross chat discussing Bennett's forthcoming exile to the south of Spain.

The Ex-Army Man's replies to questions were brisk, direct and thorough. Harris continued to speak with great relish and authority on the subject of purchasing a bar on the Costa Del Sol. He would not be drawn into discussion on any other area of Spain, as this was the only region with which he would be willing to responsibly comment on. This was the hunting ground he had known for the last twenty years and had made him a millionaire. He described the weather prospects month by month and continued to discuss profit margins, the cost of living, and the projection figures for the tourist trade for coming seasons, making particular references to certain hotels and resorts up and down the coast from Malaga to Estopona, south of Marbella.

Taxation, he explained, was almost zero and no comparison was to be drawn between the respective lifestyles of Great Britain and the south of Spain. His singular caution to Bennett was to be careful when purchasing and offered to introduce the printer to a long standing colleague of his, an estate agent specializing in the sale of businesses, a Mr. Jean-Claude Fernandez. Harris explained that over the years he had entrusted him with most of his speculative transactions. Now was the time to buy, when bars are closed for the winter season; that it was possible to buy at a discount and be prepared for the April-October tourist stampede.

By five o'clock, Howard Bennett had booked a one week all in packet vacation to Torremolinos departing Gatwick in three days. Harris called Fernandez and arranged for the estate agent to meet the Bennetts personally at Malaga Airport on their arrival. Howard Dusty Bennett left the Ariel Hotel a contented man, slightly inebriated but drained by euphoric expectation of what the future would hold for him on the Coast. For the first time in his ordered life Howard Bennett felt a compulsion to 'get going'.

Three days later Flight BA 642 touched down at Malaga Airport five minutes late. The aircraft was packed to capacity with retired British making their escape from the damp English weather to nurse complaints of arthritis and rheumatism until midsummer. As the Bennetts disembarked the warm breeze reminded them of one of the many comforts of Mediterranean living. On reaching the arrivals foyer, Bennett assumed the tiny figure carrying a placard bearing the word "Bennett" was Jean-Claude Fernandez.

The Spaniard was most gracious in his introduction disembarked, the warm Spanish breeze bore testimony to one of the comforts of a Mediterranean, bowing slightly to Bennett while shaking his hand, the gesture a little more pronounced when pecking the back of Debbie Bennett's right hand. Introductions complete, he called the lobby car and had the baggage transferred to his white Mercedes, which was conveniently parked outside the automatic sliding doors. The Spaniard engaged in idle conversation as he gunned the convertible out from Malaga airport.

Within fifteen minutes they had passed along the southbound coastal highway into Torremolinos, through the resorts of Monte Mar, La Carauela, and stopping outside the main entrance of the Hotel Los Palmeras at Benalmadena. The Spaniard's attire was noted by Debbie, an open necked bright yellow shirt and white linen pants pressed razor sharp. She disliked bright audacious colours on men; smacked of shallowness, cheapness; lacking in both intellectual and moral fibre. The thought passed, for now. They then entered the white marble-floored foyer, Fernandez gesturing towards the empty cocktail bar and restaurant and settled into the evening's business.

The conversation opened with trivialities such as the flight, the weather, and then broadening into considerations such as Spain's future in the European Common Market. Matters of interest such as medical insurance and other services were discussed in some detail. They agreed to meet next morning and bade their goodbyes.

The following morning Jean-Claude Fernandez was waiting in the lobby as arranged and was accompanied by a tall, stout Englishman who was introduced as one Brian Walker. It soon transpired that Walker had played Rugby League with Halifax in the North of England and had been a substantial scrap metal dealer, operating from Grimsby for some twenty three years. The crux of his business was that of buying up iron ore from the many liquidations and bankruptcies which occurred in the mining and garment industries in the North of England.

Walker Scrap Metal Limited was one of the thousands of small operations destined to suffer the brunt of Thatcher's relentless pursuit of tax dodgers. The ore was shipped at healthy profits in hard foreign currencies to willing buyers throughout Northern Europe and Scandinavia and later the Japanese, who transferred their heavy production to Europe for lack of metal back home. This move discredited European propaganda of the "jap bean can" and was later to seriously dent passenger and commercial vehicle production throughout Europe. Walker threw in the towel when after some forty visits by Her Majesty's Tax Inspectors; he was served a civil process, commanding him to appear at Grimsby Crown Court to defend proceedings seeking an estimated judgment in respect of £175,000. The securing of this judgment would render Walker bankrupt, resulting in the seizure of all the company's equity and assets. Brian Walker maintained that it was simply a Tory ploy to destroy him and hand over his self-made operation to his main competitor, Hull Scrap Metal Ltd. In hindsight, he was proven correct.

Walker was a big man on the field of play and a bigger man off. At all times during those twenty three years, he conducted his relationship with his employees with concern and genuine caring. Throughout the North he was adored, always willing to give a job or listen to a sad story- a true man of his own people. His business acumen was built on simple principles: he was always in a position to buy with hard cash, and always before the dreaded government liquidator would move in and freeze all assets. Long before the "briefcase brigade" could formulate an inventory of disposable assets, the same ore would be shunting its way down a production line in Northern Europe or Scandinavia. Walker did not present himself for defence at Grimsby Crown Court on the questionable advice of his solicitor. He cleaned out his bank account two days previously and was in the Costa Del Sol on the day of that hearing. Brian Walker maintained he was simply on the wrong side of the fence at the wrong time. Being of a gregarious nature he concluded that "all is fair in love and war." The Bennetts immediately took to him.

The company departed from the Los Palmas just before noon for Walker's villa.

"Life is for living," Walker would toast as the alcohol seduced his conscience into the pleasure zones of impaired optimism "and this is the place to live it!

Over the following hours Walker attempted to answer Bennett's questions as best as he knew regarding foreign exchange control, prospective resale, medical insurance, and work permits. Howard Bennett retired early that evening determined to call Jean Claude Fernandez the following morning to tying up a deal before returning London on the following Saturday.

Somewhere, in that dark slumbering part of his reason, he felt he was behaving against his better judgment, but alas like most mortals, chose to ignore his first mind.

Chapter Four

In the tiny village of Arroyo de la Miel, wrested from the mountain behind the resort of Benalmadena, a celestial morning sunshine hushed the village in a vacuum of dead heat. The old men of the village sat shaded and sipped black coffee laced with crude Spanish brandy as their offspring walked and cycled to their local places of toil. How peaceful in this off-season, Bennett pondered... what a wonderful life of quietness, of peace, the serenity of it all, and the azure ocean. A passing flash thought compounded his presence here in that the only things he would miss would be the rugby club and the couple of close friends he had left behind. He had arranged the appointment by telephone from Walker's villa one hour before and left Debbie with Brian and his wife, Pauline. He stepped inside the reception area of Propidad Del Sol, the boiler house of Fernandez's money spinner.

The floor area was finished in shining grey marble tiles, the walls painted in a cooling off-white, broken here and there with a variety of French and Spanish prints framed in chrome. The young receptionist approached Bennett with a broad, warming smile, her huge brown eyes open and eager.

"Buenas dias, Senor."

"Good morning. I have an appointment with Mr. Fernandez."

"Bueno, un momento por favor." The receptionist ushered Bennett through the busy workstations; through the line of desks neatly piled with contracts for sale, property deeds bound in pink ribbon, official papers and correspondence bearing the heading Propidad Del Sol. Several United Kingdom names and addresses did not go unnoticed and brought the Printer further comfort in what was a friendly but busy environment. The tiny figure of Jean Claude Fernandez rose from behind the mahogany oval desk to offer his hand to Bennett.

"Good morning, Mr. Bennett, how are you today... tea or coffee?'

"Coffee sounds good," replied the Printer, "Milk, no sugar."

Fernandez addressed the young woman in a quiet but officious tone. "Por favor, una cafe con leche... una cafe solo." The Spaniard opened the meeting by making idle chit-chat remarking on the weather, and the Britishness of Brian Walker.

"So you wish to purchase a little bar or business?' Fernandez sprung, with matter of fact directness. "Well, I must ask you," taking the first sip of his coffee, "do you have any experience dealing with the public... bar work, you know. If I don't think you can work a bar, I cannot sell it to you."

"Yes... enough, I think," replied the Printer.

"And how much do you wish to spend?' Please quote me the lowest figure," the Spaniard bantered on, offering Bennett a Ducado, the popular black cigarette of Spain, flicking his gold lighter.

"Twenty thousand Sterling," replied Bennett apprehensively. "I just want something very modest- just to make a living"

"Of course," replied Fernandez, picking up the buzzing phone. "Excuse me, Mr. Bennett. I have a call." the Spaniard's brow furrowed.

"Hello?' Yes, hello, Mr. Hurwick. How are you?' Yes, everything is completed. Can you give me the account number of Barclays at Highgate, so I can transfer the money?' Yes... 14-65-80-42... yes. I have got that." Fernandez continued raising his voice to clarify the account number. "Yes, that was a very good deal for you. I told you so, didn't I?' You're welcome... goodbye. See you in April. Adios." Fernandez replaced the receiver softly. Smiling, he gave the phone a confident touch with his forefinger. This gesture did not go unnoticed.

"Good," he quipped.

"Excuse me Mr. Bennett... an English client of mine. Now, I must say that twenty thousand is not a great deal of money to purchase a business, so therefore, we will certainly have to consider a trespasso, which is leasehold, not a freehold; as freeholds are very expensive, and you understand that you therefore have to pay rent to a landlord and will own the trespasso under certain rights and obligations such as maintenance, insurance, property tax and so on. Also, the cash gain of a trespasso will not be as great as that of a freehold if and when you sell." Fernandez concentrated for a few moments in silence. "You understand I must give your case particular attention as you are a friend of Peter Harris, and Peter's contacts in the United Kingdom are the strength upon which my business here continues to expand successfully."

The Printer responded accordingly. "I am indeed grateful for your personal interest, Mr. Fernandez. I can see you have my interest at heart in both the short and long term here."

Fernandez rose from his seat, opening his hands in invitation. "Now," he said," I could show you ten or twelve bars within this price, but I am only prepared to show you two. At all times, of course, you are free to contact other agents and view other properties. New agencies, I can tell you, will sell you anything. The properties I invite you to inspect are long established and possess the essential ingredients of substantial ongoing goodwill. I am the only agent on the coast who will provide you with a set of certified figures, and a profit and loss accounting balance sheet. All other agents sell on location only, which means nothing. However, we can inspect both bars tomorrow. I can pick you up at say, noon?' Does that suit you?'

"Perfect," said Bennett.

Fernandez continued pacing his office confidently. "Now, one bar is open. This bar trades for twelve months a year. The other is closed from November to March. It's a seasonal trade which makes enough to close for the winter. Both have figures and genuine reasons for selling. Alf Tebbit, the owner of "Alf's" is buying a bigger place in Marbella and also a villa. He is tired of the twelve month trade. The other bar is the "Andy Cap." Andy himself is ill. Even so, he took in a small fortune last season on a very healthy profit margin. He has his money made here over the last five years."

"What about living accommodation here?'

"I will take care of that for you, not to worry. Now, Mr. Bennett, if you will excuse me, I shall see you at midday tomorrow."

"Fine, and thank you for a most enjoyable meeting, Mr. Fernandez. Goodbye." The Spaniard accompanied the Englishman to his office door and shook hands vigorously, waving goodbye as Bennett reeled out into the midday sun.

"Howard! It was Brian Walker crossing the busy road, his huge frame dodging the morning traffic. "Coming for a game of golf? I've squared it with the women!

By one o'clock, the pair stood on the first tee of the magnificent Los Rampas golf course, set off the main coastal highway, between Fuengirola and Marbella. Agreeing on the handicap, the men spent the following three and a half hours in golfer's bliss, the Mediterranean breeze cooling the lush course, which was manicured to perfection and not a soul in sight to interrupt Walker's continuous jovial banter. Bennett holed the last stroke of the game of eighteen holes at 4:30. Walker offered his handshake of fair play. Once showered and inside the clubhouse bar Bennett noticed the list of club captains since the club's formation in 1974. He read the name Peter R. Harris, listed opposite the year 1990. Both men settled into pints of Cruzcanpo lager, Walker commencing to outline his future plans in Spain, explaining that he was the owner of a block of eight studio apartments south of Marbella. This investment, he explained, would give him a very tidy income. Walker had considered buying a bar, but reckoned he would drink the place out himself. The conversation continued to evolve around Spain's entry into the European Community in 1986, a subject with which Walker was most familiar, particularly in relation to future growth in manufacture and export, thus high consumer spending would follow. Large numbers of Europeans would come to live with the introduction of open access to free movement of labour and social security benefit entitlements for the vast and growing numbers of retired throughout a unified Europe.

Bennett felt compelled to salute Walker's indefatigable optimism albeit the notion of a utopian Spain or Europe was just too incredulous.

Chapter Five

Afragile Brian Walker stepped into the pool the following morning, his brain pounding from the unknown number of Cruzampo beers he had bolted down the previous evening. The big Northerner couldn't remember the exact number and was long past as much as giving a thought to any such details. Bennett joined him twenty minutes later, not feeling much better. The prospect of viewing both bars had been dampened from the prolonged drinking session the night before at the Las Rampas Golf Club. They had awoken to an empty villa, the wives and having gone shopping from the note on the refrigerator. Walker's car was missing from the driveway, hopefully Pauline had taken it- he couldn't remember driving home- just the occasional blurred flashback of making fair speed up the coast from Fuengirola. Walker submerged himself a dozen times under the heated water. Climbing the ladder gingerly at the deep end, he made for the open shower at the pool side, standing directly under the jet of ice cold water for a couple of minutes. Bennett dreaded the thought but followed likewise out of pride and desperation to quieten the racket in his head. Neither man spoke much. Sudden loud noises and demands on the concentration are obstacles to overcoming these occasional setbacks in the pleasure of alcohol and both Brits laboured in silence.

Fernandez arrived on time, allowed himself a cup of coffee, and left with Bennett some fifteen minutes later, handling the Mercedes expertly down the winding mountain road from the villa. On reaching the beach front highway, he turned right in the direction of Fuengirola. Bennett neglected to mention that both he and Walker had been on the same carriageway in the early hours of that morning. Fernandez opened the first conversation of the day reeling off the description of Alf's Bar, his eyes fixed on the highway.

"The property I am about to show you is in Los Boliches, just one hundred yards before Fuengirola. This is the twelve month trader. You will see that the reason for this is that it is situated in the very centre of a densely populated residential area. The clientele is mostly your own people and some Germans. The opening hours are from midday until midnight from October to February, six days a week. There are two Spanish staff employed during the season. In the off season the bar is run by Alf Jones himself and one part-time. The certified total figure for the trading year to date is... in Sterling, 60000 realising a net margin of 30% and a net profit of around 20,000. I have in my possession the necessary bank lodgement slips, receipts and so on for your consideration, if you wish. Fernandez shifted the Merc into third gear and swung a right turn at Los Boliches, continuing up the side street for just sixty yards and came to a stop outside the packed bar.

Immediately, Bennett noticed the clientele were elderly people. It was a lively place, the dart board in full swing, groups of three and four people sitting around tables chatting and laughing, playing cards and dominoes. The television was pounding out the previous week's title fight. The commentary was in English. First impressions told Bennett that this was a friendly place; good conversation, nice people, a sort of home from home for the retired people who resided in the huge complex of twenty storey apartment blocks immediately contiguous to the premises. Next door there was a busy estate agency specialising in short lets within the various surrounding apartment houses.

Fernandez introduced Alf Jones, the owner, a middle aged Cockney sporting a dated white tee shirt bearing the word "COCAINE," a gold necklace and lots of gold rings. Alf explained he was an ex seaman, having spent thirty years with the Merchant Navy. Jones was single, and made no secret of his indifference to any form of moral compliance.

"I'm pissed off with this joint and all these doddering old geezers," he hissed without making any effort to adjust his loud Cockney volume. The punters who heard him roared laughing. The Cockney turned to Bennett and prodded his finger into the Printer's chest.

"Guess how old I am mate, the truth now!"

"About forty five to fifty." Bennett lied, having given the Cockney his full consideration.

"Am I- fuck! The Londoner recoiled in laughter. "I am sixty two years of age. Now son, have a drink on me, what's it going to be," he offered, elated by the judgment.

"Brandy and ginger ale, please," replied Bennett.

"And yourself, SENOR Fernandez?' emphasizing the word "Senor" distastefully. For a moment Bennett wondered at the reason for the rude sarcasm.

"Scotch please," Fernandez replied, embarrassed.

"Anyway," continued Alf, preparing the drinks, "I want thirty grand Sterling for this joint, son. Now I'm pissed off talking about it. If you wanna buy, you talk to this geezer," nodding at Fernandez, who winced sheepishly. The Cockney cackled on. "And all these old fucks come with it. They can't walk no further than here" Again, everyone overheard. "But you'll get plenty of ol' crumpet in the summer, son, especially them Scandinavian birds!"

The Spaniard then invited the Printer to stroll around the local area. Crossing the road outside and making their way down to the beach, Bennett viewed the deserted shoreline, the relentless rumble of the Mediterranean raising the volume of their voices.

"During the season you cannot get a deck chair here after eleven am," the Spaniard explained. "Perhaps you would like some lunch, then we can return to my office?'

"Splendid," replied Bennett, his mind buoyant with the rhythm of the snow-capped breakers. The men strolled back an alternate route by way of the tiny whitewashed streets, the Spaniard bidding the odd person a gracious Buenas dias through an open half door here and there. Fifteen minutes later, Bennett ran his eye down the extensive menu of the "Restaurant Piscados" in Monte Mar, tucked in a picturesque shaded back street directly behind the bar. The owner, who Fernandez introduced as Luis spoke perfect English.

"My friend, Mr. Bennett was looking at Andy Cap's," Fernandez remarked.

"Good bar. Very, very busy in the summer," said the Restaurateur.

The company fell silent for a moment as the huge frame of Hans Kramer, a local German bar owner darkened the small doorway. As the company settled down, Bennett asked the German about living and running a bar on the coast.

"I own ze Hambeurg Bier Kellar, across the road from Andy's. I only vork from Abril to Zeptember; then I shtop, und go back to Ghermany feur two months feur ze holiday. I come back here for Christmas and to prepare feur ze season. I love ze life here- and plenty of money to enjoy ze off season!

Bennett continued to prod Kramer on the likely turnover at Andy's, the cost of stock and outgoings. The German's answers were explicit to the point of boredom and made sense in relation to the figures which Fernandez had given him. During the return trip, Fernandez explained that Kramer was previously employed on the oil rigs from the Gulf to the North Sea. During his last annual three month round of debauchery in Spain, he impregnated a young Spanish girl. Whilst making his escape at Malaga one foul Saturday night, he was greeted by a reception party of restless Spaniards. Ten days later having wired his wad from Hamburg, he stood in a packed church of St. Catherine the Suffering in Fuengirola muttering the words "I do." Kramer then purchased a business and seemed to be living happily ever after. Actually, he seemed to be an easy-going sort, one of those people who adjusted quite naturally to any set of circumstances which befell him. Bennett liked him even more having heard his amusing story.

Buyer and Agent stepped into the office of Propidad Costa Del Sol as the descending dusk shadowed the narrow streets of Aroyo de la Miel. Fernandez handed Bennett two files bearing the headings: Alf's Bar- Los Boliches and Andy Cap's- Monte Mar. The meeting was brief, Fernandez requesting his client to study both files and let him have further queries or his decision in due course. He was not a man to waste time in small talk. Fernandez drove Bennett back to the villa in seven minutes flat and did not come up the driveway, explaining he had a golf appointment at Los Rampas at 5:45.

The noise of laughter and the splashing of water directed Bennett round to the back patio to find the party relaxing around the pool. Never had he seen Debbie so happy away from the constant shadow of her parents and soaking up the pleasure of genuine down to earth friendship. She was beginning to tan, already attempting the most basic Spanish on Pauline's tutoring. She gauged her words with condescending patience, followed by the iron firmness of a fully wrung counsellor, "I believe you may have been right about this Spanish idea, Howard, but please, I beg of you do not pass one penny to that Spanish agent fellow. Don't let yourself think about it, just don't do it. Take your time, we have some money, look at other bars. Relax, enjoy yourself, God knows you deserve it. Could it be possible that we could really live here?' I have never been so happy. Brian and Pauline have invited us to join them at a cocktail party later this evening, up the mountains in some friends place. Will you come... please?' She purred.

"I can't, Deb," Bennett replied. "I've got a lot of work to do, but you please go... it'll be good for you to get some time away. I really would like to get the business done here as quickly as possible.

"You just will not listen to me...will you? If you go over my head and this thing goes pear shaped because of that agent yoke you can whistle Dixie pal. I told you I don't like him, I don't trust him, and I don't want him involved in our affairs in any way whatsoever...period. These 'agents' are all gangsters down here, can't you see that. Buy a business directly from the owner with some guarantees. Protect us first. I'll say no more."

"First of all, I haven't decided to buy anything yet, Deb. That's my point. I need to be alone to think clearly while I go over these figures. So go, have a good time, everything is under control." She felt the resentment swell in her, but allowed it to pass.

Bennett like so many times in the past just did not get it and took the view his wife simply did not know what she was talking about. It was past midnight when he retired to his bed. From his six hours study of both files he had come to certain conclusions. The format and summary of both sets of accounts were executed by the same accountants insofar as both contained a daily cash book, full inventory of stock and purchases, receipts in respect of petty cash outgoings, rent receipts, electricity, rates, community charges and monthly bank statements and deposit slips. This data was finalized and expressed in the annual profit and loss statement which accompanied each file and signed by the same firm of accountants. Bennett reckoned that bank statements do not tell lies, hence in his mind both statements could be presumed to be a true and correct summary of the business he was about to purchase. He decided against even trying to explain all of this to Debbie, not because she would not understand the details, indeed she had a better education than he, but when she took a dislike to someone he knew her first instincts would be irrecoverable. He would make a decision as to which premises to purchase tomorrow, although his instincts told him it would be "Andy Cap's."

Intermittently, his mind flashed to the fact that he had outlined clearly to Fernandez that he only had 20,000 Pounds to spend and opted to put the question of how the balance would be raised to the back of his mind as he eventually dozed off. The next morning he called Fernandez, impatient to hear his view on the matter of raising the balance.

"We can arrange something, I'm sure, but let's cross that bridge when we come to it. May I assume you have decided on either of the properties?' The Spaniard queried politely and patiently.

"Well, yes. I prefer Andy Cap's, mostly because of the shorter trading year. Perhaps we could discuss it?'

"Yes, but I am playing golf this morning with an English client at Los Rampas. Perhaps you would like to join me later at the bar there, about 3:30 this afternoon. Please do not bring any papers into the club- you understand. In the meantime I can make enquiries about financing the balance."

"Fine. I'll be there at 3:30. Bye."

Brian Walker appeared from the kitchen with a pot of coffee. "Is everything going alright for you, Howard?'

"Yes, fine. I think I have a place- Andy Cap's in Monte Mar. What do you think of it, Brian?'

"Well, I don't frequent that area. It's too busy in the season and in the off season it's closed. It must be okay if they can afford to close half the bloody year," the Northerner replied, trying to be agreeable but really not knowing.

"I was also looking at Alf's in Los Boliches?' Bennett queried.

"That's a great place," replied Walker laughing. "But Alf himself is the life and soul of that business. He's some character- real Cockney."

"I believe he's bought a night club somewhere down around Marbella."

"That'll suit Alf... y'know what I mean. Anyway, you've got to take some chance. I'm sure it'll be okay. You'll make a good publican, Howard. I know it." The reply gave Bennett confidence.

"I've to meet Fernandez at Los Rampas at three-thirty, Brian."

"I'll drop you. I feel a lot better today- hardly any beer last night; just a couple of cocktails. There were ten or twelve people there. We played poker. The women yapped 'til they turned blue. I couldn't wait to get home. I'd have much preferred to have a couple and a chat with you, Howard."

"I'd be grateful, Brian, if you would have a look at these files for me, maybe we'll take a run up to the place before I meet Fernandez?'

"No problem, Howard. We'll go now."

By one o'clock the men had inspected the outside of Andy Cap's, Bennett taking his friend for a stroll down the same route by the beach front. An hour later Walker was slouched on the bar in deep conversation with the proprietor of The Black Lion, one of the few bars which was open, situated some four hundred yards down the strip southwards from Andy Cap's. Brian knew the landlord from having met him at Los Rampas Golf Club, one Martin O'Brien, an Irishman in his early fifties who had made his money sub-contracting in London in the lucrative 1970's. The Irishman rattled on in a lilting brogue.

"Trade at that end of the strip is chock-a-block from March to September, anyone there is okay. We're not half as busy at this end and last year we did okay. Fair enough, I'm open all year, but I've nothing better to do, even though it's not worth my while in the off season. You'll be okay up there- no problem," the crusty Irishman bantered on.

"I know Andy Tebbit well, loves the birds. Nice guy, but an idiot when he got used to the money. I'd say he'll go back to his sister in London for a while, he has his money made- he's single and not growing any younger." Martin O'Brien closed the conversation without showing any real interest or excitement at the prospect of a new neighbour. In the lobby of the Los Rampas, Bennett invited his friend to sit in on the meeting with Fernandez. Walker accepted the invitation with enthusiasm, the Printer having outlined to Brian the entire state of affairs including Fernandez's undertaking to raise the residue of capital.

The Spaniard continued to explain that he had been in touch with Andy Tebbit that morning and his asking price for "Andy Cap's" was 30,000 Sterling. Tebbit would be prepared to accept 18,000 on deposit, and take the balance over a five year period at

13. 5 per cent, three per cent above the current Spanish bank deposit rate. This balance was to be paid directly to his current account at Banco Bilbao. The strength of the business was such that he did not require any guarantee or security on the balance. The purchaser would be free to operate under the existing license until June 31st. The property was debt free including electricity, rent, rates, social security payments, creditors, etc; in fact the bar was fully stocked with spirits, enough to last two months or so in high season.

Fernandez, in closing the meeting, stated that this was the one and final offer, and Tebbit would not be willing to consider any counter offer whatsoever. The Spaniard required a decision on or before the following day at noon, together with a non-refundable holding deposit of not less than 500 Pounds. Fernandez confirmed he was in receipt of another offer in cash on that very day from another English client. Bennett knew he would need cash for stock, a deposit on an apartment and a variety of other miscellaneous outgoings, although he was confident enough of raising capital from his own bank using the house in Belmore Terrace as collateral. The following day he would seal his interest by signing the already prepared contracts and promissory notes, at 11:30 sharp. His only problem now would be breaking the news to his wife.

Debbie sat in the tiny kitchen having listened to her husband's account of the affairs of the day and opened her hands in total disbelief, absolutely furious. 'Well, well, well... Mr. Entrepreneur, Mr. Bennett, you have done it again. You simply have never listened, won't listen now and will never listen to me anyway. I am not going to allow myself to get angry, to wonder why you do this time after time after time, or why you would take the word of a black stranger over mine. What's the point?' But this is the very last straw. I don't care if that yoke hands you a pot of gold, promises you the sun, moon and stars. He is bad, bad, bad. You have chosen to do business with a closet sybarite, a minotaur with that unctuous voice, slimy as a bed of eels, window dressed in all things new, vile and disgusting. No substance, fibre or values of any description or type. A real 'nobody' with 'nothing to loose' and all to gain. As always you choose the way of least resistance and for that my man you will pay as sure as the sun rises tomorrow. I am going to the beach with Pauline and a few friends this evening and we will drink wine...lots of wine. You will give me the housekeeping expenses each week and all will be well until the penny drops and then I think you should know I am gone. Do we understand each other Mr. Big Shot?' Don't even dream of asking me to take any part whatsoever in your self-decreed doom. Both my father and my brother, both whom you loath, would run country miles from that clown. I am sorry, but that's the difference between my upbringing and yours; you want to believe everyone, I believe no one until my suspicions are well proven to be wrong. And if I get a bad feeling about someone for whatever reason, I don't debate the matter; I just rid myself of that feeling by walking away, thank you very much. And I should add it's a pity, because things could have worked out here if you had just listened just for once. But No! So now, we carry on regardless and, believe it or not, I wish you the best of luck, you're going to need an awful lot of it." She left unfettered, calm but resolved that it was only a matter of time.

Bennett stood frozen at the anger and finality of the impasse but nonetheless, as usual persuaded himself against his better judgment in that the undeniable figures were there, along with the volunteered testimony of fellow long established bar owners. Why wait, she will be fine when things get going. But for now he daren't say a word.

Fernandez handed over the keys as a gesture of goodwill, should he wish to browse around his new acquisition before departing for the United Kingdom on Saturday. The formality of signing the contract the next morning took twenty minutes, the remainder of the day lounging around the immediate area and playing pool in The Black Lion.

Howard Bennett felt he was departing from his true home as he stepped down the boarding tunnel of flight BA 764 for Gatwick to the goodbyes of his wife and new friends.

Chapter Six

T he following day Bennett made his rounds, the first being to his bank manager Mr. Peter Hoddle with whom he had applied for a term loan of £5000.00 by telephone that morning. Previous to his departure he had outlined his intentions to the manager, a conservative middle aged Englishman who bade him make contact as soon as the arrangements in Spain were concreted. The Printer didn't anticipate any problems as his credit was five star and had dealt with Hoddle many times in the past. He calculated he would need a term loan of £5000.00 to be on the safe side.

"Everything in order so far, Mr. Hoddle?' Bennett enquired with a ring of anxiety. He hated banks, government offices and appellate confrontations of every description and type. "I'll be back in a few hours then."

"Very well. Everything will be ready for you by then". The Manager wished to be accommodating. The Printer ate a ploughman's lunch and made his way to Hayes Estate Agents placing his house, 35 Belmore Terrace, on the letting market quoting 500 Pounds per month on a one year lease. Bennett signed the standard lease document at the agents that day to avoid having to return and instructing them to collect the rent personally, to deduct their fees and lodge the remainder with his bank. That end of things done, he returned to see the bank manager. The property was snapped up two days later by four air hostesses working from Heathrow Airport just three miles away.

Peter Hoddle turned to the computer display on his desk and wrote on the pad in front of him.

"Now, I shall make the drafts out to... here... one draft to Jean Claude Fernandez and the other to Andrew Tebbit," Hoddle tapped the pad with his fingertips. "What's the reasoning for this, if you don't mind my asking, Mr. Bennett?' the Banker queried. Bennett rattled out the explanation.

"Well, Mr. Hoddle, I understand that the vendors always under-quote the sale price of property in Spain. The reason for this is twofold. One, in Spain the landlord is entitled to fifteen per cent of the sum contained in the contract for sale. The vendor will save fifteen per cent and secondly, the purchaser, being liable for stamp duty at the rate of ten per cent will pay less." Bennett opened his palms and continued uninterrupted. "Also both parties will realize further savings by reason of the solicitors being only at liberty to charge a fee of five per cent, on the consideration quoted within the contract. As we have no foreign exchange control at this level here in England it will be comparatively simple for Fernandez to cash the draft and pass over the cash to Tebbit, having stopped his fees etcetera. So it makes good sense."

Hoddle allowed himself a wry smile and sarcastic snigger. "Well, I have to agree. One certainly would not get away with such an arrangement here, Mr. Bennett" The Manager recited his instructions coldly into the intercom. Ten minutes later both drafts were placed on the desk in front of Hoddle. "Well, Mr. Bennett, I think that concludes matters for the moment" handing the Printer the drafts placed in a plain white envelope.

"Well, goodbye Mr. Hoddle, and thank you indeed for everything."

"You're very welcome. Mr. Bennett. The best of luck to you, keep in touch" They shook hands and parted.

The Printer treated himself to a supper of prawn cocktail and a fillet steak, washed down with a bottle of Cambertann '79. As a matter of courtesy, he called Gordon Fraser at Browne's to thank him for the contact, and the pending purchase. Fraser being a conservative person thought the purchase a little hasty, but retracted the remark by way of commenting on the sluggishness of the British legal profession and the general ineptness of politicians and industry.

"God help us when these Spanish chaps get going in the Common Market," he quipped, bidding his ex-manager good luck and thanking him for taking the time to call. The Printer walked over to Hayes High Street to Costa Holidays and booked a one way flight to Malaga, departing on Friday from Heathrow. Having finished his business there, Bennett confirmed his appointment for the following day at the Spanish Embassy on Great Portland Street, just off Oxford Circus. He then made his way home to 35 Belmore Terrace.

The phone rang out of the silence as Bennett settled down to read through the magazine "Spanish Living" he had purchased at the newsagents on the corner.

"Hello, Mister Howard Bennett?'

"Yes, who's calling?'

"Please excuse me for having called you at home. I am a client of Jean Claude Fernandez- I have just sold my bar down there in Fuengirola, and I have been looking for another one preferably up in Monte Mar. My name is Paul Romeril. Fernandez told me that Andy Cap's is sold to you. Can I ask if that is so, Mr. Bennett?'

"Well, yes, Mr. Romeril. We're closing the deal on Monday," the Printer answered, somewhat puzzled and annoyed at the disarming query.

"Yes, the contract was signed last Thursday or Friday. To be quite honest, Mr. Romeril, think this call is a little high-handed. Where did you get my number, and precisely what do you want?'

"Oh, please forgive me, Mr. Bennett. I should have explained to you. I am an old friend of Andrew Tebbit, the owner. I didn't know he was in hospital. I put my place on the market four weeks ago, and it sold within ten days, much quicker than I thought. I have had my eye on Andy Cap's for a while now, as it's only a seven month trade. It's a great bar. I attempted to contact Andrew about it, but they would not let me see him in hospital. The nurse relayed to me if I was interested in the bar, I should get in touch with Fernandez, which I did on Monday when I discovered the place was sold to you. I pleaded with Jean-Claude for your phone number, which he refused to give me until he got your permission.

He told me he tried to call you a dozen times over the last couple of days, but said there was no answer. Eventually, I got the number from him."

"Really... this is all very new to me. What's the nature of your proposition, Mr. Romeril?' Bennett inquired, dumbfounded and mystified.

"I want to buy Andy Cap's from you. I know the bar for four years now, and I am prepared to offer you 500 Pounds cash to opt out of the purchase. Unfortunately, my timing in selling my own place and trying to purchase a good bar before the season starts was bad, to say the least, then Andy of course hit the bottle and is in hospital as you know, whereby I could not even contact him to find out what the situation was. Anyway, do you have any interest in my offer, Mr. Bennett?'

"Well, I'm afraid not, even if I was, your offer would be any use to me as I already have a non-refundable deposit of 500 on the place at the moment and further expenses." The phone went silent. "Hello... Mr. Romeril, are you still there?"

"Okay, then. I'll make it 1500. That's letting you out with a free holiday and something for your pocket. That's my final offer. The tone lost its pretentiousness. "Could you think about my offer and call me by this time tomorrow if you have any interest"

"Sorry, Mr. Romeril, but I am declining your offer and now I need to finish this call. Good luck with your endeavours"

Bennett re cradled the receiver and thought the call a 'strange one', pulling a couple of cans of lager from the refrigerator and settled back into his magazine.

Chapter Seven

Great Portland Street had always been an area of London of intrigue to Bennett. The elegant buildings lavishly furnished, flying the flag of one far off place or another. Without checking the bronze name plate, he ascended the granite steps over which flew the Spanish flag. Inside he was greeted by a strikingly attractive Spanish receptionist who directed him to a room on the first floor.

Bennett filled out an application form for residency and signed an undertaking that he would not seek gainful employment until his work permit came through. The clerk took photocopies of all his documents and returned the originals.

Leaving the embassy, he made his way to the end of Oxford Street, turning left down Park Lane and over to Hyde Park Corner into Knightsbridge and down into Sloan Square. This would probably be the last time in a long while he would visit his friend Ken Samuels, a rare coin and currency dealer on Sloan Street, where an exhibition of mid-nineteenth century Chinese notes and coins was about to commence.

Bennett had been collecting notes, coins and bonds since his schooldays. His late father, a merchant seaman, stirred the boy's interest by regularly returning home with a variety of small value notes and coins from ports of the oceans. The Printer had become a personal friend of Ken Samuels over the years, having first made his acquaintance when he had won a prize for a thesis during his final year at the London School of Printing. It was a treatise on Chinese currency printing techniques from the inception of paper money in the early twelfth century.

Bennett had formed and chaired the Hayes Society of Banknote Collectors for three full years after his return from Germany, but found the position too demanding on his domestic responsibilities. He continued to attend seminars from time to time, particularly when a collector of any importance would be invited to speak.

Ken Samuels was saddened at Bennett breaking the news of his departure and promised to forward him the monthly Hayes Society newsletter. Samuels conducted the affairs of his life as if he did not have a worry in the world. A short plump balding man of dignified bearing in his mid-fifties, he had taken over the brokerage of W. H. Smith: Coin, Note, and Rare Bond Dealer from his stepfather, now long retired in his summer cottage snuggled on the south coast of England between Brighton and Hove. Along with his hand tailored double-breasted suits which complimented Samuels trusting smile which could light up the gloomiest of life's corners, Bennett always thought of him as a complete and contented person who had filed the art of living to a razor's edge, an aspiration to which the printer had yet to attain. As with all persons who came in contact with Ken Samuels, Bennett treated him with the uttermost reverence. On so many occasions he had sat bewildered at the volumes of hard, current and past information this man could unravel at will on a bottomless reservoir of topics. Ken Samuels was a person who had an unyielding mental knot around the expanse of the volatile world of which he was an intricate part. There was one word with which to describe Ken Samuels, and that was the word 'solid'

The exhibition proved unusually interesting and the pair adjourned to The Sloan Arms for a chat and a final farewell. The Printer had never forgotten that Ken Samuels had once offered him a position of employment; it was an offer that Bennett had always equated with retirement or an unexpected change in circumstances.

Chapter Eight

T he flight Captain announced touchdown in twenty minutes at Malaga Airport. The Printer had left a rain-swept London behind him. The sight of the scorching wastes of central Spain whetted his appetite for the rolling thunder of the Mediterranean. He had called his wife on leaving Ken Samuels and was pleased to find her acceptably civil enough in their new surroundings. A rugby colleague had driven Howard to Heathrow, the Printer being unable to manage the six large suitcases by himself. Debbie, Walker and Pauline met him in arrivals, beaming, sun drenched and spirited at his return. The party made their exit from the arrivals lounge without as much as a scintilla of a thought that there might lurk in their futures anything other than the high-spiritedness of those moments. The weekend was spent lounging about the pool, the men getting in a couple of rounds of golf up at Los Rampas.

Jean-Claude Fernandez telephoned and made his apologies for having given Paul Romeril Bennett's phone number, explaining he was pestering him to a point that he really had little option, particularly as he had explained he had some sort of a proposition for the Englishman. Bennett dismissed Fernandez further attempts by accepting the apology graciously.

The matter of transferring the title was surprisingly short and simple. Senor Ortega, Fernandez' solicitor and occasional partner, explained that the deed was just an ordinary lease more or less the same as any lease in the United Kingdom. The documents were in Spanish, but Ortega assured Bennett that all matters were in order. However, a further document had to be signed recognizing the fact that promissory notes had been executed by the purchaser, and further recognizing that the title deeds would not be witnessed by a Public Land Registry Lawyer until the notes were honoured.

On handing over the bank drafts, plus stamp duty and one month's rent in advance, Howard Bennett became the proud owner of Andy Cap's Bar of Monte Mar, on the majestic Costa Del Sol. The Bennetts spent the remainder of the evening viewing apartments in and around the vicinity of the bar from the letting list that Fernandez had handed him earlier. By nightfall they had decided to rent a modest one bedroom apartment in Edifico Saggitario, just five minutes from Andy Cap's. He would tie up the odds and ends with Fernandez the next day.

Chapter Nine

Two weeks after the opening it was obvious that the printer had made the worst decision of his entire life. Ask any failed sole trader why the unthinkable has happened and the tendency is, in order to sidestep blame, to provide a litany of unforeseen unfortunate events wholly outside the trader's control. Bennett's single absolute conviction just 10 weeks later was, a root and branch exception to this convenient trend in bankruptcy explanations. The entire sordid business was the handiwork of a contemptuous cabal, disposed against the workings of chance, home baked entirely from local ingredients of the most profound psychopathic evil. It was a punishing ten weeks later that an aged Howard Bennett pored over a record of turnover figures since the re-opening of Andy Cap's, and on this day those figures made calamitous reading. Four weeks after opening it was plain to see that not alone would the venture fail within a very short period of time but as a consequence Bennett would be homeless, broke, jobless and probably wifeless. The pressure had been sudden and relentless since just after the opening night. In attendance were the Walkers, the staff of the travel agents from upstairs, Byrne the Irishman from The Black Lion and his wife, a few local journalists and twenty or so elderly retired English residents. At most, Bennett assessed the business would only be capable of taking in barely enough to turn a profit. The total expected turnover was nowhere near the figures repeatedly ringing into his head provided by Senor Fernandez's worthless paper.

Bennett had spent a small fortune restocking. The bar had enough spirits on the shelves for six weeks. Fernandez had suggested a combination waiter, bartender, assistant manager who was available to allow Bennett a margin of freedom in establishing himself as a host and to serve as a translating liaison with local suppliers. Pepe Montez was introduced after a litany of favourable recommendations.

The on-going goodwill with the travel agents never materialized. Bennett was told on inquiring that they had changed their plans regarding champagne welcoming parties and other entertainment arrangements. Bennett was crestfallen and suspicious, although he did not take issue on the matter with Fernandez.

Then there was the hard nuts to be cracked: the bar stock, the food, the utilities, the sundry items that seem so insignificant until their necessity becomes apparent and become a real expense; the wages and social security payments for Pepe Montez, who had to be let go after five weeks, Bennett's living expenses, the monthly rent, utilities, and community charges for the apartment, and of course the looming first promissory note that would become due in little over one month, now as sobering as the sword of Damocles; these to be paid with with one quarter of the expected gross.

Brian Walker arrived into the bar late one evening. He too was shattered from worry and constant heavy drinking. Bennett pulled him his usual pint of Cruzcanpo lager.

"What's the matter, Brian?' Bennett queried softly, aware of the strain on the big man's countenance.

"I don't know, I just don't know, Howard." This was the first time that Bennett heard the big man use language. Walker blundered on. "That Fernandez has withheld the last month's rent from my apartments in Estepona in lieu of legal fees to get the fucking title which I've already paid for. I don't like that man Howard ... it's only dawning on me now. I think he's a fucking con man." The printer allowed Walker to continue.

"I'd like to twist his head off- fucking twist it to the left and then twist it to the right and then twist the fucker right off," Walker boomed and slammed the emptied pint glass on the bar.

"You're losing control of yourself, Brian. Take it easy. There must be some explanation," Bennett replied urgently, gripping Walker's shoulder.

"There is," Walker bellowed, burying his head in his hands in despair. "I've been fucking conned by him! Conned! Bennett stepped to the outside of the bar.

"Brian, I'm worried myself. This place is doing nothing. I didn't say anything about it to Fernandez yet, it's a bit early, is it not?' The season doesn't start until the first of next month. We should be taking in somewhere near to the averages of other bars, but 25% has been the top whack so far. I'm worried- even the wife is beginning to notice. I don't want to get her wound up and at my throat at the moment."

"Look, Brian, don't drink anymore, you might do something stupid. Go back to the villa. I'll follow you up at ten or so. I've called Pepe to mind the bar tonight. There won't be much doing anyway; we can talk things over, okay?'

"Okay, Howard. Thanks. I'd really appreciate that." Brian left Andy Cap's as Howard Bennett had never seen him before, a very disturbed and potentially dangerous man.

At 9:15 the same evening, the empty bar was visited by two men- plainclothes Guardia Civil flashing their shields.

"We would like to inspect your permiso de trabajo, you're work permit and opening license, please?' Bennett offered a drink, which they refused, and attempted to explain that his work permit had not come through from Madrid, not that it was all that important as he was in business for himself. He then presented the opening license, which was still current until the 1st of June. The policemen took lengthy notes and left half an hour later.

Bennett distrusted them. He wondered at the sudden efficiency of the Spanish Police, particularly at night for matters that could easily be attended to by day or mail. He hailed a cab for Walker's villa. Entering the villa by the back way, Bennett was greeted by Brian, as Pauline and Debbie sat in silence offering a faint welcome. Bennett chose not to mention the police visit earlier.

"Well, then. What's new?' Bennett gingerly broke the silence.

"We're broke," Pauline shuttered through the tears.

"How so?" The Printer feigned ignorance.

"You know damn well what I told you, you moron street idiot." Debbie hissed without apology.

"Sorry, but I'm only trying to help if I can."

"You're not kidding, the best is yet to come for us, believe me" Debbie added, calm, collected, prepared.

Anger was festering in Bennett. "Will somebody tell me what the hell is going on?'

"I'll tell you," volunteered Walker lifting a cigarette and filling his lungs, steadying his nerves for the litany of disaster he was about to unfold.

"You know that I had to get out of the United Kingdom. They probably have issued a warrant there for my arrest for tax evasion by now. When I got down here on a two week packet holiday, we were introduced to Fernandez by a guy called Peter Harris, who we met at the Los Rampas Golf Club. We bought the villa through Fernandez, and paid in cash. Then we bought the eight apartments at Estapona for what he said was a discount price. Again, we paid in cash. This block of eight two-bed apartments at the time of purchase had eight tenants on one year leases. Fernandez told us the previous owner was ill in the UK. These leases were due for renewal in five days.

The reason I bought was because they were supposed to be on year round lettings, at decent rents. Also, before I bought, Fernandez presented me with letters from six of the eight tenants informing me that it would be their intention to renew their leases. Actually, two of them offered to purchase their apartments outright. Ortega, Fernandez's solicitor said the title could not be finalized until we satisfied the Spanish Central Bank that all of the rules of foreign exchange control had been adhered to. I briefed him on my previous career in the United Kingdom. He said he would sort it out himself- no problem. I believed him on the word of a few of his so-called clients who said they had much of the same problem.

Then today, he told me that only two of the existing tenants would be renewing their leases, that he would be holding last month's rent for fees involved in sorting out the title. I am now absolutely convinced that the whole thing was a big scam. The money is gone; the money for the apartments, for this place and another fortune just squandered on furniture, the car and a good time, believing all was well. I have no title to either property. I'm in no doubt whatsoever that there were never any bona fide tenants in that building with the exception of the two families who have been there all year round for the last three years- the other six tenants were just set up, planted there when I was viewing for a couple of weeks. The letters of offer to purchase and renew leases were just trumped up to instil confidence in the property.

Also, when I told him the details about the money I got out of the United Kingdom. God, I was drinking and I let it slip out in the form of a brag. He decided to use that as a device to withhold my deeds. The so-called clients who had supposedly the same problem with Foreign Exchange Control were just set ups as well. I haven't seen them since.

So, he's got the deeds, all my money- the properties and he's also got me over a barrel insofar as he can drop the word to the law about hot money anytime and that's me fucked-there is not a thing I can do, not a fucking thing." Brian sat wearily on the sofa and dropped his head in his hands in despair. "Now there is nothing except the rents from the two families, which is piss. There's not a prayer of re-letting these flats now at this time of the year, not a prayer." There followed a tense silence.

"I hope to God he hasn't done the same to you and Debbie." Pauline spoke. "I'd have a very careful look at the entire affair now if I were you, before it's too late, if it's not too late already."

"It is too late, you can rest assured it is long too late" Debbie commented matter of fact, arms folded, calm as a court copper.

The printer shuddered as a strange terrifying reality suddenly overtook him. At first the reality thrashed through his mind in a microsecond, like a bolt of high voltage electricity. He rested his hand on the wall to support himself. The second phase of the attack passed more slowly, the reality sinking to the core of his reason as the big picture fell into place piece by piece. The phone call in England from Paul Romeril offering to buy him out... Peter Harris... Byrne, the Irishman... Luiz, the restaurant owner... Hans Kramer, the German... the bank drafts... the withholding of the title... the promissory notes... the accounts. The company sat down to spend the next five hours in heavy open discussion on Senor Jean Claude Fernandez. The Bennetts spent the night at the villa, the printer decimated and humiliated, Debbie completely unruffled, resolute but inwardly planning 'where to now'

Bennett slept three parts awake that night. In one uneasy dream he stood numbly while the inside of a huge flexible pipe was forming in the distance, approaching him, growing taller... closer. The observation turned to helplessness as the towering tunnel swallowed him, sloshing him about in a shrinking conduit for a sickening finite moment. As with all nightmares he awoke as a bullet from a gun, drowning in sweat; terrorized but saved.

He opened the bar the next day showing the first real signs of a nervous breakdown. Most people stupidly take breakdowns of this sort on their feet and refuse to face facts until it is too late. Behind the door Bennett picked up the officious envelope bearing the stamp of the Guardia Civil. It was a notice demanding he present himself at Torremolinos Police station at 11am that very morning.

The Englishman arrived promptly and waited for three hours until the police officer dealing with the case arrived. He was to wait a further hour until the policeman would see him at two o'clock in the afternoon. Outside the filthy reception area, the midday sun melted the deserted pavements. It was high noon...Siesta.

"I have this notice from you," Bennett opened.

"You need to pay for some fines, Senor Bennett."

"What fines?' I don't know about any fines," the Printer gasped.

"For the work permit- you know you can be deported for working without a permit, but as this is your first offence you will only be fined and the bar will not be closed. "

"What- closed?' I have it under good authority that the work permit was a mere formality in my case. It's my bar. I am not an employee!

"Your source of authority is mistaken, Senor Bennett."

Bennett muttered the words "Fernandez and his crew again" under his breath. "How much is the fine?'

"Fifty thousand pesetas- and of course you cannot work again until you have your permit, which may now be delayed," the policeman answered indifferently. "Now the other matter, the opening license- this is a very serious offence not to have an opening license."

"But I have an opening license," the Printer snapped.

"No you don't, Senor. The current license is in the name of Senor Tebbit; before you can use this license you must deposit the cost of the new license which is past due in at the Town Hall in Torremolinos."

"And how much is that?' Bennett queried.

"Five hundred thousand pesetas, plus a fine for late payment"

"And?''

"Two hundred fifty thousand," the policeman replied disinterested, his head now bowed behind the desktop.

Bennett hissed, "May I ask which court decided all these fines and when were these cases heard?'

"These fines are already determined by statute and there is no appeal. You must pay two weeks from today," the Guardia rambled on disinterested.

"And what if I cannot pay right now...what if I need time?'

"We will put an embargo on the bar and will close it the next day."

"For how long?' Bennett thought he was detecting a sneer forming on the Guardia's face.

"Until you pay, but if you don't pay in two weeks, there is a further fine for late payment- so it is better for you to pay."

"What then?'

"The property is returned to the owner; usually that is the end of the matter".

Howard Bennett reeled out into the blinding midday sun and stumbled down to the waterfront, his body dripping in stinging sweat. He slumped over the promenade rail to take his view of the rolling Mediterranean he once so loved. He threw his eyes to face the cloudless heavens allowing the sun to penetrate his closing eyelids in a kaleidoscope of changing colour. Then he opened the bloodshot eyes; the cadaverous face now grey as a channel fog hollowed with rage; like a man hell bent on an orgy of destruction. He saw his life over, crushed to ashes and dust, the resentment in Debbie's eyes and the plight of the Walkers, and then the handsome, wealthy profiles of Harris and Fernandez; the confident surfing vibrations of their voices. The lilting sway of the ocean calmed him momentarily and then he was back in reality as an old walrus-moustached Spaniard bid him good day and crunched on down the rough sand in the direction of the fishing pier. The Printer chiselled his face in sadness, and returned the compliment the best he could muster as the solitary figure stepped out of earshot. A burning tear slid along the crevice of his nose as he realized the simple gesture was the only decent thing that had happened to him for longer he cared remember.

That good stuff would have to come later. It was time to deal with Fernandez and the Spanish legal system. He grappled with the figures as he slouched up the deserted backstreets drifting into the shade to catch a cab. He ran the figures through his mind again as he tried to subrogate his ever revolving tortures.

"Let's see... 50 thousand for the work permit, 250 thousand for failing to lodge for the license, plus 500 thousand to lodge for the license- my God, that's 4,000 Pounds. I haven't even got that, and the stock and promissory notes are due on Friday! On paying the driver, Bennett stopped to observe himself in a plate glass window. He sniggered crazed eyed to the reflection, like some fence jumped psycho as the homeward traffic of Torremolinos sped behind him in the evening dusk.

Chapter Ten

Brian Walker had been pacing his living room like a caged animal for hours. Unable to sleep, he had stayed up all night thinking and drinking heavily; by now he was a man drifting within a rudderless violent delirium. As the alcohol and wrath stultified the brain he would gaze aimlessly to the ceiling to allow the scenes of mayhem brewing in his mind to form against a blank backdrop.

The imagination climaxed as he quaffed down another three fingers of neat scotch from the near drained bottle, and pointing to his image in the full length mirror, the voice lowered to a near whisper, as the next brainwave presented itself from some black repository, the distorted words being sieved laboriously through the anesthetized senses.

"I'll grab him by the hair and twist his head round a couple of times, and then I'll pull the fucker clean off... just like pullin a cork from a bottle... no... that's not wha I'm really gonna do... whad I'm really goin to do's this... I'm goin' down to the petrol station in five minutes 'n I'm buyin' a gallon of premium. Then I'm goin' to 'is office 'n I'm goin' t' fuck th' juice right over 'im... but none's gonna get on 'is cheque book... then he writes th' cheque... which... we cash round at 'is bank... then me 'n Howard '... 'n th' women's outta here tonight 'n that's how it's gonna be!

Walker searched deep in both pocket for the petrol money, the dangling hands rummaging aimlessly, the huge beer gut protruding above the buckling legs, the flabby jowls resting thankfully on his collarbone as he swayed back and forth. He turned his crazed eyes to the door, and although his sights were in that direction the legs spiralled off in an angular motion crashing into the wall unit. With prolonged breathlessness and physical difficulty he got to his feet, he grappled with the lock and reeled on out into the glaring sunlight. All attempts by Pauline to pacify the big Northerner had failed.

"Leave this to me; just leave this to me," he bellowed. She had seen him like this on a couple of occasions during their ten year marriage. Once, when the owner of Palard's Mill in Bradford had double sold scrap which Walker had already paid for in advance, he had stalked John Palard for three full days and nights, eventually tracking him down in a nightclub in Blackpool. Within minutes, Walker had removed four of his teeth, smashed his jaw, and demolished half the right side of his ribcage. The matter of damages to Palard and the nightclub were settled out of court. Brian Walker never regretted things like that. Besides, he later sued for conversion and breach of contract.

The Northerner careened down the mountain road like a roller coaster car off its track. The petrol idea vanished with the problem of keeping the car on the road. Curb-jumping the vehicle dangerously up onto the footpath, he threw open the car door with such force that it rebounded, smacking him in the leg and face. He lunged up the path, through the aluminium entrance, and marched straight through the startled pool of typists, kicking in the Spaniard's office door. Fernandez sat behind his desk, telephone in hand. Before he could utter any protest, Walker pinned the Spaniard to the filing cabinet, yanked the phone away and looped the cord tight around his neck- the caller's voice still evident at the other end of the line.

"You little piece of shit, you give me my fucking money now! Walker screamed, burying his forehead on the bridge of the Spaniard's nose, causing immediate heavy bleeding. The Spaniard cringed in terror, unable to speak, choking for his breath, his eyes ballooning from their sockets as Walker with brute strength suspended the torso from the floor and at the top of his alcoholic stupor roared his commands... "Now open that safe quick... and I swear to you, one funny move out of you and on my father's grave, I'll fucking kill you stone fucking dead!

Half an hour after Walker left with the cheque, twelve Guardia Civil arrived at the office in full riot gear. Fernandez filed charges of robbery, trespass, grievous assault and battery, together with a detailed and lengthy statement relating to violation of Foreign Exchange Control requirements. The affidavit was witnessed by Ortega, and Fernandez' sometime partner, one of the secretaries, and the patrol leader of the Guardia Civil. The statement was typed on the standard form used by the Guardia for the purpose of service of an arrest warrant which Ortega always had in his briefcase. Six copies were typed, a copy for Brian Walker, the court clerk in Malaga, Ortega the prosecuting solicitor on the civil end, one for the Guardia Civil with a wad of new peseta notes neatly folded inside, and one copy for Walker's defence counsel. Walker was arrested and taken into custody under the most severe duress; first to the police station at Torremolinos where he was charged and then to Malaga Prison. The Englishman's only reply when asked if he had anything to say was: "The next time I see him, if there is a next time, I'll fuckin' kill him! The policeman took note of his reply knowing the Northerner meant what he was saying.

Pauline Walker arrived at the bar at 7:25 that foul evening. Bennett was initially unable to make any sense of her delirious raving. The woman was broken, out of control, tugging at the roots of her hair to subdue the emotional pain and the anxiety. She gripped his arm like a vice, sobbing. Bennett thought it better to allow the frustration to take its course before attempting to calm her. He remained cool and locked the doors; the bar was empty anyway. For a moment he was tempted to ask whether Brian had died or been in an accident.

"Pauline, just tell me what has happened. Where is Brian?' The explanation emerged slowly through the constant sobbing. All he could make out was that Brian had been arrested by the police and beaten into a green police wagon an hour before. He could not make out the wrinkled arrest warrant she handed him, except the name Fernandez, whose name appeared on the four page document. Bennett drew a long breath and asked Pauline to wait while he phoned Debbie to come down, promising to clear up exactly what the situation was and what could be done about it. Debbie arrived a little later and set about calming her friend.

The printer made his exit and skipped across the moving traffic to the roadside cafe where he captured the attention of one of the English speaking waiters to make the telephone call to Torremolinos Police Station, explaining the details and the questions he needed the answers to. Moments later, the waiter handed Bennett the telephone explaining the arresting officer could not alone speak English, but wanted to speak to Bennett personally. The contents of the following conversation would forever extinguish any notion of staying in Spain for one minute longer than he had to.

"Senor Bennett, I cannot help you with the Walker case. The arrest is complete and he is due for trial, sometime this year. What I want to speak to you is of your own pending arrest. Unless you are able to pay these fines within the next seven days, it is my duty to arrest you, and I have to make it clear to you that the crimes of tax evasion, illegal operation of a business and working without a work permit carry heavy mandatory sentencing and automatic deportation once the sentence and accrued fines are satisfied. Upon arrest it is unlikely that your case will be heard for at least a few months. Do you fully understand what I have told you, Senor Bennett?'

"For Christ's sake, I thought I had time on these fines. There was never any mention of arrest or jail, or anything remotely like that!

The Guardia shifted the wad of notes in his pants pocket that he had retrieved from the envelope containing the Fernandez affidavit some hours before. "I think before you try to help your friend Walker, you should think about helping yourself first. Let me give you some good advice. If you cannot pay these fines, I strongly advise you to leave Spain, and never come back. I think I have explained myself fully, Senor Bennett. Adios." The line went dead.

A bolt of fear churned in Bennett's bowels, weakening him. He replaced the receiver and sat at a nearby table wiping his brow with a napkin. The waiter sensed trouble in the Englishman, offering consolation by suggesting he should perhaps go directly to where his friend was incarcerated.

The cab ride to Malaga Prison was the most exhausting five miles the Printer had ever endured, the highway chock-a-block with traffic returning to the city from a day on the beaches. The journey was in vain. He was refused admission to the Malaga jail and all inquiries on the matter were to be directed to a Senor Montez Perez- Walker's appointed attorney. The cab journey back was traffic free. Bennett felt some relief, his second wind fuelled by pure anger as the cab hurled past the endless double lane of vehicles on the far side of the highway. He caught the lawyer as he was about to leave his office in Plaza San Miguel in the centre of Torremolinos.

The Spaniard was irritated at Bennett's late request for a brief as he bade the Englishman be seated.

"Now, senor," he opened coldly and unconcerned, "What can I do for you?" eyeing his gold-strapped wristwatch annoyingly. He was a man of Bennett's age, but morbidly overweight; the unsightly mountain of blubber hanging from below the ribcage, the tiered cushions of flesh of his neck spilling over the collar of his sheening black mohair jacket, which atop was a Medusa face with tiny darting zealots eyes. This was one mendacious fucker the Printer thought. Bennett, at that moment couldn't have cared less if he kept him all night, and continued to stare down the lawyer aggressively. The Fat Man stared back, but smugly.

"Mr. Perez, the police have informed me that you are acting for Brian Walker, who was arrested this evening and taken into Malaga Prison, awaiting trial. What is the nature of the charges on this matter?'

The Fat Man leaned back on the leather swivel chair, placing his bloated hands on the desktop. "Ah, you must be Mister... eh- Bennett?'

"That's correct, Senor Perez."

Perez took a deep tired breath and opened his palms to commence the details. "Well, Mr. Bennett, I don't see what you can do. Mr. Walker is being held on very serious charges of assault and battery, trespass on property, criminal damage, robbery, and a number of other charges relating to Foreign Exchange Control irregularities and fraud. So what do you think you can do, Mr. Bennett?'

"When is the arraignment?' What about bail?' The Printer knew that the Spaniard did not wish to be helpful.

"Bail... what is bail?' I do not understand, Mr. Bennett?'

"Forget it." Bennett was at a loss for something to say. He felt hopeless. The lawyer shrugged his shoulders, signalling his departure and rose clumsily from behind the desk. Bennett felt the adrenalin pump and his fists flex into bricks of tensile steel. Luckily, he just about held onto himself and did his fighting with his mouth. Rising from the chair he outstretched his hand and raised his voice with the cold iciness of a man on a very short fuse.

"Sit down, Perez"

The lawyer winced at the reference. His black eyes fixed on Bennett's clenched fists attached to a man one hair's breadth from cutting loose. The attorney began to sweat profusely and blew a breath of relief as Bennett opened his fists slowly and placed his hands on his hips. Allowing a full half-minute of silence to pass, he spoke like a man looking for some straight answers, not the forte of Spanish lawyers.

"How much?"

"I know the lawyer for Senor Fernandez; perhaps I could talk with him, if you like," leaving the onus of decision to Bennett.

"Lift that phone, and start talking- now! Bennett's tone was low and laced with an undercurrent of extremely nasty possibilities.

The mysteries of the Spanish legal system were exposed over the following twenty minutes. Perez had no problem in contacting both Fernandez and his lawyer, Ortega. The pretentious bantering was conducted entirely in Spanish. Bennett sat on the desk side chair, cradling the back of his head in his clasped hands. His position remained unchanged as Perez cradled the receiver some 25 minutes later.

"I have some good news for Mr. Walker."

"No kidding, what?"

"Senor Fernandez is prepared to drop all the charges, but of course under certain conditions." Bennett laughed to the ceiling. "I'll bet there are certain conditions!' He quipped sarcastically and urged the lawyer to continue.

"First, Mr. Walker must agree to be legally deported. Secondly, he must relinquish all property and assets in Spanish territory and last, Mr. Fernandez demands the return of the cash."

A thought crossed the Englishman's mind that it was a lot better than rotting away in a jail cell in Malaga. "Then make it be possible for me to see Brian now. I think he might go for the deal." The Printer spoke less aggressively. Twenty five minutes later, both men waited in the visiting area of Malaga Prison. The sound of shuffling footsteps signalled Brian Walker's arrival behind the tiny pigeonhole.

"Brian," the Printer shouted a whisper, "Is that you mate?' Can you hear me?' It's Howard. I have some news for you." Bennett leaned his face near the tiny garlic and puke-reeking mesh. The voice behind it sounded like a man not in the full faculty of his senses; the words came slow and stammered through a stupor of pain and despair. The Printer could see Walker's right hand supporting the underside of his stubby jaw.

"Howard... get me out of here- I want to go home... tell Pauline not to worry. Get me out, Howard... just get me out any way you can!

Bennett explained the terms of release in as comforting a fashion as he could. Walker's reply told him he was a broken man.

"Anything, Howard, anything. Just do it now!

On the return trip to Monte Mar, Bennett instructed Perez to have the papers drawn up immediately and keep him informed. The Printer lied in his teeth when he told Pauline and Debbie that Brian was in good shape and would be released in a couple of days. The following hours of conversation with his wife and Pauline told both women that the Spanish pipe dream had come to an abrupt and terrible end. It all seemed so surreal. Over the next couple of hours the Bennetts helped Pauline to pack. Then, out of the blue, Debbie announced she would be flying back with her.

"As I told you I'm going home to my parents and going back to work" she told him matter of fact. "I will be in touch with you."

There were no loving embraces or kisses goodbye in the departure lounge of Malaga Airport the following morning. He had seen Debbie like this before, but not to the same degree of absoluteness. Dusty Bennett remained calm. He knew he would be leaving Spain in the next few days, and certainly before the Guardia Civil came looking to arrest him. Just as Debbie was about to step into the aircraft tunnel she turned and paced back in his direction. On reaching the security barrier, she stood rigid and pointed an accusing finger at her motionless husband. To his astonishment, and in full view of boarding passengers, she rasped the words that had long laid silent through hope for the better and fear for the worst.

"I intend to settle things with you. Stay away from my parent's house ..... and me ... you blundering moron" turning on her heels to the plans for her future.

Chapter Eleven

Three days later the British Airways Boeing commenced its decent into Heathrow Airport. Near the tail of the aircraft, the Englishman directed his sight to the jagged graph line of the white cliffs of Dover arising like miniature giants against an empty cobalt sky. A hopeful morning sun mottled the patchwork fields of southern England as the aircraft bumped and dipped to make its final approach. Bennett anticipated the aircraft's next sink to Terra Firma, as he fixed on at the dim lead-in lights outside the window, flickering like candles in the morning sun, and then they came closer and closer until the little bump, and then a smaller bump again, and then the lurch along the runway until the blast of the brakes brought the aircraft to that final cushion ride to its designated apron.

Thirty minutes later, he sat in the airport bar gazing aimlessly at the untouched black coffee he had ordered. In his isolation, he felt outcast from the mainstream of society, the bar being crowded with joyous holiday groups returning from elsewhere, being greeted by various welcoming parties.

The escape from the Guardia Civil had been nerve racking, particularly at Malaga Airport. Each uniformed policeman loomed larger than life, increasing his paranoia by the second. He had spent the forty five minutes waiting time seated in a men's room cubicle until the boarding notice crackled over the intercom. And now he was alone, his mind scrambled in a thousand thoughts, his body shattered from lack of sleep, and relentless panic attacks. The cheerful holiday groups laid further credence to the hopelessness of his circumstances... his wife... his life's savings... his debts. Brian Walker's ruin. His wife's yet unknown future actions were just too painful and convoluted to contemplate. There was nothing within him to negotiate, not one redeeming grain of good to which he could hold on to. She had been right and whatever their futures might have held in Spain, she did not deserve this. Yes, she had been right in her evaluation of her husband's infuriating immaturity and sense of judgment. In matters of the world he knew he was a complete moron. In matters such as these he was wholly undeserving of her, and worst of all she had given him a free rein. He broke down, making a hopeless attempt to hide his disabling anxiety from the world about him. The barman approached him immediately.

"Are you alright sir?"

"Yes, I'm sorry. I'm okay- I beg your pardon."

"Anything I can get you, sir?'

"No, thanks, I'm alright now. Thank you very much." Allowing the hyperventilation to take its course, and now on 'the safe ground' of home, the hour was fast approaching when the nuts and bolts of a grim reality would need to be addressed. The money in itself was bad enough, but it was the slimy cunning of it all which pained him most. He drew a series of long breaths to relieve the stress. All he had to his name was 140,000 pesetas he had taken from the register before he absconded.

Having cashed in the pesetas at the airport bank, Bennett took a cab to 57 Batley Lane, Chalk Farm, London NW7, the home of Mr. John Walker, to introduce himself and relate the details about the man's brother, Brian. As the black cab rumbled through London's morning traffic, the morning London masses going about their business brought a brief 'tranquillity to the moments' in that he might again be one of them.

He tipped the cabbie and stepped inside the wrought iron garden gate where he was greeted by a huge man of the same age and mould as Brian Walker with a no-nonsense north of England accent. John Walker listened impatiently and turned to the Printer, the big man looping a friendly arm around Bennett's shoulder.

"Listen, Howard, you looked after my brother. I'll see you're looked after and don't say no or you'll make me mad! He stared at the Printer between his sad eyes. "We've a lot to discuss. Let's go round the local and have a pint, mate!

Ten minutes later the pair bid each other cheers at the bar of the Rose and Crown Pub, High Road, in Camden Town, John's regular watering hole. This pub boasted no lounge, just one long battered hardwood bar of some forty feet, the punters standing two and three deep, mostly drinking pints of Guinness, the brackish black stout of Ireland. To the back there was a stage area with live Irish music. Bennett noticed an absence of slot machines, pool tables or a juke box. It was Thursday, pay day. Money was flying around like leaves, Guinness being downed in copious quantities, steadily advancing the customers into a happy drunken stupor by the hour. The Printer inadvertently noticed several items of decor to the back of the bar. Faded photos of football and what he thought were hockey teams, although the stick was much different than a hockey stick and a framed text, bearing the heading PROCLAMATION whatever that meant. He toyed with the pronunciation in his mind. The Irish Triple Crown Rugby Team, he immediately recognized.

By closing time Bennett was feeling little pain, and found himself joined by two people for the after hour session at Walker's place; Dennis Reid, a Cockney bricklayer and the other an Irishman of the same trade, one Sean McCahan. The group adjourned to John's house bringing the atmosphere of the Rose and Crown with them and settled into drinking and the unravelling of the Spanish affair.

The Cockney was from West Ham, London's East End, and offered his standard version of "I'm Forever Blowing Bubbles," followed by a string of hilarious but filthy jokes. McCahan's repertoire was a world apart, consisting of the complete recitation of "Dangerous Dan McGrew" by Robert Service, and two ballads, "The Boys from the Old Brigade" and "Sean South from Garryowen." Bennett related to neither, but McCahan later explained that "South" was an Irish rebel gunned down by the Crown Forces in the fifties. The company eventually settled down to discuss the Spanish affair and Brian Walker. The Printer eased into his new found company who spoke the same language and possessed identical feelings of repulsion at Bennett's account of the Spanish affair. Brian Walker's imprisonment in Malaga was discussed at great length, the Printer explaining that he was not at liberty to outline the horrendous settlement he was forced to negotiate with Fernandez to effect his brother's early release. The Cockney jumped in when Bennett finished his explanation.

"Look, mate, I can get a couple of villains go down and sort that out no fucking problem."

Bennett continued to outline in some detail the events of his life including his career with Browne's and his interests in note collecting and rugby. McCahan listened, his bright blue eyes locked in concentration. McCahan would spend the following four hours until 6 a.m. questioning the Printer's account of the story. His attitude was of genuine concern and inert curiosity. The questions were clear, logical and presented in the belief that somewhere, somehow, he could be of some help. McCahan's face turned to pallidness when he learned of the collapse of the printer's marriage. Bennett had, undoubtedly helped by the alcohol, broken down during that period of the conversation. The Irishman examined every avenue of possible remedy including the British Embassy, the penetration of the Spanish legal system, finding another purchaser or at the end of the day... extortion. McCahan was not drinking and Bennett instinctively recognized an icy reality in the Bricklayer's suggestions. This was a very scary guy. The Printer boldly inquired the reason for his intense interest in the problem, the answer was immediate.

"Something similar happened to me once, Howard, but there was nobody around to help. The big difference is that I was single" The Provo was relentless in his pursuit of a solution to the point of aggravation, suggesting to Bennett that he could simply return to his profession and start life afresh. The suggestion was dismissed sharply.

"In my present mental state I am not employable in any capacity whatsoever," the Printer replied softly, explaining that his profession demanded a high level of concentration and a capacity for on-the-spot decision making. The Printer could not help but continue to outline the intricacies of his trade to his most receptive listener. McCahan demonstrated a high intellect and unique concentration in that his queries always directly related to the very core of the subject. The discussion weaved through Bennett's career, his interest in notes and bonds, the history of printing techniques and the ancient art of paper making. Bennett, again alcohol induced swung the conversation to his favourite topic of fascination, the printing of currency, the stages of technique application and security. The Irishman arose to stretch his legs.

"Howard, that's been a fascinating conversation. I have a couple of very old Irish notes from home. Would you have a look at them for me?' They might be worth a fortune. I might even buy that bar in Spain off you! He screamed laughing, showing his three front teeth to be missing, which always made McCahan appear more comical than he actually was. One night in Birmingham, many years ago when he was leaving one pub to go to another to pay wages he was relieved of £10000 together with his upper front teeth; and the notion of replacing them never as much as occurred to him.

"Tell me this, and tell me no more," the Provo continued, downing a full glass of stout. "Would it be an easy thing to counterfeit money in this day and age?'

Bennett smiled. The number of times he had been asked the very same question. "Absolutely, but here's the catch... provided you've got about a hundred grand plus to set up the operation. "

"Oh, that's a pity," replied McCahan jokingly. "I'll have to go back to laying bricks so." By this time the other pair had been long snoring on the floor.

"Y'know, Sean- I've never seen this side of life," as he smiled at the sleeping drunks. The dawn broke through the curtains, accompanied by the chirping of birds and early morning traffic. "It's different. I have to say I quite like it," Bennett reassured himself. In two minutes he joined the snoring chorus. Sean McCahan did not sleep but made his way quietly out of the house to the nearest public phone box and dialled a number in Reading.

"Hello." The voice was female. "Any message?'

"Tell him we've found our man. The one who speaks all languages!

Chapter Twelve

Don Jose Ayala wiped clean his plate of Octopus Tapas, and washed down the moist garlic bread with a bolt of Rioja, the rich red wine from the Provence of Rioja in the fertile north west of Spain. It was a clear spring evening in the old port of San Sebastian. A cluster of seagulls swooped and fluttered frantically round the bow of a moored trawler unloading its catch of the day. Along the main promenade of the harbour burning charcoal and a hundred species of seafood permeated the night as families of three and four generations ate like wolves amid the din of troublesome children. Away from the main activity, the prostitutes plied their trade at the darker cauldrons of the waterfront to protect the identities of both themselves and their customers. All was normal as the old port sank into the darkness to the pulse of its own ancient rhythm.

Ayala, forty three years old and contentedly married with three children was the owner of a small local restaurant and tapas bar in San Sebastian. The business had been given him by his father some five years ago. He was a Basque, born and reared. His father had been jailed by Franco in the Civil War and later for his part in the setting up of "El Sindicado Nacional de los Trabajadores Espanoles", the national union of Spanish workers in Franco's Fifties. On being released he immediately joined with the new ETA, the freedom fighters of the Basque region of the North of Spain. His son's involvement in the movement was disguised to the extent that Spanish Intelligence had not once darkened his door.

"Don Jose, llamada para ti" his wife shouted from the small, busy kitchen.

"Una momento, por favor," his voice both loud and husky from the fifty Ducados he sucked into his lungs each day. The Basque's arm appeared around the kitchen doorway groping for the receiver in its usual place on a shelf. He plugged his free ear with a finger.

"Ola."

"Hello, Jose. This is McNiff. How are you?'

"Ah, McNiff la magnifica" the Basque beamed in delight.

"Como estas, que pasa amigo?'

"Everything's fine, and you?'

"La cosas estan bien, everything is good. What can I do for you?' Wait a moment please. I will take your call from the office."

Jose Ayala's father, during the Spanish Civil War, had established a lifelong friendship with Colm McNiff's father, one of the famous Fifth International Brigade of Irish Republicans who fought against Franco. The old man had never forgotten the Irishmen who came to their aid in one of the bloodiest Civil Wars in modern history. His grandchildren later were sent to Dublin to study English and stayed at McNiff's sister-in-law's house in Dublin's Donnybrook, one mile south of the city centre. McNiff happened to be staying there during Jose Ayala's visits to see his children and the pair formed a friendship immediately, their common interests being politics and culture. Ayala was eventually introduced to leading members of the newly formed breakaway group "The Provisional IRA" in 1969 and returned to the North of Spain to set up the infamous "Barcelona Arms Run." The system was simple. Illegal arms emanating from Libya and Eastern Europe would be intercepted by a Spanish trawler somewhere in the vicinity of the Balearic Sea in response to a mayday call. The arms would be transferred to the Barcelona-bound trawler, and then moved overland to Santander.

The cargo would then be shipped to Cork, and then picked up by a Dublin based Spanish trading company. This avoided passing through the dreaded Straits of Gibraltar.

A second option was to unload the arms onto a Dublin-bound truck via Lyons, Paris and Le Harve. This route was later busted at Le Harve, causing the expulsion of two diplomats from the Russian Embassy in Dublin.

"Where were we, Colm?'

"Well, Jose, I want you to do a little job for me" inquired McNiff cautiously.

"Sure," the Basque offered eagerly. "But the last job ended up in big trouble, Si?' the Basque commented, referring to the Le Harve bust.

"No, not that kind of job Jose. I want to send you on a little holiday to the South, to Torremolinos to do a little surveillance for me, nothing dangerous, just sightseeing,?'

"I know. What are the details, just call out all details to me."

"Okay, got a pen?' Fine... now listen." The brief was simple.

"I need everything you can get for me on a certain Jean Claude Fernandez; a property dealer trading under "Propidad Costa Del Sol" in Benalmadena Torremolinos, and in particular his relationship with one Howard Bennett. Present yourself as a potential purchaser of a bar. I'm sending you money to cover the expenses. Get back to me in London as soon as you can with answers"

"Don't bother sending money. You can fix me for expenses when I get back to London. I will call you when I have news. Adios" The Basque put down the phone apprehensively and pulled a fresh bottle of Rioja from the shelf. His wife wondered at the smile on his face.

An hour later Jean Claude Fernandez entered the plush bar at the Los Rampas Golf Club, carrying two files, one relating to a deportation order and settlement with a person known as Brian Walker and the other a signed contract for the sale of a bar in Los Boliches to an unwitting Scot. The barman attended to the Property Dealer immediately.

"And how are you today, Senor Fernandez?'

"I could not be better, Pepe," he replied smiling, tapping the files contentedly.

How little do men know sometimes?'

Chapter Thirteen

The Rose and Crown was packed, the stage set for a five hour drinking session. Bennett was puzzled at the earlier activity that afternoon; open back trucks and vans coming to a halt at five minute intervals unloading six or ten men still in working gear, some sporting the safety helmets of one construction firm or another. The printer learned it was the run up to the long Easter weekend; sub-contractors paid out salaries early on Wednesday to allow for those men who wished to go home to Ireland the time to book their traveling arrangements. Few actually did.

Bennett came to be liked and well accepted by all and sundry, and had even spent a few evenings serving behind the bar. Over the last couple of days he had been offered work by three different contractors without any reference to his experience or capacity. Bennett turned down the offers graciously saying "I don't know the first thing about it." Bennett marvelled at their sense of entitlement in corralling the heavy construction labour market in the UK, and their unbridled determination to trash through life on their own terms.

The Printer made his way to the toilet. Within a moment the door swung open. McCahan brushed past him and positioned himself next to Bennett at the trough.

McCahan spoke in a nonchalant manner from the side of his mouth as he zipped his pants and made his exit from the urinal. "When are ye comin to do a bit of work with us?'" he joked without losing the sincerity of the offer. Once outside he pulled Bennett to the quietness of back exit door,

"Now I need you to do something for me Howard"

"Of course, sure, if I can, what is it?'"

"I'm not a great man with the pen so will you write out what you told me about making the money that time at John's.....I remember what you said but I can't write it out. It's for a couple of boys I know, they don't know you and you will never know them and besides I owe them a favour, could you have it in a few days for me" he asked as nonchalant as asking to light a cigarette.

The Irishman pushed a very large wad of notes into Bennett's breast pocket giving no option of refusal. "Grand so" he ended, and before Bennett had a chance to respond he had joined his group at the bar.

The Printer stood dumbfounded. He fingered the wad, enough to choke an ass, and knew now he had no decision in the matter.

Later that night, Bennett quietly sat in John Walker's kitchen. His benefactor handed him a can of lager.

"You look a little peaked, Howard, are you feeling alright?'

The Printer paused as if in deliberation. "John, how well do you know Sean McCahan?'

"Well, we're not the closest of friends but he's been a drinking buddy of mine for the last couple of years. Why?'

Bennett took a long pull on the beer. "On the day I arrived, you, myself, and that chap Dennis and Sean ended up here feeling no pain. While you and Dennis slept, Sean and I continued to make friendly conversation, part of which dealt with my professional background as a security printer. The subject turned to the art of counterfeiting, and I thought nothing of it when he kept prodding me about it. I realize it's a subject that evokes that which dreams are made of. So I indulged him like anyone else because while I make it sound easy, the reality is that it's not. Anyway, tonight Sean comes up to me at the Rose and lays a wad of notes on me, sort of demanding me to write a recipe for forging currency for some "friends" John Walker laughed. "Sean is a seven day a week drunk. I've never seen him one hundred per cent sober. And his workmates are just the same. It is the only life they have ever known. Laying bricks all day, drinking themselves into comas at night, back at it the next day, and this is going on for years and years, always looking for handy money. I wouldn't pay him any mind!

"What about this money?"

"Well, you got me there, Howard. Look- say what you're saying is true. Think about it; he must have told his boss some wild tale, and his boss being an Irish fly-by-night contractor decided to throw a few quid at McCahan and have a look. Some of these contractors have so much hidden cash, what do you care?' You don't have to sign your name to anything...besides you will have long disappeared when life settles back which it always does. Take the money, are you fucking stone mad!

"Yeah, OK, I suppose you're right. I like Sean, but he is one of those people who you just know could be a very very scary guy"

Chapter Fourteen

CARTOGRAPHY OF A PLOT

T he clouds broke scattering periodic showers over the city the following morning. Bennett was seated in his box room at John Walker's, under the glare of a desk lamp mapping McCahan's demand for a strategy for the forgery of currency. He would continue to write until five o'clock that evening.

PREAMBLE.

The purpose for which this draft is written is to acquaint the unprofessional with the various processes, plant materials and difficulties incorporated in the copying of paper currency. The forging of currency to an undetectable standard is not impossible. The contents herein should in no way be related to the numerous abortive botched attempts over the last half century, with the exception of "Operation Bernhard," the German forging of British banknotes during the Second World War. Throughout the draft, I shall be referring in considerable detail to the following topics:

Capacity- professional background and knowledge of the forger, standards.

Plant and machinery.

Materials - including ink and paper.

Watermark, security strips and numbering techniques.

Security, circulation life and probability of detection.

A personal opinion on disposal devices.

Counter measures to avoid detection and arrest.

CAPACITY.

There are few professional currency forgers throughout the world capable of executing this task to a standard likely to succeed. It is highly unlikely that a trained person in any one of the trades within the graphic industry would singularly be capable of executing a job incorporating such a wide variety of crucially exacting disciplines. I can say it is only by reason of my involvement in security production and the standard to which I have perfected my profession that I can write on the subject with unquestionable authority. Fraud squads and Central Banks have no problem detecting the work of amateurs or capable professionals within only one area of discipline, such as multi-colour printing. I can therefore say that the standard to which I shall be relating is of an unprecedented level of accuracy with the exception of notes produced by "The Bernhard Operation" and one or two other successful attempts in Third World countries where the original standard of the notes are poor.

In closing this brief topic of standards, I say that the aspiration of the forger at all times should be to produce a note destitute of specific flaws such as to pass the litmus tests of detection devices, at the consumer market level. The note must be produced to accuracy where detection will only be possible by a professional such as a chemist. The note must pass all examination at consumer level. This is the degree of accuracy to which such an operation must be conducted if it is to achieve any degree of success.

PLANT, MACHINERY, PREMISES.

Any printing process employed in the copying of notes other than the original process must inevitably fail. Whilst there are many fine alternatives to a Gorby press available on the market such as Heidleberg ideally, the work should be carried out on an existing premises, with a four-colour plate making and colour separation capacity and above all the very best scanner that money can buy...the...cost £100,000 plus. I appreciate the requirement of an existing working premises would be difficult and cause security problems, but this method is infinitely more preferable than that of a new start-up situation. Also, the premises should have a top class electronic guillotine capable of being per-programmed. I will not elaborate on the reasons for this presently. On the subject of personnel, fewer the better. However, in the interest of time saving, the services of a first class pressman would be most beneficial particularly from the point of view of preparation of plates and "make ready" which is the time spent on the highly skilled exercise of manoeuvring the variables on the press to correctly establish register, ink flow, feed and delivery. Although the machine to which I have referred incorporates electronic surveillance on output, competent attendance for the usual minor alterations and servicing during running time is critical.

MATERIALS, INK, PAPER.
All the necessary materials for the run should be within existing premises such as lining up tables, touching up facilities etc. All recent attempts at copying currency have not paid attention to specialty inks and paper, resulting in notes being detected at a very early stage of circulation and more importantly, the forgeries were capable of being detected by members of the public, rendering the operation a failure. Inks are usually subjected to security measures by the addition of invisible fluorescence and magnetic loaders in the case of US Dollars. Chemicals are added to inks so that when exposed to ultra-violet light, the note should behave in a certain manner. Therefore, it is imperative that copies of the notes to be forged should be analysed by a competent chemist to define the ingredients which are contained within the ink which must then be made up to this specification. The ink will then pass the crucial tests of the Central Banks, the notes therefore requiring extensive testing to define minute inaccuracies. The paper used by security printers is of a very high quality and must be made to specification because it must be able to withstand handling during circulation.

WATERMARK, SECURITY STRIP, NUMBERING TECHNIQUES.
During paper manufacture, several security features must be included. Watermarks are incorporated during the paper manufacturing process. In America, after the 1988 Series security

threads about the face of the note are favoured. Bank note paper may also have invisible fluorescence, which is a chemical in the paper which will react under ultraviolet light. Normally, the fluorescence will be the denomination spotted on various parts of the note. Again, the paper in question must be analysed by a chemist within the industry to supply the instructions for manufacture. The purchasing of inks and paper on the open market is totally unacceptable to the master forger. The forged note should behave the same as the original to within a hairline degree, under the following tests: light fastness, weight, behaviour under handling and the various counter-security tests including exposure to ultra-violet light. The counterfeit note itself will be subjected to these various tests before being circulated. There is no reason why notes of a high denomination in 20/50 Pounds or Dollars should not possess a circulation life of four to five years. Security strips and threads are inserted during paper manufacture in many currencies. It is possible to purchase the chemical analysis and specification for any paper or ink in the Far East. They will also manufacture both at a price for what I personally would have in mind. Standard numbering boxes will not be used. Again it is critical to directly reproduce a set of numbers from the original note and have special boxes made up, then print onto the completed forgery in a separate run. This method achieves two advantages.

The numbering style will be an exact reproduction of the typeface used in the original note.

The new box can be assembled in such a way as to include only those letters of the alphabet currently in use by any given Federal Bank in the case of Dollars. Therefore, the forgeries shall show a maze of numbers and letters which will prove impossible to identify for a very long time, resulting an extended circulation life.

SECURITY, CIRCULATION LIFE.

The International Monetary Fund is a special agency of the United Nations set up by forty five countries after the Second World War with the aim of preventing a recurrence of the disastrous events of the Thirties when competitive devaluations and trade restrictions led to a slump in world trade. The fund became the guardian of the free world's monetary system, and its articles of agreement provided for an important framework of rules for exchange rates, balance of payment policies and other key factors. A forgery of the magnitude I would envisage could disturb a currency's credibility within the system and cause a counter-detection operation of unprecedented magnitude. This consideration must be borne in mind when deciding the currency to be forged and the extent of the operation. Circulation life will be determined by the quality of the notes and the inability of the public including financial institutions to detect on sight or common detection devices. The disparity must be of such minuteness so as to severely stretch the most exhausting searching tests of fraud/forensic squads and laboratories of the Central Banks. This objective will render these institutions incapable of advising the consumer market as to specific points to watch out for and circulation life could continue until all of the forgeries are returned for disposal ... the perfect crime. It is highly unlikely that a Central Bank would venture to alert members of the public to the existence of near undetectable notes. It might cause shock reaction and severely dent the movement of paper money or cause people to move money away from the system in pursuit of other currencies. The effect of releasing such news would not be prudent. I feel the treasury of any country would keep quiet and opt to wait a few years until all notes were returned for disposal. With perhaps two exceptions there has never been a forgery which has caused any national treasury any real problem.

DISPOSAL DEVICES.

A personal opinion. Successful disposal of forged notes is totally dependent on two factors. The quality of the notes and knowledge of the money system. I have dealt with quality in the previous topics. There are a number of fallacies within forgery folklore. This is due to a combination of ignorance of money movement and a lack of professional capacity in the production. Any professional forgery should be confined to the currency of the country where the crime is committed. Therefore, the currency chosen should command international repute and have a high exchange rate such as the American Dollar, the Deutsche Mark or Sterling. Forget the method of home dumping. International currencies ideally should be disposed of in any country other than that of the country of the forged currency and the only way for any serious professional forgery to seep into the system is by the employment of global money launderers who will apply every test known upon any cash deposits for processing.

COUNTER MEASURES.

Measures to avoid detection and arrest. Members of the public are usually the last people to spot highly professional counterfeit notes. Central Banks and fraud squads are not. In this draft the public will not detect the forged matter but the Central/Federal Banks eventually will. Then they will react. Concerned at the quality and absence of detection by the public they mount a huge investigation. Fingerprinting and extensive forensic evidence will be recorded. The origin of the paper will be known within days if not hours through water analysis of the note. It is imperative that the foregoing activity be considered before it occurs in order that the forger can deal with it in due course. It is in this light I must impress the following points:

In the matter of personnel, do not use the services of personnel working in the jurisdiction where the job is to be done. Fly a man in from overseas.

Always remember that cross-examination by the fraud agencies like the Secret Service will definitely occur, so appropriate contingency should be devised for this certain eventuality.

There is no need to mention the importance of wiping down and cleaning up. The forensics will go through the place with a fine tooth comb if they have any suspicion whatsoever.

The maximum cost of the operation I have outlined would be £200,000 at worst but a lot less depending.

The extent of the crime should be in the region of 350 million, preferably in American Dollars, all of a high denomination.

Only half of the counterfeit should be numbered should the Treasury or Central Bank take the unprecedented decision to release to the public the full list of genuine numbers of the forged issue, which I very much doubt. If that be the case, there's no problem in printing unquoted serial numbers on the non-circulated stock. The Treasury will not have anticipated this move. The quality I refer to will render the courts unable to prosecute any member of the public.

Remember, disposal must be effected through the laundering system, individuals talk too much. States, including Central Banks are under a constitutional obligation to produce paper currency to an undetectable standard.

The test at common law in both the UK and the USA is that of a person being 'knowingly' in possession. This must be proven beyond reasonable doubt. On the presumption that fraud squad specialists will have extreme difficulty in defining the disparity, then how could it be possible for a person to be "knowingly in possession?' This prosecution would never get near any court of law anywhere'.

Bennett would stop writing from time to time and consider use of the personal pronoun "I." During his membership of the International Society of Paper Money and Bond Collectors, the area of forgery was discussed in open forum. Indeed, the self-same society had been responsible for exposure of numerous counterfeits of rare bonds and share certificates presented for auction in London. The Printer sat and gazed outside the first floor window, as convoys of crammed London buses made their way north to Camden Town, Kentish Town and Highgate. The time was 5:30 p.m. and the traffic chock-a-block, the rain falling heavier now in the spring evening, the activity mundane and all in pursuit of the small packet that most people receive on the Friday of each week. Then, out of the stillness, Bennett winced in concern, his brow wrinkled into new inscriptions of age, defenceless to the attack of anxiety which shot to his consciousness like a bolt of evil; his family ... his savings ... the coldness of the Spanish Police ... Brian's voice of hopelessness in Malaga. The attack took its turbulent course and quelled a few minutes later. The use of the pronoun "I" did not bother him anymore. Bennett stubbed out the cigarette and began writing his second last topic of the draft. He dropped the ball point on the small bedside table, stood up and stretched his creaking limbs, yawning. Opening the small suitcase, he pulled out the portable typewriter and began to key the text. Bennett finished typing and folded the finished draft down the centre of the A4 sheets and inserted it into a sealed brown envelope. The draft was handed over that evening at The Rose to an anxious Sean McCahan, who retired to the toilet to peruse the contents. The Printer continued in conversation with John Walker, offering forty Pounds for the use of the room, which Walker refused. The Irishman appeared from the toilet some ten minutes later, his face beaming, the missing teeth and gum line framing the portrait of one very happy individual. "Be Jeses, I can't write too good but I can read like yerself ," he whispered in the Printer's ear as he downed a three-quarter pint in one gulp, and left immediately, explaining that he had to price a building extension in the suburbs.

John Walker purchased a Chinese take-away and the pair walked round to the house. "Some chance of McCahan and his friends coming up with one hundred grand" Bennett reassured himself as he dozed off at one a.m.

As Bennett slept soundly, the four IRA men sat down to study the Bennett's draft. McNiff, the chairman, was the first to speak. The usual dour tone of a man whose best days were far behind him began to finger the closed envelope as if it was some unwelcome mail. Being by far the older of the company, his principles and attitudes to speculative ideas had been firmly cemented many years ago. Years of highly dangerous involvement in the struggle for Irish freedom had taught him hard lessons. All reasoning outside the engaging militarily in a war of attrition was a lost cause and doomed to failure as far as McNiff was concerned. His five year stint at the Curragh Internment Camp in County Kildare in the fifties combined with several ferocious beatings from the Security Forces had long cemented his self-pronounced credo. The other three knew this would be his attitude, having spoken without as much as reading the first page. McNiff knew he would be at cross purposes with the others, and blundered on, "I don't know what you people think, but let me, in no uncertain terms, tell you comrades about forgery and forgery attempts within this movement," and continued to outline a discouraging chronology of botched forgery attempts within the movement since its inception. His words made painful listening. "The price we'll have to pay in our best men being jailed is to my mind unacceptable," his voice rising in volume fuelled by his anger. McNiff sat, pushing the unread file to one side. The silence of the room told him he had not convinced his staring comrades. Bob Millar knew that once his Commander did not see the words "arms," "bank" or "assassination" on the first page, he would not bother to read the draft. The financial outlay was a distinct disincentive. The schoolteacher Bob Millar then rose to his feet and would speak for one hour. "There is no doubt in my mind, Commander, that you did not as much as bother to study this crucial draft."

"I never said I did," interrupted McNiff sharply.

McCahan and O'Toole eyed each other with displeasure.

"If I may continue," the Teacher addressed McNiff with glaring annoyance, "You have outlined in your address this evening exactly what is wrong with our previous attempts at the counterfeiting of currency. The author of this most professional draft spent a very great deal of time in warning us about this debauchery of his craft, but as you have not bothered to read and study the draft, I see no point in addressing you directly on the entire matter. Having said what I have to say, I shall be requesting volunteers McCahan and O'Toole to voice their views. Then we shall take an open verbal vote on three initial questions ... One ... Should the operation go ahead?' Two ... Who should oversee?' Three ... Should Belfast be informed now or later for security reasons?' If we cannot agree, we'll refer the entire draft and decision to Belfast. Are we agreed on that?' The reply was a unanimous "Aye."

"I recently spoke on the escalation of the struggle and the possibility of purchasing Stinger missiles. Our funds are dwindling and eventually will terminate subversive activity and more important still, moral. This incredible crime, the undetectable forgery of such a magnitude will speed up the British withdrawal and save many young lives on both sides. I say we have a military and moral duty to carry out this forgery. The professionalism and ingenuity of the writer of this draft is without question. I am at a loss to understand why the movement has not come to the same conclusions in view of our disastrous track record in the counterfeit area. Not one person during my twenty years active membership has even scraped the surface of what this Englishman is talking about. No doubt about it, their professionals are to be admired in every field of endeavour. If you want to service a Rolls Royce, get a Rolls mechanic, and nobody else. I wish now to request the chair for a vote. "Turning to McNiff, who was by now buried on page three of the draft and not having heard a word of what the schoolteacher had said. All those in favour say aye." The threesome stiffened as McNiff answer in the positive without raising his head from the draft and turning to page four. "I wish to put myself forward to oversee the operation," volunteered McNiff confidently. "All those in favour," McNiff said again, undisturbed. "Carried" the Commander said, raising his head from the draft. He continued, "I don't think we should mention this to Belfast at the moment. The fewer people know the better. Can we vote on that?' "Carried, now down to details?' What about the machine and premises?' O'Toole asked, his mouth stuffed with half a burger and drooling with tomato sauce. McNiff replied, breaking his attention from the fourth page. "That's no problem at all. We have an ex-volunteer who owns a printing firm in New York. If necessary we can give him the money to buy a machine. I'm sure he will offer his premises, provided we follow this man's advice and take all the necessary precautions. He'll want a hefty fee, of course, and I wouldn't blame him. He might have to do a "runner," and not for the first time. I'll take care of that anyway. I'll call him later." "The next problem seems to be the ink and the paper," Millar continued taking charge of the discussion from his standing position. "I don't know anything about the Far East; we need to look into that. I think we might consider approaching Dublin on that. We have a person with some experience out there, but I don't like the sound of the Far East. It's full of whores and heroin dealers. How could you trust people like that?' We'll need a man who knows the ground out there." "There's only one professional around here as far as I can see," said O'Toole, washing down the last bite of burger with a mouthful of coke. "And that's the guy who wrote that draft." Niall O'Toole was three parts mad and to all appearances was absent of any natural nervous system. Unknown to himself, he possessed a clarity of thought which could flash to the core of any problem without fuss or explanation. He was also feared and admired by his colleagues. Although he was still just a lad, the Troubles had deprived him of any semblance of normality. Life was a sort of continuing game of Russian roulette to O'Toole, who had over his time on active duty cultivated a twisted thrill from staring the cold face of death from very close distances, and so far he was winning. Suddenly, the phone filled the room with sickening noise at 3:45 a.m. The Provos eyed each other as O'Toole shook the bottle of ketchup. "There's someone on the phone, will I answer it?" he inquired as if it was midday on the London Stock Exchange. "No, it's okay. I'll answer it," said McNiff picking up the receiver sharply. "Who the hell is that?" he queried, pretending to yawn. "Buenas Noches" the husky voice boomed from the other end. "I been phoning all day today and yesterday. You sleeping all day or something, eh?'

"What's the news, Jose. What's the news?' the Fenian queried with impatience. "Plenty. I am coming to London early, in five days. I have all I need to know, I think. Everything checks out no problem, but it's better if I come to talk to you, okay?' See you at Heathrow. Flight BA 676, arrive 8 p.m. Friday. Adios"

"That was Ayala from Torremolinos. Everything is okay. He'll be in on Friday."

"Did our Mr. Bennett check out okay?' asked McCahan.

"As far as I know," McNiff replied. "We'll know the whole score on Friday. Be God, I hate phones. Now let's get back to business" Millar re-addressed the meeting. The four were by now tiring, .the room breathless from the electric fire; the ashtrays full, take away boxes scattered round the table. The sudden phone call had all but killed off any enthusiasm to continue, although O'Toole could not have cared less. "This boy Bennett knows his onions," said Millar.

"Bring him in," McNiff ordered, addressing the Bricklayer. Sean McCahan nodded in agreement.

Chapter Fifteen

T he chirping of the birds announced a new dawn on April 24th as the first prisms of sunlight split the darkness of cell 207/8 at Malaga Prison. As of all places of human confinement, the musty walls bore the scribbling's of past incarcerated. It was a stifling cauldron, with a nauseating stench of all things putrid. Brian Walker lay ball wrapped on the stone floor of the bed less cell. It was his final refuge from the ferocious beating he had suffered the night before from the Guardia Civil. The face had been bathed clean of blood, the ear and scalp sutured. The man in the white coat finished his examination and nodded at the man behind him who tapped at the door. It swung behind them and the guard slid home two enormous steel bars. Forty minutes later, the cell door burst open as two Guardia Civil poked at the half-conscious lifeless body. Walker opened his eyes at the sound of marching boots and the dragging of his feet some thirty meters down the first floor wire mesh catwalk, being supported under the armpits by two Guardia. He sensed there was another behind him. The wing was still, the quietness broken only here and there by the uneasy noises of sleeping prisoners and the odd wail of a terror driven nightmare. Across the empty yard Walker collapsed, causing a gathering of seagulls to flutter harmlessly and perch in wait on the surrounding walls to finish the leftovers from the kitchen bins. Minutes later, Walker was gazing at a figure sitting behind a metal table. Senor Montez Perez - Abogado, cackled on in a lengthy litany of Spanish, both policemen still to each side of Walker. "One ... Deportation order, duly executed by Malaga Court, dated April 23rd ..." The Guardia to his side reached for one of his huge array of rubber stamps without looking, and stamped each document with well-practiced momentum as the details were hurriedly cackled. "Two ... Details of agreement between Mr. Brian Walker and Jean Claude Fernandez signed and duly witnessed; "Three ... Statement of withdrawal of all charges of Senor Jean

Claude Fernandez's versus Brian Walker dated April 23rd ..."
(stamp!). Perez jangled on.

"Four . Discharge of all rights to property, assets and equity on
Spanish territory dated April 23rd ..." (stamp!) "Five ... Agreed
inventory of all personal property of Mr. Brian Walker which has
been moved to Malaga Airport for collection on or before April
24th, 12 p.m." (Stamp!) He handed one of the policemen the
release document duly completed. "Release him. You are a very
lucky hombre," he said, turning to Walker who was then frog-
marched down the corridor and into the release area, where he
was ordered to stand on a red line two meters away from the small
cubbyhole, both his feet spread by Guardia, his cuffs not yet
released. A hoarse voice from behind the cubbyhole identified his
property as it appeared piece by piece through the cubbyhole.
Walker knew he had 301,200 in pesetas when arrested, and
offered no objection as the brown envelope appeared quoting
120,000 pesetas. The cuffs were released and he was escorted into
the changing room. Amazingly, there was a shower with shaving
utensils and soap ... glorious soap. The time was 5:45 a.m. Once
finished, he was taken to a Fiat Minivan with four other Britons,
two of whom were handcuffed to plain clothes Guardia. The van
followed the signs which read the word Aerpuerto.

Iberian flight IB631 for London via Madrid took off at 6:45 a.m.
Above the clouds the warm morning sun broke the monotony of
flying. The atmosphere was soothing, the aircraft being full of
happy families returning from holiday. Walker noticed a lone
Spaniard six seats away. "Fucking pig," he muttered to himself and
dozed into an instant deep sleep. The person he was referring to
was Don Jose Ayala. The jumbo touched down at Heathrow six
minutes early. Ayala spotted McNiff immediately in the arrivals
lounge fifteen minutes later. The aging Fenian was never a good
undercover man, always seeming at labour with his surroundings
and out of step with the flow of things. On this warm spring
morning McNiff as usual was wearing the 56 pound crombie he

had purchased and nurtured since his release from the Curragh in 1959. His had the black brogues soled and heeled every September before the hard weather. McNiff had a habit of doing things by dates rather than climatic conditions. The Fenian rose to greet Ayala, his hand outstretched. "Jose my friend. how are you?'

"Very good, Colm, very good, and how are you?' Formality complete, the pair adjourned to the lounge bar of the Trust House Forte Hotel half a mile away. Inside, transient people wandered here and there. Languages of the world filled the bar. The pair found an empty booth. "Well, Jose, what's the news?' he inquired impatiently as he paid for the glass of red wine and his own beverage of choice orange juice. McNiff possessed an aversion to alcohol- a trait he inherited from his high minded Catholic abstinence.

"Colm, I have much news for you. This fellow Bennett is genuine, everything checks out. Senor Fernandez is an embezzler, one of the biggest on the coast. He has been in partnership with a fellow called Peter Harris who arranges all the introductions from the United Kingdom. This ploy gets Harris off the hook. The system is so simple. Harris finds the client and introduces him to Fernandez, who lodges cash every day into a number of bank accounts under the trade names of the various bars he is selling. This means that any bar will show a first class cash flow, backed up by bank statements. Also, he bribes or blackmails various mouthpieces to give the prospective purchaser a good independent story about any given property. I understand that sometimes he will organize a phone call or two to persuade the potential purchaser to pull out of the deal for a fee. This will usually convince the victim to buy." The Basque continued as he mapped out the scheme on his notebook. "It is imperative that Fernandez settles the sale for more than the purchaser has in cash. He will then supposedly offer a loan from the seller over a year or two, always to be paid by way of promissory notes. This means that the purchaser will not take up the deeds until all the obligations in the contract are fulfilled. As this shall prove impossible, the seller will repossess the entire business without any refund whatsoever. If the purchaser wants the deeds, then he will have to pay up the value of the notes in one lump sum, so Fernandez is on a winner as the property will have been grossly over-valued anyway. Presently, he has fifty or sixty such deals rolling over with the vast majority going bust within a few months. The purchaser has no chance. So, I met Fernandez myself personally. Remember, the actual seller seldom meets the purchaser face to face, where there exists a seller; otherwise he sets up a fake seller to say all the right things and play out the scam. He has been known to sell property that he doesn't even have legal title for."

The Basque continued, "This man is absolutely ruthless. He has been directly responsible for much distress and hardship on many innocent people, with help by some local police. But here's some good news, I think." "Tell me."

"Mr. Fernandez deposits most of his embezzled money here in London at Lloyd's Bank on Shaftsbury Avenue. The reason for this, I think, is that he could not deposit United Kingdom drafts in Spain, as the profits are huge and the tax liability would be also. So, always he insists on being paid in two equal drafts. He deposits one in Spain to pay off the seller and take his fees and the other he sends directly back to the United Kingdom. Being a non-resident and non-national, he is not liable for taxation on cash deposits for 26 weeks. There's presently 180,000 Sterling in his deposit account at Shaftsbury Avenue, and I think we might be able to get our hands on all of it," the Basque stated firmly, his perfect white teeth sparkling a mischievous smile. "How did you get the information" McNiff asked

"I dropped in after hours, so easy...the place is not even alarmed!

"Hope you didn't leave anything behind....please go on anyway"

"Simple, provided he has not met the manager personally, and I don't think he has. I saw some statements and correspondence on his desk relating to various lodgements. He must change banks often. You see, I think he is obliged to move his money out of the U.K. every twenty six weeks to avoid tax. Check it out. However, one piece of correspondence says the following; I took it from his "out" tray and this is it...the original. He will think it was taken and filed by the secretary and she won't miss what she never saw. Look at the date ... two weeks ago."

Dear Mr. Fernandez,

I am indeed pleased to have received your cash transfer from Barclay's Bank, St. Helier, Jersey in the sum of 178,484.54 and have noted your instructions regarding withdrawals at short notice. I am sure you appreciate that you shall be liable for taxation in respect of interest earned in excess of 20000.00 per annum at the rate of 26% after 26 weeks. I note that you may be in London in the near future. I am looking forward to meeting you. Do not hesitate to call me anytime. Yours sincerely,

Andrew Glover - Branch Manager

"Well, what does it all mean?' enquired McNiff, jingling the ice in the empty glass. "We're going to have to take a chance, Colm. Just one chance that Fernandez has not met the manager yet, or is not previously familiar with any of the staff, and there's only one way to find out." "How?'

"McNiff," the Basque queried seriously. "Could you have some drafts forged?'

"I would think so... why?'

"About 70,000 - say three twenties and one ten. Let me explain. There are two possible ways we can clean him out, provided he has not met the manager or my story doesn't fall down. Suppose I call him, pretend to him I am in Spain but am coming to London to lodge 70,000 in drafts, just to give credit to the scam. I can detect from the phone call whether he has met Fernandez before or not. Let's be optimistic. Suppose he has not personally met him before. Then I can do two things. One, we can have a passport forged here in the name of Jean Claude Fernandez, I look like the guy anyway, and present myself with the forged drafts for lodging, then withdraw the existing cash he has on deposit. Give him a story ... even that I just need the cash. The drafts will inspire confidence. That plan might work, but I think it's a little optimistic. It's a lot of money. He might call Fernandez in Spain, just to be sure. Then it's blown. The plan does avoid a further trip to Spain. However, it's risky, but quick and clean. I'm only afraid that Fernandez might have called him since that letter. That's just another chance. He might have called him. Fernandez had not got the letter out of his filing system for nothing although I think it was new mail, but I cannot be sure" "Jose. It all sounds very risky to me. Why not just send a couple of lads down and frighten the shit out of him," McNiff suggested in a business as usual manner. "I think that could be even riskier, Colm. Anyway, that can be done anytime. Now, the other plan is also dependent on any communication between them. But if I had all Fernandez's correspondence in a file in front of Glover including passport, credit cards, cheque book, and a bundle of legal matter such as property deeds, insurance policies etcetera, then I don't think he would suspect a thing. I am Spanish; copying his accent is no problem. Actually, I have a tape of a conversation we had in his office, and as I said I don't look at all unlike him. The signature is no problem. This plan means we'll have to lift him, clean out all his papers and put him asleep for a few days until we've got the cash. But remember, it just takes one call to screw the whole thing up. So what do you think, Colm?' "I don't know yet," McNiff replied, not persuaded. "Pity we couldn't lift him here in London. Actually, we really need some of this money to finance a little job, one third sound okay to you, Jose ... whatever scheme we decide on?' "Done. Now what should I do?' It is a ... what do you say, 'Hobson's choice' at the moment anyway, so I may as well take the bull by the horns. What to lose, eh?' The Spaniard had made up his mind. "I will phone Glover at the bank this morning anyway. Get those drafts, we'll need them anyway. I can arrange the passport here in London if need be, but better to use his if you get your hands on it", "Are you going to book in here, Jose?'

"No, I think I better get lost in the city. I will call you later."

Chapter Sixteen

Ayala switched off the pocket recorder for the last time, confident that he could turn Fernandez' vocal nuances on and off like a faucet and dialled the bank from his room at The Winston Churchill Hotel on Great Portland Street. "Mr. Glover, please."

"Just a minute, sir. Who may I say is calling, sir?' The voice was female and appropriately firm but pleasant. "Jean-Claude Fernandez," the Basque allowed himself a nervous smile. He had long been a connoisseur of edgework. "Hello, Mr. Fernandez. Glover here. I'm delighted to hear from you. How is the weather down there?" The Manager opened. "It's very nice, Mr. Glover - but a little chilly in the evenings; have you sent on the confirmation I was speaking to you about last week?' The Basque was lost - but blundered on out of instinct. "No, I have been extremely busy, and I have to be in London on Monday. I'll have it with me so I can give it to you when I meet you. I did want to ask you, Mr. Glover, is there any particular way I should express the confirmation, in Spain it is very strict. You have to fill out a special form." Ayala wrinkled the crevices of his face, locking his jaw in anticipation of Glover's answer. "Not at all. Just state 'I hereby instruct you to transfer to Mr. Peter Harris, account number such and such the sum of' - what was it?'' The manager babbled on nonchalant.

".... mille," interrupted Ayala, hoping Glover would not understand. "Yes, Mr. Fernandez - 14,000 Pounds?'

"Oh, I'm sorry, Mr. Glover. I am, preoccupied. I forget I must speak English to you. Fourteen thousand. I'll have that prepared. Now, Mr. Glover, I shall be making a large cash withdrawal and I will also be lodging 70000 Sterling with you in bank drafts. I must ask you to have the cash ready for me. One hundred and sixty five thousand. I shall be lodging about 70,000 on deposit." "Excellent. I thought we were losing you there for a moment. Let me take a note of that. You say 165,000 Pounds in cash?'

"That is correct. But please, have the cash ready. That is why I called you today, to give you time. So, what time shall I call Monday ... about two o'clock, would that suit you, Mr. Glover?' "Two o'clock will be fine, Mr. Fernandez. Oh, just one other thing. Can you bring along a copy of your last statement, please?' It would save me a little trouble. I want it for the revenue people here as it is the end of the financial year, and they wish to quantify tax due on interest even though you've only been a depositor for a couple of months. I don't want them getting up my back for failing to file. There is a copy at headquarters in the computer centre, but it would take a week or so to get that, the system you understand." "I'm afraid I'm not sure if I can locate it just at the minute, Mr. Glover," Ayala blurted. "Perhaps you could have a look and I could call you tomorrow, Mr. Fernandez?' "Well ... one can only do one's best under short notice ..."Actually, Mr. Glover. I just remembered where I put it. I'll have it for you Monday. Anyway, I am leaving for Barcelona today for a meeting and flying out tonight, so I won't be available by phone. I will see you Monday at two o'clock. Bye for now." "Fernandez" terminated the conversation with deft diplomacy. Ayala replaced the receiver sharply. "Fuck him and his statement. Should I take a chance and tell him I couldn't find it?' No, I won't, just in case. I'm going to have to pay you another visit, Mr. Fernandez - and quick." The Basque dialled McNiff's number.

"Hello?'

"Ola, Ayala here. Colm, get on that phone and book three returns to Malaga leaving tonight. It's got to be a rush job. Organize the usual I.D.s' for the other two. I'll wait here for your call. Those drafts have to be done by Monday morning. Adios." Don Jose Ayala picked up the phone an hour later. It was Colm McNiff. "Hello, Jose. I've booked the tickets for Millar and O'Toole. McCahan can't go. Look, it's better if you could book separately. Just give them a call. It's a discount shop in Kensington - Budget Fares. Get on BA 494 - departing tonight 7:45 p.m., return Sunday, arriving Heathrow 11:45 p.m. Do it now. They tell me there is a rush on three day returns with the golfers, who all have their own apartments so they book flight only. Call me back in fifteen minutes to confirm, and then you can meet the boys this afternoon to fill them in. Is there any equipment you need?' "Yes, now that you mention it. We will want, say, 30 milligrams of morphine, say two fluid ounces of chloroform, some scopolamine, and better get two-three dozen pairs of surgical gloves. I think that's it, can you manage that?' Oh, and a half dozen hypodermics. That will take a few hours. Call me as soon as you book the flight." The Basque returned the call ten minutes later. "No problem, Colm. I've to pick up my tickets at Heathrow. Could you meet me with the others at 6 o'clock, here in the Churchill?' It shouldn't take too long to tell them the details. I've got to go now. I have to call Spain. Don't skimp on the equipment; it's essential." A matter of equal importance flashed into Ayala's mind. He placed his hand on the receiver and concentrated for a few moments. Then he picked it up sharply and dialled Glover's number at Barclay's Bank. The Basque was put through to Glover immediately after the secretary's usual polite but inquisitive greeting. "Hello, Mr. Fernandez. I have organized the cash for you for Monday. Did you find the statement?' The banker was polite and seemed to be in good spirits. It was Friday and within half an hour he would be free of the drudge of work for a full two days. "Yes, Mr. Glover. My secretary has located it. I am already en route. However, the reason I called is to ask if I can bring forward my appointment on Monday," Ayala lacing his tone with a hint of demand. "Of course, but I can only give you half an hour at 10:30 a.m. Other than that my diary is filled for Monday, unless you would like to leave it until Tuesday." "No, Mr. Glover. I have most urgent business on Monday and into the week. I'll take the 10:30 appointment. Perhaps you would join me for a meal some evening when you are free?' I shall be in London for at least three weeks" the Basque ventured, lying in his teeth. "I'd be delighted, Mr. Fernandez. Until Monday then"

The Banker was in a hurry to get off the telephone.

"Have a good weekend, Mr. Glover. Bye" Ayala replaced the receiver. Sporting a broad smile, he jumped on the coffee table and clapped his hands in rhythm, rattling a few steps of a Spanish dance, a sort of personal coup-de-gras Spanish-style, a ritual he exercised when in receipt of good news. Jean-Claude Fernandez picked up the phone five minutes later. He had just returned from his siesta. "Buenos Dias, Senor Fernandez" The conversation continued in Spanish. "Hello, Mr. Fernandez. This is Luis Gumez," opened the Basque. This was the name he had been using during his contact with Fernandez. He continued. "I have changed my mind about buying a bar there. I am particularly interested in three bars, the one in Los Boliches; the one in Fuengirola and the one in Torremolinos. I am coming down from Barcelona on Sunday. Perhaps you could meet me." "Well, certainly, but you must bring a booking deposit with you, say 500,000 pesetas anyway, because I am in advanced negotiations on these bars at the moment," said Fernandez lying, his pulse quickening but remaining ice cool.

"That's no problem. I can bring this in cash, but I must see you Sunday. I have to be back in Barcelona on Monday for a meeting with the solicitors to sort out my mother's estate." The Basque's tone was both demanding and serious. "Can you meet me at my apartment at Edifico Del Sol at 6 o'clock on Sunday evening?' It's just across the road from your office as you know, number 271." Ayala had not handed in the keys before his early departure for London, and the rent was paid up in advance. He continued, "Please bring with you the papers relating to these bars, including the contracts which I can sign."

"Very well, Senor Gumez. I shall be there at six sharp"

Chapter Seventeen

" I've never been to Spain before," said Niall O'Toole, thumbing through the glossy holiday brochure. "Will we be able to have a swim?' The Provo picked up the surgical gloves at Boots Nationwide Pharmacy. Then he was off to a small cafe opposite St. Bartholomew's Hospital for a clandestine meeting with a stoic-looking Irish RN. The small ampoules containing the drugs had the word "Insulin" stamped officiously on the face labels, the covering letter on doctor's notepaper confirming that the bearer was a diabetic lest Customs be suspicious. Millar would carry the drugs; years of study and continuous late night meetings made him look frail anyway.

The threesome met in Reading at 4:45 p.m. Within two hours they were parking the car around the corner from the Winston Churchill Hotel on Great Portland Street. They made a fine sight, McNiff in his crombie as usual, carrying a battered dated briefcase, the type with brass buckles and locking device. Millar hid everything with a black raincoat, the American type buttoned at the neck and a hold all sporting the word "Adidas." Niall O'Toole also had a hold all of the same type with the words "Glasgow Celtic." It was green and white - very bright and sporty. Also, he wore a sleeveless tee-shirt and a pair of good quality stone washed jeans, his two inch polished brown leather belt trimming off the youthful presentation. The bomber jacket was slung through the hand grip of the hold all.

Five minutes later, Ayala was briefing the men in his room. For this purpose he had purchased a small dry board, water base markers and a map of the area of concentration. In the first instance, he ordered that both Provos should immediately take on the identities of both the American passports, and he would not be disclosing his true name at any time in the future. The instructions were brief.

"We depart tonight at 8:45 p.m. from Heathrow. I shall be travelling separately. Do not under any circumstances approach me or speak to me until you arrive at the apartment where the target is to be abducted, on Sunday at six o'clock. I will now outline the procedure. If you have any questions, you can ask when I have finished."

The IRA men sensed a aloofness and certainty about this phantom Spaniard, who complimented the lush furnishings of the room perfectly, sporting pure silk black polka dot shirt with black mohair slacks, impeccably pressed, which touched his black leather slip-ons. The jewellery was simple but expensive, contrasting appropriately with his light olive skin. The only objection a voyeur might have would be his continuous hacking cough from chain-smoking. His opening sentence stamped the level of discipline he was to demand of the two Irishmen. Lifting both American passports, addressed Millar and O'Toole thus:

"Mr. Flinn and Mr. Richards, you will arrive at Malaga Airport at approximately 11:45 p.m. Spanish time. During the flight do not speak too much to any particular person. Just stay low and join in the atmosphere." He pinned the map of Spain on the built-in wardrobe and placed the small dry board upright on the dressing table.

"When the plane lands and you clear Customs, do not use a cab; take the train from here," pointing to the train station, across the taxi rank, one hundred metres from the airport exit.

"If the flight is delayed, take a cab if you must. Then, get off at this stop ... La Caraheula. It's just four stops, then go to "Hotel Plaza Sol" ... here. You will see the big neon light; you can't miss it. Do not ask for directions, especially to the Guardia Civil. You will get a room there. Book in for two nights. Tomorrow, Saturday, you will take the bus south ... any bus to Fuengirola will do and get off when you reach Edifico Sol on the left hand side. Again, do not request directions. Enter the building through the back entrance and go to the swimming pool. Do not use the elevator and meet me at apartment 271 at ten o'clock sharp; it's on the third floor. I will fill you in on the rest of the details then. Any questions, Mr. Flinn- Mr. Richards?'

"No questions." the Provos replied in harmony.

"Bring the drugs and surgical gloves with you." I would like two pairs myself, please, before we leave for the airport." Millar handed them over from his inside pocket. "Now if you don't mind, I would like to inspect the drugs and needles." Millar opened his shaving kit and spread the goods on the coffee table. "The chloroform is the one with the letter 'A' under the base of the bottle and the morphine is the one with the 'M' stuck underneath. The scopolamine solution is unmarked. "

"I am told the stuff is pharmaceutically pure," interrupted McNiff.

"Well, that's it, gentlemen. You make your own way to the airport." Ayala distributed the tickets accurately checking that both were filled out to the appropriate aliases.

"Guard these tickets with your life. It may depend on them. If you lose them it could be very serious. Now, about the money. We should have enough to cover lost airline tickets or anything else. How much do you both have?' "Two Thousand, Five Hundred Pounds Sterling between us."

"Just one thing," Ayala snapped. "That Glasgow Celtic hold-all is not an American team. Change that bag now! The team broke up at 7:15 p.m. Ayala travelled to Heathrow Airport alone by subway, followed by O'Toole and Millar twenty minutes later.

Chapter Eighteen

B rian Walker had stepped from the Jumbo that morning anticipating that the police would be waiting for him at Heathrow arrivals. He was astonished that he had not been escorted on the flight, but where were the others; he did not see the handcuffed Britons since Malaga Airport. They were not on the flight - perhaps they got the Manchester or Birmingham departures later on. The Guardia had escorted Walker at close range, while he was picking up his property, six large suitcases and one large trunk which would need to be weighed and duly paid for as extra baggage. He had to pay 600 Pounds between legal fees and fines at the prison earlier.

He had been ripped off, and wondered who had paid the air fare, although he did not care. If there were no police waiting to arrest him at arrivals he would live to tell the tale and perhaps someday carry out his promise on the evening he was charged at Torremolinos Guardia Station. He was exhausted. The two hour snore in the plane only further weakened him when he awoke to the airline breakfast, which he devoured in four mouthfuls. Picking up his baggage on the trolley, he walked through Customs as if they did not exist and quickened his pace in the direction of the taxi rank. He could not believe it. There was definitely something out of order, he thought. A period of six months was granted to Walker's solicitor to establish his whereabouts for the purpose of drafting his defense. No arrest warrant had been issued, and there was still a month to go to file the appropriate documentation. The cabbie was pleased at a run from Heathrow to Camden Town, unusual these days since the introduction of the Heathrow-Central London tube link.

Immediately on entering his brother's hallway, he called Pauline in Wolverhampton, John and Bennett dumping the luggage in the living room. Naturally, his wife was blissful to the point of tears at her husband's return. After all, they still had some money left and more important, they had each other. Bennett envied them. Brian spent a full forty five minutes speaking to his wife and replaced the receiver having said "bye love, see you tomorrow."

Turning to Bennett, the big man embraced him in a friendly bear hug. "Don't worry, mate. We're not finished by a long shot." The conversation drew on, hour by hour. The relief and excitement of being home gave Brian a second breath. John had made a hearty breakfast of steak and eggs, washed down with a couple of pots of strong tea and a batch loaf of white bread with lashings of butter. John produced the bank draft which he had picked up from Barclay's, explaining that his brother would have to cash it in person. It was made out in the amount of £30,000, the residue of the various imposed settlements with Fernandez. "I won't bother cashing it today; I'm too tired. Anyway, I still have a few Pounds," Brian remarked yawning. "I'll leave it until Monday. Pauline is coming down from Wolverhampton tomorrow. Perhaps yourself and Debbie would join us for a night out, be just like old times, what do you say, Howard?'

"I'll let you know, Brian. Things haven't been too good between us since. She's at her parent's. It's all very crushing; although I do feel a lot better in the last ten days or so since I got back. I'm sure I could pick up a job quite soon but not just yet. Then I can rent a flat and hopefully get back to normal again. I'm so grateful to John here for putting me up. I've certainly learned a lot and met some really comforting down-to-earth people." The Printer turned to Brian's brother. "I'll make it up to you sometime, John. Thank you for everything." Bennett offered his hand.

"Put it out of your mind mate. It's nothing; nothing at all." The men shook hands heartily. Bennett continued enthusiastically. "I'm so relieved to be home. It feels like I've just finished a term in prison, much like you - what value freedom! That Irish crowd down at the Rose and Crown would put anybody out of their misery. Life seems to be just 'come day, go day' to them.

111

I'd love someday to go back to Dublin for a Rugby International. There really is something very special about the 'Rose."

"Well, you never know Howard, perhaps we might even go into business together. You're a professional and I still have some money, although I'd have to be a silent partner. I do have a hell of a lot of good contacts here in England still. I could definitely flood out a small printing operation with work in a very short time. We'll talk about it when we get sorted out."

The conversation swung round to the subject of the Spanish situation. There seemed to be little they could do. Walker was afraid to go to the Spanish Embassy or any authority because of the "hot money aspect." Bennett was more concerned with pulling his life back together again.

"Well, I'm going round to the Rose for a drink. Then I'll go for a good sleep. Ring me around seven, will you?' Brian asked. It was two o'clock in the afternoon. John had a free afternoon and joined Bennett who had an appointment with Ken Samuels at four o'clock. He had made his mind up to sell his treasured Ming Note, gauging he would need the money for a deposit on the flat he would rent in the near future. The pair spent a carefree afternoon lounging around Hyde Park, Kensington and into Sloan Square. Samuels was overjoyed to see his friend so soon.

The Printer did not elaborate on the reasons for his early return to London, just saying, "It's not all it's made out to be, Ken. I'm back here now for good. I put the bar on the market. It should sell soon enough lying. I'd like to do a little business with you, Ken. Could we talk?'

Samuel's showroom was small and purposely laid out for the informal browser. Smoking and children were prohibited. The floor was covered in a deep red carpet purposely fitted to preserve silence and improve concentration. The front window was dressed out in red velvet, skilfully terraced to give an interesting effect to the variety of notes and coins on display. Both walls were covered with aluminium cases to hip level and trimmed off with a line of counter-type viewing cases to floor level on each side. The ceiling was in the Italian Pergola style, modern bronze with an array of spotlights concealed to give best effect to the more expensive notes. To the back of this area there was a Louis 14th occasional table which had a variety of current magazines and newspaper articles which were free of charge. Also, there were lists of banknote and bond dealers, clubs and auction houses. Every fifteen minutes the silence would be broken by the slow loud chimes of the French baroque clock which was placed at the far right-hand corner of the viewing area. Samuels once remarked it was the best investment that he had ever made in that the quarter hourly chimes were an inescapable reminder of the value of time. The occasional table stood against the single tinted glass partition behind which was Samuels' office. Again, the office was small, only twelve by fifteen feet, but furnished in Louis 14th pieces. The back wall was covered in framed bonds, notes and various articles which Samuels had written throughout his thirty five year career. Samuels requested his secretary to prepare coffee for John and show him around while he would speak to Howard Bennett in his office about the most precious of all his material possessions- a Ming Dynasty note for one Yi Guan, issued in 1368 A.D. - which he had deposited with Ken Samuels some years before. He had acquired this note in Hong Kong as a handshake while installing a printing machine. Samuels paid him a nominal retainer for exhibition purposes. The note was insured for 5000 Pounds "Ken, I would like to sell my Ming Note." Samuels eyed his friend in suspicion and disbelief.

"You're behaving imprudently sir," the dealer stated firmly. "Why do you want to sell?'

"I'm going to need the money," Bennett grovelled. Samuels fixed his eyes on Bennett in concern.

"Listen, Howard, we've been close friends for a very long time. I don't know what has happened to you in Spain, and I shan't ask. I've had an offer from a collector in Yellow Springs, Ohio, for that note. I posted the offer to your address in Spain last week. If I were you I would not sell."

"What's the offer, Ken?'

"Four Thousand Five Hundred Pounds. Look - I'll tell you what I'll do. If you need some money, I will advance you whatever you want within reason. Keep the Ming in any case."

"Maybe you're right. I'm not really desperate just yet. I appreciate your offer of a loan, Ken, thanks so much. I'll mull it over and see you again in a few days. I'm not right lately between one thing and the other. Thank you for talking me out of it ... that note was a token of gratitude from some good people in Hong Kong ... back when I was a happier man."

Ken Samuels extended his hand to his colleague. Bennett reciprocated; Samuels punctuating the exchange of friendship by wrapping his other hand to enclose Bennett's. Samuels peered intensely into the Printer's eyes.

"I take back what I'd said before. I can see you are deeply troubled. Please, Dusty, if you need anything or you need to just talk and get things off your chest, please know you can rely on me"

Howard Bennett attempted a reply, feeling sheepish, albeit now fully aware of the extent of his long association with Ken Samuels. The Printer tightened his grip. "I just need time to sort myself out, I'll settle out in a few days. Thanks again, Ken."

Bennett did an about-face and walked to the reception area to interrupt John Walker's fleeting attempts to chat up the secretary.

"Y' know, Howard?' When I was a kid I started up a little stamp collection. Lost interest of course, but the stuff here really fascinated me ... the coins ... and the currencies ... with those little cards besides them, with the history and such"

"Sure, John." Bennett caught himself being abrupt, but he felt he needed to shift gears. "Let's get a drink."

The two sauntered through the bustling streets of London, now approaching dusk, the target being the Rose and Crown.

Sean McCahan greeted the men as they entered the pub. "How are ye" the Bricklayer's toothless smile aglow.

As Bennett dozed off at 1 a.m. the thought occurred to him that 200,000 pound outlay mentioned in the draft apparently did not seem to bother McCahan and his so called "friends,"

"I hope I haven't got myself into anything," was Bennett's last thought as the darkness descended on another day in his troubled life.

Chapter Nineteen

The booked out British Airways departure for Malaga had taken off on time, five hours earlier. Bobby Millar was tense. He had never before been on active duty, spending most of his time questioning his ability to stand up to a cross-examination about his American identity from the Spanish Police. It takes a certain inward conviction to put such considerations out of mind when going into battle. Millar was an over-cautious man, a trait that is sometimes dangerous on operations like this one. O'Toole was incapable of any such meanderings of the imagination. A hardened terrorist of finely calculated recklessness, he was now for many years more than capable of shaping his thoughts to the whim of his will. As far as O'Toole was concerned, he was on the way to Spain to have a few drinks and a swim. If he met a girl, that would be a bonus. Sometime on the way back out to the airport on Sunday, some prick was going to be lifted and put asleep. On Monday when they got back to London, the Spanish guy was going to clean out a bank, that's all ... what's the big deal?'

Ayala's mind worked differently. He was a gambler through and through with that instinctive sixth sense for good and bad risk. It is the sort of logic that is nurtured out of the will to survive and win, which is even tastier against the odds. Ayala possessed an unnatural ability to sense trouble at great distances. He did not have that feeling as he flicked through the "El Pais" fifteen minutes before touchdown.

After passing through Customs without a hitch, Millar headed for a taxi without thinking. "What the fuck are you doing?' rasped O'Toole, in a good American accent and headed straight for the train station. Once inside the apartment, O'Toole showered and changed immediately. Millar was pacing the lounge, not having removed his jacket.

"What's the matter with you?' Have a shower, come on out and have a few beers. Did you see the action down the road ... no end to it" O'Toole smacked the Teacher on the shoulder. O'Toole's attitude gave Millar confidence. He needed it. As the night moved into the early hours, the pair grew easier with each other, the Explosives Man constantly laughing off the job as a joke. He meant it, and by two a.m. he had Millar convinced. Niall O'Toole was a good wingman to have on your side in times like these.

O'Toole woke first the next morning at 8:20 a.m. to the sound of laughing voices and the rumbling of the Mediterranean. He stepped out onto the balcony, shielding his sleepy eyes from the glare of the morning sun. The beach disappeared into the distance on either side of his vision and was already becoming busy. Two pleasure cruisers were docked on the beach, their owners touting for business, their day's work well begun. Millar woke half an hour later. The two went down to the pool bar for rolls and coffee, and arrived at the Basque's apartment at ten o'clock sharp as arranged entering by the pool stairs. Millar pressed the button on the intercom. The door opened a moment later, Ayala greeting both Irishmen with a silent smile and waved them to the lounge which overlooked the rolling ocean. The room was absent of a lived in feeling; Ayala explaining that he would not be unpacking except for the daily couple of shirts and change of underwear and pants. The room was sparsely furnished in crude wooden Spanish pieces. The tiled floor added to the emptiness. The Basque spent the next hour explaining the steps of the abduction. The drugs were laid out on the coffee table. O'Toole moved uneasily in his seat, the adrenalin pumping through his veins as the Basque went through the action, using Millar in the place of Fernandez.

"The target will arrive at this door at six o'clock sharp tomorrow evening. He is very small, about five-foot-four and weights maybe one hundred twenty Pounds. It is essential that he has his keys which are always on a key holder on the left-hand side of his belt. I've never seen him without them. I will open the door; if I see the keys I will say to him the words 'Buenas Noches.' I may continue to speak, but if my first words are 'Buenos Noches,' then the following action shall be taken. You, Mr. Flinn," pointing at O'Toole, "will be in the bathroom here. When he comes in, I will have my back to him leading him into the lounge and probably speaking. Simply stand out, without arousing him and place the cloth I will give you over his mouth and nostrils like this. You should not release the cloth until he becomes limp. It will take about fifteen to twenty seconds. You will be wearing surgical gloves. Then take the body into the bedroom here, the first door on the right, just at the end of the hallway. Place him on the bed and I will then inject the drugs and remove the keys and search his pockets. While I am doing this, both of you should be cleaning up my prints. We will rub down an hour before he arrives anyway. Mr. Flinn and I will change into these two boiler suits. These are the jump type and light blue with the words Benalmadena Constructiones printed in red on the back. Meanwhile you, Mr. Richards, should gather up the drugs and needles and pack them in your shaving bag. Then take the holdalls and get out to the departure bar in the airport by cab. If I am not there by 7:25 p.m., you should check in and travel alone. I should say that your position will be in the wardrobe here. With a bit of luck he'll be knocked out before you see him. Remember this is the action we take if my first words are 'Buenos Noches' If I say anything other than that simply stay in your positions. What happens then, I'll decide when it happens. We'll just have to play it by ear. Any questions?' 'Ayala addressed the Irishmen with both hands on his hips, looking calm, confident, ready. "No questions- very good. I would like you both to be here tomorrow at three o'clock in the afternoon. Have you got the airline tickets with you?'

"Yes, I have them," said Millar.

"Give them to me now; bring all your gear at three o'clock and wipe down your apartment and the escalator. Give notice of leaving. Tell the receptionist you're on your way to Morocco for a holiday. Come here the same way as today, using the bus and backstairs. Everything okay?"

"No problem. See you at three o'clock then. Here are the tickets." Millar handed them over. The Provos left by the back stairs unnoticed.

Chapter Twenty

Ayala waved from the balcony as the lone Fernandez arrived on the dot of six o'clock. The target waved back, the glisten of chrome keys dangling from his belt flashing in the evening sunlight. The Swindler made his way up the public stairs. The Basque told the hidden Provos he had the keys and the operation a 'go' as he opened the door after deliberately waiting a few seconds after the chimes of the doorbell.

"Ah, Buenas Noches," continuing in a blaze of speedy Spanish. Ayala turned his back on the target, Fernandez followed. Niall O'Toole slipped out from the bathroom in his stocking feet and pounced on his prey, suffocating the mouth and nostrils with the chloroform-soaked cloth, locking his head and neck in a vice on his chest and forearm. O'Toole locked his other arm around the Spaniard's chest which prevented his immediate reaction to pull away the cloth. The Swindler's eyeballs ballooned, bulging from their sockets during the five or six seconds of the ordeal, the tiny legs pumping like pistons as though some maniac was bending his bones. Moments later the body slumped lifeless. The Basque administered the intramuscular doses of drugs from the hypodermics without fuss. A search of his pockets revealed a wallet, two Spanish cheque books and a purse containing a few notes and mixed coins. The briefcase contained papers relating to a bar in Los Boliches. No one spoke. It was all over in fifteen minutes including the rubbing down for prints. The lifeless body was placed in the closet, made comfortable with some pillows and a soft down, some food and water, the door locked.

Giving himself a final shrug, Miller flushed the toilet. He was relieved to have done his part, if only to take the heat off O'Toole, who might have aroused suspicion travelling alone. The others made their way across the main road to the office, Ayala carrying a large tool bag into which he had put his briefcase. The lock opened easily.

Once inside, Ayala made for the filing cabinet; again it was locked, but opened easily. The Spaniard passed O'Toole the bunch of keys and he got to work on the desk drawers. Within five minutes they had what they wanted, plus a bonus: six bank drafts in the amount 42,800 Pounds - all drawn on English banks. Both the carrying case and large tool bag were stuffed with files relating to bank statements, correspondence, cheque books and credit cards, insurance policies, title deeds and contracts for sale. And then, bingo; Fernandez's passport. The jump suits folded into a very small bulk and were stuffed in the tool bag also. The office was left undisturbed, the filing cabinet and desk drawers re-locked and the entire areas of suspicion, inside and out given a final wipe.

The pair walked to the train station and reached the departure lounge separately, well inside schedule with almost too much time to spare. The Basque had told the Provo to purchase one business attaché case at the airport shop and meet him in the men's room, where the files were transferred from the tool bag. Ayala remained in a cubicle until ten minutes before check-in. The final few minutes he spent organizing his forged papers for presentation at check-in. Wiping down the cubicle, he checked to see he had not forgotten anything. Ayala washed his hands and checked in at departure gate number 4.

By 10:15 p.m. that evening, the three men were looking across the oval desk at a gleaming Colm McNiff. Seven forged bank drafts were laid out on the desk, 128,846.84 in amounts ranging from 16,000 to 22,000 Pounds Sterling.

"I hope to Christ everything goes all right tomorrow at the bank," he said addressing Jose Ayala. The papers made startling reading. There were fifty four files relating to weekly cash injections into various bank accounts. Twenty five files related to serious allegations of misrepresentation and fraud from clients - British, American and German mostly. There was one very recent file which contained an agreement between one Brian Walker and Jean Claude Fernandez and referred to a deportation order and

121

prison release. A further six files outlined the movement of a single large amount of money from various banks in the U.K. and offshore including the latest which was headed Lloyds Bank, Shaftsbury Avenue, London SW1. This was the one Ayala wanted. Luckily, another file had photocopies of all personal legal documents in case the originals got lost or stolen including passport, driving license, current credit cards, flying licence, birth certificate, Spanish residences and work permit. As with all professional swindlers, Fernandez was a meticulous person, although foolishly he had left six bank drafts, three credit cards in the top drawer of his desk - all English, Probably only used these cards when travelling. The up-to-date statements from Eurocard, Visa and Diner's Club were also in one file.

At eight o'clock, the Basque began to sort the papers for presentation to Glover. Ayala chose one of Fernanda's' genuine drafts and skilfully made the last number in the year indistinguishable. The draft was handwritten in blue ink, but very clear. The lettering was large and in a script style. It was easy to change. He placed this draft which was for £19,800 on top of the 6 drafts for £42800 from Fernandez's office and then under these the seven forgeries. He then packed the attaché case with files relating to bank correspondence. Glover's file was on top. Underneath and first visible he packed four sets of title deeds neatly bound in pink silk strips. The passport and various identifications, cheque books and credit cards he placed in the various transparent compartments in the wallet. Beneath both brass locking devices he stuck on in gold ultra-set the initials J.C.F. - accurately lined up.

The total for deposit in drafts would be £128,846.84 in forgeries and one genuine draft for £19,800, plus the 6 genuine drafts from the Fernandez's office for £42800 totalling £191446.84. The amount currently on deposit was £78,000 bringing the grand total up for looting to £269446.84. He then wrote down the details for the cash withdrawal slip and practiced the signature over the next twenty minutes

The time was 9:15 a.m. McNiff and O'Toole were in the kitchen making breakfast. The Basque checked through the papers again and again, spending intermittent one minute periods free handing the signature at speed. It was perfect. He was concerned at being requested by Glover to fill out the cash withdrawal slip freehand. Time was short. He decided to ask Glover to do it; then he would sign it. The Basque got back down to the figures. The total lodgement in drafts would be £191446.84. Therefore, the amount on deposit having lodged the drafts would be £269446.84. Bank drafts are credited at the end of the day and do not require clearing. Glover had £250,000 in cash waiting for the Basque which meant that the account would still show a balance of £19446.84 credit at the end of the day's trading.

Ayala calculated the odds in his mind and the possibility of getting out if things went wrong. He was ready. Picking up the attaché case, he went to the kitchen. The atmosphere is always the same going into battle. McNiff shook hands and said he would be praying for him, chewing on his last sausage.

"Are ye right?' O'Toole demanded bluntly dangling the car keys. The last piece of equipment the Basque took was the snub nose FN Browning which he put in his left inside pocket, having pushed home the clip and flicked the safety.

Barclay's Bank on Shaftsbury Avenue stands proudly at the centre of an endless street of Georgian buildings. Almost Baroque in its elaboration, the basement is broken by an ornate doorway with scrolled pediment carried on consoles. Above, standing on the first floor parapet were four giant Corinthian columns running through three floors. From the far side of the furious thoroughfare one could see the iron and glass roof and tall chimneys rise above the triangular pediment. Once inside the main marble reception hall, the visitor was met by a strikingly bronze sculpture by one John Henry Foley of "Ino and the Infant Bacchus", which was life size. The Basque took the three marble steps and entered the reception area as if he owned the place. Without hesitation, he made his way up to the main banking hall to the open counter with the notice "Enquiries." Before having finished his introduction to the clerk, he spotted a middle-aged man approaching him smiling his hand outstretched.

"Good morning. Senor Fernandez, I presume." They shook hands vigorously, the Banker pulling over the flap door on the counter with his free hand, ushering the Basque to his office. "Come this way, Mr. Fernandez." The Banker opened the office door, allowing the Spaniard to enter first. "May I offer you a cup of coffee or something, Mr. Fernandez?'

"Oh, that's kind of you, yes. I would very much like a cup of coffee - black with one sugar, please." Glover instructed the young secretary in an officious tone, his smile disappearing, his voice more urgent. The Banker pulled a packet of Dunhills to calm the atmosphere, which is always uneasy with first face to face meetings. Ayala declined the offer of a cigarette but flicked his gold lighter before Glover had the cigarette in his mouth. Both men engaged in idle chatter of the world until the coffee arrived two minutes later. Ayala's first sip rang the bell to take control.

"Now, Mr. Glover," cooed Ayala "these are my credentials, my passport and my flying license, and this is the confirmation which you requested, which has been duly witnessed by my solicitor in Spain. I hope it is in order."

"Absolutely perfect, Mr. Fernandez," the Banker said before finishing reading the short statement.

"And here is the original statement you require for the Revenue people - I have a photocopy, so you can keep it." The Basque was keeping the momentum going with deft skill and timing.

"Good man. Could you just sign this cash withdrawal slip which I have made out."

Unknown to himself, the Banker broke Alaya's continuity. The Basque picked the gold pen from his breast pocket. For a second his thumb pricked the safety catch on the rod. He continued, "Where should I sign, Mr. Glover?' searching the slip with the ball point.

"Just here, Mr. Fernandez at the X." He marked from the far side of the desk. The Basque signed perfectly and at speed.

"Here I have eight bank drafts from various English clients of mine which I wish to deposit, Mr. Glover. This one for £19,800, I must ask you if it is okay to be deposited. As you can see, the year on the date is a little smudged."

"Oh, I'm sure it should be okay. It's a draft. A draft is a draft in this country, Mr. Fernandez." The Banker wished to be accommodating.

"Please, Mr. Glover, I would prefer if you would call this bank and check. Last year a draft was not honoured for eight weeks because my name Fernandez was misspelled, it was spelled 'Fernandez'. Would you clear it for me, please?' The Basque's tone was polite, but business-like.

"Certainly, Mr. Fernandez; of course! The Manager pressed the intercom. The girl arrived seconds later. Glover handed her the draft. "Special clearance, please - immediately!

Ayala took up the momentum again. "The total of the drafts is £138,646. Can you check my balance, please?'

"Certainly" At this point Glover was working for the Basque and eyed the visual display unit. "It reads £178,000, so therefore you can have on deposit, including the drafts, - he toted on the pad - £316,646.

"Fine. I shall in future be lodging all drafts by registered post when I am not in London. Don't worry; they're insured. I would be obliged, Mr. Glover, if you could just call me every two weeks or so in Spain and let me know the state of my account. I will, of course, pay whatever fee is necessary. For the coming year's trading I shall be lodging in excess of £500,000." The buzz of the intercom interrupted the flow of conversation again - the Basque heard the message clearly.

"That draft is cleared, Mr. Glover," the secretary's voice crackled through the intercom. "Fine, thank you. Your draft is cleared, Mr. Fernandez, all these drafts will be credited to your account at the close of business this evening."

"Fine. That's all for the moment Mr. Glover, except to invite you to join me for dinner during the week. Which evening would suit you?'

"That's most kind of you; I would love to. The only evening I have free is Friday - usually I go for a few drinks and a game of bridge at the Banker's Club at Berkeley Square."

"Fine, I play bridge also, but I won't impose on you. Perhaps I could call you on Thursday; then we can decide. How is that with you?'

"Splendid, Mr. Fernandez, splendid." He picked up the phone - "Miss Roberts, please bring in the folder for Mr. Fernandez." The girl opened the door and placed the folder on the desk, leaving immediately. "Here's the cash, Mr. Fernandez, there's no need to check it, I can assure you." Fernandez opened the plastic zip and placed the wad in the attaché case with the other assortment of papers which were on the desk. "You know, Mr. Fernandez, I am most concerned about your security, carrying all this cash. I do not wish to be rude, but have you taken some precautions?' If you would like I can have the porter drive you to your destination."

"That would be absolutely splendid Mr. Glover. That's extremely kind of you. Thank you very much." The porter called five minutes later, stating that the car was ready in the rear courtyard. Banker and conman both shook hands vigorously and bade their goodbyes over a couple of moments. The manager then escorted Ayala through the back office, and said his last goodbye at the door to the courtyard which was filled with staff cars. The Basque saw the black Jaguar XJ6 purring at the exit, the black suited porter standing by the opened back door.

Five minutes later they were hurtling down Park Lane at high speed in the furious London traffic. The Basque gave the porter a ten spot as he stopped the car outside the Hilton close to Hyde Park Corner, and disappeared into the traffic saying "Anytime, sir, anytime" in a pleasant Cockney accent.

Like any bustling international city, London is a difficult place to hide with a bag full of hot money. The Basque knew that every single note could not only be accounted for, but traced. He hailed a taxi immediately outside the Hilton and headed for Victoria Station. If for some reason, even just a phone call from Perez, Fernandez's solicitor, enquiring as to his partner's whereabouts, then the job would be blown. The Basque called McNiff from the nearest pub, instructing him to tell O'Toole that he could not make it back to the car. O'Toole had called in three minutes before, suspecting that the Spaniard had left town with the loot.

"Look, Colm, wait for O'Toole to call in, then meet me at The Royal Gardiner Pub in Pimlico. It's just past Victoria Station, he can't miss it! I'll have the money split. We're reasonably safe for the moment, but for how long I don't know. I'd advise you to get that money through the system immediately - in the next couple of days. If you don't get here by 2:30 p.m. which is closing time, I will call you. Call me if he's on his way, the phone number is 60542, the code is 049. I want to get rid of some of it this afternoon and return the rod. Okay, Adios." McNiff called half an hour later, they were on their way.

Immediately after every crime there is a delirious frenzy laced with creeping paranoia within the rising vibes of a serious fear. Unsuccessful criminals, blinded with euphoria and temporary elation do not as a rule confront and deal with these essential elements of criminal activity. Mindless spending, alcohol, drug abuse and loose talk usually account for the fingering of suspects in a comparatively short space of time. Once fingered, life gets most uncomfortable. The persistent interrogation on points of minute detail, the extension orders for detention and vicious cross-examination at all hours of the night usually break the suspect even if he is only a source of information. The vast majority of suspects will sing when being confronted with charges for the withholding of information etc.; but not the IRA. Their breaking point is far beyond that of the sixty hour a week policeman with a pension, wife and family. The Special Branch will then move in, who are experts in interrogation and are usually specially chosen, single and very persuasive. Their techniques vary from torture and beatings to psychological warfare. The Provisional IRA are specially trained to deal with this as a matter of course, and they play to their strengths. Firstly, their politics take the view that their interrogators are the hired-heavies of a regime for which they have hate and loathing. The mind will depart from the body and freeze. This ploy will eventually bring frustration, anger and confusion on the interrogators who will then out of frustration resort to violence. When this inevitably occurs, the IRA will have won. Hours will pass rendering the admissibility of any statement questionable. The suspect will then be discharged and run to his legal counsel to commence counter proceedings. Special Branch know the ploy so well.

Ayala's was in deep concentration as he waited for O'Toole and McNiff in the "Royal Gardiner." Had he left any prints?' Not likely. He had waxed his fingers and handled all paper matter with the most delicate touch. Had Ortega called from Spain?' There was a good chance that he would call tomorrow - Tuesday. The Basque went through the procedure in his mind. The forged drafts would be discovered on Tuesday evening or at best on Wednesday morning. Glover would be telephoned immediately. All hell would break loose. He would call Fernandez immediately if he had not been on to him already. The Fraud Squad, Forensics and Special Branch would be on the premises within the hour. The staff would be rounded up and hundreds of statements taken after closing time at three o'clock.

Ayala's every step and movement would be gone over again and again. The tape from the Bank's video would be studied and dissected with a fine tooth comb. A highly accurate photo kit would be compiled which would be released immediately to the Spanish Police. The apartment where the abduction took place would be gone through by the Forensics and a file would be opened probably with the words "Abduction of Senor Jean Claude Fernandez."

Receptionists at hotels and guest houses up and down the coast would be presented with the photo kit and asked whether they had seen this man on or around a given date. The kit would then be circulated around the Spanish surveillance network for wanted criminals. With luck they would turn up with nothing. Glover would insist that the wanted man flew out from Barcelona. This would later be found to be untrue, the conclusion being that the passport was forged. Fernandez's offshore money would be exposed. He would crack under interrogation, but the Swindler being a Spaniard knew he would probably be able to cover up the entire matter with bribes, if he had any money left. No doubt clients of Fernandez in the United Kingdom would be interviewed by the British Police and a cabinet full of allegations of fraud would also be exposed and probably further investigated. Who would have to pay up, the Bank or Fernandez? The case would decay in a confusing muddle, Spain not yet being full members of the EEC with no direct access to the civil or criminal courts within that jurisdiction. But more than anything else, there was just one niggling suspicion at the back of Jose Ayala's wandering mind that day which caused him to shutter in anguish. It was a long shot, but a highly dangerous improbability. Had some supervisor at the Communications Centre for counter espionage at Cheltenham detailed listeners to tape United Kingdom/ Spanish telephone calls that night when McNiff called him in San Sebastian?' Was that call somewhere amid the thousands of memos bearing tapes of overseas calls made that evening?' It was highly unlikely, but possible, and possibilities tend to blow out of proportion in criminal activity.

O'Toole and McNiff arrived separately half an hour later. They were both smiling, but tense and unable to chat naturally about the trivialities of the world.

Ayala split the cash in the toilet, £83,000 for himself and £167,000 for the cell. O'Toole had brought his hold-all. The company parted ten minutes later. Half an hour later, Ayala was lost up in the city visiting every bank and bureau de change in sight. At 6.30 p.m. he wolfed down a five course meal at Cafe Du Paris in Kensington. The Basque managed to change £25,000 during the afternoon and adjourned to the Playboy Club on Park Lane that evening and gambled £35,000. The Basque showed a marginal profit of £900 for his five hour stint at the Roulette wheel. He had booked into the Lancaster Hotel at Lancaster Gate earlier in the afternoon by telephone. The night porter let him at 3 a.m. Ayala blacked out immediately and slept for ten hours leaving instructions not to be disturbed. The Provisionals had finished distributing their cash by 4 o'clock in the afternoon. Their method was simply to distribute the cash to ten persons in equal shares on 10% commission. They would have the lot changed by the next midday.

Chapter Twenty One

T he late London afternoon had darkened to prison grey as Sean McCahan waited impatiently in the Rose and Crown. Bennett arrived at half past four o'clock as usual. An eerie silence descended on the streets of West London making the sounds of chatter and traffic more prominent in the muted stillness, natures warning of a gathering thunderstorm. The Provisional got straight down to business, eyeing the Englishman with purpose. "Howard, I'd like you to meet a couple of friends of mine tonight. They just want to have a chat, y'know" he rambled on in a matter of fact fashion. Bennett was stone sober, fresh and alert, responding immediately, his tone serious and tainted with resentfulness, punctuated by the persistent wagging of his pointed index finger.

"Listen, Sean, I did that draft for you purely as a favour, as you put it so bluntly to me ... that's all. I don't know who you or your friends are. Sean, you've got to level with me here; this is serious shit you're dealing with. To tell you the truth, I regret having anything to do with it. Now I'm telling you, that's as far as it goes. I am positively not getting involved, that's it. Do I make myself clear?' He stared the Bricklayer accusingly.

"For Christ sake, Howard, calm down. I would never dream of asking you to do anything like that," McCahan retreated in pretence and rambled on convincingly. "They just want to ask you a few questions about the paper is all. They'll give you couple hundred Pounds for an hour or so of your time, don't say you can't use the cash so." the tone of the request sotto voce, indifferent.

"Come clean and tell me what these friends of yours are about or you can forget it, Sean."

"To be honest, I am embarrassed to tell you, but I am doing the brickwork on an extension for a family of market traders, decent people but they buy, maybe steal and sell everything and anything. They are a real 'Fools and Horses' outfit. I was telling them at the tea break about printing money. They don't have twenty thousand, never mind two hundred thousand ... but they gave me twice what I gave you ... so come on ... get me out of a hole ... I would do it for you Howard!

"Well why the hell didn't tell me that the first time, coming off with all that mystery and intrigue stuff?' All you had to do was tell me ... that's all. OK ... take me to Reading then."

The evening outside had now changed for the worse as McCahan slugged the old Ford into first gear. The afternoon rays of the April sun were by now blotted out by the looming grey clouds. A sudden wind blew up, shaking the sky into cracking thunder, people scurrying for cover into the shops fronts and bars. McCahan remarked it was usual weather for April as he eased the old banger into the nearside lane of crawling traffic, the frayed wipers trashing to and fro beating off the driving rain. They drove west towards the centre of London, the conversation sparse, McCahan having to concentrate fully to keep the clapped out motor out of trouble in the treacherous conditions. By 7:15 p.m. they were crossing the bridge over the River Thames into Reading, retiring to the "Horse and Plough" public house, where they would be picked up at 7:45 p.m. The whole arrangement was a waste of time and professional information as far as the Englishman was concerned. Niall O'Toole arrived half an hour later, his curly dark hair and light green bomber jacket showing evidence of the teeming rain outside. McCahan did not introduce the stranger. Bennett sensed an immediate gut feeling of arrogance about the young man.

"How's it going, Seanie boy?' Did ye bring the doctor with ye?'

"Aye, I did, surely. This is the man ... in persona," McCahan replied boastfully, accentuating the Latin reference. The threesome left, tucking into their coats and bursting into a short sprint down the side street towards the parked vehicle. O'Toole opened the back double doors of the black transit and gestured both men inside. The diesel spluttered into life and slid efficiently into the stream of traffic on the main street. They drove for at least half an

hour at varying speeds and intermittent gear changes. Every so
often the transit would come to a stop to clear traffic lights or
approach main roads and intersections. From the back of the van,
it was impossible to see through the clouded windscreen, which
was serviced only by the single driver's side wiper. The
Englishman had no idea where he was and he did not particularly
care. Suddenly, the rattle of the rain on the roof and the noises of
traffic stopped. The diesel cut out in a dying hiss. The back doors
flew open a couple of seconds later by O'Toole, and to the rear,
the clang of steel doors being anchored with draw bolts by a
third man. This person was well dressed in a smart black
raincoat, but could not make out the details of the face which was
concealed behind tinted spectacles and a black scarf.

A tinge of uneasiness pricked the Englishman and he said so to
Sean McCahan. The suggestion was passed off with the whispered
remark "don't be ridiculous", which did little to assuage Bennett's
paranoia. O'Toole led the Printer, Sean McCahan and the third man
in through the rear entrance of the house, and continued up a
single flight of dark stairs and onto the first landing. Bennett was
not at all relaxed, plunging both his hands deep in his raincoat
pockets, shuffling his feet to calm his nerves and give the
impression of nonchalance. O'Toole knocked gently on the oak-
panelled door. A voice bade enter. The Printer was instructed by
O'Toole to follow directly behind him.

Once inside, Bennett could see the room was oblong, about
twenty by fourteen feet; elegant, Victorian. The immediate reaction
to search the area with his eyes to try and establish his
whereabouts or unearth some clue as to the identity of his new-
found company proved fruitless. There was literally no object or
person upon which to feed the racing appetite of his curiosity. The
two white ceiling centre pieces and cornices were just visible and
well preserved. The large velvet drapes at either end were drawn
and a radiant coal fire sent the giant shadows flickering around the
opposite walls. This was the only source of light, except for the

bright reading lamp which was positioned to one side of the oval mahogany desk at the far end of the room. Behind, there sat one man who had his head bowed in concentration on the papers directly under the reading lamp. It was Colm McNiff. He invited the men be seated in the three comfortable chairs spread directly to the front of the desk and eyed the Printer momentarily over the top of his bifocals as he continued to finger the draft.

Once seated, the door opened to their rear. The Printer was seated in the middle position, with O'Toole to his left and Millar to his right. McCahan was somewhere behind him, he hoped. The man to his front clasped his hands to the praying position, the joined index fingers tapping the button of his nose, and sighed, still concentrating intently on the draft. Finally, between the flickering shadows of the fire and the lamplight, Bennett could see the man was middle aged, perhaps late sixties. The fair hair was receding to the centre of the crown of his head. The bald areas were heavily freckled as were the backs of his hands. On the right wrist was strapped a thick brown leather watchstrap and a polished copper band on the other, the mark of a superstitious arthritic cure. The lapel of his dark tweed jacket boasted a simple gold circle.

Unbeknown to Bennett this was a fáinne, the symbol of a fluent Irish speaker. Intermittently, he would raise his hand to clear his throat, breaking the silence in a slight cough. Neither this individual nor the others smacked Howard Bennett as criminals, or so called street traders for that matter.

Neither did the person to his right. Rather than stare him in the face, as it was obvious this person sought to guard his disguise more diligently than the others. Bennett could see that his shoes were polished to a shine, the razor sharp press on his grey pants tipping the knots on his shoelaces. Both hands were hidden, plunged in the pockets of the raincoat. It was the American type, buttoned and covering the trachea. The arrogant youngster who had picked them up in Reading sat to his left. As Bennett turned cautiously to view him he was greeted with a wry smile and a flash wink of his eye. This was the only hint of communication and Bennett was thankful for it. He returned the gesture as convincingly as he could and changed the position of his feet nervously, not making a sound on the thick pile carpet. There was a framed notice on the wall. It read "Poblacht na hEireann." He had seen it somewhere before. Behind the desk there were two flags standing upright. There were definitely stars on one and the other was predominantly white. Bennett could not make out the other colours. The only sound was the ticking of the mantle clock and the rustling of the papers which McNiff continued to finger. Without lifting his head, he slid two wads of crisp new ten pound notes across the polished desk top. He did not speak. Bennett did not react. The Printer could now see his draft clearly. Each page had been pasted onto a larger sheet.

The excess margin was filled with notes and figures. McNiff broke the silence suddenly. The voice was slow, articulate and soft-rounded. "Mister Bennett, thank you for coming here this evening" lifting his head and removing his glasses to take the Englishman into full view for the first time. He clasped his hands and continued: "I will not be introducing any person here to you. There is no point. We have given your draft the most extensive consideration and have decided to proceed with the crime outlined. What is your immediate reaction to that statement, Mister Bennett?'

The word "crime" stunned the Printer, though the question was totally disarming. Christ, these people are deathly serious. Bennett crossed his arms and took a deep breath in relief at the break in silence and opened his first sentence in a loud, confident tone - more a statement of fact.

"Well, I can definitely say it will have been the first time executed properly, at least in Europe anyway, but do you have £200,000 or so to set up the operation?' queried Bennett, gaining a little in confidence.

"Yes! O'Hara replied from the Printer's left. The reply was raspy blunt..

"Well, in that case there should be no problem, from the production end anyway. Security and disposal is an entirely different matter, as I have explained. To be quite frank with you, I don't see what further help I can be to you." The Printer was anxious to get the hell out. The wad of notes on the desktop was now very far from his racing mind. There was no reply to his statement. The atmosphere was becoming extremely tense as the mantle clock counted the long seconds of silence. Unable to focus his eyes in any given direction, he took a deep breath to calm his nerves. Clasping his hands, he fixed on the sanctuary of his shoes, petrified in that surreal twilight between the rising vibes of a fatal fear and the minds surrender to a new and terrifying reality; his chest pounded; he dared speak.

"Sean, if you are there behind me, will you tell me what is going on, Sean, are you there?' The Englishman flexed his eyes in despair. There was no answer. It was as if the room had taken a collective oath of silence. McNiff leaned forward, shoulders square and in full view.

''Mr. Bennett, or... I prefer to call you Howard. Who and what we are is irrelevant. We no more wish to be here with you than you with us. Just think of this meeting as an inevitability of fate because that is what this is. I ask you try and to be neither nervous nor frightened because I am telling you there is no reason to be, unless you make that reason yourself, and we do not want that and neither do you I am quite certain. We know more than you do about the recent events in Spain, and the whereabouts of your wife. If you cooperate with us, and I believe you will, I assure you all will be well, and if not you leave us no choice as you have enough information if placed in the right hands, even as we speak, to cause us untold damage."

A Glock 17 9mm automatic appeared from the darkness and placed gingerly on the polished table. McNiff continued.

"Our intentions here this evening are both simple and twofold. We are placing you in full control over the execution of this plan" tapping the draft, "and you must give us your solemn word, under pain of certain death you will not now or ever breath a word of this to anyone. You will have all the time and resources that you will need and you will be protected in every way including from a legal stance insofar as you will never have been a willing participant in this venture. We will swear to it. We will, as an incentive, whether you accept or not, be returning the money you were swindled of in Spain. Arrangements will be made to protect your cover. All daily matters will continue as usual including the issue of your wife who you will be in contact with you, or you her with sooner or later. That contact will need special attention from the security position. We think it better you call the tenants at your rented house and check if you have any mail. This way you can gauge the position from a safe distance. Also we will arrange a small flat for you. Your cover will be copper fastened for the job duration and perhaps for life. We are not, probably much to your surprise, criminals, murderers or power mongers, so we will be trying to get you to trust us; we have in the 'trust business' for a very long time. Now, Howard I we would very much like what you have to say" opening his hands in *fait accompli.*

The Printer took steadying breaths, felt a quaver of fear and plunged. The pieces of evidence flurried in his mind. The speaker's accent smacked of that of refined rounded highland Scottish, pronunciation, clarity and choice of words dignified, even pedagogic, obviously an educated person. He tried to put the gun to the back of his mind. From nowhere, a sense of 'self' overcame him as a distant thrill began to rise from the bottom of his nature. He was now becoming a cog in some self-appointed People's Tribunal, and that destiny was, in increments, pulling him closer to membership of a 'de facto' brand of brothers in arms'. He would therefore, as best he could muster, address the speaker in the same manner as the speaker had addressed him, frank, truthful, calm.

"Well, I am not at all sure where to begin sir, other than to say you have made it very clear to me that I have a Hobson's choice here, either I choose to live or I choose to die, or even perhaps worse I spend the rest of my life looking over my shoulder, So, it follows this operation will go ahead, with or without me, but it seems you insist I manage it, which terrifies the life out of me. Your familiarity with the Spanish disaster and my entire personal background could only come from one source ...or maybe there is more. I won't ask." Bennett craned his chin, shoulders square to his listener, hands clasped. "I implore you to know this before decisions are made, this operation will certainly be busted after, I would say two years. We will be arrested sooner or later. What the outcome of that eventuality may be I cannot say, but you can put your last penny on it ... we will be busted and prosecuted ... have no doubt. If the bust is for the Dollar you can rest assured that powers outside the normal ambit of any police force, judge and jury will be on our track. That said, it is also obvious I have no choice but to do as I am told preferably with an agreeable attitude. So, there is little more to say or discuss now; these events of the last few hours as I am sure you understand have me quite scared and absolutely exhausted"

The old man closed the meeting asking Bennett in a calm pacifying tone,

"Howard, get some rest, sleep in the upstairs room, can you eat"

Bennett awoke some seven hours later to the sounds of human voices. The curtains were drawn, the glowing coal fire warmed the room. A lampshade in the corner was the only light. O'Toole was sitting beside it, arms folded, legs outstretched, the pistol resting harmlessly on the side table.

"How are you, Howard?' O'Toole said.

Bennett rose to his feet slowly and sat again, noticing that he was wearing new pyjamas.

"We had to pour you into them last night" O'Toole joked

O'Toole stood up and steadied the printer, both hands on his hips.

"Take it easy; everything is fine. There's no problem, Howard. Just rest. I'll get you a cup of tea." He tapped the floor with his heel.

"Fine ... everything is fine ... just fine." The Printer shaped a vacant grin as Millar entered the room a few minutes later with a tray which he placed on the dressing table. Using a mini krypton bulb flashlight, he examined the Englishman's eyes.

"How are you feeling, Howard?' Do you feel okay?' We had to give you something to calm you down" His voice was monotonous and condescending, muffled by the scarf that hid his visage from the bridge of his nose down to the trachea. As he turned to the tray and poured a cup of tea,

O'Toole helped Bennett to sit upright, placing a couple of extra pillows behind his back. Millar offered the tea which Bennett accepted gratefully, his hands shaking. He sipped at the hot liquid, turned on his side and fell into a deep sleep.

"He'll be alright," said Millar. "He'll wake again in an hour or so. I'd better get Colm up." He took the tray and left the room. Bennett woke two hours later and sat upright without assistance, stretched and yawned. He addressed McNiff, more sober than before.

"Well, here we are....where to now?'

Over the following forty minutes the reality became clearer. The printers first impression was, these three men behaved as normal as a workmates tea break. The masked individual both struck Bennett as being well educated, articulate and extremely mild mannered. The conversation went on for a full hour. It was all just so surreal. Howard Bennett had by now fully reached the conclusion to accept his circumstances, as he had no foundation either of security, stability or value to negotiate within himself.

Over the following hours, downstairs he paced the floor in full control of his dumbfound audience, losing himself in long and detailed monologues, offering argument and counter-argument on strategy. The history of forgery since 1900 was condensed to a ten minute address. Notions of saving money here and there were dismissed with persuasive concrete facts. The crime was methodically analysed from beginning to end. The Provos furiously took notes, the tone of their questions almost apologetic. The conclusions took the form of four headings: "Premises," "Machine," "Paper," and "Ink."

McNiff looked at his notes two hours later, four pages of muddled details, garbled notes on dates, names, telephone numbers and figures with the words Dollars, Deutsch marks and Sterling. The scribbled place names ranged from London, New York and Dublin. A place called Ballymun was mentioned. Ali Halid, Joe Kilkenny and a John Sullivan of N.Y.C. were among the names. The meeting ended. Bennett was told he could go. O'Toole was instructed to drop him at Reading train station. He would be contacted the next day and would not see Sean McCahan again. Bennett could not believe it. He was led out by O'Toole who suggested they go for a pint on the way down. Colm McNiff picked up the phone ten minutes later and dialled a New York number. The voice at the other end was a mid-Atlantic American drawl

"Colm here. How are you, Joe?'

"Great Colm, and yourself. What can I do for you?'

"I have to talk to you. I'm coming over in the next few days. I'll call you from Kennedy." McNiff replaced the receiver in its cradle. Smiling, he addressed Millar. "The move is on."

Chapter Twenty Two

Bennett reeled into the Rose and Crown on that Tuesday evening. The April evenings were drawing longer and the dusk only now beginning to fall at 8.45. The bar was quiet, Bennett's thoughts marooned in the incredible events of the past thirty hours. Waves of reality, disbelief, and acceptance streaked across his mind's eye in rushes, between intervals of torpidity in which hazy monotonous lilting voices spoke, something inside him replied and lights shone through his closed eyelids as bright as the sun. Brian Walker was at the end of the bar with John and appeared dizzy with excitement as he caught sight of the Printer.

"Hey, Howard, where have you been?' You've missed everything! He approached Bennett and lapped his huge arm around the Printer's shoulder. Walker was out of control with happiness as he frog-marched Bennett to the far end of the bar.

"Where the hell have you been ... you've missed it all ... did you hear what's happened?'

"What's the big news, Brian," the reply lacklustre.

"Wait for it, Howard. You won't believe it. Fernandez has been turned over for a quarter of a mil - he's been turned over for TWO HUNDRED AND FIFTY GRAND, Walker's voice ascending in delirious volume with each word.

"You're joking - you must be joking," said Bennett in a half query ... "How was he turned over?' How did you find out?'

"The police were over at the house an hour ago. I had to make a statement. They knew I was in the nick out in Malaga and everything. They're looking for you. You'll have to make a statement. You'd better go down tonight. What do you think?' his huge frame lunging to and fro in undiluted pleasure.

"I don't know what to think, quite honestly, Brian. Listen, I had better go round and make that statement, get that out of the way anyway. I'll be back; then we can have a good natter." Bennett left without saying goodbye. As he paced in the direction of Camden Town

Police Station, he knew he would have to stop and think. He made his way across the traffic into a fast food joint and ordered a burger and chips. Thirty five minutes later he braced himself, cleared his tangled thoughts as best he could and paced into the reception area of the police station like any mortal about to produce his driving license. The interview by a middle-aged Detective Narrowmoor took longer than he had hoped, a full hour in fact. Litanies of details were recorded relating to his period in Spain. Bennett answered all the questions calmly and accurately.

Narrowmoor appeared to be summing up. "So you believe you were set up to fail by Fernandez and the others?'

"Absolutely ... and I see little chance of proving it. Would you be able to tell me about Fernandez being robbed?' I came here straight away after Brian Walker told me you wanted to see me and didn't get the full story."

Narrowmoor replied: "We usually ask the questions here, but I see from Heathrow flight lists that neither you nor Walker were in Spain at the time, so this much I can tell you. Basically, Fernandez was kidnapped, drugged, and trussed up in a closet for a few days across the way from his office. Apparently during that time, his office was burgled of certain valuables and records. His secretary alerted the Spanish police on Monday morning and a search for Fernandez ensued. Fortunately for him, when he awoke some time that evening, a family on holiday in the adjacent apartment complained of the racket next door to the manager, who found Fernandez trapped in the closet. After being seen by a doctor, the police there interviewed him and with his assistance inventoried the items taken. Their investigation intensified this morning when they determined that a Spaniard posing as Fernandez had cleaned out his account in a London bank early Monday morning."

The Printer burst out laughing. The Detective squinted, searching for any trace of conspiracy, and sensing none, relaxed his guard and grinned. The printer began calculating at the words "kidnapped, drugged," and abandoned any notion to focus his on the remainder of the policeman's monologue.

"Poetic justice," said Narrowmoor. The Detective offered his condolences about the unfortunate experience and dismissed Bennett, who was relieved to get out of the place.

"You feeling alright, mate?' Walker asked as Bennett sat in silence staring at the last pint of the night. "You do look a bit shook, son."

"Don't worry, Brian - it'll pass." The Printer forced a smile. The Walker Brothers and Bennett lumbered the usual take-away around to the house. As the company made their exit, the Printer was called aside by the barman.

"Howard, some chap phoned about an hour ago, just after you left. He said you were with him earlier and you're to meet him at the Railroad Cafe at Victoria Station in the morning at 8:30 a.m." Bennett thanked the young barman and bid him goodnight with the words "Ah, sure - no problem. I understand." The following hours were spent in serious discussion speculating on the Jean-Claude Fernandez affair. The conversation bored the pants off Dusty Bennett, who knew full well who was responsible, and froze at the speed and accuracy with which such a complex mission could have been successfully executed..

Howard Bennett did not have any problem picking out the man in the fading crombie at 8:20 a.m. the following morning at a table in an empty section of the station cafe. The ride had been taken by Underground, half awake, more asleep. The self-service food counter was busy with a steady queue ordering tea, coffee and snacks. The Printer could see the Irishman tucking into a full English breakfast with The Times perched directly to his front supported between the sugar canister and milk jug. Bennett ordered coffee and joined him.

"Howard. Good to see you're early. How are you today - alright?'

"Well, better than yesterday anyway." Bennett did not know the man's name.

"Well, where do we go from here?'

"Dublin ... to have a look over a few details and that," replied McNiff, in a matter of fact sort of way, spreading the paper to the next page." "I'd like to have a chat with you on a few aspects of the job. We're anxious to get it moving."

"Fair enough" Bennett was agreeable but seemed lacking in enthusiasm. The Provisional sensed this and folded the newspaper.

"Bennett, I think you had better get a few things straight. One ... you don't have any choice in the matter. Two ... if by any remote chance the job is bust you won't serve a day; and three ... so you might as well get on with it and get finished. Everything you need will be provided. Now, I want you to go through the entire operation from start to finish in order that I can make all the necessary arrangements."

"Good, but I think it would be better if you didn't take any notes - there's no need. By the way, what have you done with my typed report draft?" Bennett's first demonstration of some wilful co-operation which guided the old man to a less adverse disposition.

"It was destroyed along with the copies," the provisional replied. Once again the Printer commenced the lengthy monologue. By degrees he again pieced together the numerous ingredients of the crime. Much as he tried to discard his mounting excitement, the conviction of the certain success of a crime of such magnitude could be only executed with the use of his talents, and his talents alone. Outside the cafe, Bennett surveyed the masses of 'employed' of Victoria Station scurrying here and there. He was a voyeur dislodged from the landscape of clock driven citizens.. Fears for the future and profound regret about the past weighed heavily, as he continued probing McNiff.

"I need to know now if the money for this is available.

"We have the money. That's the least of the problems. Getting the job done right; that's the real problem,"

"Alright. Let's take it from the start. There are basically four items we require ... a suitable premises, a suitable machine, the proper paper, and the ink. The premises must have a camera and plate making capacity. We will also need another printer, and a good one. The entire job will run approximately ten days on a twenty-four hour shift. The other man will have to be capable of the following tasks: operating a camera, making plates, achieving register and watching the run and the quality while I sleep. Also, it must have a suitable guillotine. I will be able to instruct you on all of this when I inspect the premises. The machine itself should not be a problem. It's just a matter of finding one and installation, although if there is a suitable machine on the premises that would be perfect.

"What about the paper and ink, Howard?' McNiff spoke very quietly, clasping the freckled hands under the button of his nose.

"Well, the paper and ink is definitely 'the' problem. The paper will need to be manufactured to specification.. I don't see any possibility of getting this done here in the United Kingdom or indeed in Europe or the States either. It would be too dangerous to even attempt it. There is one possibility however. If you can get a paper chemist to analyse the paper we require, then we would have the exact specification for manufacture. There are in Thailand, and other places in the Far East several clandestine mills which I know have the capability to manufacture almost any paper product in the world to any specification, but to get them to do it to our specification and at what price is another matter."

"How long would it take to make?'

"I'd say about two weeks, although there is another problem. The paper for the forging of Dollars does not contain a visible strip or thread until series 1990. That series began using a polyester interwoven security strip, but there are at least 360 billion Dollars in circulation from the previous series of 1988 that have not yet been fully processed for replacement. That is why I say the entire job should be executed in Dollars. This is the last window of opportunity for any professional forger to prise this singular weakness in the world's biggest currency security system. Do your

145

people have any contacts whatsoever out there?' If we could get an introduction we would have a better chance."

"I understand. I'm sure we'll come up with something.

What about the ink?'

"The ink is not such a big problem. Again, we'll have to have it analysed and manufactured. That's not going to be difficult. But not so difficult as the paper. It might not be necessary to manufacture at all ... it's up to you."

"What do you mean exactly?'

"If you want to achieve the maximum circulation life of the notes, say five years or so, it would of course be better to use original specification ink. But against that we'll have to consider the difficulties and of course the security risk. There's no way we'll get it made here.

"What exactly would the effects of using ordinary inks be?'

"A number of things. The quality and colour of the finished note will be easier to detect. Even so it is reasonable to assume that detection will not occur until the notes are returned for disposal. Also I will only know after I get the analysis of the ink is security loaded and if so, with what. If at all possible, we really must have the inks made up."

"You speak about numbering boxes in your draft?'

"Numbering is critical. Most forgers have made the fatal mistake of using only a few different serial numbers. The reason for this is that it is impossible to purchase numbering boxes of the exact same style as those used on genuine currency. Therefore, it is imperative that these boxes are specially made up. We can then print a maze of initials and numbers. The Treasury will be unable to advise the public as to what a bona fide number is because the variety of forged numbers will be so vast it would take volumes to quote them. I suggest that we only circulate half what we print - then wait to see what happens." The Printer smiled at McNiff who smiled back.

"Dollars then!'

"Absolutely, but pre 1988, close fisting the table lightly to concrete the point.

"Of course, but depending on how the arrangements go in respect of the ink and paper manufacture. Dollars are infinitely easier to produce, and it's the easiest currency to dispose of fast. Also all the denominations are the same size with the same colour content which means we can produce all the notes on the one run, say twenties, fifties and hundreds. The varieties on the note such as serial numbers, district numbers and the Federal Reserve seal will be over-printed in the letter press process. There are twelve Federal Reserve areas and we can cover them all. For instance, F-6 represents the Federal Reserve area of Atlanta. On that issue alone, I would hazard a wild guess that there is possibly 30 billion Dollars in circulation per issue. Therefore, it's fair to assume that there is say, twelve times that amount in circulation in the twelve areas which is 360 billion. In 100's alone, fifty million would constitute a minute fraction of the total currency in circulation. It's nothing. Also, it's a currency which is easy to sell at a discount if you are dealing with the laundering system. The first thing is the premises."

McNiff looked at his watch. It was 11:10 a.m. Bennett continued.

"You mentioned legal issues, what do you have in mind?'"

"Well, we are all in the risk business - you are not a stupid man. I do not know what steps you may have taken to protect yourself ... perhaps a letter in a deposit box to be opened on your death, the last thing we want to do is eliminate you - unless, of course, it's absolutely necessary. Just play ball and everything will be okay. We're going to have to trust each other. Perhaps we might even get to like each other, who knows?' Suffice to say we are advised that if certain rules are strictly followed then this will be an almost impossible case to 'prosecute'. We are also informed that much depends on the extradition arrangements with us and the Americans. We are also considering numerous other measures and actions to keep all of us out of jail. But you don't need to worry yourself about that right now. On the cash side I told you the Spanish cash is to be returned to you as an incentive. The actual amount of any other money is not the issue but rather providing you with enough money to live modestly for the rest of your life on the one hand, but on the other not to allow you to be tempted to lose control of yourself and thereby expose the existence of these funds earlier than we anticipate. The amount itself will be decided largely by our measure of your character." The men settled into a light lunch and the conversation grew less tense. Bennett enquired matter of fact , "A Lloyd's bank was ripped off in London by some Spaniard just the day before yesterday. Do your people know anything about that?' The pause in the Fenian's reply answered the question.

"Don't know what the hell you're talking about, Howard" not raising his head to avoid donating any credence to the question.

Chapter Twenty Three

T he Printer had called the tenants before he and McNiff took off from Heathrow arranging his mail would be picked the next day.

Fifty four minutes later the aircraft swung in over a glistening Dublin Bay to make its descent. Bennett could see the speckle of fishing trawlers bobbing on the Irish Sea, busy in the business of drawing in the catch of the day. He observed the coastal village of Howth as the aircraft dipped over the tiny landmass of Ireland's Eye to make its descent into Dublin Airport. His concentration shifted to the discipline of landing. Ironically, the flight was packed with English rugby supporters over for the annual International game with Ireland. This match had been postponed in late February because of bad weather. There was nothing at stake other than national pride, the French having won the grand slam. Rugby people will know that this does not in any way interfere with the very special atmosphere of an international. The remainder of the flight was taken up by salesmen and undefined hired hands envious at the prospect of a carefree weekend. Much as he would have liked he could not bring himself to join in the singing of "Swing Low Sweet Chariot," the anthem of English rugby.

Ten minutes later, Bennett found himself squashed in the back of a cab between two twenty stone English supporters. He had lost the Provo in the rush for taxis as they travelled separately as always. The rugby fans were booked into the Burlington Hotel also. Bennett declined the offer to join them and opted for a single room. The bar was jam-packed, the atmosphere carefree. Bennett could not help but join in. An hour later he heard his name being paged through the hotel intercom. He was requested in the foyer. McNiff was there with another man. By this time, given the atmosphere, the Printer had put the outlandish set of circumstances to the back of his mind. The other man was tall, good-looking, about thirty five, custom fitted into an expensive lightweight blue suit; a low key individual with piercing dark eyes giving him the look of a hunter. McNiff pulled Bennett to one side before attempting an introduction.

"This fellow knows nothing, Howard. He's going to drive us to meet someone who might know something about Thailand, okay?'

The black 2.8 litre Ford Granada cruised out of the packed car park and headed north, down the opulent Dublin night club district of Leeson Street into Stephen's Green and elegant Dawson Street across the River Liffey to the less fashionable north side of Dublin City.

The Ford continued out to Glasnevin and eventually negotiated the roundabout which introduces the concrete maze of Ballymun, reckoned to be one of the most criminally infested ghettos of the city of Dublin. The motor came to an abrupt halt in the shopping mall car park, to the left of the roundabout. The threesome marched inside the shopping centre, the stranger leading the way. His walk was authoritative, vigorous and business-like as he burst through the doors of the Ballymun Bar.

McNiff and Bennett followed at a slower pace, being unsure what lay ahead. Leaving the evening spring sunshine outside, the Printer blinked his eyes in amazement. The bar was huge, seating some two hundred and fifty people, almost all male. The darkness was such that the walls, floor or ceiling did not boast any colour other than a brown varnish of nicotine. All forty tables were overflowing with pints of beer, untended ash trays accompanied with meaningless banter and loud jeering laughter. As the three men paced up along the bar, silence fell on the tables nearest them as they passed. The Printer heard the word "Provos" whisper across the drink laden tables. A wave of silence jailed the premises; all eyes were now on the trio. O'Doherty nodded his head sharply in the direction of the far corner. The only sound was that of gunfire from the huge video which was showing one of Eastwood's aged spaghetti westerns. A tiny frail man rose from his seat and walked down along the silent alley of tables, turned right and made his way to the exit. O'Doherty and the other two followed. Bennett being last, heard the noise resume as he released the swinging glass exit door to close. The man they had picked up was in his late 30's with a dishevelled mop of long tangled mousy hair.

He was dressed as the homeless in a nondescript jacket at least two sizes too large and a pair of dying wrinkled filthy jeans. This man was small, about 5'6" and weighed around a 130 Pounds. The slight limp on his right side he had acquired some five months earlier from a "kneecapping," standard IRA punishment for drug dealing.

He seemed terrified by the presence of the 'stranger. The car moved out of the car park and turned left at the roundabout to head north, towards the open country. The man of no name drove, the ex-drug dealer sat in the front, Bennett and McNiff in the back. Nobody spoke. Taking a left turn five miles out, the Granada crunched into the empty gravel car park of a small country pub.

Without guidance, the Dealer shuffled across the car park to the small lounge. It must have been a rendezvous before, Bennett thought. The pub was empty except for the sleeping collie by the fireside. The stranger tapped the bar with his bunch of keys. A young man of about nineteen appeared through the kitchen door behind the empty bar.

"Hello there. What can I get you?'

"Well ... I'll have a pint of stout myself, and what can I get for you?' He turned to the Printer.

"The same, thanks" Bennett's cockney English accent so obvious in the quietness of the country pub.

"And a glass of orange," O'Doherty barked without asking Colm McNiff. The boy walked into the bar area to prepare the drinks. Without turning to address the drug dealer the stranger began to speak.

"Murphy, who were you buying heroin from in Thailand?' The Dealer paused, lifting one hand from his pocket to scratch his chin.

"His name is Chan Wong. He operates from a camera shop in Bangkok on The Ploenchit Road, in the central shopping arcade."

"And who were you dealing with in London?' Do you still have contact numbers?' Can you contact these fellows?' McNiff interrupted.

"I think so. What do you want me to say to him?' slung his hand back in his pocket, a little more relaxed at the atmosphere of the interrogation. For the first time he might have something they needed and there is always the possibility of a little cash. Bennett amused himself, patting the sleeping dog. McNiff sat on a floor stool, his hand clasped on the briefcase atop his lap. He replied:

"Tell him you want to buy some stuff and ask him if he has any contacts in the paper making business." McNiff blurted pig iron blunt and ham fisted as usual.

"That sounds terribly naive and stupid! McNiff gazed in amazement. It was Bennett who spoke from his bunkered position patting the dog.

"Well, what should he say?' You tell him what to say, Howard." The Printer rose from his position and rested a hand on the Dealer's skeleton shoulder.

"Listen, mate, will you have a drink on me?' The stranger stiffened at the offer.

"Sure," the Dealer said, appreciative at the gesture of friendship. "I'll have a pint of stout please, thank you very much ... me name's Murphy."

"Okay. Now, you have had some experience with the underworld in Bangkok, is that so?' You are not in any danger, just give me all the information you can, okay?' The forger now calming the fractured ambiance

The Dealer now receptive, now relaxed, in the belief he had at least one ally in the group. The drinks arrived. O'Doherty joined McNiff and allowed Bennett's private conversation to continue.

"When you call this guy in Bangkok just ask him to enquire if it would be possible to get some special paper made. Tell him there could be a lot of money in it for him. What sort of bloke is he?'

"He's a smack dealer, big ... very big. My first contact was with his brother in London. He's an illegal immigrant, been holed up there for years now. At first I used to score off him and just bring the gear to Dublin and deal it. That's until the Irish Drug Squad got me. Then he asked me if I would do a couple of donkey runs to Thailand to mule gear back to London for him. That's how I met his brother in Bangkok. They make big big bucks...into the millions maybe. "

"That much?' Bennett replied.

"Oh, yea - sure I made at least 300,000 in two years dealing full time."

"What did you do with that kind of money?'

"Got involved in it ... that's it ... y'know what I mean?' Murphy pulled up both the sleeves of his frayed jacket. Both arms were mapped with ropey calluses resembling half submerged earthworms. "Once you get involved it's all over. The heavies did me a favour in a way." Murphy nodded in the stranger's direction.

"His brother in London, tell me about him?"

"His name is Johnny Wong. At least that's the name he uses. He lives in a plush flat near Swiss Cottage. I still have his number."

Bennett lit a cigarette, ordered another round and placed both his hands widespread on the bar. The drinks arrived minutes later. The young barman left the beer deciding to pick up the tab later rather than disturb his engaged customers. Having gone through the entire logistics of the problem of paper in his mind over the passing minutes, Bennett had come to a definite conclusion.. For the first time he had come to realize the persuasive value of raw power. No matter that it came from the barrel of a gun or the written word, it certainly gets things done a lot quicker. and turned to McNiff who was in deep conversation with the stranger in the far corner.

"Colm, can I speak to you for a moment outside?' The Forger and Fenian stomped outside into the cool spring evening, the sounds of nature now distinct in the gathering dusk. Bennett sat on the bonnet of the motor.

"Colm, I think we might be on to something here. I have no doubt the paper can be manufactured in Thailand. The dealer in Bangkok could be the key because he has so much to loose. What if I go out there with Murphy and get an introduction as a dealer from England. Let's say we set up a deal using shipments of paper as a front. We tell him the drugs can be secreted in the shipments after a few runs to see if the first few shipments clear. I'm sure he can find somewhere to have it manufactured to spec. It's not an easy job, but very doable for the smallest of custom paper-making outfits who know their stuff. All we need is a few hundred reams of paper, maybe just a few pallets, which could be shipped by air. I could sort it out when I get out there. There is no watermark or security strip as such in the paper employed in the Dollar except the post 1988 series, which still doesn't present much of a problem. The notes will still definitely not be exposed until they get back to various Federal Reserve Banks. What I'm saying is that a trip to Thailand is definitely worth a shot. The odds are all on our side, even if we have to spend a little money and involve ourselves with this guy who would have the contacts to supply us with this paper. Everything out there just has a price the same as anywhere else"

"That makes good sense. Once we have the paper we're gone. I have complete confidence in you, Howard. Whatever you say goes. I told you that." The older man for the first time looked the Printer between the eyes and gave him a slap on the shoulder. The relationship was growing. McNiff continued. "The first thing we ought to do is to have Murphy telephone the contact in Thailand. He'll set you up as a prospective purchaser, make an appointment to see him and let him know and that Murphy will be travelling with you. We'll see what happens then."

"In the meantime we will have to get the notes to be analysed. Could that be arranged in the next few days. I simply must have the paper specification, and what about the ink specification and numbering boxes?'

"I'm sure I can arrange both. The boxes I'll have to think about. As Murphy will be travelling to Thailand with you, he'd better get himself cleaned up, a haircut and a bath would not do any harm; get him some clothes also out of the 300 quid I'll give you. Feed him. Actually, I have to get a passport for him ... his own passport was re-possessed. He's only out of the nick 14 weeks." Bennett could see the old man was not without some sympathy for the hapless youngster.

"It might even be possible to get this paper made up legally - a straight order. There's nothing illegal about that. Say if we got a few bogus quotations from paper manufacturers here and took them to Thailand with me to make things look up-front, I could say that the paper was for a security job, or give them some story anyway. They might just do it. Even if they suspect it's for currency, they won't know which one, but I doubt they'll cop it. It makes good sense to buy anything in Thailand anyway, everything is dirt cheap.

"Now you're talking, Howard. We'd better get him cleaned up. I'll leave him with you. Get him a room in the hotel. He can make the call tonight."

Bennett and Murphy were back in the shopping centre fifteen minutes later. The stranger and McNiff drove on into the city. It was 7:30 p.m. The shopping centre would not close until nine o'clock. Both men had a haircut and Bennett purchased a couple of cheap suits, a dozen shirts and a few sets of underwear. The pair got a taxi across the city to the Burlington where Bennett booked a single room for the Dubliner across the hall from his own.

An hour later Murphy picked up the phone and dialled Wong's number which he knew from his head, drug people never use notebooks. International dialling was a troublesome business those days, the caller being at cross purposes whether the series of bleeps indicate an engaged tone. Murphy knew all about it. He'd dialled the number hundreds of times in the past. The receiver was picked up almost immediately at 1am. Thai time..

"Ploenchit Camera Arcade." An oriental English accent vibrated from half way across the world.

"Hello ... this is James Bond. Is that Chan?'

"No ... Mr. Bond. He na hea at da momen. You ca the numba - 251-5141. He at da Ambassadorial Hotel, hokay?'

"Yeah, okay. I'll call him now. Bye." Murphy dropped the receiver and turned to Bennett. "He's not there, pal. He's at a different number. They must be using the same code names. The guy on the phone recognized mine straight away. Will I call him now?'

Outside the open window, the sounds of Dublin's streets were becoming more sparse as a hazy cool dusk descended over the pavements and rooftops. Bennett nodded in agreement from his outstretched position on the single bed. Murphy dialled again and waited.

"Ambassadorial Hotel."

"Hello, could you page a Mr. Chan Wong, please?' This is long distance." Murphy could hear the soft music being interrupted and the name Mr. Chan Wong echoing throughout the foyer. A minute later the receiver broke into life.

"Chan here."

"Hello there. This is Bond. How's life?' Murphy enquired in a flat Dublin accent. Bennett rose from the bed and put his ear alongside the receiver.

"Ah, James how are you ... long time, no hear from you. You back in business?'

"Yeah. I'll be out shortly. How are things?'

"About the same, about the same."

"Good - good. I'll call you when I get in. By the way, I'll have another guy with me, okay?' Gotta go now. See you when I get out."

"That is okay. I talk with you when you arrive. Bye bye, Bond. Good to hear from you! Murphy replaced the receiver and looked to the Printer. "Well, Wong is still in business. He'll talk to us when we get out. It's not a good idea to be too specific on the phone; he ok'd it when I mentioned bringing you."

The Printer rose from his hunkers with the notion - how small the world really is. He tapped Murphy on the shoulder.

"It's a start anyway. Fancy a drink, Murphy?' the Printer offered, becoming more familiar with his new partner.

"I'd love one ... me nerves are all shattered, the thought of them heavies make me freak." The Dealer was serious, crouching into his tiny frame and blowing a whistle of alarm.

"You're not one of them, right?'

"No, I'm not."

"Well, I want to give you a bit of advice pal. I don't know what the score is, and I don't want to know, but don't stand on their corns, I'm telling you; you fuck with them and guaranteed they'll fucking blow you away in a heartbeat, just like that," clicking his fingers and twisting his mouth to convey the message.

Chapter Twenty four

I n Boulder, Colorado, you could until recently buy a brand new Armalite rifle over the counter. It would be yours provided you convinced the gun dealer you weren't a criminal or a nut. But as always, if you buy privately you don't have to prove either. The assault rifle, capable of firing thirty high velocity bullets just as fast as you can pull the trigger, would be basically similar to that used by American GI's and the Provisional IRA - the only difference being that their guns can fire in bursts. The stock model, however, can be easily modified to do the same with an aftermarket device. Both weapons are lethal at distances up to four hundred meters and can pierce armoured vehicles, such as the ones used by the British and the Royal Ulster Constabulary in Northern Ireland.

The liberal firearms laws in the western American States and the deep South had provided rich pickings for illegal gun dealers. Samuel Abraham Guttrie was one such man. The scorching mid-western sun and stagnant humidity had brought the town to a standstill. The telephone purred in his motel room.

"Yeah, what is it?'

"Sam - Colm here. How are you keeping?'

"Hey, Colm, how ya doin', great to hear from ya."

"Is that phone of yours okay?' McNiff's first question.

"Yeah, it's alright."

Colm McNiff had never once had a cordial word with this individual. Sam Guttrie was a key player in the movements Armalite arms Colerado run, though he hadn't hooked up hardware for McNiff for a long time. Like most illegal arms dealers he was a man tempered by greed; a man destitute of any moral yardstick. Guttrie was small time; a one man operation, although from time to time he proved himself capable of tapping bigger contacts. Since his return from Vietnam in '72, he traded, albeit fronted as a mail order firm selling ladies and children's garments via catalogues from manufacturers in New York. Guttrie and regular work departed after he got shot in the butt patrolling the Cambodian border. For this inconvenience he received a disability pension in perpetuity. Single and semi-retired, he was morbidly overweight and for the most part bald. The limp from his wound made his look more cumbersome; the stubby fingers and mean mountain jaw forming an impression of social isolation and obsessive self-service. Guttrie was a man ever vigilant to any opportunity for unearned reward.

"Sammy boy, I want you to do something for me."

"Yeah, sure, babe, the arms man slid his calculator and notebook across the desk top nearer to him.

"I want you to collect up a few Dollar bills for me. I want twenties, fifties and hundreds. Get me three notes of each from all twelve Federal Reserve areas. The more 88 series and before the better, nothing past 1990, but I need a complete set of 88's"

"What?' You want three of each bill from all twelve Federal areas."

"That's right. Can you handle it?' the Fenian emphasising his request huddled in the public international telephone section of the General Post Office on O'Connell Street in Dublin. Guttrie rose from the leather swivel chair, holding his forehead with the palm of his hand, struggling to adjust his mind to the request.

"I'm not sure I understand. You want three copies of new twenty, fifty, and one hundred Dollar bills from each of the twelve Federal Reserve areas, pre '88 series if possible, is that what you want?'

"That's it - you've got it."

"What the fuck do you want 'em for, babe?' That's a big heap of dough you're talkin'! "Can you do it or not?' McNiff was final. The arms man was already tapping his calculator, one of the few skills he had perfected to hairline accuracy. "You're talking $6,120 for a start ... and it's goin' to cost me. Let's see." He paused for a couple of seconds. The Provo listened eagerly. "It's going to cost me ten grand - how's that?' I'm just doin' you a favor. It's no big deal."

"You're a top heavy there, Sammy."

There followed a lingering silence. The arms man responded to justify his first attempt at barter. "Look, babe, this is the way it is. First, I need some people, one from each area, okay?' They gotta front $510 apiece. Then they gotta run around sorting out the 88 series which might take a few passes. What's the big deal with the 88 series?'

"Stop right there, Sammy. I want you to do the job personally and discretely, do you understand?' You yourself - maybe one more. Will you front the dough, Sammy boy?' I'll mail you a check. It'll take a couple of days but I need those notes fast."

"Okay, I'll front, but it'll cost you an extra grand."

"OK" Sam. "I'm mailing the money now. Get the paper here pronto. Don't play games with me, Sammy boy."

"Hey babe hey, cool down. I don't want problems"

You'll get the bills okay. Where do you want me to send 'em?'

"Your last stop is New York. Leave the stuff at the reception, The Empire Hotel, Columbus Circle. I will be told in 30 minutes day or night.

I will need you in Dublin in the near future. "We'll cover the cost. Call Dublin at the usual number when you've got the notes. Remember, be discrete. Good Luck"

"Call in a couple of days, eh, bye." Guttrie replaced the receiver, looked to the ceiling blowing a muted whistle of relief. "You don't mess with them guys"

The Arms Man was becoming fascinated and began to shoehorn the problem into perspective. So many factors to be covered like security and expediency. He began to pace the tiny apartment, wandering from room to room, chugging his beer and smoking heavily, pausing now and then to allow his mind to digest the train of thought. McNiff was certainly in a hurry to get those Dollars. Why?' Why would a big roller in the IRA want a load of new Dollars of certain denominations and series for each Federal area?' The conclusion came almost immediately.

He gazed at the ceiling and slowly twisted his mouth into a contorted grin of the 'all knowing' and spoke to the ceiling light as if addressing McNiff: "You ol' son of a bitch, McNiff. You're gonna forge'em … that's it! The Arms Man buckled over, holding his huge beer belly with his free hand to steady his gut from the uncontrollable laughter. He collapsed into the couch, breathless and hacking, wiping the oozing sweat from his forehead.

McNiff paced across the main hall of the General Post Office, where years ago a band of martyrs struck a blow for Irish freedom, its exterior still showing pockmarks here and there left by British guns. The Provisional pulled an aged cheque book from the First National Bank of Colorado and wrote a cheque for $16,120. This account had been dormant for two years. The signature read Michael Horan. Having slipped the cheque inside the A4 envelope, McNiff mailed the packet extra special three-day delivery, addressing it to Guttrie's P.O. Box number in Colorado.

Chapter Twenty Five

Lansdowne Road Stadium in Dublin was, as usual packed to capacity for the international with England. As the first dropout hung in the air, the Englishman could feel the excitement grip him. The atmosphere reminded him of a time not so long ago when he was reasonably content but for the not irregular skirmishes with his wife. Much as he tried, he could not evict his bizarre set of circumstances from his mind and reasoned, crazy as it might sound, it was a lot better than Spain and decided to give the game his full enthusiasm. Murphy had gone with McNiff earlier that morning to arrange travelling papers. They would be back in the Burlington Hotel at six or seven o'clock. As Bennett engrossed himself in the excitement of the game the suffocating panic attack began, choking him with unyielding suckered tentacles. From some unknown space, the overpowering scenes appeared in black and white shadows of thirties movies, the encrypted voice of the Mynah bird dictating his inescapable doom. He tumbles into a devouring vortex of criminal courts, wigged judges and barristers, his prolonged pleadings of the condemned ignored. Now weakened and gasping for breath minutes pass until the visions reassemble and unify into an inky blob that streaks away into nothingness like the phantasmagoria of a fevered dream. Reality returns, the roar of the crowd, his hands gripping the rail for dear life, the blast of Spring rain in his face. He now knew for absolute certain he must not allow himself be alone for too long at any one time, at least not in the immediate future.

Bennett quenched his thoughts abruptly and tried to join in the deafening excitement as England won a five yard scrum with a minute or so to go in the first half. The Irish found a relieving touch from the loose ruck which gave the Welsh ref ideal opportunity to blow half time with the score at two penalties each. The showers of April rain became heavier which was to have its usual effect on the second half which turned out to be nothing more than a dog fight for possession of the football. As usual in tight internationals, the last quarter brought out the best in both teams, the Irish having gone ahead with a splendid drop goal from the fly half in the twenty-eighth minute. Three minutes later, the English full back cannoned a Garryowen directed to the bowels of the Irish defence, the oval ball swirling and dipping in the vicious cross wind, a fullback's nightmare the world over. The Irish fullback was stampeded and discarded like a lifeless carcass. The English pack wrenched possession from the loose ruck and fired a long accurate ball back to their stand-off, who had all the time in the world to drop the daintiest of goals and tie the game up at 13 points each. Bennett knew the feeling. He had kicked so many in his playing career. The Welshman blew time up five minutes later. Bennett comforted himself in the variety of familiar accents which surrounded him - a group from the Coventry Club in the Midlands and another from Bath.

Equally, the Irish intermingled in good spirited cross-conversation. There were a dozen or so men from the Cork Constitution Club and a very large contingent from the famous Garryowen Club in Limerick. The post-mortem on the game commenced in the Burlington Bar half an hour later. As usual, the discussion matured into open song, and later, optimistic intoxicated aspirations of getting lucky. Many a rugby supporter has been known to have found himself within 'circumstances of the needy' the morning after an international. An hour later, as Bennett stepped up at the urinal in the packed noisy toilet, a notion struck him that this game of rugby football was one of the few things he could cling to in life, one of the few solids he could isolate from the ravages of his disposition.

There are a lot of people in this world that would have agreed with him. As Bennett entered the bar he could see Murphy approach him, his grey heroin racked face beaming. The 'off the shelf' navy blue suit, haircut and white shirt and tie doing wonders.

"Howard - we're going Wednesday week, Colm is in the restaurant. He's got all the gear, tickets and all. I can't wait."

"Should be interesting to say the least," Bennett replied, taking in the Dubliner's new image with admiration. He pulled Bennett aside with a nod.

"Listen,. I've knobbed a couple of English broads over there, got 'em eatin outa the palm of me hand ... now just stay cool and go along with what I say and we'll be laughin' - ya got it?' and scurried back to the bar, not giving Bennett an opportunity to reply. The Printer viewed both ladies with surprise, definitely somewhere around the thirty-five year mark and middle-class by the expensive camel duffel coats and expensive silk neck scarves. The Englishman wanted to bolt.

"This is my partner, John Stephens. John - this is Amanda, and this is Sandra. They're both from Cheltenham, John."

Bennett pretended the best face he could, but knew immediately they were on a loser at the limp handshake and lifeless "How d'you do." The conversation continued into the most pretentious, boring chatter. Murphy did not help matters at all. People notice nicotine-stained fingernails peeled to the scut with the word 'love' tattooed across them. The huge gold-coloured sovereign ring was not having any impression on the 'trespassed upon' frozen company. They looked to each other white eyed in alarm as the Dubliner downed a full pint of Guinness with one mouthful and bawled at the busy barman impatiently.

"Hey, pal - give's a round of gargle here, will ya?'

The ladies both made their exit at fair speed, making the excuse they were going to the bathroom. Thirty minutes later, the two men both sat on the vacant seats in defeat. Murphy chain-lit his twelfth cigarette and broke the prolonged silence.

"You're absolutely useless, pal - you scared them off. I thought you were a better bloke than that, pal. Otherwise, I wouldn't have asked you into the company, Jeses - I had it all set up."

Bennett addressed the Dubliner, unable to break his continuous laughter. "Murphy, I am not qualified to give you a lecture whatever be the science of seduction but I'll certainly give you nine points for effort. Now I'm going into the restaurant to see 'our friend'. Wait here; I'll be back when I'm finished. Keep to yourself, that's an order."

"Oh yea, wait 'til ya see me in Bangkok pal, then we'll see who's who and what's what," giving the 'arm under elbow' gesture.

"I'm sure Murphy; I'm sure."

The Printer shuddered at the thought of the Dubliner's previous female company and left the determined Casanova behind him and stepped to his tip toes to try and spot McNiff through the crowded restaurant. A few seconds later his eye caught the man standing in the crombie waving furiously from the far corner. McNiff was not alone and rose from his seat to introduce the attractive lady he introduced as his niece.

"Howard, this is Miss Fiona Geraghty."

Without rising from her seated position she offered her hand and peered momentarily over the top of her glasses, the smile pretentious and short lived. Bennett felt an immediate aversion to this person. The Fenian continued the introduction which was placated with the reverences older men sometimes lavish on younger women. Bennett sighed an impatient breath and folded his arms at a loss to understand the purpose for her presence.

"Howard, Fiona is a Professor of Economics at Trinity College," clasping his hands around the coffee mug. He continued the introduction with smiles of admiration, of a man transformed and bade the company retire to Bennett's room.

"Fiona has extensive knowledge of the international money market and has undertaken to advise us on disposal techniques"

Bennett exploded. "Wow.....Wow..... Wow.....Stop right there..... right now. One, I don't have a bulls notion what you're talking about, and two, if I ever needed a lecturer in economics I am quite capable of acquiring one myself.

The Englishman tugged forcefully at the collar of McNiff's crombie.

"Come out here you, I want to speak to you! McNiff had not seen the Briton so infuriated and duly excused himself, following Bennett, who thundered out through the exit and into the packed corridor. Suddenly, McNiff found himself pinned to the wall by the towering furious Englishman, chin in his face, shoulders squared to the enemy. Bennett had one hand on his hip and the other across the McNiff's shoulder beside a floodlit print of Dublin's O'Connell Street.

"What the fuck are you doing....you fucking doddering lunatic, what the fuck are you doing?' Bennett boomed in rising rage.

"What's the matter, Howard?' the Fenian queried with a hint of guilt. The answer came fast and furious.

"What's the matter?' I can't believe my fucking ears. You never told me about 'Miss Prim' in the restaurant. Who the hell does she think she is?' Now our cover is blown, the whole fucking deal is bust and she's sitting in a box being cross-examined about association, Colm, association! Did you ever hear that word association, Colm?'

"Howard, you've a lot of pressure on you. That's not going to happen. We don't recognize the courts anyway."

"I can't believe this. What's the fucking difference if you do or not when we're going down for thirty years. And on top of all that, you tell her my real name. Come to that, you've told me your own real name so now we're all buddies in the club together. If anything happens now, I'll go down just the same as the rest of you. The protection you promised me under anonymity is blown. As far as I'm concerned you've done more damage in the last five minutes than all the fucking police in the world. Thanks be to Jesus you don't take a drink, you blundering fuckin' idiot! you owe me you horses arsehole" Bennett eased up and stood away from the wall. The time had come to lay some hard facts on the line.

"It seems to me Colm, that neither you nor your people have any comprehension of the security which is 'beyond words' imperative to get this fucking nightmare over with properly. And let me tell you: that I don't give a shit about your veiled threats or what you might have done to me personally. Let me tell you something pal ... if you or your people do anything like what just happened it'll set back your cause by a hundred years ... that's been taken care of. I'm the man going to do this job and in future nothing but nothing happens without my being told ... got it?' This job will be a success, executing it is academic, shoring up evidence for the massive investigation takes brains, logic and foresight and you have neither. Any more schoolboy shit and I'm out of this. Now that the damage is done you can tell your niece inside I will speak with her just to see what the extent of the damage is. I'm going back to the bar to keep an eye on this other fucking peanut brain you gave me, check if he still has a beating heart"

"Fair enough, Howard. I hope she's still there, and pulling a few letters from his inside pocket handed them to the forger. That's your mail we had picked up" McNiff walked to the restaurant in the certainty that the days of frightening the Englishman were now over. The Printer fanned the few items of mail and then saw the cruncher with the usual solicitor's details in the top left corner. He opened it and speed reading the contents knew his marriage was over, which came as no surprise. The words 'reckless', 'irreconcilable differences', 'ex parte', 'terms of separation' jumped from the page. He had seen it all before as many of his friends had been through the same ordeal. He joined Murphy in the bar who was alone, drunk, ranting on and on that he could not wait for Thailand. McNiff joined them fifteen minutes later saying that Fiona Geraghty would be 'looking forward' to 'talking' the next day here at three o'clock and sincerely hoped that the next meeting would be more amicable.

Chapter Twenty Six

Next morning the atmosphere of the International had passed save for the usual few plane and boat missers, who lingered around the empty bar here and there making alternative travelling arrangements.

Fiona Geraghty arrived at 3.10pm.

"Good afternoon, Sir. I am reliably informed you do not have a name ...for now anyway"

The Printer turned to greet his interrogator of the previous day "Good afternoon, Miss Geraghty. Can I get you a drink?' The reply was speckled with a spark of humour.

"I think you'd better, Sir! Bennett felt a quiver of confidence at the reply and continued the mildly good-willed banter. "Call me Howard, I'll call you Fiona. What would you like?'

"I would like a brandy and ginger ale please, Howard." The Printer stood from his bar stool and ordered, suggesting they both retire to the back lounge for privacy. No man can honestly pretend indifference on initial meetings with beautiful women. On stepping from the stool, Bennett was surprised that Fiona Geraghty stood same height as him in half inch heels.

The Printer had the barman run a tab and ushered his companion into the lavish empty lounge. Seating themselves in the far corner the economist placed her slim briefcase on the table and lifted her glasses to the perched position above the forehead, revealing the left eye ever so slightly turned. The forger noticed the attractive characteristic and could not help but peer into the briefcase. He folded his arms in expectation at the heading on the cover of a rather dated International Business Week Magazine dated March 18th, 1991 - "WHAT CAN BE DONE?' Fiona Geraghty stared at Bennett whilst continuing to arrange the papers on the table.

"Howard, before we get on with this I would like you to know certain things. My inclusion yesterday was totally innocent, and I honestly feel that you jumped to a hasty conclusion in presuming it was anything other than that. Anyway, let's leave that behind us." She continued in a softer tone. "I have been briefed on your domestic circumstances. Colm, as you know, is my uncle. My father was on active duty with him in the 'Forties and early 'Fifties. While l deplore violence no matter what the motive, I have to say to you that I am in full support of any form of economic warfare - anything you say to me shall be 'never have been said' and I cannot honestly conceive of any interrogation in the future unless it is in the form of a plea bargain. I am not going to expand too much but in strict legal terms there is no case against you. I would like you to know that Colm McNiff educated both my brother and I out of his own pocket after my father's death. This is not the first time both my brother and I have contributed in our own way to the cause. Howard, if I may commence the business of the day."

"Of course, Fiona," Bennett replied, pulling a pack of Rothman's from his pocket to calm his nerves. Geraghty declined the offer of a cigarette with the words "don't smoke." However, he did notice her pouring the ginger ale mixer with an experienced hand and down two fingers of brandy without any evidence of discomfort. "Thank Christ she takes a drink anyway," he said to himself, lighting the cigarette and pitching his first question through the exhaling smoke.

"What do you wish to know about this job anyway?'

"What job, I don't know anything about any 'job' as you put it." She tapped both her thighs in determination, "Being an economist, I was quite simply asked by my uncle if I knew anything about international money laundering, just the same as any student doing a thesis, that's all. Colm asked me to give you this" she said matter of fact, handing him an unopened white envelope. I don't need to know the contents"

Bennett opened the envelope impatiently and commenced reading the contents at blistering speed. "Where on earth did you get this?' Bennett still buried in the text.

"From Colm, I told you. Please don't read it here"

The contents contained a complete scientific analysis of the United States 20, 50 and 100 Dollar bill from the Federal Reserve Area L6 of Atlanta, Georgia. The analysis had been obviously executed by three unnamed persons - a paper chemist, an ink specialist/chemist and a printing technologist. The first page read thus:

"I have today analysed the samples enclosed herein and outline the paper specification and manufacturing procedure in respect of these samples only. I can state that these samples do not vary from the ink specification outlined hereunder. The following page consisted of a professional ink analysis. "A further analysis would of course be necessary to establish ink specification for the remaining eleven Federal Reserve areas. The above specification refers only to the samples presented."

Fiona Geraghty excused herself and made for the bar as Bennett read the report in. Rather than continue onto the next piece he could not help but stare at his new acquaintance as she spoke to the lone bartender and pointed a finger in Bennett's direction, without turning, the eyeglasses still perched on the crown of her head. Bennett's gaze followed Fiona Geraghty as she stepped towards the door marked "Ladies," the sleek form obvious through the shimmering black dress. Her stride matched her height, long and elegant, a lissom form of undoubted grace and a damned expensive education and position to match. It was only when the door closed behind her that he noticed her hair swept to the back of her head and fixed with a simple hair slide. The Printer could feel himself bite his lip but banished any thoughts of an advance, at the certainty of failure, or McNiff hearing about it ... or both. He thumbed to the next page of the report. Again the content was short and specific.

"The process employed in the printing of the three denominations herewith is intaglio. I have separated all six images for colour separation and can state that the colours employed are those quoted in the ink specification only. Only the relief plate reproduction shall be possible to approximately .001 efficiency by way of 10:1 blow-up of origination. Touch up and metal letterpress relief plate production at this quoted 10:1 size. The blow down to effect the quoted .001 efficiency should be taken from reproduction proofs from the 10:1 engravings. An efficiency level of .0001 could be achieved, but this will depend on the camera equipment employed and quality of the reproduction proofs to be used for the blow down and of course the efficiency level of the touch up and machine operator.

I am astonished that the overall quality compared to other currencies is extremely poor. The serial numbering equipment is non-standard. However, in order to attain this level of reproduction it would be necessary to have reproduction proofs from a perfect original blown to a size of 10:1, from which the blow down to actual size will reproduce superior to the sample enclosed."

Bennett's concentration broke suddenly as he saw Fiona tower over his seated position in front of the table, a pint of Guinness in one hand and a glass of brandy in the other. She smiled.

"Well, where were we?'

The reports were perfectly formatted and typed on a superior paper from which the heading had been blacked out The International Accreditations at the bottom of the page certified the laboratory as bona fide.

The Printer scented a combination of soap and perfume as he leaned a little closer to re-observe the written notes. His eyes drifted to her hands which were lightly tanned and slender, the fingernails manicured and varnished in 'patriot red'. The left hand did not boast an engagement or wedding ring. She braced both her hands around the chin of her folded legs, just below the kneecap, and stared Bennett for a reply, the moist open mouth and button nostrils dampening any failing hope to serious concentration. Pretending the best face he could, he continued to sneak a momentary focus at the soulful brown eyes of angelic perplexity, which by now he wished would invade and save his tormented soul. He jailed his brow in one open hand. She rescued him from the rising despair.

"I know what has happened in Spain and a very sketchy account of your being here. Colm is very fond of you, I think you should know. I should tell you that from my uncle's descriptions of you I was cautiously looking forward to meeting you. From what I am told, I do believe that all will be well. At least we have met which I think is a good thing and I would like you to feel likewise. Enough for one day, why don't you eat and get some rest. I would look forward to seeing you again tomorrow, say at noon, if that be OK?'" handing Bennett International Business Magazine which contained a long and detailed investigation into international money laundering.

Chapter Twenty Seven

Across the Atlantic ocean, Sam Guttrie chewed on the last mouthful of a ten ounce burger in the Homestead Saloon, just outside Boulder Colorado. Rubbing his inflated fingers with the napkin, he concentrated on the piece of paper to the side of his plate. The flashing juke box was thumping out the Kenny Rogers hit, "The Gambler" at full volume as the clusters of mini coloured lights flashed in the darkness. The joint was a labyrinth repository of the very worst of American kitsch; cheap framed prints of 'The Duke', James Dean, Munroe, Frank, Elvis, and Garland, hundreds of plastic miniatures varying in size and stature of Laurel and Hardy, Charlie Chaplin, Babe Ruth and other sporting heroes. Mostly cowhands, retired vets and sometime prostitutes made up most of the sixty or so people at the nondescript bar. It was a sort of watering hole-cum-eatery and snack stop. The Arms Dealer's mind was far from his surroundings.

The heading read FEDERAL RESERVE AREAS - and underneath in a single list: A1- Boston B2- New York C3- Philadelphia D4- Cleveland E5- Richmond F6- Atlanta G7- Chicago H8- St. Louis I9- Minneapolis J10- Kansas City K11- Dallas L12- San Francisco.

He tucked the list of areas into his shirt breast pocket. Heaving his huge frame out into the clear night to the old Chevy in the parking lot, he belched and settled into the deep self-made dip in the driver's bucket seat. Guttrie drove north for two miles up the Denver Highway to The Cherry Creek Motel. The arms man had a single room apartment leased on a yearly basis, which worked out at a moderate ninety five bucks per week and turned the key to room 16 which was purposely on the ground floor to avoid the climbing of stairs.

Once inside, he pulled a six pack of beer from the fridge. Lighting a cigarette, he sat at the dining table, the only sounds being those of the intermittent footsteps of the hookers who used a specific number of rooms on an hourly basis. Sam Guttrie laid out sheets of paper in front of him. The first sheet had a detached list of queries relating to travel and accommodations.

The second sheet had a series of quotations from several airlines. The three quotes for an interstate twelve city ticket were about the same. The terms and conditions were also similar; valid for sixty days, two stopovers only; first departure within twenty one days of issue.

The third sheet contained a blank map of the United States with the twelve Federal Reserve areas marked with a red dot. A blue ball point line linked up the flight path. Guttrie rose from the table, wiping the sweat from his brow.

"Not as easy as it sounded, not so easy at all. There has just got to be some easier way"

His first consideration was that of spiking the operation. Maybe he would do a deal with the CIA or the Secret Service. The thought sent his head shaking vigorously and he drew a prolonged whistle of the dreadful possibilities. What if he told McNiff that the operation of rounding up these Dollars was proving almost impossible; that the security end was wide open and an investment of, say, twenty grand would be necessary to cover all the tracks; would he go for it?' Guttrie decided to give that angle some thought later. On the other hand, why did McNiff want to see him in Dublin, fares and expenses no object?'

The last time Guttrie went to Dublin, McNiff argued for two hours over $300 on a ten grand deal, and refused point blank to contribute to any fares or expenses. On the province of probability, he decided on playing ball all the way for the moment in the certain knowledge he would be one of the first in line if things went OK. Besides, he could use the information anytime in the future provided it made sense, but he knew in his heart of hearts the notion of ratting on McNiff was just idle thought. How could he even think such a thing?'

Guttrie would not sleep that long night, spending the next five hours pacing the floor, smoking and drinking beer. He was not that concerned with the matter of rounding up the bills, but rather the subsequent investigation when the forgery would be blown in a year or two, as all counterfeit jobs are sooner or later. The Arms Man had a clean slate. He had never been suspected of any association with crime or subversive activity. Leaving aside the mercenary streak in his character, he was a rogue of very sound perception and common sense logic.

The crime of counterfeiting bills from all twelve Federal areas made worried Guttrie because knowing the Irish as he did, he knew they would not think twice if they had the wherewithal. When the notes would be eventually exposed, he knew heads would be rolling at the Secret Service and the Treasury. Counterfeiting currency is a crime against which society has little or no defence, which justifies the gravest punishment on the offender. The most serious pressure would be put on the Secret Service and the FBI, and probably even the CIA and at that point it is end game. He concluded he would have to talk to McNiff personally for both their sakes. A flash of paranoia; what if the Provo got paranoid and suspected he was trying to manoeuvre a more profitable angle ... maybe even a hint of blackmail or extortion?' No thanks. The Arms Man was shrewd enough to know without question they would immediately send some 'Mad Mick' down from the Big Apple or Boston to blow his head off before any word got out.

"Jesus," he groaned to himself, "this is getting to be a fucking nightmare. When those notes are spotted, all hell will break loose. There's no way they'll stop until they bust the operation, no matter how much it costs or how long it takes.

The early morning stream of trucks had well begun to roll outside, making their way down from Wyoming through Denver and Colorado Springs, some going on to Santa Fe and down through New Mexico. The Arms Man knew he would not sleep until he struck on a satisfactory formula for the gathering up of these gad damn Dollars. He decided to shower, shave and eat breakfast.

By 5:30 a.m. he was doing just that at "The White Fence Restaurant," on the Denver Highway. The double helping of scrambled eggs and pot of black coffee helped to offset the creeping tiredness. The diner was empty and quiet except for the odd noise of crashing china being loaded into the dishwasher for the morning rush. The TV was buzzing at quarter volume, reviewing the previous night's sports events and scores.

Guttrie did not notice the Colorado State Police cruiser roll up into the car park and lurch to a silent halt. The car's body raised a couple of inches from the ground as the two State Troopers eased themselves from the vehicle.

They stretched, fixed their gun belts and made their way into the restaurant at a slow drag, leaving the windows open to allow the cool breeze to circulate through the vehicle. The driver was known as "Big Bob" Jenkins. Guttrie knew him well. They had both served in the 'Nam in '66 and '67 although the only time they had met there was by chance in a brothel while on "R and R" leave in Thailand. The other trooper was a nondescript rookie by the stiffness of his uniform and the newness of his leathers and hardware. Jenkins' mouth curled in a beaming smile under his sunglasses on seeing his alumni. Sooner or later the conversation would end up in the 'Nam. Jenkins was the exception to the rule in that he truly wanted to be a good soldier, and he was the very best, capable of dropping a mortar on a dime at 300 yards and handling a bazooka like a peashooter. He was probably the toughest and bravest man that Sam Abe Guttrie had ever met during his chequered lifetime. Of all the hundreds of men Guttrie had met in the 'Nam he couldn't recall a single soul that had come out quite the same as he had gone in, and Big Bob Jenkins was no exception. Guttrie knew it was better to allow him a wide berth to ramble on.

"Yea, Sam, we got big problems. It's these drugs ... coke, mostly."

Guttrie was always interested in what Bob Jenkins had to say, particularly about his job and called for a round of cold beer. The big Trooper whipped out his notebook and opened a blank page.

He was to spend the next half an hour explaining the current spate of drug activity in and around the state of Colorado.

Guttrie listened carefully, his hands braced around the empty coffee cup. He had never forgotten that Big Bob Jenkins had inadvertently tipped him off well in advance about the Tobacco and Firearm Agency moving in on the Armalite run eighteen months ago. The Arms Man prodded the Trooper to keep talking.

"Go ahead, Big Bob, I'm listening ... this is unbelievable."

"We're arresting around a hundred guys a month in Denver alone for small time dealing, y'know?' These guys deal just to keep themselves in stuff ... crazy. Actually, I need to be in Colorado Springs court at 11:30 a.m. I've got two guys up for possession. They'll get cut loose and thrown in a drug rehab program. Actually, one guy was in the 'Nam. His name's Luke Conrad, runs the pool hall in Pueblo ... ever heard of him, Sam?'

"Nope. Never heard of him, Big Bob"

The rookie turned his back on the pinball machine and approached Jenkins.

"Okay, son, we gotta get movin' The Trooper downed his beer, smacked his lips and let out a sigh of satisfaction. The rookie was already outside reporting in on the radio which crackled round the empty car park.

"Okay, Big Bob, I'll walk you to the car." Outside, they both shook hands and embraced for a moment - a common gesture among veterans of the 'Nam.

"Now, you remember Sam, anything I can do for you, just gimme a holler, y'understand?'

The Chevy roared off out of the car park, raising a fifty yard cloud of dust before bouncing onto Interstate Highway 25 southbound for Colorado Springs. The Arms Man plunged both his hands in his pockets and trajected a stream of saliva through his front teeth mumbling the name Luke Conrad. Raising his head to shade his eyes from the blinding sun, he tracked the Chevy by now the best part of a mile up the straight spine highway.

"Big Bob, old buddy, you just done me one hell of a favour, but you ain't never goin ta know nothin bout it"

Chapter Twenty Eight

Luke Conrad got a lot of phone calls at his job in the pool hall in Pueblo, mostly concerning small drug deals, stolen goods, and illegal gambling. Earlier that day, Big Bob Jenkins had testified to the grand jury that his prisoner hadn't resisted and was willing to cooperate. Big Bob extended himself only out of Conrad's commendable service in Vietnam. The ploy succeeded in having the charge for possession written off. A probation period of eighteen months was applied, together with a six month suspended sentence. Conrad also agreed to undergo counselling during the probation period. Most small-minded criminals will not appreciate a good thing and Luke J. Conrad was no different. He both looked and behaved like a vagabond cowboy, his high-heeled leather boots and stone washed denims blended with the Doc Holiday moustache and shoulder length torched hair. Entering the pool hall, he was immediately surrounded by a half dozen of his cronies enquiring as to the outcome of the case. Conrad raised the hand in the air sporting the 'V' for victory sign.

"No sweat, babe, Eighteen months' probation; any you guys want a good attorney; you call and talk to lil' ol' Lukey here."

"There's a call for ya, Luke - ya wanna take it?'

"Yeah, gimme it." He picked up the phone from the booth beside the bar. "How do?' Luke here. Who dat?'

"Hi, Luke. Never mind 'who dat,' I wanna talk a little business with you."

"Who the fuck is this, what do you want?'

"Don't be getting so excited Conrad, I just wanna talk a little business, that's all. There's good bucks in it for you and it's legal!

"Listen, who is this?' What the hell are you shittin' 'bout?" Conrad shuffled his boots nervously on the wooden floorboards.

"Are you interested in earning a quick couple a g's or not?' If you're not I'll get someone else. You interested?' It's dead straight!

"Can I call you back?' Conrad replied, trying to unearth a phone number.

"Nope."

"Okay, okay. What's goin' down, whoever the fuck you are! The din of the juke box and pool tables caused the Cowboy to shut the booth door and continue his habit of fidgeting with his beer doused moustache. He tried to place the muffled voice and so reckoned the call was long distance. Sam Guttrie continued to speak from the phone booth in the foyer of a hotel in downtown Cheyenne, just across the border in the State of Wyoming.

"Okay, Luke, buddy. You're interested?'

"Yeah, sure. Provided it's straight - no dope."

"No, no dope. Just want ya' to round up a few bills."

"I don't understand. But I do understand that you know me and I don't know you, pal."

"Alright. I'll lay it out for you. I want you to get the following bills for me, just listen. I want three of each ... twenties, fifties and hundred Dollar bills, before 1988, from each of the twelve Federal Reserve areas." Guttrie was not surprised at the arrogant interruption.

"What?' Why can't you just git'em youaself?'

"Just listen. All ya gotta do is a five day flyin' trip to each area. It's a piece of cake. I was going to do it myself. But I got no time. Maybe you have some way of rounding these bills up some other way with less flying time or maybe no flying time. Problem is I need these real fast. But 88's are easy. Every third or fourth bill is an 88 because of the year which is close to maturing. There's two grand in it for you, Luke."

"Do you know me, pal?' What's these bills gonna be used for, anyways ... I don't like the sound of this pal," the Cowboy groaned, knowing he would not get an answer.

"To tell you the truth, Luke, I don't know myself. They're for a dude in Europe someplace," the Arms Man left his reply hanging.

"Don't bullshit me, pal. Betch'ya them bills is gonna be fer counterfeited - you Mafia?' holding the receiver with both hands.

"That's dangerous talk Conrad!"

"You doing the favour or not boy?' Guttrie's tone became cold, and laced with unpleasant possibilities. The silence lingered.

"Don't sound to me like I have much choice, Mister, does it?'

"You said that, boy." The Arms Man knew that Luke C. Conrad was getting just plain scared.

"Listen, Mister, can you call me in an hour?' I can't talk right now. I'm in. I'll do it. Call me in one hour."

"Don't worry about a thing." Guttrie wrote the number on his hand.

"Sure, Lukie babe. I'll call you ... I don't have to, eh, y'know - tell you to be a good boy or nothin?'

"Naw, no sweat. I'm a good ol' boy, Mister." The line went dead. Guttrie smiled and made his way to the nearest bar, ordering a Manhattan. The place was packed with families staying over for the annual Grade A Rodeo in Cody. An hour later, Conrad picked up the receiver in his apartment knowing the call was from his unknown employer.

"Yeah. Luke here. That you?'

"Yeah, it's me again. "You on?'

"Yeah, no problem. You frontin the cash?'

"Yeah, we'll front." The word "we" confirmed Conrad a shiver of fear. He listened on. "So, Luke. This is it. I'm allowing you a hundred bucks a day personal expenses. You gotta get three of each bill, right?' The three bills each of twenties, fifties and hundreds comes to five hundred and ten for each area, right?' Each is five hundred ten bucks, okay?'

"Wait a minute. Hold on, will ya?'

"So, multiply that by twelve is, eh, $6,120 - right?'

"Yeah, right."

"Plus your ex's of six hundred is six thousand seven hundred and twenty, for starters."

"Yeah, that's right. What about my dough?'

"Just a sec, Luke boy ... don't be hasty. Also, you have to get an interstate airline ticket. That'll be seven-fifty. So, that's a total of seventy-four-seventy. Now, I'll front a grand of your commission 'cause I'm a nice guy ... that's eighty-four-seventy; the other grand you'll get when the job's done. That's the job at the worst ... you may not need to do all that travelin'. The twelve area bills are everywhere but chances of pickin' up faster is in the state of issue"

"Sounds okay. Where have I gotta go and where do you want the bills dropped?'

"Okay. Here's the flight path. Just one thing, if you can get the bills of Dallas and San Francisco Federal Banks somewhere in Colorado or in the next State, then you won't have to fly to 'Frisco or Dallas. Anyways, just do it your own way. Here's the flight path. Gotta pen, Lukie Boy?'

"Yeah, go ahead."

"Say you begin at Denver ... then you go to Kansas City ... Saint Louis ... Minneapolis ... Chicago ... Cleveland ... Boston ... Atlanta, Georgia ... Richmond, Virginia ... Philadelphia and last stop New York City. When you get the bills you'll deposit them as I said, to be picked up at the Empire Hotel at Columbus Circle in New York, to be marked for the care of Mike Kennedy. Your name will be Frank Winston."

"Yeah, sure, no sweat. But I can't see me getting 'round in just six days, Mister. Things can go wrong, y'know. I'd say this job's gonna take longer than that"

"Okay, okay. I'll put an extra five hundred for expenses. Now, that's where the buck stops Luke, ya hear?'

"Got it. I'll handle it. Where's the dough?'

"You get it in the next day or two. I'll have a note in it for you. It'll be all in the note."

"Okay, pal. I'll be waiting to hear from you."

"Right ... so long." Guttrie dropped the receiver and gave the phone a friendly last tap whispering to himself. "Where there's a will, there's a way! The time was 4:30 p.m. Mid-West time. The Arms Man lurched the old Chevy onto Interstate Highway 25 southbound for his office in Boulder whistling "She'll be Coming Round the Mountain" in a slow monotonous melody which helped him concentrate. While he had succeeded in nailing Conrad to collect the bills, he was left with the delicate task of arranging some contingency in case the Cowboy did a run with the money. Approaching Boulder by the back highway running alongside the Rocky Mountain National Park, Guttrie decided that Luke C. Conrad needed a little closer looking at.

He stopped briefly at his office and picked up McNiff's check, which he stuffed in his breast pocket. Instinct told him not to cash it for the moment. An hour later, he fingered his way through the list of members at the Veterans Club on West Colfix Avenue in Denver. Conrad's name came up immediately; the address which current as Conrad was on the mailing list was described as 1050 Nth Desert Drive, Pueblo, Colorado. The Arms Man then made his way down the avenue to the County Hall, known as the City and County Building. The afternoon sun was dropping behind the gold-domed Colorado State Capitol. The grassy mall was dotted with shaded trees and park benches were now almost empty except for the clutter of birds here and there pecking at the leftovers of the lunches. "Shit" he whispered as he mounted the thirty shallow granite steps which led to the imposing double mahogany doors. Once inside the marble hall; he stopped a few moments to catch his breath and made his way to the counter marked Marriages, Deaths and Births. The attractive girl with native Indian features approached the counter glancing at her watch.

"You're a little late, sir. Closing time is in fifteen minutes. What can I do for you?'

"Sorry young lady, I'll be as quick as I can. Could you please do a search for marriages and births in Pueblo?'

"What is the name, sir, and the middle initial if you have it?'

"Eh, Conrad, Luke C. Conrad."

"Shouldn't be too much trouble, sir" She returned five minutes later.

"Sir. Here you are. Is the address 1050 Arkansas Avenue, Pueblo?'

"Yes, that's correct, ma'am." The girl handed the Arms Man a printout.

"That's all we have, sir. Will that be all, sir?'

"Yes, ma'am, and thank you very much." Guttrie read the slip immediately and smiled. There were four names. Luke C. Conrad of 720 Pine Springs Avenue, Pueblo 2/8/49 to Jennifer Christine Chapman 12/7/52 at Pueblo Registry Office 12/12/76.

At the base of the sheet were the names of the children:

1. Catherine Maria Conrad, 10/12/77 at Colorado Springs Maternity Hospital.

2. Jennifer Christine Conrad. 11/25/79 at Colorado Springs Maternity Hospital.

The Arms Man paid the two Dollars search fee and reckoned it was the best couple of bucks he ever spent. By 7 p.m. he was back in his apartment at the Cherry Creek Motel. Pulling on his surgical gloves, he grabbed a wad of notes from the floor safe under the refrigerator and commenced to count out the nearly nine grand in mixed denominations being careful to wipe all matter for prints and packed the bills in the padded envelope. He pulled McNiff's check from his breast pocket. Fingering the check for a few moments he pulled out his lighter and set the check alight, quoting himself the words "no names, no packed drill." He watched the paper burn out in the kitchen sink and brushed the ashes down the drain. The explanatory note he had promised Luke Conrad simply read in assorted black newsprint:

DAD - WE LOVE YOU - MOM, CATHY, JENNY.

He addressed the envelope c/o Luke C. Conrad, Pueblo Pool Hall, 5097 1st Avenue, Pueblo, Colorado. 45034.

Chapter Twenty Nine

The following morning Bennett awoke refreshed from the first quiet sleep he had for months. As he opened his eyes to Dublin's morning sunlight, the first thought that rang through his mind was the words "Fiona ... The Buttery, Trinity College ... noon." He rose immediately, anxious to eat breakfast and get through the article in the International Business Week Magazine. The purr of the bedside telephone broke the stillness. It was McNiff, the message short.

"Howard, we're going to New York on Thursday morning to check out premises. I'll be in touch. If not, I'll meet you at Dublin Airport at 7:30 a.m. sharp in the departure bar. Your papers, ticket and visa are in order"

Bennett showered slowly, allowing himself an extra couple of minutes under the cold spray to hose off the waking drowsiness. He then shaved twice for closeness and treated himself to an extra splash of after shave which he had purchased in the hotel gift shop the day before. Choosing a white shirt, he opened the window to test the cool of the morning. Concentrating on the car park, and on out onto the main road, all was still except distant fluttering of birds from some unseen treetop, He decided on a navy blue suit and black leather slip-ons. He would not need an overcoat and made his way down the corridor towards the elevator.

Passing Murphy's room, the Englishman decided to check on his prodigal sidekick. The room reeked of stale beer and tobacco. Murphy lay sprawled on the bed crucified, mouth wide open snoring like a bear and fully clothed, the bedside radio playing away at fair volume, a dozen empty Guinness bottles scattered here and there about the room. As Bennett entered the empty restaurant he was curious as to where Murphy was getting money to buy beer and checked the wad of notes in his inside pocket. Everything seemed in order. "That guy worries me, he's a fucking scourge."

"Jesus, I'm dyin! Murphy's flat accent from behind as Bennett stirred the first coffee.

"Don't startle me like that, Murphy. What's the matter with you?' and gestured the seedy Dubliner to the seat opposite.

"Is the bar open?' I need a cure," Murphy stuttered with all the symptoms of a really vicious hangover.

"No, it's not. Why don't you fuck off go take a shower. I wish I could get things done without you. You are a danger, a menace and a fuck up, I don't what's going to happen next with you"

"Jesus, that'd kill me altogether. Who's the bird you pulled last night, pal?'

"Mind your own fucking business, what have you got for me" Bennett replied abruptly.

The Dubliner spoke through a prolonged yawn. "Yeah, I was talking to Wong last night on the telephone. We'll be meeting him on Thursday week in Bangkok. Flight's a killer; it's a full 24hours with the connection!

"For Christ's sake, why can't you stay off the beer and straighten up. If you keep this up I'll have to tell him that I just can't trust you, can't work with you"

"Yeah, you're right. I'll straighten out. McNiff will be here this evening at six o'clock with the papers and tickets and all that. I'd better be in shape for him. We fly to London first, then we catch a midday Air France direct, the grub's nice anyway."

"Okay, Murphy. Listen, I've got to go. I'll see you this evening. You've got to get a grip on things otherwise I have to tell himself I can't work with you and by the way, where are you getting all this money for all this beer?' Bennett asked, sporting a dry smile of suspicion. Murphy's vacant stare told the Englishman he was searching his flogged-out brain for an acceptable answer which came almost immediately. "I picked up me dole." Bennett spent the rest of the morning until 12:30 p.m., lazing around Dublin's Grafton Street area and by the lake in delightful St. Stephen's Green anticipating meeting with Fiona Geraghty again. Crossing the miniature stone bridge to the west side of the lake, he could not help but join a group of schoolboys bouncing flat stones across the still water. Unashamedly, he chose a stone from the shore and tried his luck. The missile hopped some seven or eight times and earned him a sarcastic round of applause. There was a certain magic in the moment, he thought, sort of like re-acquiring an old touch or the beginnings of something new.

At the same time, Colm McNiff paced up along the cobblestone entrance leading to the eighth unit apartment block of Ailesbury Mews, Ailesbury Road, Dublin. Brendan Geraghty, Barrister at Law, resided alone and unobtrusively at unit number 21. The Fenian nourished a consummate loathing for this particular vicinity of his fair city. His blood pressure always rose a couple of points on passing up along the elegant detached foreign embassies of the Merrion Road. Like any freedom fighter, as he liked to describe himself, he took the view that the occupants of such places were nothing other than the gutless hired hands of power and corruption. The British Embassy held a special place in his animus and on passing would raise his right hand in military salute to mock the Irish Special Branch, who unfortunately knew him well. The cab driver of the day would always freak in paranoia at the postured punter, suspect he had just picked up another fifty fifty and hope for the best. The words always broke reverently through the silence: "We will never forget ye," referring to his brothers in arms of the inglorious past.

Fiona's brother, Brendan Geraghty was thirty nine years of age, single and a distinguished barrister. His father had died of a heart attack whilst interned at the Curragh Camp with McNiff for his part in the infamous Border campaign of the forties and fifties. His mother died soon afterwards of a broken heart, having unsuccessfully attempted suicide by gassing. Both Brendan and his sister Fiona were then fostered by Colm McNiff's sister Eileen, a secondary school teacher specialising in Irish, European history and economics. At a very young age, Brendan Geraghty showed intellectual promise in winning a State Scholarship to secondary school at the age of twelve. Eileen McNiff recognized his qualities of unmovable determination and a huge appetite for hard work and academic competition. His sister Fiona was less brilliant mostly by reason of her feckless attitude to the serious matter of concentration and study. At the time she seemed more inclined towards the less demanding areas of the arts, particularly literature and drama. Eileen McNiff hounded Fiona into repeating her leaving certificate at the age of eighteen, having achieved a modest two Honours at her first attempt. Her stepmother thought she would never live the result down among her colleagues and knew that Fiona had not made a really honest effort. The following term proved a relentless hell for Fiona. However, the discipline earned her a university scholarship and she duly compromised with Eileen by opting to take political science and economics, earning her Masters at twenty eight years of age. Brendan's career prospects took longer to mature. He achieved an Honours B.A. without fuss but was still at a loss to settle down to a chosen field. It was the following twelve months he subsequently spent lounging around Dublin which introduced him to the law. With his stepmother going up the walls in frustration at his conduct, he found solace in his daily excursion to Dublin's Four Courts. Quickly, he insulated himself in the legal system and on each edition of the legal diary, would choose his cases and duly attend in the public gallery just like any court reporter. By the following October, Brendan was enrolled at Dublin's King's Inns and was called to the bar two years later having achieved first class Honours B.L. LLM. He was never in any doubt as to the role he would play within the legal system. He simply wished to be a first class practicing barrister, his area of specialty he would discover by trial and error. Colm McNiff was always good for a modest loan anyway.

The Barrister welcomed his elder guardian and knew that McNiff would decline the offer of a glass of port. His profession had long thought him there are occasions to be direct, disarming and sometimes quite callous in extracting information. This apartment always gave the impression of an untidy occupant. McNiff had to clear space on the button back leather couch. For security reasons, Geraghty did not employ a maid and always passed off any criticism with the explanation that he preferred the lived-in look. Every available space was heaped with files, transcripts, books and magazines. More often than not current material on which he was working could be spotted in or around the fire breast where Geraghty spent most of his time at home.

"Now, Colm, I understand you are about to embark on this madness Fiona told me about" The Barrister blabbered off dismissively.

He picked a pen from his breast pocket and sat on the couch opposite, manoeuvring his feet into the only space between the scattered files on the floor. Without lifting his head, he continued in the same precise, impersonal dialect.

"You must realize Colm, that if anybody gets wind of this, they'll quite simply track you down like a dog and lock you up for the rest of your life. I've had a look at Fiona's brief and that the lunacy is to be done on the premises in Brooklyn, New York of one Sean Kilkenny this August, and Kilkenny himself has no knowledge of what's going on, is that correct?' The Barrister rapped out the facts as boorish as a speaking clock.

"Correct," McNiff answered obediently, "Assuming the forger approves of the facilities."

"And that the production is to be executed by this English chap... Mr. Bennett, who is being held under duress and one other young man not from within the ranks, a printer in other words, to help Bennett out, is that correct?'

"Right, Brendan. I'm sure Fiona has told you everything." "I'm not sure. The paper matter is to be manufactured in Thailand or someplace and the various other constituents to be used within the job such as numbering equipment; etcetera is to be obtained from sources outside this country." The Barrister continued to take speedy notes uninterrupted. "I spoke to Fiona for some two hours on this nonsense on Saturday. I have all the dates and times here but as yet I don't have a copy of the U.S. Prevention of Forgery (Amendment) Act, 1976 so naturally I am not aware of what perimeters the Act covers in respect of any forged material, or substance. However, I shall for the moment presume the Act covers the crime of the forgery of Dollar bills by a person from outside the jurisdiction of the United States. I spent all of damn yesterday trying to compile an opinion on this matter and I have to say that there are simply too many gaping variables. Also I have been unsuccessful in locating any precedent cases"

"What do you mean exactly, Brendan?' The Fenian enquired, knowing the explanation if any would be short and dismissive.

The Barrister rose to his feet and began to pace the floor slowly, both hands clasped behind his back. A short time after he qualified, he was commissioned by McNiff and others to complete his dinners at the English Bar, and was called two years afterwards. Specializing in criminal law and the highly delicate area of offences against the State, or the Prevention of Terrorism Act, as it is known in Great Britain. During his thirteen years practice, he was a well-known Republican sympathiser and an open opponent of the non-jury Special Criminal Courts in the Republic. Being one of the few barristers qualified to practice in Great Britain and the North of Ireland, he was the foremost authority on crimes within the definition of political offences in both jurisdictions. He was also an active advocate of law reform in those areas. McNiff could not recall the number of times Geraghty had coldly exposed the law as an ass for better or worse depending which side of whatever issue he was representing.

"In the first instance Colm, you must realistically decide on what the chances are of being caught. As you well know, under the provisions of the Prevention of Terrorism Act, which are emergency powers, there is no onus whatsoever on the State to be in possession of firm evidence other than suspicion. This gives effect to detention and application for extension. That point aside, my most grave concern would be the elements of forensic evidence; statements and association. Also, the Americans will initially be looking for people there and not on this side of the water. This is why I would advise you most strongly not to attempt to dispose any of this matter in any other jurisdiction other than the United States. To my mind it's highly unlikely that the Secret Service, who are responsible for protecting The Treasury would therefore have any reason to look further than their own borders. Clearly, there is no point in my speculating on the merits or weaknesses of any prosecution's case in this matter. The best advice I can give you is simply to ensure that it never gets that far, if any loose bricks are laying around, they will be falling on your shoulders. I'm sure I don't have to expand on that."

"No, you don't."

"To continue, I don't for the world of me, see why it would not be possible to dispose of the notes to a retailer, someone who would have the capacity to wash the bills and disappear. It would be worth his while ... so making it well worth his while." Geraghty continued to walk the floor at the same controlled pace, his mind piercing at he fulcrum of the complex issue. He stopped for a moment and opened his palms in query at the seated Provisional.

"Forget about legal considerations, Colm. What's to stop you calling one of the money laundering chaps in the States. I was reading an article in one of Fiona's magazines on Saturday, which stated one man washed $124 million in eight months and only on a five per cent commission although that was bona fide legal tender deposited through the banking system. If these notes are as good as you say they will be what's to stop that being done?' So hook up with such a person ... anonymously, of course, and put a deal to him, on commission. You can call or contact as many of these people as you wish. You can access them, but they don't know you. Anonymity must be preserved at all times. Just keep the cord cut. The forged money can be wired directly offshore; then you can move the bona fide cash anywhere you like. When the notes are detected the Secret Service will eventually track down the laundering people and come to a blank. But even that will take a very long time. The bird should well have flown by then. This is all provided the notes are good enough. You seem confident they will be. I will be watching things as they transpire and offer any advices I deem appropriate" the Barrister clapped his hands in confident conclusion.

"I have to agree, Brendan. The scheme you outline would leave the Secret Service and the rest running around in circles in the States. They would probably tone down the investigation eventually. The only thing that worries me is that the laundering people would know the destination of the deposits which will of course expose the identity of the offshore banks, and then perhaps the laundering operation and the actual depositor"

"It doesn't make any difference; even if you wire the orders yourself they will still know the destination when the records are checked. The imperative point is anonymity. Professional launderers form the offshore account in aliases, but which stand up. Then you either spend or rewire elsewhere. Just don't put all your eggs in the one basket. If one or two accounts are eventually discovered, well that's too bad. Besides, the authorities will still have to establish jurisdiction offshore and from what I read that's not on in the immediate future anyway. Besides, I believe the

Bulgarians and Libyans are willing to take hot money; check it out. The entire success or failure of this crime will depend on the standard of comparison of the forgeries and the expertise of the launderers. I understand this English chap knows his business."

"Yes, Brendan, he does. I think he has taken a liking to Fiona, believe it or not." The Barrister looked to McNiff in surprise and allowed himself a humorous snigger.

"As if the man is not in enough trouble already, he has my most sincere condolences. How bad can it get?' First he looses his job, then he gets stung for every dime he has, then the wife runs for cover, then he meets you lot and is locked into something he could possible do 30 years for, and he's not finished quite yet....then he meets Fiona, the poor unfortunate bastard. Anyway, it is absolutely imperative that your forger is kept in the dark literally as much as possible, for both his sake and yours. The less he knows under whatever interrogation may occur, the better for him and even more so for you. He must be concealed during transit as much as possible and must never be able to identify people, places or objects. I do appreciate that this would be nigh impossible but every step must be taken from here on in. If he cannot answer the critical questions, and passes a polygraph which he will almost certainly be compelled to take, then he becomes a dead end, and this job calls for dead ends. Also it would be of very substantive value to any defence if this forger was paid a substantial sum which he would never touch and be able to prove that fact. This would make the essential of any criminal case dormant as the 'intent' of his actions would be impossible to prove. Any prosecution will then undoubtedly seek to establish that he had numerous opportunities to go to the police so therefore it must be made clear to him in a very persuasive way that such an action will result in certain death or perhaps worse in some ways, spending the rest of his life looking over his shoulder. So it follows he must make his whereabouts known at all times when this matter is finished. If there is anything else I can think of I will let you know"

The barrister changed the topic.

Colm, everything that can be done for this unfortunate man must be done, I need you to promise me that"

On the other side of Dublin, Fiona Geraghty stood before the mirror in the ladies room of the faculty lounge at Trinity and let slip the hair slide, allowing the shiny tresses to adorn her shoulders. She applied some 'patriot red' gloss to her lips, turned against the mirror to inspect the shape of the butt which curved and dipped behind the sheen of the black pleated chiffon skirt.

Chapter Thirty

Dusty Bennett browsed his way down Dublin's bustling Grafton Street in the direction of Trinity College. By now the midday sun had induced the masses of bank, government and office people out of their places of work to sample the first breaths of summer. Taking the time to huddle in the horseshoe audience and concentrate on the young banjo playing street busker, the Englishman becoming drawn in by the melodic magic of the series of Irish reels. The heat of the sun and clarity of the banjo's ripping twang suspended the Englishman into a trance as he eyed the young musician finger the frets in union with the hypnotic sound. He drifted. There are times in every person's life when his creator will decide he be granted freedom to realize certain truths of his inner self. There are moments when an individual will aggregate all the proper factors to attain self-worth, self-purpose; as this lad has. But he cannot sustain them for long, as the soulless drudge of daily life vanquishes him. It is by then too late. Through love and guidance, every child must find his passion before the world destroys him. Staring the youngsters infantile fingers pick the fret he whispered the words from some old blues song which occurred to him. 'Bless the child who has his own'

Who were these men, his jailors?' The Irish Republican Army, these people who would lay down their lives for what they considered to be a noble cause. Noble causes were back in the age of chivalry he believed. What drove men to such extremes of atrocity?' Where lay the reasoning of the totality of the sacrifice in the face of such overwhelming odds?' He toyed with the sequence of issues in his mind. And then, out of his passing trance the only great forgery of the twentieth century emerged, The German 'Bernhart' operation of British Pounds during the Second World War. He caressed his jaw staring to the clear blue sky, blinking his eyes against the rays of the sun, contemplated there has not been in history one single successful forgery of currency perpetrated by an individual. Bennett dropped his gratuity into the banjo case, turned his back on the raptured audience, waved a friendly salute of goodbye to the youngster with the words "Thanks, young man, the very best of British luck to you."

As he reached the bottom of Grafton Street he could see the high granite wall topped with elegant green Georgian railings which marks the boundary of Trinity College, Dublin. The emerald leaves of springtime shimmered on the great oak trees of its perimeter. He had by now lost all inclination to protocol or pretence and paced bravely in through the famous arched gateway. By his slim form and distinguished step he could have passed for a mature student or faculty lecturer. He was still ten minutes early and took the opportunity to view a rugby match in progress. The noise of applause, together with protruding stilts of the goalposts behind the high brick wall directed him to the pitch. Leaning over the wooden barrier he immediately recognised the Irish scrum half of the previous Saturday's International. Time was getting short; he would see Fiona in two or three minutes. A pipe-smoking corduroy attired student directed him to The Buttery.

A nippy wind was beginning to blow and Bennett had not brought an overcoat. He walked briskly across the paved path to the cobblestone forecourt and followed directions by turning right to the Buttery. Through the restaurant window he could see Fiona Geraghy seated alone, to the back of the canteen, her attire nondescript by the flowing teaching gown. She waved from the window, probably in the suspicion that the Brit was not sure of his geography. Folding his jacket over his arm he walked confidently into the canteen. She stood so tall, statuesque, her stance piratically parted, with a canine smile that could save mankind.

"Well, why don't you come with me to the Four Courts?' I have a short hearing which should only be ten to fifteen minutes, then we can have the rest of the day together unless you have some other arrangements. The mysteries of Irish jurisprudence will be unveiled for you"

"I'd love that, Fiona. Let's go."

Fiona Geraghty presented herself as an expert witness for the State at 2:15 p.m. that afternoon in Court Fifteen of the High Court, confirming that the conduct of a certain savings and loan society could not be described as anything other than outright fraud. Bennett sat mesmerized in the public gallery. He could not have known it was Brendan Geraghty B.L. who had delivered the opening for the prosecution. The barrister noticed his sister leaving with a tall slim fair haired man and again repeated his condolences with the phrase 'she will have his guts for garters'

The pair stood in the circular domed foyer of Dublin's Four Courts, the ghostly wigged black gowned stoical figures armed with chest held wads of mysterious files swooning around, their instructing scrubbed solicitors in their repetitious tiresome attire, sprinkling piecemeal useless divinities on their groups of terrified foreboding litigants. Their only connection with the human race 'sparketh into life when the time cometh to hack up the booty' Truly a grim godawful comfortless place, a clearing house for the misfortunes of fate, to be avoided at all costs by the honest, the good and the kind-hearted. The pair exited through the main entrance to the spilling rain and the sickly brownish River Liffey. They walked towards The Clarence Hotel, the most ungarlanded but excellent eatery in Dublin, which was later bought by the most famous Irish rock band in world. Fiona fished out a canvas covered umbrella from her handbag which when opened formed a complete half dome supported by an interior Elmwood frame, centre stem and hooked handle. Bennett could not help but comment.

"My word Fiona, I have not seen one of those for many years"

"I know, I treasure it, I have had it since I was a teenager"

How beautiful thought the forger, to have preserved such a simple object for so long; still in pristine condition; the mark of an upbringing of values.

With that she instinctively slung her forearm under his, linked him, matching his every stride not with the maladroit march of the catwalk, but the natural unfettered heel and toe stride of a congenital athlete. The forger retreated into himself searching for some justification for these moments of salutary bliss. Now seated in the comfort of the hotel restaurant the forger nonetheless felt out of his depth, adrift of his moorings and the economist sensed this. She lazed her next comment.

"Don't let that place across the road or all the fuckin ejits in it intimidate you. I'm sure you must have noticed it's all just well-rehearsed business as usual window dressing nonsense. I hate the place, sorry, perhaps I should not have taken you there. Now Mister, there will be no talk of 'washing money' today. I really should also keep in mind your circumstances which understandably have you in tough spot but maybe not as tough as you may think," she rambled on scrolling the wine list. "That's my favourite, 19.50 in this joint and 6.99 in the off license, there's economy of margin for you" and she smiled that mischievous smile and then smiled again.

The forger took a deep breath, and jumped.

"Indeed...I am out of my depth...with you...not them, but that's OK, I'll just go with the flow, what the hell. You know a great deal about me, would you like to tell me a little about yourself?'

"Not a lot to know really, I heard a terrific phrase from that aging Swedish actress recently, Ingrid Bergman, she said, as we get on in this life the best advice I can offer is to take care of the body and cultivate a terrible memory". Of course there have been a few men, a marriage and then a few more, same old bag of dust, I am sure you know exactly what I mean.

Bennett jumped again, the non-pretentiousness of her delivery emboldening him.

"I am just surprised you are still single...or are you?'

"If you are asking why I am not married, I will answer your question with a very fair counter question, what's the point of marriage, exactly....like....you tell me, but please try to be brief?' She had thrown down the gauntlet.

Bennett froze, searching for a compelling reply to rescue him, but there was none. He felt foolish to have asked the stupid question in the first place.

"I am not at all surprised at your silence, because there is no answer. Here's my take on it anyway" she had saved him again.

"All people are married from birth anyway, some to wealth, art, music, the seven deadliest and so on, and some are content in the contractual obligations of marriage, and that's all there is to it. Agreed?'

"How well put. Yes, Agreed absolutely. I would be very interested in your thoughts about my circumstances" he asked, now sliding unconsciously into a subordinate neediness.

"That's an interesting one", she pondered. "Destiny, destiny indeed. All living things are the subjects of this phenomenon we conveniently label 'the chain of fate' and, as Churchill put it, we can only deal with it one link at one time. Your fate is as inexplicable as the bullet that ripped into Franz Ferdinand in 1914 and started the First World War, or the later emergence of an idle psychotic madman whose only reason lay in the ravings of Wagner's 'Wrath of the Gods' and the decrees of some middle age obscure Austrian Teutonic cult; or the ruin of Alan Turing, one of the finest minds of the twentieth century solely because he was homosexual. I could go on and on. Take your pick. Neither science nor philosophy has as much as attempted to investigate the mystery of destiny, the core and mystery of all life, simply because it cannot. The only progression to date lies in the foggy ravings of Nostradamus, the mathematical formulas of the insurance actuary or the starting odds at your local bookmaker. There's progress for you! So try not to worry about it"

The forger sat fascinated, heart and soul seduced by the grace and intellect of this quite wonderful person. Would she not be apprehensive about keeping company; albeit platonic; with an 'about to be' the world's greatest forger of currency.

"I have to ask are you not scared about being seen with me...you know" he asked sheepishly.

"No, I don't know...anything. My uncle asked me to provide some information with which an economist might be familiar and I provided it to him, that's all. In doing that I happened to meet you and we spent some time together. That's all. I am entitled to my privacy. Jesus, even some black smocked half -baked self-deluded theologian perched upright in a screened pine box is granted that. Where do they get the nerve. Fuck off" she barked as if to an intruder on her civil rights.

Bennett keeled over laughing uncontrollably, his ribs cracking at her continuing running commentary of the extensive 'miracles on offer' by the Vatican. It was hopeless, he just could not control himself; it was just too raw; too hilarious; too real; too absurd and too much to take; especially when delivered by this brilliant bawdy irresistible raconteur Professor of Economics, wild as a March hare. And the more he tried to stop her the more she laid it on. "Did you know most of them become closet alcoholics when they learn how to turn the water into wine. They have gone deep undercover these days you must know, I spotted one of them yesterday, disguised; checking out the criminal courts whizzing past on one of those skateboards" and she just bantered on and on with a continuous monologue of super high grade rib cracking gut wrenching comedy.

Three hours later they stood on the rain drenched granite steps leading to her flat on the west side of Dublin's delightful Merrion Square, the forger holding the prized umbrella in his right hand. She leaned to him, eyes closed and placed her hot lips on his rain soaked cheek, and whispered. "You may borrow my umbrella but please return it along with yourself in one piece" As the forger opened his eyes from the trance the massive Georgian door whispered closed followed by the soft 'clump' of the massive mortise door lock. Now elevated to her lofty bower and sweet solitude; there he stood, drenched, enlightened, emboldened, humbled, seduced, denied, randy as a warren of rabbits. The only connection to her was that umbrella, an item of undoubted high fetishist value, but alas under instruction to be returned as received... post-haste.

Chapter Thirty One

COSA NOSTRA

J ohn Sullivan sparked up his fifth Pall Mall of the morning and
ran his finger down the list of names on the daily work sheet
for Manhattan's West Side Piers, infamously known as "Hell's
Kitchen. Below, on the ground floor, some 700 members of the
Longshoreman's Union had assembled some 30 minutes before for
the daily "shape-up" for varied parcels of work designations, if one
could define it as such. McNiff's call had come at 11.30 p.m. the
night before.

They were a happy bunch, and for the very best of reasons.
Only some 100 men would toil that day, mostly the newer and
youngest members. The remainder would make their exit, their
union books stamped; to homes, bars, and side work in the
knowledge that their salaries and benefits remained intact for
life, by reason of the most extraordinary settlements ever
effected in the annals of American trade union law.

Since New York's dockland began to take shape in the middle of
the last century, Manhattan's lucrative West Side waterfront had
been controlled by the Italians and the Irish. Their existence has
been chequered with the usual dockland chronology of gang
warfare, power struggles, bloodshed and mass pilferage. To the
south, across Buttercup Bay, the equally lucrative docklands of
South Brooklyn and Red Hook was controlled by New York
Mafiosi, and both groups have since enjoyed a long and relatively
trouble-free association. Since the forming of the International
Longshoreman's Association the presidency has been held by an
Irishman and the vice presidency by an Italian, usually on 'no
show' high salaried positions It was in the mid Sixties when
container cargo was introduced and over half of the ILA's members
were threatened with redundancy, the association's real
bargaining leverage, the mafia controlled massive Teamster's

Union joined forces and demonstrated their awesome power, plummeting the world of shippers, industrialists and the US Government into chaos and eventual submission.

As is always the case in labour settlements, the cost was passed down the line to world shippers, whereby every mortal downing a shot of imported whiskey or imported foreign car indirectly pays for the thousands of salaries paid out in perpetuity to idle longshoremen on the Friday of each and every week. Thus, the age old longshoreman's skill of "swinging a hook" faded into history.

It was a normal morning as Sullivan stepped down to the smoke filled hall. A greeting of raucous applause, as usual, rose in unison. Huddles of men directed their attention from the racing pages of the Daily News and Post to focus attention on the call-out, which would be no more than a mere formality. As Sullivan reeled off the names for work, groups of eight and ten of the younger men made their way to the exit and out into the sunshine.

Sullivan had finished the call out by 7:45 a.m. Now the hall was empty but for a few huddles of longshoremen engaged in lingering chatter. The Irishman made his way back to the first floor office and commenced the paperwork of the day, squinting at his watch every now and again.

Sullivan was a gentle giant of a man, socially well-disposed and soft-spoken, only the devil horn grey curls in his jet black hair bearing testimony to his 64 years. The deep set dark eyes gave him the calming presence of still waters. Sullivan had achieved the position of shop steward of Piers 26 - 31 through hard work, dedication and singular pursuit of his goal. Throughout the ILA, Sullivan was known and trusted as a trade union negotiator of inordinate skills. His quiet demeanour never allowed him to get ruffled. Shipping executives feared him, for they knew that while Sullivan always spoke softly, he also carried one great big ass scary stick, The Teamsters Union.

Sullivan did not go to that bar that morning for his usual game of pool and half a dozen shots of Seagram's Rye Canadian whiskey.

Instead he eased the Buick out of the rear car park and drove west across midtown Manhattan, swung a right at Chinatown and on over the Manhattan Bridge into South Brooklyn. Sullivan reflected on the conversation he had with Colm McNiff the night before, and felt a tinge of excitement run up his spine as the glistening Manhattan skyline loomed behind him in the rear view mirror. Taking a right at Atlantic Avenue, he hurled the growling six cylinder two miles up Fourth Avenue until he reached The Mariner Bar at fifty second street.

Inside, the joint was jammed with longshoremen. The long bar was laden with shots of rye whiskey known as boilermakers and beer chasers. Both pool tables were in full swing, the respective blackboards bearing long lists of chalked initials awaiting their turn to play. This bar was buzzing, its occupants engaged in the serious business of the morning's agenda of idleness. Some marked off their tips for the afternoon's meeting at Aqueduct, while others checked their lotto numbers against the results in the morning newspapers. Here and there money changed hands in repaid loans, side bets- and fresh advances. The Mariner Bar bounced on merrily into another of its days to the punch of its own special tempo. Sullivan stepped on up to the far end of the bar, his dark eyes patrolling the groups in search of the person he was to meet, one Tony Delicado. The Sicilian stepped out from the telephone booth and beckoned to the Irishman through a haze of smoke.

"Hey, Irish, how 'ya doin'?' Both men retired to the back room which only boasted a small shabby table, two skeleton chairs and a single naked light bulb dangling from the centre of the ceiling. They had been friends for twenty five years, and there was no apprehension in either man's mind as they both sat to either side of the table for the 'sit down', Cosa Nostra's slang for face to face meetings, having closed and locked the door.

Delicado was immediately identifiable as a Sicilian by the scalloped edges of his English, and the fine head of cropped silver black hair swept directly back from his noble forehead. The full brush moustache and manicured fingernails belied his station in life as shop steward of Brooklyn's south docks. He was a small man, of broad shoulders, stocky build, the excess twenty pounds around the midriff and chest laying credence to his love of food and wine. The Sicilian began the meeting in silence by opening both his hands in question, the lines of his forehead growing more profound. Sullivan spoke quietly, both his hands clasped restfully on his penguin chest.

"Tony, I have to ask you a favour. I have to speak with your uncle immediately; can it be arranged?' Delicado shrugged his shoulders in nonchalant agreement.

"Of course, Irish, but he may want to know why you wish to see him first, capire?'

"Please, Tony, I can't tell you." Delicado again shrugged his shoulders and opened his hands in acceptance. Sicilians understand these things. He continued, rising from his seat and caressing his moustache: "Today, Irish is it that important?'

"If possible"

Delicado left the room returning ten minutes later, his tone was sharp and alert, "Okay, Irish, show time," and turned on his heels walking briskly through the crowded bar to his Cadillac parked outside. The journey to Port Washington on Long Island's North Shore was pleasant. By now the mid-morning sunshine discharged any threat of rain. As the Caddy rolled smoothly out along the north shore, Sullivan eyed the marinas jammed with sumptuous ocean-goers with indifference. All that idle money looted from the great unwashed.

Delicado followed the meandering road to the far side of the charming town and turned left down to the water where he pulled into an empty restaurant parking lot. The gleaming black Lincoln Town Car parked in the far corner did not escape the Irishman's wily attention. Both men were allowed inside the closed premises by a man in his early thirties. At the far end of the dressed tables sat the lone grey figure of Don Giancarlo Delicado and to his side his consigliore, the family advisor who must be one hundred per cent Sicilian. The old man rose to greet his two visitors with gracious silence.

Sullivan had met the Capo on just two or three occasions in the past through his now deceased uncle Joe. The Irishman had never forgotten that way back in the early 70's, Giancarlo had personally come to his aid when his wife suffered a difficult and expensive pregnancy with their first child. Sullivan's medical insurance had maxed out and the pending hospital bills would have made him to dispose of his modest house in Marine Park on Brooklyn's south waterfront. The Irishman had spoken to Tony Delicado out of none other than reasons of sharing the problem. Two weeks before the birth, John Sullivan was informed by the hospital authorities that all the outstanding balances were paid in full. His subsequent investigation into the matter was met with silence and an index finger crossing the lips of Tony Delicado. His only reply was "omerta gumbatta."

Don Giancarlo Delicado attended the christening, along with his wife, left an envelope containing $3,000 and made his exit prematurely. The Capo was a man of three score and ten, and to a great degree the events of his life were shrouded in mystery. The family's interest in construction, private carting, trade unions and gambling were well known and Don Delicado was profoundly proud of the fact that he had never spent a day in jail. He was now thin haired and slim with age- but the depth of his eyes told a man that behind the gracious figure lay an ocean of knowledge, experience, and awesome power. His first questions to Sullivan always related to family matters, health and educational progress of the children. The Irishman's answers were as usual quietly spoken, serious and explicit. The capo listened in silence, the fixed concentration of his eyes and nodding of his head showed his caring. His countenance remained unchanged as he gestured his nephew and bodyguard to leave the company with a wave of his hand; and as always to his side his consigliore, (family advisor).

"And now, my friend, why do you come to see me so urgently - tell me?' The Don leaned his back on the leather armchair, crossed his legs in expectation, his penetrating stare never leaving the Irishman's eyes as he lifted the anisette.

"Mr. Delicado, I have been sent to see you by some people, Irish people, and friends of my uncle Joe to ask a consideration of you." The Don nodded his head and urging the Irishman to continue. Sullivan lowered his tone and continued to speak over the next five minutes without interruption. "These people are about to execute a very large forgery of American Dollars. Even the paper itself has been specially manufactured to comply and the forgery will be in denominations of 20, 50 and 100 Dollar bills, evenly spread over the twelve Federal Reserves. Each note will possess a different serial number, and all of the ingredients of the real Dollar will be contained in this forgery to a point of perfection where neither any detection device, bank nor financial institution will be capable of exposing these notes before disposal. I don't think it should be necessary for me to further dwell on the accuracy of the counterfeit or the competence of the forgers. The amount will be in the region of 300 million plus. The reason I am here is to ask you on their behalf whether laundering arrangements could be provided."

The capo rose from his seat and began pacing the floor slowly and in silence. Then he asked the golden bullet question turning his back on Sullivan. "Now, tell me- tell me about these people. No names, of course. First tell me about the people we might be dealing with. Do I presume correctly in guessing it must be the your uncle's army...the IRA. The accusing stare in the Capo's eyes ran a shiver of voltage up the Irishman's spine. Sullivan should have known better than not to have mentioned the involvement in the first sentence. From experience he knew that whenever doing business with a Sicilian, particularly a high ranking capo within the Cosa Nostra one has to be extremely careful with the choosing and placement of words; with the meaning and weight of inclusions and more so omissions; with the timing and the chronology of facts. If a boss gets any whiff of doubt the 'sit down' stops, the suspicion of disrespect can raise its head which is paramount stuff with Sicilians. In usual circumstances that meeting would have been terminated right there. Sullivan would have been checked for wiring and sent his merry way with serious doubts about his future. No normal non family person would ever get near a boss no matter the reason. Such a meeting, even with such a proposal, would certainly take weeks if not months to arrange, and probably not at all. The information would be gathered by underlings and then brought to the capo. A meeting such as this is known as a 'sit down', and 'sit downs' at this level with non-family are few and far between. The Cosa Nostra have terms of conduct long built into their feudal system. No boss or underboss would ever allow himself exposed to the incriminating language which inevitably would occur in a 'sit down' such as this. There are so many myths and inaccurate images of the Mafia, Cosa Nostra, and Organised Crime created for the benefit of television, film makers and so called journalist and documentary makers. Cosa Nostra does not parade around in public shooting people and flaunting their wealth. There are of course exceptions to this past and present, but these have very short tenures. The real old school successful mobsters like Sam Giancana out of Chicago; who is believed to have handed JFK the Chicago vote; Carlo Gambino who once headed an army of over one thousand foot soldiers in New York, never spent one night in jail, and Salvatore Catalano one of the big players who ran the famous 'Pizza Connection' importation of one and a half billion Dollars of heroin, just to mention a few. Calvatore went to his small bakery every day and put in a day's work just the same as everyone else. Delicato would have an interest in many legal businesses such as carting, haulage, pizza parlours, night clubs and the list goes on. Like the rest he would have the same daily problems of staff, screw ups and all the other hassle the goes with the territory.

Also when dealing with a boss, or an underboss decision making is very fast and utterly final. The capo re-seated and continued. "I must decline. Out of respect for your uncle I will explain. These people are reckless beyond comprehension, their incentive is love of country and hatred of a regime and ours is family who coexist with regimes of power. There is the difference. If we do business with these people, we deal with an unknown quantity-and their strength of conviction is perhaps stronger than ours insofar as if something did go bad we could be involved with a force more than capable of hurting us and our interests. This is the point I put to you, capire?' The capo relaxed both his hands in the praying position round the bridge of his nose, his piercing stare penetrating the Irishman's soul. He urged Sullivan to respond with a beckoning of his hands.

For a moment, the Irishman felt raped, his head adrift of its moorings, his thoughts thrashing in inertia and confusion, and looked to the ceiling for some sanctuary. This was not a good move, shows uncertainty. He retreated within himself, and striking a chord of salvation, he continued.

"These people don't know who you are, who your people are. They know and accept that I would never betray my contacts; my loyalty to you, Mr. Delicado. My instructions are quite simply that these people are in possession of paper, serial numbering boxes and above all, the expertise to carry out this forgery to an unprecedented standard of accuracy. I have been asked to explain that the standards I have outlined are guaranteed and they are willing to do business on a very flexible basis. Such is the confidence that I have in them that I put my life on them, I give you my life." The Don narrowed the furrow of his brow.

"My friend, please.... you are family; we know you many years. We could never hurt you, your papa was one of my closest friends. We went through many things together, like a brother I loved him- and your mama, like a sister. I have known many things about the IRA since the time of your papa. His heart never rested easy in

America. Often he told to me about the old country- about his beloved Dublin town and the courage of the men he was forced to leave behind." Don Carlo rose to his feet and again began his habitual routine of pacing the floor slowly, staring to his feet, gauging each step with purpose, his hands clasped behind his back. Sicilians are masters of creative negotiation and the more profitable the enterprise the more masterful they become. For all of the inter family Mafiosi wars that have happened since the turn of the century it is seldom that members of the public are interfered with other than loan sharking and illegal gambling shakedowns. Whilst these in themselves are extremely lucrative operations the Cosa Nostra's real power lies in the cohesiveness of the multi-tiered levels always available to resort to violence which threads like a needle through the fabric of most American cities. It is solely within this ability to resort to highly organised violence Cosa Nostra insures its piece of any action to which it feels entitled. Any person who sees the Cosa Nostra as anything other than ruthless predators is a fool. Whilst occasions are reserved for gestures of so called friendship and celebration with non-Italian associates the mafia inner sanctums have always been and always will be prohibited to outsiders. Like all predators of the wild Cosa Nostra is exactly what it says, "Our cause" and exclusively preys on the weak and the isolated. Never will the organisation hunt a stronger adversary directly, but so cunning is the Sicilian instinct that it has succeeded over and over again in gouging corporations and interests many times the Mafia's strength in power and numbers. Their secret lies through in the control of the most critical key in any endeavour, labour. Once labour is under their control the biggest giant in industry can be brought to its knees. A classic example of this would be when "Lucky Luciano" organised a troop ship to be torched on the Brooklyn docks from his cell where he was serving 20 years on prostitution and racketeering charges in 1942. As everybody knows Luciano was freed and deported to Italy in return for his guarantee for the security of Brooklyn's dockland where more than 60% of American soldiers and arms were assembled before sailing for the battlefields of Europe. Also Luciano was able to guarantee safe passage for the allies' invasion of Sicily. It is also all but impossible to hide from the mafia unless extraordinary precautions are taken. They have a saying, "our reach is far and wide" and it is. The Capo's evaluation of Sullivan's proposal was now expanding in that direction, 'far and wide'.

"This is what I would like you to do John. Go to your boss, and first give him my respect. Tell him the truth, exactly what I said, where I see the weakness in his interests. But I want you to tell him this. I know that he will find a launderer in the USA without too much difficulty. But with respect your people are nowhere near as organised as we are here in the US, and I think we can be of very valuable assistance. We will oversee the transport, handling, and the security aspects of the transaction. The launderers will be in no doubt that it is Cosa Nostra they are dealing with and that Cosa Nostra will be ensuring that our clients are properly protected. Our fee will be 2 million Dollars in good notes when everything is finalised. But I believe your people will have a much bigger problem and that will be a problem of credulity. Because of the condition of anonymity I cannot imagine any launderer taking your people seriously. If this problem arises you have my permission to come back to us but this fee will be very substantial and I will only discuss this with your boss.

The capo pecked the Irishman on the right cheek and ravelled his hands as if to wash them with the words "Tutti terminadi" the traditional Sicilian closure to any 'sit down' and gestured the pair to the exit.

Sullivan called McNiff on his return to Brooklyn and relayed the details of the arrangement explaining the services which were to be provided by 'Organised Crime'.

Chapter Thirty Two

J ohn F. Kennedy Airport was bustling as usual three days later. The Printer and Fenian, having travelled separately passed through Immigration without a hitch. Bennett had never been to the United States before. By now he had grown used to the company of unscrupulous men, whose single-mindedness had well begun to shake the dust from some of his sacred scruples. His lifelong notions of effort and reward, good and evil were by now in unnoticeable increments recalibrating themselves within the 'id' of his make-up.

The JFK Express thundered into Penn Station on 34th Street and Eighth Avenue at 8:35 a.m. McNiff had instructed Bennett to leave the train first and book a single room at the Penta Hotel on Seventh Avenue and would contact him later when he had met with Joe Kilkenny. McNiff was alone in the carriage, which had been crammed with foreign tourists and Americans returning from God knows where.

McNiff spotted Kilkenny immediately in the centre of the huge circular foyer. Joseph Kilkenny always wore the same trilby as long as McNiff could remember, and spent half his time filling the barrel pipe, wrested to the side of his mouth. Kilkenny was a small man, about 5'7" and plump, weighing some 220 lbs. McNiff surmised that this was due to the lifestyle to which he had become accustomed over the last twenty plus years as the owner of "Red Hook Design and Print, Inc."

Kilkenny had always dressed impeccably. Dark colours and simple, but well cut lines, which he was convinced gave a level of credibility to the wheeler-dealers of the advertising and graphic industry, whom for the most part he viewed with consummate loathing. Joe Kilkenny had worked for the Movement in the middle and late Fifties. The Irish Coalition Government of the time had caused thousands to emigrate with draconian economic policies. Kilkenny was a letterpress pressman and found hard work, long hours and industrial pay not to his liking. Four months before emigrating, he was charged with forging tickets for an All-Ireland football final, jumped bail and emigrated to the USA, never to be seen in the Republic of Ireland again. Arriving in New York City, penniless and a wanted man, his whereabouts were known only to McNiff and a couple of other close friends. McNiff came to his aid with a small loan and through IRA contacts in the States, providing him with a new identity.

Kilkenny had never forgotten this, although he sometimes doubted whether be would have been allowed to. After his arrival in New York, he cultivated an unquenchable appetite for hard work and monastic discipline. Within five years, he was pressroom manager of the Premier Print and Box Company, on Manhattan's Upper West side. The firm went belly up and Kilkenny started Brooklyn Design and Print out of his savings and severance settlement. The beginnings were modest; one Heidleberg Platin in a leaking corrugated iron shed on which he had difficulty paying the eighty bucks a week rent. At this time, McNiff was doing five years at the Curragh Camp. People say there are skeletons in every man's closet, and Joe Kilkenny was no exception. The real cash which put the present firm on its feet was generated out of small time forgery for the IRA. During his years in the United States he had executed several forgeries for the movement, the most important being the printing of $200,000 in Federal Food Stamps which were distributed throughout the State of New York at twenty per cent of face value. Joe Kilkenny was a Republican sympathizer of sorts, but basically he was a likable con artist with a sharp eye for the ladies, and an appreciation for the better things in life. By now he had cultivated the Brooklyn accent. His greeting never changed.

Hey Colm, what 'ya say?'

McNiff always exercised the short military salute and Kilkenny loved the protocol of it all which he believed bestowed upon him an inclusive status within the movement. The pair retired to the

Penta Hotel across from the circular Madison Square Garden complex. Kilkenny gestured to the far empty corner of the bar.

"Shot of brandy, and a beer chaser on the side and a glass of orange juice. Heavy on the rocks, pal." He had long stopped asking McNiff his drink. He filled the pipe slowly and sparked up, eyeing the old Fenian with curiosity through the rising blue smoke.

"Well, Colm. What's it to be this time?'

McNiff was hesitant, gazing at his orange juice with the inquiring eye of a connoisseur. It was definitely better quality than the stuff on the Far Side, by the fragments of real orange floating around the surface. He downed a mouthful, allowed himself a sigh and dangled the ice at the bottom of the glass. McNiff had this habit when he needed to concentrate. Without replacing the glass on the bar, he turned to Kilkenny who was now striking the second match.

"We need a little cooperation Joe. You and the staff go on vacation during the first two weeks of August, is that right?'

"That's right. Same every year" Kilkenny nodded, chewing the stem and releasing a small cloud of purple smoke suspended in the atmosphere. McNiff gathered his thoughts.

"You don't need to know any details about this operation Joe, but we might be using your premises during the first two weeks of August." For the first time in their long association Kilkenny was being told he would play no part in whatever was about to happen.

"Well, Colm, I know by the sound of you I don't have much choice, but there are a couple of things I do want to know. One, how are you going to cover my ass, and two, is there anything in it for me?' He continued, 'There is no holiday time as such, thousands of people come and go week in week out , twenty four seven, all year even holidays and Christmas. Supply and demand rules in this town. The industrial estate as you would call it is vast, over one hundred buildings eight stories high manned with industrial elevators capable of shunting five tons in one lift. There is literally no security except at the front gate which is only for help with directions and container check in. This place has been here since the twenties and before. It was the gathering point for most of the troops in the Second World War. I have never as much as seen the cops here except to break up an in house fight or remove the odd drunken employee. That's it. From the security angle you couldn't get better unless you will be bringing in containers of illegal stuff and even that wouldn't be anything unusual." Kilkenny was laying out his stall, emphasising the plus points to justify a bigger pay day.

Kilkenny paused and fired up another pipeful moving the match in looping arcs to ventilate the flame. McNiff could detect that Kilkenny was thankful not to be involved in whatever was about to take place. Once he was well covered financially he would play ball. His thoughts were now far from criminal activity and more concentrated on doing the best deal possible from his one bite of the cherry and continued to put his best foot forward. 'If my plant will be needed that's fine. You can tell whoever, there is one 5 year old Heidleberg GTOV with full plate making facilities. That's all he would need to know I think. Can you remember that. But I will need to make arrangements to get rid of the couple of staff. The way things are over the past years in the advertising business I only hire on short contract basis, almost job by job from the agencies. I am still non-union otherwise I would be out of business a long time ago. I am guessing you will need a vacant shop which can be done but I will need to arrange with the girl who takes care of all the paper stuff. She is three days a week anyway, won't be a problem. There are just two guys there today finishing a job. They will finish at 3.30..

"Well, look, I don't even know yet whether your place is suitable. But I'll be able to tell you after my guy checks it out. Could he could have a look at it after five then.

'Sure, I don't need nor want to be there but I think it would be wise to take every precaution to conceal the location and any evidence inside which could be used against you in the future. I need to get out there now to get that done myself" Kilkenny handed McNiff his business card, keys and the alarm code advising the inspection should be called off for now if on the outside chance any hassle from security or anyone else.

The men parted minutes later. Kilkenny left alone by cab, McNiff heading for the elevator.

Minutes later Bennett listened gobsmacked as the he felt his energy levels awaken as McNiff detailed the meeting with the contact, especially the mention of the four colour Heidleberg and the plate making facilities. It felt like he was returning to work, back to some gradient of normality. The aggregates of his professionalism and his leadership qualities reinstalled his sense of dignity, releasing him in some measure from the imprisoned state he had endured over the last weeks if not months given the Spanish debacle. Now he was King of his Universe, fully in control and in control of all others. He, and the he alone was about to let slip and blood his hounds. And now the hour and the man were upon him. The words of Churchill occurred to him when after years in the wildness when he stepped through the doors of Buckingham Palace to accept his credentials. 'It seems as if all of my previous life has been but a preparation for this trial and for this hour'

McNiff thought the time a good opportunity to familiarize the forger with the security precautions which must be placed upon him for his sake and everybody else's. Bennett appreciated the reasons and the logic of all the precautions and indeed thanked McNiff for having given the matter the time and consideration that he did. From henceforth all the forgers movements which were thought could injure any and all those involved were to be 'blacked out' McNiff explained a van would arrive in one hour and bring him to and from the premises. He would not see the driver. Bennett would be required to wear business tinted glasses and take all precaution to conceal his identity, and at all times to be aware of the danger of leaving fingerprints; this was for his own sake after all.

Bennett returned to McNiff's room three hours later....beaming. He just had two words, "It's on".

Next day Kilkenny peered through the belching blue smoke across at the Fenian in the lounge of the Penta Hotel.

"Joe, we will be using your premises during the first two weeks of August"

"OK, Colm. I can tell you here and now I don't even want to think what's going on. Thank God, I'll be down in the Bahamas or Puerto Rico sunning myself when all this is happening." Kilkenny was upbeat sensing the irresistible draw of cold unearned cash and this was exactly how McNiff wanted him.

"Okay, Joe. I'll call you in due course with the details. The cash payment is to be twenty thousand Dollars. Don't even dream about arguing with me. There's no more we can do now, so drink up. "

"You go ahead Colm. I think I'll stay on for a few." Joe Kilkenny made his exit at 8:15 p.m., a little intoxicated. As he turned the key in the ignition of his Lincoln in the underground parking lot, he scratched his forehead with his free hand, puzzled and bewildered, whispering to himself through the odour of brandy and Clan pipe tobacco. "Well, what the eye don't see, don't hurt the heart and swept the motor up the hotel ramp and into the furious traffic.

The Printer paced up and down Room 447 of the Penta Hotel, and had been doing so for the last two hours, his mind jumbled with details, paper, ink and security, to name a few. He was impatient to get to work. On his return, he had been careful to dodge the receptionist and make his way quietly up the stairs to the first floor elevator. The spring sunlight broke through the drawn drapes, forming a laser of rising smoke across the room. The television was on. Bennett had devoured a half pint of vodka; the packet of Pall Mall showed he had three left..

In times of decision, it is sometimes difficult to sort the wood from the trees. This particular job was stretching every area of his professional capacity to breaking point. To make a wrong decision in any of edgework decisions would be disastrous. It could cost him his life. The visit to Joe Kilkenny's premises had gone so well that he wondered in his own mind whether the owner of the factory knew anything about the job. The factory measured approximately forty feet wide by one hundred feet oblong and situated on the third or maybe the fourth or fifth floor. He had no idea how he got there, or how he got back to The Penta. The journeys were just a blank of sitting in the back of a blacked out van holding a set of keys and alarm instructions. Bennett gloated with pleasure as he surmised the itinerary of plant and machinery.

On entering from the rear, the Forger stood in the preparation area which had two light tables, two state of the art composing units, the art section and a stone for the servicing of the letterpress section. This preparation area was divided from the machine printing room by a studded partition.

Leaving the preparation area, the camera and darkroom was to the right. The Printer had memorized the list of the equipment. To the centre, the visitor would see a maze of machines. First, side by side, were one 2-color Heidleberg and one four colour Heidleberg GTOV litho units. Behind the machine on the left was a Heidleberg letterpress crown cylinder used for numbering, perforation, embossing and cutting. To the right of this machine was a small letterpress Heidleberg plating machine, for small one-off jobs and a Multilith 250 with a specialized T51 head, which gave the tiny press 2-color capacity. To the back right hand corner behind the camera and darkroom was the guillotine and a folding machine. The exit for finished goods was on the centre of the back wall which was a single steel door opening onto the corridor and huge industrial elevator. The Printer considered the factory a first class unit for good quality general jobbing, professionally planned and well run. The plant had been chosen to allow for improvisation of staff and a very high production level. Bennett felt he could improve on the layout, but not by much. He had taken special note of the lighting arrangements. There was no natural light in the factory, which was entirely lighted by forty twin fluorescents. The effect was adequate, although print purists would not necessarily agree with this. The windows to the front of the building were at five foot and blacked out. There was not one scintilla of evidence with which he could ever place a location on the premises.

McNiff entered the hotel room.

"Hello, Howard," he said in a friendly tone. "I see you've been having a drink ... ah, sure you might as well. When do we start the job?' McNiff inquired excitedly, removing the crombie. Bennett answered, requesting he sit down, relax and listen. Bennett remained standing and commenced his dialogue while pacing the room.

"The premises are excellent. Does the owner know anything about this?'

"No, Howard of course not. Besides I gave you my word on these matters. Forget you ever heard that name, I should never have mentioned it. He could never be trusted to handle anything like this. You surprise me, he's what we call a useful hanger on....forget him" There was an undoubted ring of trust and respect buried somewhere in McNiff's statement and Bennett appreciated it. "We fly to Dublin Sunday morning at 7:45 a.m. so let's eat and get a good night's sleep,' McNiff closed out and pointed to the restaurant. "Enough for one day" he said with a prolonged yawn.

Chapter Thirty Three

T he first time Murphy had gone to Thailand on a heroin operation, he had made the cardinal mistake of calming his nerves with copious quantities of free Chivas Regal then available all long haul flights. Thai Customs, like all customs officers have honed skills in the pinpointing of drug people. Murphy had never forgotten the three and a half hours he had spent in the small office to the rear of the airport building, blundering through a cloud of alcohol, about the purpose and general circumstances of his visit.

Miraculously, he was released, having convinced his hosts of a life- long ambition of sampling the more licentious services on offer in Thailand. That was some four and a half years ago. He had since made some dozen excursions, and on each occasion had waltzed through the Customs as if they did not exist. Murphy had since kept his powder bone-dry when entering or leaving Don Muang airport.

Bennett sat beside him in seat B46, just alongside the right wing of the huge Air France jumbo, flicking his way through the contents of his briefcase. The command to fasten seat belts and prepare for touchdown brought the soft music to a sobering halt, as the 747 began its approach. The Printer could see the vast Gulf of Thailand to his right and the mountainous terrain of Southern Burma to the left.

Bennett was not unfamiliar with Bangkok. Some five years ago his Hong Kong-bound flight connected here while in transit to install a six colour offset press on the premises of The Hong Kong Times. "Funny old world," he thought to himself as the flaps dropped for the last time and the revolutions reversed to make final approach for landing. Bennett noticed the smugness of the other travellers, from the expensive clothes, jewellery and conservative formality during the long hours flying time. He was relieved Murphy was at last settling in. The passing through customs was nerve-racking with each entrant being briefly interviewed. Both their British passports passed undetected and Murphy was careful to keep his long sleeved shirt cuffs buttoned lest the officials spot any needle track marks on the inside of his arms.

It was Murphy who spotted the small oriental in the arrivals area with the word "BOND" on the placard. The tiny frame in the standard neck high black Chinese collar business suit, white shirt and black pallbearer tie. The tiny circular shades blotting out any expression of humour or personality. Five minutes later, both Europeans were seated comfortably in the back of the limo, crossing the Chao Phya River on the western fringe of the bustling metropolis of Bangkok. Murphy remarked that traffic was bottleneck as usual, which gave Bennett time to view the city's night action through the open tinted window. It took thirty five minutes to ease the mile and a half down the Ramai Road and park up outside the Bangkok Plaza Hotel off the Ploenchit Road on the far side of the city.

Having dropped the couple of suitcases in the lavish foyer, the driver made his exit with a sharp obedient bow. Bennett was glad to be rid of him and always suspected that one hundred and twenty pound, five foot Orientals had some hidden resources ... like breaking every bone in a man's body in ten to twenty seconds. The Forger changed pound Sterling to Baht at Reception and invited Murphy to a meal in the Pat Pan Grill, one of the four exclusive restaurants in the hotel. Both men were exhausted and famished with hunger. In hindsight, Murphy considered his appointment with Chan Wong to be too hasty. He should really have left it until tomorrow. The pair opted to stay safe, avoid local hot spicy food and ordered fillet steak, a simple side salad and coffee, which proved acceptable. Forty minutes later they tipped their brandy glasses in a clink, Bennett toasting:

"Well mate, it's now or never."

The Englishman gave Murphy 2,000 Baht, instructing him that he would be waiting in the room. The Dealer walked briskly out of the hotel and down the Ploenchit Road, dodging the flow of small motor cycles, sometimes stepping onto the street to continue his pace through the crawling mangled traffic. The alcohol level in his blood had by now almost worn off probably for the first time in many months. He did not feel tired and surprised himself at the lightness of his step and the clarity of his thinking. Michael C. Murphy, Esq. was ready for business and no better man when the odds were right. He continued his urgent pace oblivious to the rambunctious night life and the all-consuming maze of temptation which eventually breaks the will of the most well-meaning onlooker. The Dub had seen it all before. There were urgent matters on his mind as he took the steps of the sumptuous Ambassador Hotel. Once inside the foyer he slowed his pace to a near standstill and slung the file under his armpit.

Plunging both hands in his pockets, he browsed across the deep pillow carpet to the elevator stabbing the button which showed the arrow in the upward direction. It took eight seconds before the double doors silently slid open on the landing of the top floor. The Irishman reeled to the end of the elegant corridor and rang the bell on penthouse number four which boasted the bronze lettering "Chan Wong - Permanent resident. Do Not Disturb Unannounced! Signed, The President- Ambassador Hotel Group."

The white panelled door was slid open almost immediately by the slim oriental girl. Without showing the guilt of a stare, Murphy took in the deep cheekbones and wide inviting smile. The single pink flower tucked behind the tiny jewelled earlobe contrasted perfectly with the ankle length silk sarong which glistened by the body length floral embroidery on a quilt green background. She clasped to the praying position and dropped her head slightly. "Mista Bond?' Welcome ... pleese comb!

Murphy smiled and stepped obediently into the world of Chan Wong. As usual, he was requested to wait in the occasional room off which there were four doors, one on each corner. The eye could not focus clearly for more than fifteen feet in Wong's tremendously spacious penthouse. The light, or lack of it, was skilfully distributed to give an immediate impression of sinister secrecy to the visitor. The skylight to the centre of the reception was the only natural light source, but Chan Wong preferred to use this to nurture his huge collection of exotic plants suspended from the ceiling, under which was a circular flower garden. The perpetual motion of gurgling water, together with the oriental music of a thousand years created a truly hypnotic experience. The residue of this reception area was furnished in a maze of the most exotic wicker work and gigantic plants, highlighted with the concealed spotlights here and there.

Without parting her hands from the praying position, the oriental girl silently tiptoed out through the door at the far right hand corner. Murphy always tired waiting for the "Coolie," who maintained an upper hand by his psychological preparation for what ordinarily should be friendly but businesslike meetings. However, he was typical of the secretive and ruthless perpetrators of the business of death on the Orient.

Thirty minutes later, Murphy rose to enter the forum at the beckon from the girl at the far door. Wong did not rise from behind the oval desk, nor did he gesture a handshake. Allowing his head to drop momentarily, he laboured his mouth into contorted smile and allowed Murphy be seated with a nondescript wave of his hand. The Dubliner often wondered at what lay beneath the mohair suits and handmade silk shirts. Physically, Wong looked like a man who had spent his life in a crack in a wall in Belsen or up to his balls in some rice paddy for twenty hours a day. The man standing to his left bore no such resemblance, and only destitute of the proverbial bowler with which he would surely decapitate a stone statue from a hundred and fifty yards. He was a gorilla of a man, 9 parts retarded, with a shining android skull, the huge frame bulging from the bum-freezer tuxedo jacket, the huge hands dangling limp at his sides, and darting beady eyes ever vigilant to any sudden movement.

Murphy had long nicknamed him the "Missing Link" and suspected someone had belted him with a hammer by the deep gouge to the front of his shaven skull. Without straightening or moving the position of his hands, the Link disappeared robot like into the far room at a click of Wong's fingers. It was the usual routine ... slow, formal and dotted with threatening undertones. The Link returned a few moments later with the same ebony box from which Murphy had so often sampled the contents.

Wong folded the box open, revealing three compartments.

To the left there was a four by four inch mirror. The centre was divided into twelve tiny glass compartments, each containing approximately one gram of heroin, duly priced and varying in purity and origin. The various utensils of administration were packed neatly in the right side. Surrounding the two unopened plastic sachets of hypodermics were a variety of cigarette papers, plastic and chrome inhalers, cigarette tobacco with a well-used miniature blood pressure device, ball shaped hand pump and a packet of silver foil used in "chasing the dragon." Murphy rested both his arms on the table and eyed the varieties of smack with interest. Same routine, Murphy had done it all so many times.

"Why not sample goods, Bond?' The Dubliner raised his nicotine-stained fingers in polite refusal. "Listen, Chan, I've got to keep straight; there's a huge deal coming up and I've just must keep it together. This is going to be the big one."

The Oriental rubbed his chin with chicken claw fingers and let a prolonged groan of surprise and interest, the black eyes revealing his search for information lest the Dubliner had other dealers to talk to. Murphy remained silent.

"You want to talk me about this deal, Bond?' He continued the tone of his sentence, prying deep at the heart of the yet undisclosed details. The room was becoming tense.

"Of course, but I only hope you can handle it Chan, this is the really big one."

"I handle the deal, Bond," he continued without hesitation. "How many dolla - how many dolla the deal?' He opened both skeleton hands, impatient. Murphy couldn't help but allow himself a smile. The coolie smiled back. "How many dolla?'

"Around five million wholesale ... cash." The Weed rose from behind the desk and babbled something into his intercom in a vexed tone. Continuing around to the front of the desk, he took the Dubliner by the elbow and escorted him out through the reception and into another room. Murphy had not been in this room before, which had all of the evidence of a cauldron of lurid vice. The room itself was small, but took on bigger proportions by the mirrored walls and ceiling. The dimly lit bar was laden with stock and the four wicker stools showed this to be a place designed for the seedy and the intimate. The low, lavishly cushioned seating could easily have been used for purposes other than idle bar chatter. A huge video screen rested suspiciously in the far corner. An empty match box with the words "The Mill Steak House, Broad Pines, Chicago" told Murphy there had been some recent visitors. Without consulting Murphy, the Coolie reached for the bottle of Chivas Regal and poured two shots. .

"Now, Bond, talk to me about the deal ... cheers."

"Okay, here's the beef. The guy is in the market for smack and has not done business in Thailand in the past. I'm doing the negotiation and I'm going to do a good job for him. He's no fool, has run with the Indians for the last four or five years and wants a complete packet which will keep him from exposure or risk. To my mind he has come up with a really novel idea, he intends to use reams of paper manufactured here as the runner. The Dub spoke with excited authority, the wily Coolie listened nodding his skull as to elevate his approachability.

"This guy wants to have original paper made here in Thailand for further processing in the U.S." Murphy handed over one of the

225

forged quotations from the Bradford Paper Manufacturing Company. "This is the specification and last quotation from a British manufacturer. In order to justify the manufacture of this paper here in Thailand, the quotation for, say, a two year contract would need to be low, but credible. The Coolie puffed on a king sized filter and nodded his head without speaking, skilfully allowing the Dubliner to continue the proposal.

"The first consignment will be opened by Customs, then the second and third and so on. Sooner or later, like all mortals, they'll get slack and avoid the hassle and just let the stuff through particularly during the Christmas season. That's when we'll hit. My client is willing to put up big cash for the first order ... that's giving you an incentive just to start the ball rolling and get the first consignment out. Here are the manufacturing specifications and a few samples. But remember, the stuff has to be exact to the specification. If it's not, the whole deal's off. He'll want a sample pronto because the paper has to pass muster with his partners, so it has to be one hundred per cent, right and proper."

The Coolie shouted orders into the intercom on the bar. The Link entering the room seconds later. Without asking the Irishman a question, Wong wrote for five minutes in Hanyu Chinese characters, the American king-size smouldering in the gold holder which dangled from the side of his clasped mouth. Carefully folding the bogus letter heading containing the paper specification with his lengthy handwritten note, he placed both items into an envelope which he handed to the Link, who took an obedient bow and disappeared out the door. Removing his spectacles he turned to Murphy.

"Okay, Bond, I sent the specification to chemist at paper mill I know. Tomorrow he tell me if possible to make the paper, how soon it can be made and for how many dolla. When do you want to pick up heroin?'

"Leave it until we get that paper sorted out. Then we can talk some real business. I'm bone tired. I'd better get back to the client."

"You no want a woman tonight, Bond?'

"Naw, not tonight. I'm beat. Anyway, the client would object."

"You call me tomorrow, Bond. Then we do big business."
Twenty minutes later, Murphy was back in the Bangkok Hotel
explaining to the Englishman the outcome of the meeting.

Chapter Thirty Four

T he Printer awoke first the next morning to the din of traffic and the drone of an industrial vacuum cleaner. Sitting upright in the single bed, he allowed his thoughts to settle.

"Okay. One, confirm the paper can be made. Two, get confirmation from McNiff that all paper used throughout the Fed areas are the same. Three, test the stuff against original. Four, quantify the order and arrange for transportation. That's it." Twenty seconds later the bedside phone shook into life.

"Hello. What is it?' The Printer had forgotten to leave the duty of answering the phone to Murphy. "I want to speak to Bond." Bennett did not bother to ask who was calling and gave the snoring Murphy a jab. He leaped out of his slumber in shock, a habit he had acquired after a lifetime squinting over his shoulder. "Don't worry," the Printer said. "It's only a phone call, Bond."

"Yea ... what is it. Bond here."

"Good morning, Bond. Chan here. I sent my man to entertain you and the client today. He call in one hour. All expenses I pay. You call me two o'clock. Acceptable to you, Bond?"

"Yea ... thanks, 'till two then," and he replaced the receiver with a nod of satisfaction. "Get dressed pal, we're going out to enjoy ourselves. Oh, fuck, what a life" and swivelled buck naked into the shower, singing his head off.

Bennett folded his hands to the back of his head and rested for a few minutes to allow the Dub to finish showering. "What a transformation," he thought to himself as Murphy began to speak through the cloud of steam and hiss of the pressurized water.

"Anytime I came down here to score smack, Wong stands the expenses; wine, women and song. Now, if ya don't wanna come, that's fine, pal. But don't be 'comin' over with all that fuckin' Mr. Perfect crap you gave me in the Burlington with those two English broads." Bennett smiled in amusement at the tiny Dub's unquenchable zest for debauchery. For a moment the printer felt overcome with that holiday feeling that the world is one's oyster.

"Hurry up in that shower, mate. I'm with you all the way. What the hell; why not?'

"Now you're talkin' pal," Murphy replied, the tiny legs protruding from under the bath towel. The Link stood stationary in the centre of the foyer, his legs apart with the slouched shoulders and dangling maulers, his beady eyes jumping here and there to catch a glimpse of the two clients who emerged from the elevator. Without any expression or greeting, he grunted and turned his back, leading both men to the elevator and the underground car park. Moments later the black limousine bounced up the ramp and into the near side lane of crawling traffic. Murphy and Bennett sat alongside in the back which was like a mini hotel suite. Bennett lay back on the sumptuous upholstery and stretched his legs as far as they could go with no problem. In the centre sat the silver ice bucket, the bottle of Dom Perignon wrapped in white cloth and glistening with chill. Beneath, the elaborate mahogany panel contained an eight-inch colour TV and hi fi system which had some fifty tapes neatly packed to each side. Murphy pulled down the flap to his front and smiled at the Briton. The line of eight bottles of first class booze were perched on the chrome assembly and sat upside down each with the gill unit ready for easy loading. Directly underneath were four departments containing freshly cut lemon, orange, olives and pineapple, together with a blinding variety of cocktail sticks, bar accessories and tiny bottles of hot sauce, Worcestershire sauce and bitters which completed the smallest cocktail bar the Englishman had ever seen. The ice box contained two dozen bottles of chilled Singha Lager beer and a tray of chilled glasses. Two white telephones were cleverly concealed in a fold-out door unit to the side of each passenger. A tinted glass panel kept the Link at bearable distance. The Briton looked in surprise as Murphy jotted a note and handed it to him anxiously. It read:

DON'T TALK OUT OF SCHOOL- LIMO HAS EARS.

The Printer gave Murphy a wink of understanding and settled down to take in the novelty of his surroundings and the adventure of the day. The Link hurled the limo out along the Pattaya Highway. By his horse-sensed rigid driving style he knew the Link had never known other than the perpetual commands of his masters. Bennett pulled down the roller blind in the dividing glass at the uncomfortable sight of the Link's searching eyes in the front mirror. The hundred and forty five kilometre drive southeast of Bangkok in the Chonburi Province took a short hour and a half.

As the Link's limo thundered up the Pattaya Highway, Chin Yan Chiu backed the iris of his eye from the microscope which focused on the tiny sample of paper matter, and turned to the specification which had been handed to him by the Link the day before.

Outside the ramshackle paper mill, the sun fried the corrugated rust-rotted rooftops of the industrial quarter, fermenting the refuse in its gutters. The aural assault of monotonous Thai music, a cacophony of cymbals, percussion and the simplest of repetitive scores of vague wind and brass; enough to dull the senses into an induced mantra which seemed to have no resolve.

Chiu's thoughts knurled his forehead into new crevices of age as he said the word "dolla," and scurried through the insect-like close quarters of the factory floor to the section of the building which dealt with sub-contractual legitimate runs of hand- made paper for stocks and bonds for specialized clients were produced. Having relayed his orders to the foreman, the staff of some 16 paper makers flurried into activity. Chiu did not return to the lab, but hunkered silent, as all new Buddha's should, to oversee the process and examine the first sample, which took but 6 hours.

Chan Wong's spine was being backward stressed by the Thai masseuse when he received the panic stricken telephone call from the paper chemist.

"You shall be well compensated for your diligence," Wong reeled off in the Thai language's ascending and descending tones.

Murphy contented himself sipping champagne and playing music. He'd seen it all before, and was not an individual interested in culture or sightseeing anyway. The Printer gazed in wonder at the endless lush rice paddies and the primitive agricultural activity of the stooped figures to either side of the meandering highway, the barrier keeping the furious traffic at safe distance. Murphy knew they were approaching Pattaya as the distilled salty air of the ocean snapped through the open window.

"We're just there, pal. Wait'll ya see this place. It's really something else! The time was 12:30 p.m. The limo gradually slowed to around thirty miles per hour and approached Pattaya, the capital's unsophisticated seaside playground. Bennett immediately knew that this was a lively and cosmopolitan place by the groups of sun-scorched jet set Japanese, Western trippers and affluent Thais. The beach was jam-packed and noisy with the sounds of music, conversation and burning charcoal on the dozens of barbecues scattered among huddled groups. The vast ocean of turquoise water was calm and still, thereby amplifying the raucousness of the beach.

"That looks inviting, Murphy," the Printer said excitedly as he leaned over to take in the paradisiacal scene. To the left, Bennett could see the endless line of expensive chain hotels, up-market motors and literally hundreds of small cylinder motorcycles, the standard unit of transport in Thailand. Five minutes later, the Link rolled the limo up to the rear of the Nipa Lodge, a "high roller only" hotel at the end of the beach road. The threesome stepped out from the vehicle and stretched. Bennett could see the private beach through the rustling palms, the tiny waves caressing the talcum sand, caressing bliss of a million years' evolution. From somewhere inside the hotel, the Link appeared with a line of three white-suited waiters in convoy. In a thrice, the folding table was placed on the paved area under a trio of huge palms and prepared for dinner. The Link grumped, and led the three back to the main building in the same single file. Murphy chose the smaller of the bathing trunks which were left on the two deck chairs. Fitting the face mask and snorkel, he took ten steps and disappeared out into the calm water, the gliding breathing hose cutting the surface like a periscope. Bennett was a strong swimmer and his stylish crawl propelled a distance of some twenty yards in a few seconds. The Englishman filled his lungs and dived deep into the world of the coral. Immediately, a huge shoal of tiny multicolored fish disappeared in a flash before his eyes. On his third dive, the shrubbery of ocean foliage swayed and shivered shocking the tiny shoals of the coral. Bennett made a hasty surface and could see the hull and engine of a boat rip apart the ceiling of the ocean in a disappearing line of foaming action. As his head bobbed to the sanctuary of the waterline, he could see a speedboat, by now some two hundred meters out to sea. He could not make out the two persons on board.

Murphy's excited roar from twenty yards away broke the intrigue.

"That's the broads, pal. Let's go in," and turned to swim for the shore some thirty yards away.

Bennett followed, easily overtaking the Dubliner. The pair took the few steps up along the hot sand and stretched on the beach cots, allowing the sun to dry them both. Murphy spoke first, choking and breathless after the thirty yard burst.

"Which one d'ya want, pal?" Demanded Murphy, hoping for a negative reply.

"I haven't even seen them yet. Are they prostitutes?' Bennett inquired facetiously.

"Not at all. What d'ya think I am?' They're escorts." The telephone broke the silence. Murphy picked up the receiver saying "I betcha its Wong."

"Hello Bond, Wong. You having nice time, Irishman?'

"As usual, Chan. Any news?' The Dubliner got straight to the point and the Englishman was beginning to like his style.

"Yes. Good news. Paper no problem. Can have sample sheet in three days, but cost you many dolla because having to change whole machine. Many people, take much time. All night tonight and tomorrow, day and night, Bond. You understand?'

"Yea, I understand. How much?' Bennett sat upright in concentration, tipping Murphy's elbow for a hint of the news.

"Five thousand dolla for sixty reams you quote on the order, Bond. You have the dolla?' The Irishman covered the mouthpiece with the palm of his free hand and spoke to the Forger.

"They can have a sample sheet of the paper in three days. He's talkin' six grand for the first order of sixty reams."

"Take it." Bennett replied without hesitation, a tingle of excitement brushing the back of his neck. The Printer's two second calculation reckoned the price at probably around thirty per cent of the U.S. price. He continued:

"Murphy, tell him it's subject to the stuff standing my scrutiny, otherwise not a cent."

"Chan?' Okay ... we got a deal, provided the client is satisfied with the quality. He'll give you a couple of grand up front either way," Murphy offered, flashing the Englishman a confident wink of his eye.

"That's okay. Be in touch with you later, Bond." The line went dead, allowing the serenity of the surroundings to recompose. The speedboat had disappeared. The hunger took over. The time was 2:15 p.m. Murphy picked up the receiver and babbled something in Thai. Bennett could not make it out precisely but reckoned he was ordering dinner. Ten minutes later the convoy arrived with silver trays of covered food. Bennett's mouth became moistened at the irresistible array mouth-watering colourful dishes were placed on the table. The menu read:

Prawn salad - the best you have ever tasted.
Mussels fried with Thai sauce - succulent, but sharp.
Pea Dook Phad Phed - fried catfish - a little dry, but surprisingly good meat.
Steamed crab claws - sickening to the unacquired palate.

Khai Sod Sai - eggs stuffed with pork and vegetables; a cold dish starter.

Coconut ice cream - a couple of spoonfuls is enough, but a really nutty coconut taste

Fruit - papaya and fresh pineapple - a good mouth wash.

Surprising - a pot of really good Mouselli Italian coffee

Perfect finish with a good dash of Napoleon brandy.

Murphy lifted his first index finger to the silencing position across the mouth, indicating to Bennett not to talk business. They both lay outstretched on the soft white sand for the following two hours, every so often stepping dazed into the ocean to cool. The conversation was sparse in the tranquil quietness of their personal paradise of that memorable afternoon.

The Link woke them both at five p.m. looking amusingly out of place in his black suit and white polo neck. The dinner table had gone. The sun was still warm but beginning to set across the hazy horizon. The Link made the shape of a woman with both his hands and plodded in the direction of the hotel entrance with the same flat-footed dumbass step. It was not until eleven o'clock that the smaller of the two Thai girls turned the key to suite 201 at the Nipa Lodge. Howard Richard Bennett followed closely behind, indifferent to protocol by a headful of brandy, and had long dismissed any pretence of chivalry or idle chatter. Removing his clothes, he lay face down on the huge bamboo bed. The sheets cooled his hot skin as he closed his eyes in restful anticipation of the darkened hours that would follow. The girl appeared from the bathroom in a shimmering blue swimsuit, the high cut from the tip of the inner thigh to the waist exposing the large sensuous torso and buttocks. Her gentle massage moved gradually to the base of the back.

The following three days were spent on trips and overnight stopovers in Kanchanaburi, one of the most picturesque of Thailand's provinces of wild jungles and rugged hills and then south to the country's oldest seaside resort, Thia Hin, the summer residence of the Royal Family ever since King Rama VII built a summer palace there in 1920. On the afternoon of that Thursday, as the limo pulled out of the fishing village of Pranburi, the car phone burst into life for the first time. The Link took the message and switched over the call to Murphy who was dabbling with the hi-fi as usual. He replaced the receiver twenty seconds later and said something to the Link in Thai, who nodded in obedience, and eased the limo up around the eighty mile mark. Murphy turned to Howard Bennett.

"The paper's ready, pal. We've need to get back to the Ambassador. He's left the samples at reception."

An hour and a half later, Howard Bennett carefully opened the large flat packet containing the samples which looked good to the eye, felt good to the touch and behaved well on handling. The second packet contained one tweezers, one scalpel, one bottle of 150 millilitres of a chemical reactor used for the purpose of comparing the quality and content of one paper with another and a small plastic bottle containing twenty or thirty tiny paper samples which had been taken at intermittent points of each sheet. There were twenty four full double crown sheets. The Printer took his jacket from the wardrobe and whipped out his wallet where he had carefully stored the $20, $50, and S100 bill samples which McNiff had picked up at Heathrow airport. Using the hairline scalpel, he cut two paper samples from each bill and purposely chosen from blank areas without any printed image. Using a sample from the plastic matchbox, he ensured that his cut-outs were exactly the same size, approximately one-third of an inch square. The Englishman ordered: "Murphy, go down to the market and get me two dozen slim glasses."

Murphy returned fifteen minutes later and commenced to wash and polish each glass at the Englishman's impatient request. Bennett inspected each glass scrupulously and re-washed and cleaned one or two, removing tiny fibres left from the paper towels. He then laid out the two dozen glasses on the coffee table in four rows of six. Taking the bottle of clear liquid reactor, he poured an even third of an inch into each glass.

"What's it all about?' Murphy ventured out of the silence, and suspected it must have been very serious business at the Englishman's sharp reply to 'shut up' and continued the ordered process. Picking up the samples from the notes, he placed one sample in each glass of the front row of six, which from left to right represented the bills as follows: $20 - $20 - $50 - $50 - $100 - $100. Into each of the remaining glasses he dropped one sample at random of the newly manufactured paper and waited, staring out of the hotel window into the bustling metropolis, rubbing his hands nervously.

"This is it, Murphy; this is it." Bennett stared at his watch for an endless three minutes and turned away from the window as the second hand passed the twelve o'clock point into the third minute.

"Hey, pal - they're changin' color. They're all turnin' yella."

"Shut up, Murphy. Get away from the fuckin table. You'll knock it over or something! The Englishman dropped to his hunkers and stared at each glass, every so often flashing his eye to the first row of six to compare the thin yellow line which topped off each glass of clear liquid.

"Jesus, it's absolutely perfect. I can't believe it." The fading colour line at the base of the glasses containing the samples represented the foreign matter of clear varnish and the odd security thread which was not to be incorporated in the manufacture of the Thai paper. The Printer checked the yellow rings every half hour for the next four hours. There was no disturbance, the implication being that considerations such as tensile strength, light fastness and the effect of end user handling would be constant and accurately reproduced in the forgeries. Murphy, having lost patience had gone to Pat Pong Road to sample a couple of massage parlours. The Printer lay on the single bed and gazed at the ceiling in deep concentration as a hazy dusk cooled the city of Bangkok. The stillness of night sharpened his concentration as he whispered his thoughts over and over again to the gathering darkness.

"So, the paper's perfect. Great. But what volume should I order?' Sixty reams is enough to reproduce approximately fifty to sixty million. If the papers used throughout the other eleven Federal areas are the same, then we're in business. Actually, we should order more, say, a total of 240 reams ... enough for say, $200 million. I wish Colm would call and let me know about the analysis on the other eleven areas. What am I supposed to order?' The mill is tooled up for production ready to roll. They want to be compensated each hour that machine lies idle while they're waiting for the final order, and I wouldn't blame them." Murphy got back an hour later and lay on the couch, exhausted.

"What's the story, pal?' Is the stuff alright?' I have to let Wong know right away!

"Yes, Murphy, the paper's okay. But I don't know how much I want. I have to wait to hear from Colm, maybe I'll call him. What time is it now?'

"Eh, ten o'clock. That'll be two o'clock in Dublin. You might as well try him. This guy Wong gets very excited when things go wrong, especially anything to do with money."

Half an hour later, a tired Colm McNiff picked up the public phone on the landing of the bed & breakfast off Parnell Square in Dublin. The sound of an English voice echoed from a world away. "Hello. Colm here. How are you?' The Fenian raised his voice to ensure contact as the city of Dublin ground on in the mid afternoon sun.

"I'm glad I caught you, Colm. The paper is perfect, but I'm in a quandary about how much to order. They want around a hundred a ream. Murphy gave them the line about the heroin arrangements, his contact went for it in a big way. I've really got to give him the final order so as we're not tying up the machine. Things could get very nasty if he smells a rat. That's what I'm afraid of. Any news on the other paper specifications?"

"No, not yet. I'll call you immediately when I hear. Look, Howard, tell Murphy to pay him for the first sixty reams. How much is that?'

"Six grand"

"Fair enough. Pay him for the next sixty reams in advance to keep them happy. Give him the angle that Customs could blow the prospective operation anytime and we'd be left with a heap of paper that cost us thirty odd grand. No way are we forking that out. Just hang in. I should have the Dollars from America and the specification on the eleven other areas in a few days, just hang in. I'll call you immediately." The numbering boxes and ink are ready by the way."

"Great. I'll play it like you said and wait for your call. All the best."

"All the best, Howard. Mind yourself." McNiff rested his hand on the wall behind the phone box and scratched his head in thought. He was becoming perturbed at not having heard from Samuel Abraham Guttrie for a full ten days since contact.

"What the hell is he doing rounding up a few Dollars?' I hope he hasn't done anything stupid." Glancing at his watch, he reckoned it would be another hour before the first National Bank of Colorado would open its doors. McNiff spent the next hour and a half drinking tea and pacing the tiny room.

An hour later he dialled the Colorado bank from the General Post Office on O'Connell Street. "Good morning. First National of Colorado."

"Good morning. My name is Michael McCann and I maintain a current account there. The account number is 046166849."

"Yes sir. How may I help you, please?'

"I wrote a check six or seven days ago for sixteen thousand, one hundred twenty Dollars. Can you tell me if that check has come in for payment, please?'

"Just a moment." McNiff could hear the soft tapping of the computer keyboard.

"No, Mr. McCann. That check has not yet been presented for payment. Will that be all, sir?'

"Yes, Miss. Thank you very much," and dropped the receiver thinking the worst, whatever that might be.

It was to be an agonizing five days later that Luke C. Conrad flew into Terminal Six of La Guardia Airport, New York City. The time was 7 p.m. Eastern time. Across the Atlantic, in the city of Dublin, Colm McNiff sat on a park bench in Parnell Square staring east like a pilgrim to Mecca, his mind knotted in a thousand possibilities.

"What the hell has gone wrong?' he whispered to himself and raised his freckled right hand to peel the last of his fingernails.

Half a world away in Bangkok, a tall blonde Englishman lay face down on the bamboo bed oblivious to the attentions of the young Thai girl to his side. From his resting position his open eye was fixed on the finger of moonlight on the silent white telephone by the bedside. The time was four a.m.

Chapter thirty Five

A lean brush blond cowboy stepped at pace in the direction of the men's room in Kennedy airport. Once inside the cubicle, he found the twenty and two fifty Dollar bills needed to complete the 1988 and pre 88 Series, and opened the hide briefcase laying the plastic portfolio on his knees. The twenty sheets of transparent plastic showed the lists and colour pictures of leather and rawhide goods manufactured by the Bighorn Rawhide and Leather Company in Cody, Wyoming. Inside each plastic envelope between the two coloured catalogue sheets were the nine bills from each of the Federal Reserve areas he had visited in the last seventeen days. Carefully, he placed the last three bills from the Federal area of New York into the twelfth plastic envelope, folded his arms and exhaled a long breath of relief.

The Cowboy placed the portfolio into the briefcase and reached for the imitation gold buffalo skull which dangled at the bottom of his necklace. He inserted one of the skull horns into his right nostril and closed the other side of his nose with the index finger. Taking a firm snuff, he relaxed on the toilet bowl for a couple of moments allowing the coke to hit the spot. Five minutes later, he spoke to the fill-in manager of the Pueblo Pool Hall from one of the endless lines of phone booths at the centre of the terminal. The message was short and precise.

"When that guy calls again tonight, tell him everything's okay. I'll be waiting for his call," as he dropped the receiver at the reply "Got it" from the far end. Minutes later, the Cowboy was sprawled out in the back of the yellow cab travelling at speed on the outside of the four lane highway. The continuous Arabic banter of the cabbie into the mike of the two way radio annoyed Conrad to the point that he told the driver to "shut up" and "do your fuckin' yellin' on your own time, pal." Good coke was expensive and its pleasure was not to be interfered with by foreigners who were being overpaid for their services. Anyway, the Cowboy was

240

distrustful of all things New York, and rested his high heeled boots on the bullet-proof Plexiglas partition to enjoy the ride in over the Brooklyn Bridge and on to the concrete jungle of Manhattan. The cab came to a stop outside the Empire Hotel at Columbus Circle. Without speaking, he saw the meter read $19.50, stepped out onto the sidewalk and threw a twenty Dollar bill through the open front window.

Inside, he broached the reception and passed the assistant manager a five Dollar bill. He advised the young man that a call would be coming through for a Frank Winston and that he would be in the bar. Five minutes later, the Cowboy sat at the crowded bar, his arms slouched in comfortable attention, his ears pricked in readiness for the sound of his name through the intercom. He reflected on the events of the previous sixteen days, which had been a disaster from beginning to end. First there was the note mentioning his family from his unknown employer. Then the suggestion of using cash dispenser machines proved impossible because a withdrawal limit of two-fifty per twenty four hours. To top it all, he failed to locate suitable bills from the Dallas and 'Frisco Federal areas in or around Colorado and thus had to fly to both cities which took three full days and messed up the whole pre-planned flight path. Then there were delays at Minneapolis, Chicago and St. Louis, resulting in expensive overnight stays. However, he did snort a lot of coke and had scored a dozen very acceptable hookers over his sixteen day blast. Conrad still had nine-fifty of his commission and expenses allowances, and he still had a grand to come. It was a full two and a half hours later as Conrad thought about calling the pool hall again that the call came through. The Cowboy was handed the bar telephone.

"How-do, cowboy. You got the stuff?'

"Yeah, mister. I got the stuff."

"Any hassle?'

"Loads a hassle, mister. You got ma dough?'

"Yeah, cowboy. When I get the stuff."

"Okay. What's the drill then ... as we arranged, mister?'

"Yeah, leave the stuff at the reception for the care of Michael Kennedy. Call back in four hours. The grand will be there in cash at reception marked for the notice of Frank Winston - no problem."

"I'd better have the stuff put in the safe, y'know?'

"Good thinkin', cowboy. I'll have the grand I owe you put in the safe also."

"Well, that's it then, mister. Nice to do business with you."

"Just one thing, cowboy."

"What's that?'

"Don't get cute."

The line went dead. Abe Guttrie repositioned his blubber frame in the public call box opposite the University of Colorado in Boulder and placed numerous quarters in the slot, dialling a Dublin number. A minute later Colm McNiff ran up the shabby stairway to the empty second floor landing of the bed & breakfast, and snatched the black receiver from the cradle.

"Hello ... hello ... hello! twisted in anxiety in the sure knowledge that the call was long distance. Abe Guttrie's voice broke through clearly a couple of seconds later.

"Colm, Sam here. Mission accomplished. Ah've got it all."

"Ah, good man; good man. I was getting worried. Sammy boy, when will you be over?'

"Well, Colm, first I gotta pick 'em up in New York."

"What the fuck are ye talkin' about, Sammy?'

"Don't be gittin' excited, Colm. I gotta dude who don't know me to round 'em up. It was the best way, Colm ... y'understand?' I thought it better not to cash your check, by the way."

"Fine, whatever. When will I see you, Sam?'

"I'll call you in an hour. I've gotta book the flights. Everything else is okay. Hang in there. I'll call you back."

"Fair enough. I'll wait for your call."

The Arms Man called back an hour later, confirming his arrival time in Dublin two days later on Aer Lingus flight EI 364 from New

York. They agreed to meet in the foyer of the Cara Airport Hotel immediately after arrival.

Chapter Thirty Six

T he forger sprang from a light sleep at the purr of the bedside phone. Murphy had by now booked a separate bedroom to allow privacy for the continuous string of stunning women which Chan Wong was providing.

"Hello, Howard?' This is Colm. I've got some news." A prism of afternoon sunshine gilded one side of his crombie, as the Fenian ground his ear into the telephone.

"Yes, Colm, what is it?' Bennett rasped, the bamboo shutters shimmering in the breeze.

"The stuff is on the way. I'll call you with the specification on the rest in about thirty hours. Be available at the phone, Howard."

"Well, of course, Colm. I'll be here."

"How is everything else, Howard?'

"Perfect; absolutely perfect. I paid over the ten thousand."

"That's grand. Keep an eye on Murphy ... see that he stays half right or you both may have problems leaving Thailand and that is the last thing we need right now!

"You can depend on me to do that, Colm. I'll be waiting for your call. Could you eh ... mention to Fiona that I am OK."

By this time the hotel room had taken on the appearance of a test laboratory. The Printer had ordered Murphy to acquire a further two litres of the chemical reactor through Wong. He had also purchased another twenty dozen slim glasses which were lined up in rows of eight deep on the three coffee tables. The Printer had insisted on the suppliers providing five sheets of the manufactured paper from each five hundred sheet finished ream. This way he was able to test the entire sixty reams for likeness and consistency. Every seven or eight hours, a courier would bring samples of the paper as it rolled off the machine. Some 160 of the 240 glasses contained a sample, and each surface of the liquid showed the thin yellow collar of success.

The job was now nearing completion. The only question which remained was whether the remaining paper used in the other eleven Federal areas were exactly the same specification. If so, then the order would be increased to perhaps 300 reams, enough to reproduce $250 million or hopefully more. The way things were going, Bennett did not see any reason why they should not both be out of Thailand in four to five days.

Murphy made his way across the dense strolling crowds of lurid Bangkok to Wong's suite at the President Hotel. Once the usual formal routine was over, the Irishman handed the two thousand he had skimmed off the top to the Coolie. Once a junkie. Always a junkie. The Link accompanied Murphy to an unoccupied apartment on the tenth floor for the handing over of the smack. On leaving the sumptuous penthouse, Wong asked Murphy a disturbing question, the gold cigarette holder dangling from the side of his bone jaw.

"Bond, what is the job client wants paper for?' Chan Wong smiled sarcastically, biting the holder between his sparkling gold teeth.

"Haven't a clue, pal. Why?' Murphy's reply was convincingly naive; he did not know anyway and never guessed.

"You tell client I like to talk with him," and turned his tiny frame in the direction of the office. The Paddy made his exit at fair speed and limped up to his own room in the Ambassadorial in heart pounding delirious excitement. Once inside, he opened the foil and separated the ounce of smack into four single units. From under the mattress he picked the roll of silver foil he had purchased earlier and commenced to wrap the white powder in four small single balls, which he then stuck with adhesive behind a decorative bath panel.

The Dub presented himself minutes later at Bennett's door. "By the way the coolie needs to talk to you about the job that paper is wanted for"

Bennett froze. "Holy shit, he's copped it." The Printer laid his palm across his pounding forehead.

"What's the problem, pal. Are ya feelin' okay pal?', Murphy inquired sympathetically.

"Yes, I'm fine. Murphy. It's just the heat. Sit down, I want to talk to you," Bennett replied. They both sat alongside on the bamboo couch and fired up a couple of cigarettes.

"Murphy, exactly what sort of a demon is this Wong?' Tell me all you can about him," the Printer asked softly. The Dubliner blew an exhaust of blue smoke to the ceiling.

"Well, pal. I'll put it to you this way. He's one of these people who gets what he wants, when he wants it, and how he wants it. He's smart, always a couple of steps ahead of the posse. I don't know the extent of his influence and power. Wong only lets you know what he wants you to know. He's got the heaviest muscle in Bangkok looking after him.

"What about his brother in London?'

"He's the same. But he's running the really big end of the business in England through his distribution network. Once the gear gets through Customs and onto the market, you're made. His brother is the guy who's making the real money for Wong." The phone rang, breaking Bennett's train of thought.

"You answer it, Murphy. If it's Wong looking for me I'm not here. You don't know when I'll be back, okay?' Murphy replaced the receiver a couple of minutes later.

"It was him. He said you're to call him when you get in. You seem a bit worried, pal. What's the hassle?' Wong never chases anyone unless he wants something, usually money."

Bennett pretended not to notice the last comment and began to slowly pace the room. The Paddy looked on in ignorance at the Englishman's broadening smile. Both hands in his pockets, he swivelled to his seated companion. "Murphy, get your gear together. You're going home!

"But..."

The Englishman took Murphy by the lapel of his suit with one hand and ripped the tiny drug dealer from the couch. "I

246

told you to get your gear together. You're going home. Now get the fuck out of here and get back here when you're ready. Did you or did you not ever mention the Provisional IRA or me or anything to Wong- ever?' He shook the petrified Dubliner like a rag doll, his cold blue eyes remaining fixed on the Dealer.

"No, never! replied a nervous Murphy standing uncomfortably close to the balcony. Bennett released his grip.

"Just go to your room, get your stuff together and get back here now. Don't talk to anyone, just get back pronto," Bennett commanded, pressing his index finger hard against Murphy's sweating nose.

"Sure, pal, sure. I'll be back in a jif. Should I check the next flight?'

"Yes. Get on the fucking flight...get back here, I need to give you money for this short notice"

Murphy left the room shaking and puzzled. The Printer sat by the phone and carefully dialled McNiff's number in Dublin. As usual, McNiff was there- eager, disciplined and ever ready to serve.

"Thanks be to Christ I've caught you, Colm. I think we may have problems." They spent the following twenty minutes in fretful conversation. Meanwhile, Murphy had confirmed a single seat on the London-bound Air France flight via Bahrain due to take off in six hours, and packed his few odds and ends in stunned hurried silence. He had not eaten for seven hours and removing his pants, sat on the toilet, forcing himself to move his bowels. Murphy then placed the four small foil balls from behind the bath panel, which he lined up on the top of the waist high cistern and commenced to shower, concentrating on cleaning his back passage. Without dressing, he took the packet of condoms from his suit pocket and opened four units, placing each foil of heroin within a single unit and continued to pull the slimy film back and forward, twisting the foil ball on each consecutive wrap. Then he cut the remaining thick rubber end with a blade and fixed the completed joint by heating the open end with his lighter and submersing it in the sink of cold water. Having dried the units carefully, he continued to coat each in mineral oil and perched his right foot on top of the cistern, coaxing each ball of heroin high up the passage to the gut using a chopstick. He straightened up and went through his usual routine of physical exercise to familiarize with the new condition. He felt comfortable. Murphy left immediately for the airport armed with the extra expense money the Bennett had given him and, the body pack of high grade pure heroin.

Chapter Thirty Seven

Three hours later, as Murphy fastened his seat belt the Jumbo eased down runway 13 at Dan Muang airport, Niall O'Toole sat alone in the crowded bar of The Swiss Cottage Tavern, London, his eyes fixed on the exclusive Cantonese restaurant across the busy junction, and in particular the silver grey Mazda XR7 which was parked in the near empty front car park. The time was 8:30 p.m. O'Toole was becoming increasingly pissed off as he fingered the ticket for middleweight title fight due to start in forty minutes at the Loftus Road football grounds.

Forty five minutes passed before a tiny, slim Oriental appeared through the front door of the restaurant and stepped effeminately towards the vehicle. A drizzle of summer rain began to grease the streets outside as O'Toole rose from the barstool and paced briskly across the busy thoroughfare leaving the unfinished coffee on the bar.

As he paced smartly to the far side of the road, and could see the Oriental inserting the ignition key into the front door lock and quickened to a tip toe trot. Within a couple of seconds O'Toole was standing, legs apart, staring the gutter of Johnny Wong's parallel neck bone and unleashed the most ferocious right hander, burying his fist somewhere around the eardrum. Before the tiny frame slouched over onto the tarmac, O'Toole followed up with a vicious left uppercut, ricocheting the head from the first punch. With one hand, he held the unconscious body upright and calmly clicked the key in the front door. So tiny was the Oriental that O'Toole felt no strain in slinging him face-down onto the back seat, much the same way as a small bag of laundry.

Without fuss, he applied the cloth over the bleeding, rasping mouth and nostrils, adjusted the mirror and repositioned the front seat. Comfortably seated, he fired the powerful motor into life and slid efficiently into the traffic, fiddling with the radio in the hope of catching some of the fight commentary on BBC 1.

An hour later, Johnny Wong was staring half unconscious down the barrel of a scratched Glock pistol in a house somewhere out in Reading. In his state of white terror, he was oblivious to the pain of a broken jaw and burst eardrum.

Chapter Thirty Eight

Bennett sat waiting uneasily in the reception area of Chan Wong's suite. Looking around, he got the impression of being in a sort of indoor jungle with moving water, dimmed lighting and bamboo furniture. The Link gestured him into Wong's office with a grunt after the usual half hour wait. Bennett got down to business without formality or introduction.

"Okay, Wong, what do you want to talk about?' He stared at the Face of Death without expression, his cold blue eyes turning to ice. The Coolie smiled for a moment, and then changed his countenance to grotesque ugliness. The Link shifted his feet uneasily on the carpet, Bennett did likewise.

"Man at paper factory say paper for making American Dolla," said Wong as he fitted the king size into his gold cigarette holder. Bennett flicked his lighter into a purple flame before Wong placed the holder in his jaw. As he lit the cigarette, Wong did not remove the threatening stare from the Englishman's cold eyes.

"So what, Wong, you got paid," the Printer continued forcefully having been seated and crossed his legs lazily as if to show indifference at the Coolie's angle on things. The Heroin Dealer replied without hesitation: "Not get pay enough Dolla ... Englishman."

Bennett stood from the chair only to experience the vice grip of the Link pressing him back into his seated position.

"Okay, Chinaman, okay. How much do you want for the paper?' and opened his hands in acceptance of his circumstances.

"Two hundra tousan' dolla, Mister Englishman." Bennett smiled at his blackmailer and quite unable to do otherwise, broke into loud sarcastic laughter. Surprisingly, the Coolie did likewise, ordering the Link to join in with a wave of the chicken paw hand.

"OK...OK...., Chinaman. I think we might have a deal, but I'll have to contact my partners. I don't think 200 grand will present a problem." The laughter died down and the Link was dismissed with the irritating click of Wong's fingers.

"Now, Englishman, talk to me about the deal Bond do for you," and walked round to the front of the desk.

"Well, Chinaman, we have to make the money first. Then we do the deal, no problem, know what I mean?' The Oriental stopped for a moment and turned to Bennett as he escorted him out to the reception.

"Oh, you make Dolla; then you deal. Very good.. Forget Bond. You deal with me direct, Englishman. Better for you, better for me, understand?'

"Sure, I understand. Is the paper ready?'

"Yes, paper ready." They both adjourned to the room of mirrors and began talking and drinking.

"Look, Chinaman, I'll have that 200 thousand in a day or two. But for that kind of money I will want 400 reams. Get the paper cleared for export and out to the airport ready for transit immediately. You have the address stickers and that, so let's not waste time."

"Okay, that is acceptable. Paper go to airport same day, you call me with the Dolla when wired to Bangkok." The pair spent the following two hours discussing the prospective methodology for smuggling heroin using the "paper run." Bennett declined the offer of a girl and left Wong's penthouse at 12:15 a.m.

By eleven o'clock the following morning he was on the daily Air France flight for Paris where he would connect for Dublin, having made certain arrangements with Colm McNiff by telephone. He knew he would never visit Thailand again.

It was as the Jumbo tailed off over the Gulf of Thailand to face west that Wong received a telephone call from London. It was his brother, babbling in Teo Chew Chinese about dangerous men with guns and the exposure of the UK heroin operation. There was a hood being pulled over his head, all supposedly because of something about paper.

Four hundred reams of paper matter were loaded into the Quantas New York-bound aircraft ten hours later bearing the final destination: Process Printers Inc., St. James Street, Atlantic City, New Jersey U.S.A.

Cargo Instructions: To Be Collected on Arrival.

Chapter Thirty Nine

Francis O'Doherty pinned out Sam Guttrie limping flatfoot across the drenched apron of terminal five at Dublin Airport. The arms man had no hand luggage other than the black folder squeezed under his right armpit. It was the very worst of Monday mornings, of the sort we recall with dread with our moms slinging on our schoolbag and then half asleep dumping us out into the big bad world. How we would have loved to have stayed at home with her on such days, on all days if only we could. The swirling rain lashed the acres of runway, and on the horizon, the looming darkness guaranteeing endless bad weather. One after another, huge aircraft showing all lights drifted and lurched uneasily from the skies, rising great even sheaths of spray from the submerged runways, their passengers grateful at the sanctuary of Terra Firma. O'Doherty turned to McNiff.

"He's in. Let's go."

Ten minutes later, the stranger eased the black Granada into the Cara Airport Hotel car park. McNiff waited impatiently at the bar as O'Doherty made some pre-arranged phone calls.

The Arms Man arrived an hour later, carrying a small suitcase and red hold all bearing the words "Denver Broncos," together with the black plastic folder. Both Fenians greeted Guttrie insensitively and retired to room 415 to get to business immediately. Guttrie passed the folder to O'Doherty who left at once, gunning the two and a half litre south along the Swords Road in the direction of the city of Dublin. Within twenty minutes he had passed the black folder to a man in a laboratory white coat at a side door of a large paper mill on Dublin's south side.

Back at the hotel, Guttrie laboured to great lengths to describe the method he had used to round up the bills and continued to explain his decision not to cash McNiff's check for $16,120. An atmosphere of potent expectation filled the room.

"You've done a good job, Sammy." McNiff seldom praised people, but when he did, he meant what he was saying, and promised to settle any outstanding money in cash.

"Well, Colm, you didn't ask me over here on a sightseeing tour. What's goin' down?'

"We want to launder some money in the States."

"How much?"

"About $250 to $300 million." The Arms Man pretended astonishment, not wanting to give McNiff any hint that he suspected a forgery of this magnitude in the making. Allowing his whistle of alarm to descend to silence, he looked McNiff between the eyes and smiled.

"Really ...." Guthrie's wheels spun like a cash register.

Guttrie discarded all symptoms of jet lag as the vast amounts of cash and intrigue of which he would take some part unfolded. Francis O'Doherty entered the room at 3:25 p.m. with the black folder and a small white envelope which he handed to his fellow Fenian whispering the words, "The paper and ink are the same. Colm."

McNiff opened the envelope in the privacy of the bedroom, nibbling at the last scut of a nail on his right hand. The officious typed report read thus:

I have analysed samples from each of the one hundred and eight notes enclosed herewith and cannot detect any inconsistency on analysis- or with the previous three samples presented recently. The paper content, ink makeup, integrated fluorescence and printing technique are likewise to a comparable ratio factor of approximately 1: 1,000.

McNiff re-entered the bedroom, handing the note and envelope to O'Doherty requesting him to dispose of it. The bedside phone purred. McNiff knew it was Bennett calling from Jury's Hotel and ordered Francis O'Doherty to collect the Englishman immediately. A few moments after O'Doherty's exit the Arms Man rose awkwardly to his feet and addressed the aging McNiff..

"Colm, I reckon I could dispose of the bills for you on a commission, provided they're shit hot like you say," opening his hands for a reply.

"How, Sammy, how?' McNiff interested.

"Well, for a slice of the action I reckon I can hook you up with a professional launderer stateside. I hear through the grapevine that the service is available."

McNiff snapped, "That's exactly what we don't want. Hooking up directly with any launderer would spike this entire operation in more ways that would not even occur to you. We are working on other arrangements and knowing you as we do and given you are greasy as a bed of eels, I believe your inclusion in the end game would be far more trouble than it is worth. At best and for now you may pass the identities of potential launderers to us. If we do business with one or any of these then we can talk. That's it, no more questions or discussion on the matter" McNiff was dismissive, final. Guttrie decided not to press any hint as to his pay-out just yet; not the right time.

McNiff gazed out the hotel window at the swirling rain as he had done for most waking hours of his five years of imprisonment and reflecting over the many years could never in his wildest dreams have imagined it could all come to this defining moment. Like so many other republicans and despite having been long excommunicated from the Catholic Church he remained a daily practitioner and searched for some divine revelation for this watershed manifestation of events. Like all unquestioning devotees he convinced himself of the righteousness of his movement's actions past and present to be one component of the promised destiny guaranteed by his sworn fealty to his Vatican masters. Now temporarily released from the indefensible culpability of his actions he decided on a softer approach to Guttrie who in the past proven himself more capable, given the chance than that of a small time bagman. McNiff decided not to comment on Guttrie's presumption that the forgery was being executed outside the United States, and decided to give the Arms Man a wider berth.

"Listen Sammy, when you locate the right launderer you will be put in contact with someone who I insist must accompany you with any contact you have with these people from day one, do I make myself clear"

"Sure, I'll handle it." The pair shook hands and waited for O'Doherty who buzzed from the reception ten minutes later. Like all people with secrets, Guttrie's plan to help himself to a skim died with the McNiff's phantom babysitter and decided to get some sleep and fly out to New York on the next available flight. McNiff made his way down to reception to one of the few men that he could trust, Howard Bennett..

"Welcome home, Howard, me boy! Saluting the Forger.

"You did a great job out in the other place. That paper is arriving in the morning at eleven o'clock in New York. We have Niall picking it up," referring to O'Toole.

"Good to see you, Colm. Have you seen Murphy- how is he?" The Englishman queried genuinely.

"Aye, he's alright, last I heard, but you never know with him"

"Are you still holding Wong's brother in London?'

"Well of course we are, Howard. We'll be holding him for a long time.. I doubt he will ever be out of our sights. We want to get all the info about the London operation, so we can have your friend out in Bangkok over a barrel in case we run out of paper if we are to do this job again"

Both men retired to the lavish lounge, O'Doherty having gone to pick up the cash to pay the Arms Man before he flew back to the States. McNiff jiggled the ice at the bottom of his glass of orange. The Englishman broke the silence.

"Well, Colm, what now. I want to see the numbering boxes. What has been done about my assistant?'

"I've found a lad." McNiff reached into his briefcase and passed the Englishman a sealed white envelope, making the comment, "I hope he suits. He is from within the ranks. I showed him the bills. He's the best we've got." The Printer opened the envelope and speed read the curriculum vitae. It read:

I am trained to do what is required but I do not have any plate making experience. My experience has been limited to letterpress scoring and numbering and, litho multicolour production of a high order. I hope my skills will be of use."

"The chap will do fine. How old is he?'

"Twenty something. He's a good lad."

"Okay, Colm, what are the arrangements now?' Let's get this bloody job finished." The Printer called for coffee and sandwiches. The thronged arrivals bar was jammed with Americans complaining about the Irish weather. McNiff reeled off the arrangements for the next few days.

"I've been in touch with Joe Kilkenny in New York. Everything is set except I need a list of materials in case we run out of something. Kilkenny said he would pick the stuff up for us himself.

"Right, Colm. I'll have it later today. I really wish you would not use that name, call him 'yer man' or something"

"The paper is to be collected this morning at Kennedy Airport. There may be a delay of a day or so on that. I believe all imported goods from that part of the world are searched for drugs. The numbering boxes are ready. I'll show them to you later on today. The inks are in London at the moment. Your assistant is available anytime- that's about it."

An hour later, Francis O'Doherty paced authoritatively up along the long bar carrying a leather suitcase which appeared heavy by the slouch on his frame. "Hello, Colm. I picked up the cash and the other- should we go to the room so as everything can be checked out," nodding at Bennett.

A few minutes later, both men went back to the Arms Man's room leaving O'Doherty at the bar. Bennett opened the suitcase and removed the four heavy boxes carefully from within. It was easy to unwrangle the knot on the heavy white twine on the first-the largest of the containers. Inside and wrapped individually in slimy, greasy brownish yellow wax paper were ninety precision machined numbering boxes. The Printer removed the first numbering box from its greased wrapping and laid the unit face up on the coffee table oblivious to the nasal snores of Abe Guttrie.

"Beautiful. Perfect. It even has the prefix and suffix letter included ... fantastic! Bennett pressed the prefix letter 'A' with his thumb. The unit clicked silently into life changing the last of the eight zero digits to the reading A00000001A. Taking his pen he again stabbed the prefix 'A' causing the unit to slide efficiently to the reading A00000002A. "Absolutely perfect, Colm." The Printer eyed the work of engineering precision in homogeneous fascination. There were ninety units in the box, lest one or two units might malfunction. The production of the original typestyle used on the samples was scrupulously exact, razor sharp and deep etched in tensile steel. The Printer opened the remainder of the boxes which contained the check letter and plate position number, the face plate unit, the series number and the back plate numbering units respectively. He turned to the Provisional and spoke with that certain tone of indomitable confidence. "Well done. Colm. I am surprised. I have not seen the bills to be used for the plates yet," Bennett said urgently.

"I have them here in my briefcase." The Provo handed the folder to Bennett who laid the bills out on the coffee table being careful not to crease or bend any of the 108 poly encased notes.

"They're first class," the Printer quipped as he laid out the last of the 36 $100 bills.

"There is one problem, Colm," Bennett ventured, pointing to the Treasury seal to the right of Jackson's portrait on the $20 bill. "The Treasury seal is overprinted in green on top of the word Twenty, so this means that I will have to separate the seal out of the word Twenty in order to reproduce both overprinted images. It's not that much of a problem, but it will take time and it has to be done really right. I would like to start on that separation as soon as I can- tomorrow, if possible. Remember there are three separations to be done, by hand."

"How come three?' replied McNiff alarmed.

"Very simple. We're going to forge three denominations from twelve Federal Reserve areas- the United States Treasury seal is the same for all the areas. So we just need to separate for the words twenty, fifty and one hundred," opening his hands to invite agreement.

"Right, Howard. How long?' Will it hold us up?'

"Each separation will take at the very least a couple of days, unless we could have the separation done by camera or with an electronic scanner. I could separate with the equipment in Brooklyn, but I would prefer to be ready when I hit the premises on the first day to save time in case we have problems."

"What's involved exactly, Howard?' the Fenian inquired in order that he could make an informed decision.

"It's as simple as this, Colm. This Treasury seal is overprinted in green on the word 'twenty' in this case. I have to separate the seal from the spelt out denomination on each of the three notes, that is; 20, 50 and 100. Lucky enough the Treasury seal is the same for all the Federal Areas. The Federal Area seals are different for each of the twelve Federal Areas, but thankfully are not overprinted with any other colour. The methodology employed for separation can be twofold but in both cases I'll need the use of a camera to blow up the original. I can separate by hand, using very fine radiograph pens."

"What do you think yourself, Howard?'

"Well, I'll try and do it by hand, but I can't guarantee a first class job. In the meantime, have a look around and see if you can gain access to a camera for a few hours. If neither option turns up, I'll do it in New York. We'll lose a few hours - that's all."

"Okay. I'll see what I can do. I'll hold on to a copy of each bill in case something turns up. What about the list of materials for yer man?' He's going on vacation. What about the thread for the face of the paper and the list of materials for yer man?' He's going on vacation in five days on August 1st. That's our deadline."

"I'll give you that list tonight. Make sure that yer man does not go to his regular suppliers with the order as there might be a blowback. Spread the order around. Besides, he'll probably have most of the stuff in stock anyway."

"Good thinking, Howard. I'll contact you tonight at Jury's." The Printer lifted the phone and ordered a cab; Destination- Trinity College, College Green.

Chapter Forty

The Quantas Jumbo from Bangkok touched down twenty minutes late at Kennedy Airport, New York. The forklift operator eased the twin grabs under the first of the six pallets supporting a wooden crate of sixty reams of paper matter and being a responsible airport employee, he stalled momentarily before reversing the fork away from the aircraft.

"It's still drizzling rain," he thought, and proceeded to protect the cargo with a plastic tarp.

"Good man," Niall O'Toole whispered to himself as he studied the action through powerful binoculars from the main terminal building- Far Eastern section. His blue boiler suit bore the words "Process Printers- Atlantic City, New Jersey" embroidered in officious red capitals across the back.

He dropped the glasses into the leather case as the forklift rumbled across the apron into the bowels of warehouse 3A and disappeared into the distance. One hour later, two sniffer dogs, an uneasy member of the narcotic squad and one uniformed US Customs officer stood in a circle around the pallets of paper. Another man arrived in a dark suit and without lifting his head from the Daily News, said the words "Open it" and marked his nag for the 2:15 at Aqueduct. O'Toole arrived at the nondescript wooden counter in the reception of Warehouse 3A one hour later. A bored middle aged man rose slowly and inched his way to the window.

"Whatta ya got?'

"I'm from Process Printers. I gotta pick up pallets just in from Bangkok on the 11:15 Quantas. Here are the papers." O'Toole handed the clerk a bunch of import dockets, duly completed. The clerk disappeared behind the hoarding, leaving the O'Toole pacing the damp concrete floor, dangling the van keys impatiently. The clerk returned ten minutes later.

"That cargo's bein' inspected by Customs, It'll be at least an hour, maybe more."

"It's fine with me; I get paid by the hour. I'll wait.

You got a pay phone around here?' O'Toole said, playing along. From previous experience, he knew if you give cargo handlers in the States any hassle one could be waiting for hours if not days. It wouldn't hurt to grease the men who actually pull the material. International cargo is placed in a secured area to be looked over by Customs, but where you stand on line depends generally by those wise enough to slip a five or ten spot in with the paperwork.

"Sure, out the door to the left. You wanna pay the freight now? Comes to one thousand three forty two."

"Yeah, I've got a certified check. Here y'are." O'Toole smiled inwardly at himself, proud of his mastery of the Noo Yawk accent. Niall O'Toole signed several triplicate documents with his alias. He received copies of these and was directed to the dispatcher's desk some twenty yards from the office. He slipped in the gratuity between the release authorization and bill of lading receipt. Just outside the caged-in Customs Inspection area, he saw that there were six others waiting about with lacklustre expressions on their faces, resigned to the inevitable indifference of the cargo handlers to their particular vision of efficiency. "I'd appreciate anything you could do for me," he mentioned as he handed the papers over with a wink.

In forty minutes flat, O'Toole was backing the van up to the loading dock, where he further tipped the forklift operator. He told the guy:

"Hey, we all gotta eat, right?'

Chapter Forty One

While O'Toole eased the van out of John F. Kennedy Airport and negotiated the last of the roundabouts, sliding onto the Belt Parkway for the borough of Brooklyn, Sam Guttrie looked down on a peaceful Dublin Bay for the last time. As the Aer Lingus Jumbo climbed into the clouds, the Arms Man mulled McNiff's brief over in his mind. Guttrie knew he would never get another chance like this one. The earlier suggestion of dumping cash around the United States now seemed hopelessly naive. There had to be a better way, more fool proof, less risk.

However, there were hitches. The first being his own self-anonymity. Then of there were the considerations of security and trust, but the Arms Man felt that the most dangerous exposure would be the actual transportation of the notes. Guttrie sieved through the delicate equation of laundering 300 million forged Dollars and keeping his and everyone's asses covered at the same time.

Close to an hour later, the attractive hostess handed Guttrie a transatlantic dinner. As usual, he was famished and wolfed down the meal in three minutes without raising his sweating head from the small pull-out table. McNiff had voluntarily given him an extra grand for his duty of care. The Southerner decided to spend this cash in tracking down a yet unknown laundering organization. Guttrie suspected he would find such a person in the city of New York. He slept for the remainder of the flight and by 9 p.m. that evening was turning the key to room 506 in the Hotel Taft on Seventh Avenue and 50th Street, just eight blocks north of Time Square. Once inside, Guttrie showered, shaved and sat upright on the single bed studying the lengthy article line for line, recording the points of interest in his mind. Under the heading "Gaping Holes," he circled ten lines at the bottom of the column, which read:

"But even with all these new laws, there are still gaping holes in the effort to stem laundering. Although U.S. officials have now more cooperation recently from such traditional banking havens as the Cayman Islands and Switzerland, authorities in cities like London, Toronto, Hong Kong and Frankfurt do not monitor large cash transactions and most international bankers want things to stay that way. Top management is less worried about snuffing out unsavoury depositors and more worried about preserving their role as an international financial centre."

He commenced his habit of pacing slowly round the room, deep in thought, chain-smoking and pausing every now and then to digest the order and logic of his scheme. It would be just plain jack ass stupid to coldly approach any laundering organization with an invitation to discuss the washing of truckloads of forged Dollar bills.

"Stinks," the Southerner continued his one man conversation, addressing the bathroom mirror. The arms man then once again drifted to the core of his cunning. The first approach would be critical he reasoned, as he Sam Guttrie is a nobody, with not even the tiniest shred of credulity to offer to anybody, never mind Columbian high roller launderers who had in the quite recent past had been proved to have successfully washed more money than God.

"Antonio Carrera was convicted in the U.S. of not filing currency transaction reports while laundering $57 million through a Miami Bank." The wily Arms Man knew if only he could find this launderer, the job could be done really professionally. Any attempt to contact this launderer would be a very tricky and possibly dangerous enterprise; also he would only get the one shot. His ten years' experience in arms trading had made him a most able and wily negotiating tactician. Hands in his pockets, he gazed out of the window of the eighth floor of the Taft Hotel to the rumble of Manhattan and then lay on the single bed, his bloated hands supporting the back of his sweating neck, the isolation and restfulness illuminating the dark corners of his racing theories.

Guttrie always used this method to awaken the predatory cunning which hibernated at the bottom of his nature. In times of enterprise the Arms Man always initially pitted the danger against the reward. There was no question on that topic in this case. As the hours slipped by, Guttrie reached for the photocopies on the bedside table and commenced to study Antonio Carrera, the man who would hopefully tick the empty squares of the wily Arms Man's plans. The profile read thus:

"Antonio Carrera was convicted in the US of filing currency transaction reports while laundering 57 million through a Miami bank. He and his brother Herman, who will soon stand trial on similar charges, come from the cream of Columbian society. Their family owned Hotel Santa Plaz in Medellin, a sort of Waldorf Astoria of Columbia. The family's vast holdings include import/ export firms; travel agencies; legitimate currency exchange houses; real estate and an international line of grain trading companies. Both men were released on personal bail of five million each. The Carreras and other big laundering operations offer more than pedigrees. They offer financial expertise and legitimate overseas contacts that drug dealers sorely lack. Through their travel agencies and money houses, such people had both the education and the technical know- how traffickers need to run their operations and had plenty of legitimate customers for their Dollars."

Guttrie studied the Columbian's photograph carefully. He was a young man, about thirty six, remarkably good looking with the typical Latin profile of Indian and Hispanic blood; highly educated, having achieved two years credits towards an Engineering doctorate before returning to the family's travel agency in Cali.

The Arms Man frowned as his eyes flashed to the single line of information at the top of the column: "For their efforts launderers typically earn a 6% commission." "How the hell am I, a two bit redneck going to explain being anywhere near three hundred million in cold cash?'

Then there was the question of anonymity. Guttrie concluded that if Carrera was able and willing to deal he would simply have to accept the Arms Man's preconditions in consideration of maybe upping the entire laundering and bank handling fee. He decided his strongest weapon lay in the reasoning that his victim would succumb to greed. Reading further into the article, the arms man knew that Antonio Carrera was a man in deep trouble. The American Crime Commission had succeeded in registering a welter of liens and seizure orders on all of his assets in the United States. Then there was the $5 million bail. In short, Carrera was; by his own standards bust; no matter what 'spin' he might put on his state of affairs. The arms man reckoned he would probably have to 'bow' to seven to fifteen years, unless he could raise enough cash to compensate the State and buy out the time. How could this guy get bail when it seemed his options were limited in the extreme or, was there some other plan being hatched behind the smoke?'

Clearly, there was no doubt that a juicy plea bargain on the basis of equitable compensation and a reduction on time in prison could be negotiated by any attorney worth his salt. Obviously, Carrera's family had money, but Guttrie was certain they would prefer not to have to save their boy's bacon, who, for all his smarts, through greed and outrageous negligence had created the entire ruinous fuck up in the first place. Any family support would be enormously expensive, and bring further disastrous unwanted attention on the families activities.

Unlike most big launderers, surprisingly, Carrera had become sloppy, real sloppy. Initially, the article said, he had employed ten or twelve first class launderers, making small deposits in banks up and down the Florida coast. These people were professionals who took the precaution of fronting themselves up in shell corporations, making deposits in up to one hundred banks each, from Miami to Jacksonville and Naples on the Mexican Gulf, right on up to Clearwater and across to Panama City. Within a short time he was being pestered if not threatened by the Columbian drug cartels for his laundering skills. At that time there was no problem. Indeed, bank managers were competing with each other to achieve the highest intake of deposits to influence their superiors for quick promotion. Such was the intensity of this competition that Carrera had his office right over the National Bank of Miami in Palm Beach. Stupidly and driven by blind greed, he fired his entire team, and continued making huge cash deposits in just half a dozen banks up along the Florida panhandle.

For all his families wealth and business acumen, plus their son's impressive education this kid could fuck up a cup of coffee. From day one the parents had placed far too much space between their boy and reality. Did it never cross his mind that this 'Kamikaze' money pinching technique of his was doomed to failure?' It was no surprise whatsoever that he was the first of many to be arrested when the Crime Commission mounted "Operation Greenback" and went after money washers with a vengeance. As the last sunlight draped the buildings of 5th Avenue the arms man had concluded four critical facts upon which any contact with the Columbian would ultimately succeed or fail. One. Would his greed seduce him into a solo mission against McNiff's iron clad instruction or equally would he pass the job to somebody else for a fee. Two. How would the launderer react to the condition of absolute anonymity? Three. How are the transfer and handling matters to be overseen and secured?' Four. Will the paper pass the expected multiple quality tests?'

As the rooftops of New York City cooled, Guttrie decided there were just too many holes, far too many unanswered questions and decided he needed to contact McNiff about that New York contact he spoke of who must accompany him anyway and who would be handling the crucial security end of things.

At midday two days later the arms man, sporting a Denver Broncos peaked baseball hat, studied the map of New York's underground and caught the 'R' train for Brooklyn, which rumbles out of Manhattan and over the famous Brooklyn bridge and on out through Park Slope to the famous suspended Verrazano Bridge, which connects Staten Island to Brooklyn. Some forty minutes later he alighted at Sixty Ninth Street and Third Avenue in the middle class area of Bay Ridge, which is made up of mature tree lined streets of three story elegant brownstone family houses. As instructed, he entered a bar restaurant over which read the name JOE MAJORS in very dated times roman hand scribed capitals. Once inside, he felt he was in another place and another time. The bar was full with exclusively well-presented retired men, life's battles long past and now approaching their twilights. The place seemed unchanged since the twenties boasting a burly hardwood back bar being tended by two white aproned elderly gentlemen, standing straight as reeds, white shirts and simple ties, tight well-kept hair. These gentlemen, manifest of the cordiality of a bygone era, once tough as be Jesus, had seen it all, from 'The Halls of Montezuma to the shores of Tripoli'; and now basking in the sunshine of a worthwhile life of sometimes unthinkable sacrifice, toil, and the struggles we must all now endure. To the rear, the restaurant of ten tables in the traditional simple red chequered covering and a black and white terracotta floor. The menu exclusively the very best original Italian food of homemade sauces and pasta priced for common folk thus the longevity of this delightful landmark establishment of old stock and square business. The only connection to modernity was the two high mounted televisions solely for the purpose of keeping the valued customers updated with racing and sports results.

A wave from the far end of the bar beckoned the arms man. The man at the end of the bar was distinctly New York Italian, pinkie ring, expensively dressed, tuned in, and asked jokingly with a pointed finger, 'so you're the guy with the Bronco's hat?' He introduced himself as Joey and directed the arms man to the small and empty function room. They got down to business immediately, The Sicilian opened.

'My boss tells me I will be riding 'shotgun' with you on this thing. When do we 'sit down' with these guys?' Guttrie, within a very short period of the 'matter of fact' chat felt very comfortable with this man who had been briefed to the smallest detail and had the smarts to fill in any minute missing pieces. They agreed they would just go with the flow, feel it out, protect anonymity at all times, and report back. The Sicilian emphasised he was told to take part in any negotiations where he felt appropriate to do so. They parted just twenty minutes later, No big thing, Guttrie armed with the contact number, the Sicilian on standby for the Guttrie's call. The time was 12.45.

Next day, the arms man sat deflated in his room. After hours and hours of speculation he came to the realisation that being a simple 'country boy' he was just plain way out of his depth on this one. There was no way he alone could make this meeting with any serious launderer to happen. Even if he tried, and failed, the price might be too scary to contemplate. The arms man was invigorated by both the stature and preparedness of this Sicilian Joey. He demonstrated a solid understanding of the entirety of the multiple and high stake manoeuvres in which they were about to engage, which seemed routine to him. Even given his inclusion, which was insisted on by McNiff, and spiked Guttries little scam, this was a very reliable and powerful minder to have on your hip, and was, at this place and time, the only option he had to pull this mission off. The arms man sucked in a lungful of air and picked up the receiver dialling the Sicilian. They would meet within the hour at the first rendezvous, Joe Majors at Sixty Eight Street in Bay Ridge, Brooklyn.

The Sicilian was there before time as usual, this time wearing a very expensive maroon zip up leather jacket, mid green wool polo neck and grey dress pants. This guy looked 'the business' regardless what he wore, and he came wrapped with that unmistakable stamp of 'powerful presence'. The arms man laboured the background details about Carrera, the article, and the multiple problems facing him. The Sicilian listened unruffled. The arms man continued, spending a full fifteen minutes wading through the hopelessly weak myriad of issues of his own credulity and the impossibility of the task before him. It was all just 'matter of fact' stuff to the Sicilian who understood every word without as much as the slightest hint of surprise or doubt. Cosa Nostra have 'black belts' in their understanding of the affairs of life, family and business and have an inherited skill of the identity and the removal of obstacles at searing speed. He answered the Guttrie's quandary with unapproachable concreteness.

"OK....we got a small problem here. I'm going to need to talk with my boss, make a few calls, check things out. 'We' got lots of contacts in Florida and with the Columbian guys down there. Seems to me this guy needs to understand 'we are who we are', what we need done, and he, or some gumbatta (associate) of his is going to do it. That's all. Maybe I 'sit' with this guy alone because if you are there maybe he's going to paint pictures in his head, cause to him you are just an 'empty suit' or worse, FBI or Secret Service. So let's not frighten the horses. I am not sure yet, but I think we need to reach out to his lawyer in Florida, and get to him that route. I can let him know who we are in a very subtle way and then he got two choices, one is good and one is not so good. Don't worry about it, sleep on it. That's it gumbatta, rubbed his hands together as if washing them and said the words 'tutti terminadi" and left.

The arms man sat dazed on the barstool at the routine display of the awesome power of Cosa Nostra. So that's how real power works, from princes to paupers. It was the most elevating emboldening experience the arms man had ever witnessed. Where the hell does McNiff get these contacts?' That Sicilian had in three minutes demolished a potential lifetime of speculation and preponderance with unblemished logic and a certainty beyond any doubt. Guttrie was dizzy with excitement at the prospect of meeting 'his gumbatta' again as soon as possible.

It was 24 hours later that Guttrie got the call that things were on track, and three days later he was told to be at the usual place at 7 pm.

His 'gumbatta' was there as usual, matter of fact as usual, straight to the 'nut' as usual.

"OK, this thing is taken care of. You don't need to know any more than that. Your end is to be taken care of by your boss on the other side. Word is you are not to call him. The Sicilian for the first time since they had met offered a handshake saying 'anytime you might need me after this is done you know where I am' and left. As Guttrie basked in the offer of friendship from a real Cosa Nostra, Niall O'Toole and another young man slept soundly in room sixty three of the Golden Gate Motel, in Sheepshead Bay next to Coney Island and Joe Kilkenny wheeled his suitcase to the American airlines check in for San Juan, Puerto Rico.

Chapter Forty Two

EXECUTION

The following morning Bennett paced the press room slowly, and methodically inspected the tools of his trade. First he stepped to the preparation light table and flicked the switch, and then to the darkroom where he again switched on the power. Over the next hour, he checked the list of materials. The darkroom facilities, the three pallets of paper, ink, varnish, and last of all the room temperature which he took a note of on his pad. It was 1:30 p.m. before the Printer turned to the most important unit of equipment, the double crown Heidleberg cylinder printing press which would be used for the numbering, defiant as an old warhorse among the metallic panels of the modern offsets and litho machines, which had for so long threatened its existence. Bennett paced respectfully around the huge chunk of cast iron and ran his fingers lovingly across the glistening stainless steel main cylinder. "This will be your finest hour, old girl," he whispered, "and mine, too, I hope."

Like all crafts which have progressed through time, the oldest principles live on and command the begrudging respect of modern technology. Letterpress printing is simple: spread ink on an image, press on the paper, and that's it. To what standard this application of paper to ink can be achieved depends on two things: one, the capacity of the printer, and secondly the capacity of the machine. A machine's capability depends largely on what is known to print purists as "rolling power." The Printer mounted the 60 year old great clump of cast iron and cranked the press into motion, the ten horsepower motor building up to maximum revolutions; the transparent rollers dropping on the master cylinder in tacky contact. The press bed moved back and forward in union with the hiss of the hydraulic air system; the suction at the paper feed contrasted with the escape blow on the chalking unit which would soon be caressing counterfeit American currency; lots of it.

The young man appeared from the back entrance having tapped the code on the steel door. O'Toole introduced him as Michael. He was a boy of 23 or 24 summers, small with wiry red hair, freckled face and sad green eyes.

Standing to attention he offered his hand in a rigid grip saying "Pleased to meet you boss"

Immediately, both printers began exchanging their respective working experiences as they meandered around the factory noting different machinery here and there as Bennett stuck with technical cross conversation with his young receptive companion. It was just another job to be planned and executed in the most professional manner. O'Toole disappeared to the front of the premises as the welter of technical jargon became totally incomprehensible to him. A little later, the forgers leaned on the work stone and studied the shining numbering boxes in admiration. Within a half hour, Bennett had established the work schedule which would be implemented throughout the crime, leaving his colleague in no doubt as to his responsibilities.

Bennett then opened the black plastic folder and carefully slid out a single bill of each denomination and Federal Reserve area to be reproduced, commenting now and again on specific points which could present problems. Once having the twelve Federal Reserve area samples spread on the table it became obvious each of the areas had either been produced in one printing plant with different shifts varying the ink density and side trim, or printed in different plants which reflected the same small differences. On further inspection they agreed the differences were the result of human discrepancy. The young man agreed mentioning the lay edge, guillotine set up and ink density would need to be varied throughout the run. He mounted the platform of the old Heidleberg which was still running, and commenced to examine the machine like an old pro, making adjustments on the suction feed and line of

36 inking keys. The huge cylinder dropped into the impression position, cranking the 15 tons of cast iron into life. Turning his back on the machine which was running at pitch revs, he alighted from the platform and addressed his boss with amused satisfaction.

"Who'd ever think an old antique like this could overprint and number money. Let's baptise it 'The Whale' I don't care what anyone says, boss, you just can't beat rolling power, although it's going to be slow."

"How slow, Michael?' How many impressions an hour, do you reckon?' Bennett inquired politely.

"We'll have to keep it to about 2,000 - certainly not more. We won't get the accuracy on the numbering and second colour on the front. Shall we go through the time schedule again, boss?'

"Yes. It looks like it's going to be tight. Okay, Michael. Let's reconsider. On each sheet we've got one bill from each of the 12 Federal areas- that's $2,040 per sheet. The entire job is to produce approximately $250 million. That's a total run of 125,000 for each application. In this case we have the black which includes the numbering on the front and also the varnish finishing. That's two letterpress applications on the front, constituting a total run of 250,000. On the back I just have one application, the green numbering and of course, the varnish application - that's two runs as the front say 250,000. I feel this old whale could handle 1800- 2,000 impressions per hour in comfort. That's another couple of hundred hours, make-ready time could be as much as, say three hours on each application to get it really right. Say we do an 18 hour day, all going half right. The drying time should take care of itself, but guillotining, packing and cleaning up will be a couple of days, so we're talking at least ten days, and that's provided you do not have any problems with the litho end of the job."

I'll start setting up The Whale tonight?' I'll have to drop all those rollers and clean them by hand; also I'd like to clean out the ducting system and change a few of the inking keys. I've brought some with me. I want to be absolutely sure that once we start rolling, there aren't any hitches. While you are preparing the plates over the next couple of days I could be making up the frames and positioning the numbering boxes and get the cylinder dressed." The Englishman was pleased at his young workman's competence and mature attitude to it all..

"OK young fella, we'll start tonight. If we work through until 6 o'clock tomorrow morning that will give us a good start. Then we can continue through Saturday afternoon, Saturday night and maybe with a bit of luck, start rolling sometime on Monday."

Bennett passed the folder containing the Dollars to O'Toole for safekeeping, switched off all the equipment and invited his young colleague to a spot of lunch, O'Toole the designated driver of the 'blacked out' Dodge van taxied the two to the empty back room of the pre-arranged diner. Like all co-exponents of any craft, the pair took to each other immediately, each concentrating on the other's suggestions and suspicions regarding any grey areas. The couple of hours intensive conversation clinically exposed a list of problems they would have to grapple with and overcome. The Englishman assured himself that he would not encounter any major ink problems as he had handled fluorescence on a daily basis in Brownings in the production of Government stamps used for the stamping property deeds. Another worrying topic was the varnish. This would be the final and the trickiest process because of the constraints of drying time and the danger of the finished sheets clinging to each other under the guillotine.

"Don't worry about it, Michael. We'll find a way," and gave him a friendly confident tap on the shoulder.

Peculiarly, the fact that a huge forgery was about to take place was never as much as mentioned. The men behaved just like any team of craftsmen about to commence a job of work with a couple of interesting obstacles. The pair entered at the premises unobtrusively an hour later. The younger man donned his overalls and began dismantling the roller section of the machine. He was well trained, responsible and diligent. One by one he cleaned and dried each roller until spotless, the centre stainless steel axle clearly visible through the transparent cone. Both men worked in quietness through that long night, breaking for tea which O'Toole brought at 9 p.m. The windows to the rear of the premises had been covered to blot out any evidence of activity. By midnight, the younger man had the rollers refitted and balanced, the cylinder dressed and ready for running. During the following hours he polished out the grubby inking duct and changed some dozen or so inking keys which he considered were not up to scratch. By 2 a.m. the great old hunk of metal was turning over like a humming bird at top revs, the moving parts having been greased and a couple of minor leaks having been patched up in the hydraulic air system supplying the feed and delivery sections. The Englishman congratulated his colleague on a fine night's work and commenced to explain his progress.

"I've finished all the negatives. They're ready for printing down. The first set of $20 bills are in. They should be ready for proofing in an hour or so. Keep the machine running, and watch that ink spread. We should have the first proofs this morning. There will be a good deal of touching up. I'll print down the rest of the negatives for the GTOV and etch the letterpress plates when I'm satisfied the equipment is working okay."

The younger man examined the serial numbering boxes on the work stone. Bennett took a double crown sheet of paper which he placed on the bright lining up table. Over the next hour, he worked quickly and accurately, drawing out six lines of six deep. The first section of 12 boxes would constitute the twelve Federal areas for the twenty Dollar bill, the second section contained the fifties and the third the hundreds. Between each Dollar box, he allowed approximately 1/16th of an inch for final trim. Working at speed, he took a tracing from each bill in the folder and retraced two boxes on each Dollar box he had drawn. These would be the positions where the serial numbering boxes should be placed in the iron chase which the lad was about to assemble. Hairline accuracy would be imperative. The Englishman handed the complete sheet to Michael an hour later comprising the border position of each of the 72 numbering boxes, two to each note; one in the top right hand corner and the other to the bottom on the left. These would be overprinted in green together with the treasury seal. Bennett continued to explain that each of the two serial boxes on each note should be tapped up to comply with the respective Federal Reserve area. On the first of the six lines by six deep the prefix letter should read: A - B - C - D - E - F; second line: G - H - I - J - K - L. This would complete the $20 series of the 12 Federal areas. The same would apply to the twenty four numbering boxes for the $50 and $100 section respectively. The lad listened to Bennett's instructions calmly and confidently, only mentioning that he would insert some spacers around the boxes for tiny adjustment. Bennett checked his watch as the chirping of the birds told him it was early morning. It reminded him of another morning not so long ago when he awoke in a strange house with some stranger people.

Fitting the rubber gloves on, he removed the first plate and greeted the portrait of President Jackson with reverence.

"Good morning, Mr. President. How are you today, sir?' and smiled to himself, wiping the plate dry. The Forger could pick out the tiniest detail in and around the portrait, knitting through the beautiful scroll work which some hand engraver had spent half a lifetime perfecting at a workbench at the National Institute of Printing and Engraving. Then he locked home the plate on the main cylinder of the GTOV. Mounting the operating platform, he took a few moments to observer his young workmate who was deep in concentration at the far stone, tapping the 72 numbering boxes to comply with the numbering instructions and lining up the boxes. Bennett called him.

"Michael, I'm just about to take the first proof.

The first proof on floated quietly at the delivery end, Bennett picking it by his thumb and index finger as it came to rest. A few seconds later each man gazed at the image through a magnifying glass in astonishment. The reproduction was so perfect that the razor edges of tiny detail laboured the eye to find fault. The tiniest hairlines weaving through the beautiful scrollwork leaned out of the image in testimony to the man that had created the original hand engraved plate. However, the five to one blow-up did show slight smudging here and there. Bennett checked the original bill and noted the serial number as F87746542B - probably the second millionth impression. Paper currency is made and printed by human beings and nobody's perfect,-unless of course, the odds are right. Therefore, the Englishman concluded, the plates which would print this forgery when touched up would be more accurate than the image on that original $20 note which a certain Luke C. Conrad had picked up in Atlanta Airport a short time before when stoned out of his brains and prowling for a woman. Should that be the case, he thought, then it must be concluded that a Federal security system would be incapable of detecting a hairline superior note, bearing in mind comparison of standards between the original and the forgery.

"Maybe we'd better not do too good a job on this," he said and laughed at the bemused young man to his side.

The lad looked on quietly. The form for the green Treasury seal and serial numbering boxes was already locked on the whale, ready for proofing. The time was 5:30 a.m. The zinc plates were processing for the following hour into a new day, both men floundering around the empty premises smoking ... walking ... praying. The young man had pulled the proof for the green. All 72 serial boxes were in perfect position and there was nothing to do but wait. The plates were then removed from the acid and locked on the machine at 6:35 a.m. The lad exhaled a nervous breath, and stepped onto the platform cranking the machine up through the revs saying. "It's now or never, boss."

In a thrice the Printers were bent over the stone, searching the proof from every conceivable angle. The great surge of delirious excitement which touches most mortals only perhaps once in a lifetime overcame both men immediately. The Provo dropped his magnifying glass, placed a hand on Bennett's shoulder and whispered the words: "It's perfect." Bennett clenched his fists, dropped his eyelids and gazed to heaven like a thankful pilgrim. "Thanks be to Christ, thanks be to Christ," he said, and meant every single word.

The phone rang. O'Toole answered as usual.

"Get the Englishman to the phone," McNiff rasped. Bennett made his way to the front office eager to know the reason for the phantom call.

"What's up?' Bennett snapped without introduction. And then the crushing news.

"Bad news, they want used stuff!

"I knew it, I knew it - I fucking knew it … shit!

"I'll call in 24 hours" and dropped the receiver. After absorbing the fullness of the blow he decided to let the job run its course as there was nothing he could do now anyway except play with some solutions in his mind. He also decided against telling his assistant for now anyway.

Seven days later his young partner relaxed in a chair keeping an eye on the old press as it churned out the numbered printed sheets in monotonous repetition. He was by now becoming bored with the challenge but continued to hold his concentration. At the slightest evidence of inconsistency in the machines performance, he would rise and check the sheets for numbering and reproduction accuracy. The forgery itself was by now nearing completion as the register clock to the side of the machine clicked to 266,748. Only the application of the varnish remained. Without referring to McNiff's call, Bennett calmly explained the problem to his seated workmate

As the forgery ground into the eighth day, the pair huddled over the work stone for the hundredth time. The work stone was now well established as the forum for problem solving. Each man suggested a variety of solutions from graphite dust application to crushing the bills some way or other. They knew they had to find a way. The pair were a first class team with an unlimited reservoir of technical resourcefulness and that winning blend of hardened experience and the freshness of youth. Such had been the accuracy of the operation that they had succeeded in producing an extra 400 sheets of the last series. The wastage on the job was minimal. As the last 50 sheets of the forgery tripped out the delivery end of the "whale," the younger man stopped rigid in his movements, pointing his index finger at the Englishman.

"I have an idea! The young man began working in furious enthusiasm, filling the chalk units to the delivery with a pint can of graphite dust. Each unit was hooked to the hydraulic system. Within the hour he had redressed the master cylinder in a scattered layer of mounds and bulges. Bennett stood motionless, his arms folded restfully as he studied the procedure with interest, and nodding his head intermittently in agreement. The idea worked; the sheets tripping out the delivery end in crinkled dust-stained mess. The texture and feeling of the notes was like that of any used currency; each note giving the impression of a varied circulation life. Bennett mixed the bills with a batch of genuine notes and requested his partner to identify the forgeries. The young man did so, but with considerable difficulty and only with aid of a microscope. The Forger instructed O'Toole to call McNiff and inform him everything was in order and to continue his arrangements. During the relative cool of darkness the forgery rolled on efficiently without unforeseen event. Across the East River, the Yuppies of Wall Street clinked crystal into the early hours at the South Street Seaport while lesser men were only beginning their day at the adjoining Fulton Fish Market.

It was near dawn that both men and O'Toole began packing the 25 steamer trunks with thousands of batches of mixed notes, as the hum of traffic grew louder on the overhead Brooklyn-Queens

Expressway. The Twenty four steamer trunks were set to one side for the "pick up" which was to be overseen by O'Toole at 9am.

The threesome spent the following 14 hours polishing, cleaning and gathering up the components of the crime into plastic garbage sacks which would later be destroyed.

All wore surgical gloves and sneakers of the same issue. Over and over again the entire area was re-examined to a point where the exercise became redundant. Bennett instructed his assistant to re-soil the ink duct, replace the old keys and drain the moving parts of the machine of service grease. The patches on the air system were removed and the rollers realigned to their previous clapped out position. The Forger drained the oil system and allowed the warhorse to grind to its original alignment. The original cylinder dressing was replaced and all and sundry left exactly as found. The final wipe down was done in stocking feet.

As the first rays of the mornings sunshine warmed the Brooklyn's rooftops the Dodge van backed up to the factory rear freight entrance with the words GOT Couriers (Guaranteed On Time) marked on its sides in bright multi coloured artwork. O'Toole and Michael dolly wheeled the trunks onto the loading dock where 3 young men appeared from the open back doors. Within minutes the vehicle disappeared out the industrial estate exit and slid into the jammed northbound lane heading for The Long Island Expressway. One last inspection of the premises in stocking feet, and the factory secured, the Dodge cruised south out along the coast road known as the Belt Parkway coming to a stop at The Golden Gate Motel. Once inside the O'Toole suggested they both get some rest telling Bennett he would be back to collect him in a few hours.

One hour later the electric powered wrought iron gateways of a mansion in Sands Point on Long Island's north shore swung open before O'Toole having been screened by the CCTV system and security intercom. As the van broached the main gravel forecourt leaving the quarter mile oak lined entrance behind, a lone figure directed the Dodge to the rear car park. Armed men appeared on the flagstone rear entrance as he cut the engine and commenced unloading the twenty five trunks which were dolly wheeled inside like clockwork. Once inside O'Toole and the three men made their way through to the huge kitchen through clusters of separated groups of young Cosa Nostra who were armed with the best hardware money could buy. Lots of Uzi's, Berettas and Glocks.

Through the colloquial multi paned window O'Toole saw the commercial chopper resting on its landing pad at the rear of the manicured back lawn. They stepped down the stairs to the darkness of the basement. Passing through the maze of dust wine racks to the clearing they were greeted by McNiff and McCahan. The steam trunks were already open to the front of the portable tables where behind sat six Latin men and two oriental women. These people were professional money counters. One by one each bundle was handed to the counter, who then opened and split the bundle of notes two or three times as one would a deck of cards, smearing any random note with the erasable ultra violet detector. The amount was then fed into the currency counter, the amount then entered into one of the four desk-top computers which was 'on line' with offshore banking havens worldwide. These were professional money counters and launderers, and boy could they count Dollar bills at blistering speed and accuracy. The momentum continued at the same pitch hour after hour in church silence. The final bundles from the last trunk were tested for ultra violet light, counted, tagged, rebound, entered into an account number and replaced into the stainless steel trunks they themselves had provided.

As the sunset descended behind the skyline of Hoboken New Jersey, the last trunk of notes were sealed with the four Chubb electronic locks. The person who appeared to be their leader rose from the seat like the rest and said the words 'OK...everything is fine, we are done and set about gathering their belongings to leave. Within half an hour the mansion was empty save the three

Fenians. O'Toole was sent to pick up Bennett at the Golden Gate, his assistant already on his way to Kennedy airport.

Two hours later O'Toole and the forger were escorted to a grand oak panelled room. It was McNiff, who greeted them. The Forger stood without speaking and eyed the packet on the polished table top. McNiff handed him the envelope, requesting him to read the contents. Bennett opened the envelope nervously. The content read thus: Rodney Anthony Lewis, The following mandate instructions must be followed in relation to all correspondence and cash transactions with the Banc du Credit Suiss, 12 Rue Rudez, Zurich, Switzerland. The cash on deposit shall be $5,000,000 Dollars, available now. The account shall be quoted as R.A.L. constituting the initials of the depositor Rodney Andrew Lewis. The access code is 178742001. The account number is 162085372. The note on a separate sheet of paper read : DO NOT DRAW ON THIS ACCOUNT. This forms part of your defence if necessary.

Bennett filled his lungs and looked at each of the men in concert. Sliding the envelope into his raincoat pocket he was uneasy at what to do except attempt a final farewell. Another man entered the room. The Forger recognised him by his missing front teeth and beaming smile. Sean McCahan offered his hand. Bennett refused and instead rose, hands on his hips and stared to the floor in concentration. Tenseness filled the room. Suddenly, Bennett whipped a wicked right uppercut to the Irishman's jaw, upending him like a sack of coal on the carpet.

"That's for Reading, you bastard!

The company looked to each other in unmoved McNiff's eyes twinkled, the corners of the mouth turning up slightly, O'Toole being a fight fan offered to do referee eager for a right good dust up. Typical O'Toole. McCahan rose slowly to his feet, holding his jaw, his legs quivering from the suddenness of the shot and braced himself. After a moment's silence he took the noble option and offered his hand with a genuine willingness. They shook hands.

"Sorry, Howard ... I had no choice ... I hope everything goes okay for you." Bennett turned to the others. McNiff was nibbling on his thumb as if nothing happened.

O'Toole spoke. "Shall we do it now?' The three Fenians escorted the Brit to the rear grounds where they formed a single line in military fashion. McNiff roared orders in Gaelic.

Bennett just stood, too weary and drained to care what might happen. The old Republican recited a statement in Gaelic. McNiff then invited the Briton to bid a last farewell. The first man he confronted was Sean McCahan, whose blue eyes stared into his soul.

"I will always think of you Howard. Sorry about Reading ... mind yourself." They shook hands and the Provo reverted to his position of rigid attention, his damp mop of curly brown hair glistening in the summer's downpour. O'Toole, as usual, had little to say.

"All the best. Take care of yourself ... God speed our day." Colm McNiff stared Bennett through the damp lenses of his ill- fitting spectacles. For the first time, Bennett noticed the lifeless depursed facial features bearing testimony to the many years of hardship "On leaving you, I ask you to think of us in our hour of struggle. We pray you find some peace after all this. Goodbye and God bless you. Goodbye son ... God be good to you ... there's no more to be said." They embraced. The Printer could feel the damp herringbone pattern of the crombie across his palms and ventured a joke.

"You ought to treat yourself to a new coat, my old mate." The Republican embraced Bennett again, his eyes glazing in that moment; Howard felt a new but familiar feeling. The face of his father, the Merchant Marine, flashed in his mind.

"Not at all Howard ... this coat is fine. I don't think I'll need it for too much longer anyway." The Fenian drew a deep breath and exhaled into a sigh. On his command the men swivelled on their heels and marched in through the rear exit from which they had come.

Bennett stood alone in the centre of the gravelled courtyard. O'Toole appeared and cranked the Dodge into life. The sky broke again into cracking thunder as he caught a glimpse of a squirrel scurrying up a tree for cover. As the rain pounded the world into subjection, the reality overcame him, as he murmured the words 'God help us' as the Dodge crawled down the foliage covered avenue, turning left at the pillared exit in the direction of Kennedy Airport and Dublin.

Chapter Forty Three

STINGER

T he world crunched on its axis, delineating the first flecks of dawn along the line of seventy degrees latitude, from the Kara Sea in Russia's frozen north on down through Kazakhstan, Kabul and west of Bombay in the Arabic Sea.

It was hot as Hades. They were indeed strange men. Bearded, rag headed, huddled in hunkered groups, crop stands of Ak47's and shoulder held grenade launchers spiked in rest to the azure heavens. Great hunting hawks wheeling above as tiny tin cups of Darjeeling tea washed down herb scented rice as goat meat spat and sizzled over the open fire.

The stranger in their midst hunched silent on the granite rock, the streams of burning sweat streamed down the crevices of weathered skin. A crombie overcoat was neatly folded over the battered suitcase, the same suitcase with which he had walked to freedom from The Curragh Internment Camp in the County Kildare in the Republic of Ireland on a dark December morning, more long ago than he cared to remember.

He was once a great warrior, a great Mujahid, their leader had been told and from a far off place fighting the same tribe their forefathers had massacred along the Khyber Pass, the ones in the red coats with the shining white hats.

The trip had been exhausting, first the turbulent crossing from Rosslare in the County Wexford to Le Harve in the North of France. Then a sleepless train ride to Paris, one of the European nerve centres of direct access to any part of the world. From there he suffered the 10 hour flight to Lahore in northern Pakistan, from where he took his seat on the sweatbox known as the Trans Pakistan Railway, which ends its journey at Peshawar, Pakistan's hub for spies, drug and arms dealers.

Having passed Customs without event, the old Fenian had been driven some miles along the Khyber and into Afghanistan, the land of the fiercest fighters on God's Earth, the land of the Mujahedeen. They had camped in wait for the Great Warrior for days and nights, under Afghanistan's darkness of cobalt skies and galaxy of stars dancing heel and toe. Immediately they knew it was HIM from the green, white and gold flags of his tribe, which were pasted on his suitcase. The tribe men descended from the old battered diesel in delirium, each laden to the pits with a blinding arsenal of weaponry, two and three assault rifles each, huge bandoliers of shells and other assorted grenades and handguns. They were tiny men, with the vigour and strength of stallions as they yelped and scavenged like dogs for an audience with the Great Mujahid from the far off place.

Their leader, Abdul Ajhilbal, took precedence. The left side of the face had clearly been the subject of some terrible fate. The cheekbone had somehow collapsed; lifeless as a spent scrotum. The flange of the lower eyelid sunk into the cavity, the iris pickled in some waxy saliva, giving rise to the suspicion of some murky substance at the bottom of his nature. McNiff was not a man who frightened easily, but the sight was alarming.

But as with many initial speculations on the character of a person, the opposite proved to be true. The fullness and warmth of the smile of welcome triggered the old Fenian into an infinitely less arresting disposition.

The Mujahid knelt to his knees and snapped both of the Irishman's wrists with the tightness of a lathe's chuck and proceeded to kiss both hands with mumblings of his dialect. The tiny man then produced the leather bound tome and the first of many old brown photographs. It was a British colonel, with a harnessed collared military jacket, seagull waxed moustache and Spartan white hat which beaked to the bridge of his nose. The Fenian moved his tired eyes to the Holy Warrior and moved his head up and down.

A great cheer rang out, magazine after magazine was emptied into the heavens in rejoicing and another squabble ensued for privilege of audience. Other photos followed, pale men with slanted eyes, who came from the north in green uniforms, leather jackboots and pancake hats with red bands. They came with tanks and helicopters and jet fighters, and they too had gone away, just like the ones with the red coats and polished boots.

The ritual of welcome lingered for a further hour. Weapon after weapon was presented with beaming smiles of black teeth, soured of stale rice, meat, and opiated hashish. But the weapon of most interest to McNiff was finally brought forward in a finely machined metal box measuring just 48 inches by 14. As the clips were undone and the hinged casket opened, another great cheer erupted, accompanied by the rattle of gunfire.

McNiff stared the contents ... his heart began to rev uncontrollably in his chest, culminating in a sharp pain that left him dizzy and weakened. Here it was at last ... the weapon of total portable destruction ... so small ... so unimpressive. A dart of golden sunshine highlighted the letters FM92 SERIAL NO. ATC798653427. The back end lay to its side and the detachable laser unit sat snug in the top left corner of the case. With McNiff's nod the box was closed and replaced with other assorted weapons in the rear of the canvas covered truck. The diesel spluttered into life and shuttered at a snail's pace down the primitive treacherous mountain road in the direction of the lush valleys of the Nabutt River in the Provence of Nangarhar.

Hour after hour they descended the lower slopes of the Karaborum Mountains, the midday sun gilding the huge sheets of granite all round them as patrols of hunting hawks glided in the parched crevices in search of their bounties of young chicks, eggs and mountain rodents. Along the veins of rock the Fenian noted the many herds of mountain goats nibbling on the odd tuft of sparse vegetation. The air became cooler as the band rounded a final turn and the lushness of the Nabutt Valley came into view, testing the expanse of ones eyesight. For further hours they passed herds of sheep, bolting clusters of wild horses, discarded Soviet weaponry and the many tent-housed villages of Mujahedeen until they finally came to a halt at the village of Balsawue, situated on banks of the wandering tidal Nabutt River.

By now the gathering dusk cooled the mud houses and dirt roads of the village as the glow of firelight roasted fresh meat and simmered large iron urns of a herbal rice broth. The constant flow of fighters to the fireside brought gifts of beads and silver and prayers scribed in Dari and bound in crude leather frames. As night fell, a galleon moon patrolled the sleeping village as The Great Warrior was laid on a straw bed in one of the underground mud houses. To his side, they laid the metal box, adorned in mountain flowers and religious objects. As they removed his jacket, a curious ring of beads fell to the floor ... many beads with a naked man nailed to two cross members of wood. This was another warrior the men in the red coats had massacred, they decided, and laid the object on his chest. Then they lit a galaxy of candles and prayed until dawn that he would live to bring many boxes to the far off Jihad.

And so now the group sat on the side of the mountain overlooking the valley in readiness for the firing of the weapon. A short time before, a group of tribesmen had been dousing the inside of a discarded Soviet tank with gas some mile and a half away high on the mountainside. The furnace had been raging for some minutes when a single rainbow flare gave the signal that all was ready. The leader rose from his squat and within seconds the STINGER was assembled and loaded. The tribesman knelt in the commando position and searched the expanse of the mountainside for his target. As the tank turret divided the cross hairs he pressed the laser button and fired. The exhaust roared out the rear of the unit, a mushroom of black smoke rose above the tank followed by roaring fire. McNiff scoured the target from high powered binoculars. Huge chunks of tangled metal ripped from their housings ... the caterpillar wheels and treads blasted apart like some abandoned roller coaster.

McNiff shuddered as he pondered momentarily on the many deaths which would be the result of the use of this awesome weapon. Then his instincts told him the weapon could indeed be the saviour of lives. The old Fenian laid the binoculars on the ground and covered his face with his hands. His mind wandered in the darkness as the ghosts of Pearse and Wolf Tone filled his vision, along with the countless others who gave their lives for the cause ... the hunger strikers and the gift of the new movement which arose out the ashes of '69, many of whom were still imprisoned behind the grey prison walls of Ireland and Britain. He would play a great part in their salvation, in the righting of the wrongs of an ancient evil.

And then he thought of the young British soldiers, of the 18 and 19 year old innocents, who if only left to their own reason at that blessed time of life would be courting their girls, playing sport and cultivating their plans of life and limb. All young pink cheeked children of God, their frames hardly moulded to maturity, their fear and terror at fever pitch ... some loving mother's son whose womb did nurture and conceive to be thrown onto the bloody streets of Belfast or Derry to fight and sometimes die for reasons beyond their understanding. And then Colm McNiff broke down, still holding his hands over the tear filled cheeks, shuddering horribly as the reality of war and death circled his mind's eye.

So here he stood, on a baking hillside in Afghanistan, the fate of so many issues mauling his conscience, persecuting his soul. The tribesmen helped him down the mountainside to the waiting diesel and crashed on down the primitive road back to the village.

The following days were spent inspecting the hundreds of STINGER surface to air missiles which were stashed high in the Karaborum Mountains. McNiff was also instructed on assembly, maintenance and firing. All arrangements for the movement of money and shipping instructions would be handled entirely by Bob Millar.

As the Paris bound Jumbo roared down Runway 8 at Lahore Airport, Colm McNiff felt his heart wrench in his chest again. He would make a point of seeing his doctor when he got to Dublin.

It was some seven days later he straddled out of his doctor's office in the centre of a rain swept Dublin, prescription in hand together with the admission slip for Jervis St. Hospital. McNiff had denied an ambulance but gave his word he would allow himself be admitted the following day. The prolonged delays in removing the stethoscope from his breast and the frowning silence of his doctor solidified the office in the unsaid that most mortals understand. Devoutly religious people like McNiff hold no fear of death. Indeed such people hold no fear of anything other than the self-maligning of the soul. The eternal laying to rest from this world of wanton sin and invariant suffering is a blessing.

The journey from Afghanistan had been exhausting to a point of near collapse. The overnight stay at a cheap pension in Paris had helped to recharge his vitality but in a flurry to catch the 6 am train to Le Havre he had to lay down the suitcase and support himself on a coffee stand in Gare Saint Lazare train station. He lost consciousness for some seconds and continued at a snail's pace.

The calm passage across St. George's Channel to Rosslare in the Irish southern county of Wexford had been used to rest, to think and to pray.

As the old diesel engine cranked and shook on the rails, the Fenian gazed on the rising dew of the dawn, to the bright meadows of Boulavogue and Shelmalier, fawning in the breeze and where once the forces of the British Crown had butchered by blade and by blunderbuss the wretched impoverished souls of his countrymen.

The Fenian fingered the Rosary beads with the gentleness of a child's touch as a tumbling white sun appeared over the Irish Sea. The train exited the tiny town of Wicklow and stiffened on its rails in a direct surge for the fair city of Dublin, 40 miles north along the fjordic coastline, which buttressed the surging sea in great volcanoes of white surf. His thoughts sunk as the burden of decision making filtered to the core of his thinking, and shivered as he pondered on the employment of the awesome military and financial power of his tiny army. Then he traced the political, military and financial bankruptcy of the North of Ireland. This would indeed mark the finest hour in the long and bloody annals of the Fenian movement. By now the gleaming fields of the harvest were active with men and machinery, some who stopped momentarily to gaze or wave at the passing convoy. Little could they have known that the sunken sickly man in the second carriage saw the gesture as their final salute. A tear moistened the iris of his eye, but even in this moment of profound emotion he could feel the glory of his dreams disappear into a lacuna, a hiatus, an overpowering slip from the knot securing their moorings, those moorings to which he had been so pure, so loyal, so indefatigable for so many decades in a crucified lifetime. Much as he tried to reason with his primitive urges, with visions of glory for his once beleaguered army, Colm McNiff, as if by some divine intervention was convinced as the train crawled into Amiens St. Station that an end to the struggle would not lie in the waging of a full blown war.

For the following six days he remained snuggled in his basement flat on Parnell Square, making sporadic excursions to the local grocery store and stroking the red coal fire as Dublin's traffic passed above him. After daily Mass at St. Patrick's he was able to take the short walk across O'Connell Street to the General Post Office where he would go to teller 6, a sympathizer who held messages from Bob Millar. It was on this the 7th day after leaving the doctor's office that the teller handed him the small white envelope. The message was simple, "St. Michan's 11:00 a.m. tomorrow Thursday"

Next morning he summoned a taxi and swept up along the quayside of the River Liffey turning right in behind the famous

Four Courts. St. Michan's is an unobtrusive facade nestled alongside Irish distilleries, a colossal stone building of the late 18th century. The church itself was founded in Dublin atop pagan druidic vaults below a sacred oak forest. The corpses lying there since Michan's time have suffered no decay outside of a slightly leathery exterior, their joints still pliable. The Fenian, being a regular visitor had long associated the phenomenon with the durability of his army through time and trial. Minutes later as the Dublin autumn hailstones rattled the stain glass windows, he sat alone in a pew, head in hands, bone weary and sore. That the church was empty only added to the pain and isolation. He prayed to his God for the strength to face Him, to remove these awesome decisions from his soul and to have mercy in this new spiritual state that his days were coming to an end. It was a bittersweet sensation somewhere between joy and relief but spiced with a desperateness to close his life in purity and to ensure that the sacrifice was not made for his own glory but to that which he believed, preservation of the birth right of mankind.

Minutes later, Bob Millar, dressed with the sharpness of a statesman, dipped two fingers in the font of holy water and blessed himself. McNiff, without turning knew the familiar footsteps on the creaking floorboards before the lone figure genuflected in the aisle and slid to the side of the sunken posture, embracing him lightly with an arm. Slowly, McNiff stirred, his eyes brightening out of the trance.

"The Phoenix has landed ... they're in." For Bob Millar to be sighted with McNiff would be a disaster. Unlike McNiff, so well-known by successive governments and special branch alike, Millar's existence and function within the movement had remained a well-guarded secret even within the ranks itself. In the past, Millar had overseen and negotiated numerous operations, the details of which were known only to him. Such was the confidence the hierarchy had in the quiet schoolteacher from Croydon.

Both men left the church separately with a rendezvous for one hour later at a small hotel in the seaside town of Dun Laoghaire, ten miles to the south of the city. The light of the day had now turned to greyness. Soon, the working populace of the city would disperse to the warm modest homes of the suburbs, to the raucous joviality of local pubs, where the events of the day would be discussed over creamy pints of black porter, and for the younger at heart there were dances, dates and other social assembly. The two Fenians fixed their eyes through the hotel window to the mist of the Irish Sea. They had eaten a late lunch of smoked cod in silence, unable to engage in idle chatter by reason of the critical importance of the events of the previous days and months. Millar looked to his commander aided only by the glow of the firelight and inwardly touched for a moment on admiration and respect he had for Colm McNiff. It was more than anything the humility and meekness of the man so giving during the course of a lifetime of thankless struggle and never ending sacrifice. McNiff squinted at the schoolteacher through the askew spectacles, the freckled hands resting on the lap of the frayed crombie which he had not yet disowned.

"Colm, I pray God in His wisdom that this will be the final military operation of the movement, we have as I speak to you numerous units in place at a moment's notice. Over the past days and indeed months I have been plagued with other matters; matters of conscience and the burden of taking decisions of such enormous consequences. The fact of these units being in place is known only by two other people other than you and I. This was a smuggling operation of unparalleled expense and sophistication. It is a fact for me to be able to say that we are in a position to wage war by land, air and by sea the consequences of which are unpredictable at this time. It is this uncertainty which has caused me to seriously alter my opinion as to the questionable wisdom of war. There exists another option and I plead with you to listen to it". McNiff agreed with a nod.

At that moment Bob Millar knew that Colm McNiff was near the end, closer his Maker than the ways of this world of darkness and danger, and chances that he would not be taking a part in the ending of the armed struggle in the North.

"Whatever you do Bobby, I have complete confidence in you. Tell me what you have in mind and then I will have to be on my way, I am so very tired." His eyes drifted to another place..

"I understand Colm, I will be as brief as I can. I have made arrangements to meet with a very powerful Irish-American caucus next week with the aid of the editor of an Irish New York weekly. Naturally the caucus members will not know my identity. I will be pleading with this very influential group to give us any assistance they may in the US to avert a civil war. I will of course not make known to them the full extent of our potency, just enough to be persuasive. I will be directing them to have Washington advise London that we are releasing an undefined number of Stingers directed at British airborne military. We will allow no more than 48 hours to set up secret negotiations via this caucus with the aim of not alone legitimizing our political wing but the Republican movement itself. At some stage we will have to offer a complete ceasefire over a prolonged period so Major can save some face and bring us to the table. If we can succeed in calling a ceasefire under the right deal, then there is no doubt that the Loyalist paramilitaries will follow suit within a very short time. I say that this could be achieved in three months with minimum loss of life. But if however we are met with intransigence, we will wage a guerrilla war the savagery and destruction of which will catapult the entire region into a new dark age made even more deathly by its utter finality. I am done; do I have your support?' The old warrior just rose from his seat, and nodded ever so slowly in the fading light. He then embraced his soldier and stumbled from the warmth of the room, hiding a grimace of pain as he clutched the doorknob and disappeared into the night. They knew they would never see each other again.

The Schoolteacher observed the old man as he gored his way through the gale which blew off the Irish Sea and vanished into the train station. The schoolteacher moved to the small table and sat, his arms outstretched, the hands expanded to fullness atop the linen tablecloth. The moments became sacred, for grief is a sacred state of mind. And then the schoolteacher broke completely into a loud shuttering wail which after a while levelled to prolonged mournful cries of unsuppressed lamentation and then to the whimpering of a fretful frightened child. Finding strength, he rose to support himself on the fire breast. He made the following promise to himself, to his commander and to his army. "If ever this damn struggle is ever to be ended, it must be ended now."

Chapter Forty Four

CEASEFIRE

The Winter of 1993 had been mild by New York City standards; a few heavy snow flurries just before and after Christmas. But even now in late February, icy mounds lingered on the city's sidewalks. A bone chilling breeze blew in from New York Harbour motivating the city's pedestrians to quicken in pace, take the odd chance at a changing traffic light, or cross the street amid crawling traffic to reach the warmth of the workplace.

Tom Byrne, Editor in Chief of New York's Irish Weekly, studied the passing traffic from his 28th floor office on Park Avenue South, tapping the window sill nervously, glimpsing at the desktop clock. Tom Byrne was expecting a visitor of some importance.

The Editor, an amiable mannered Irishman, the boyish profile defying his 46 years, the trimmed beard at one with his rich cultural background now shelved by the daily battle of balancing the dollars and cents in the toughest city in the world.

The phone call he had received two days before had been the most important and unnerving during his lifetime. For many years, and first as a young journalist in Dublin, Byrne had cultivated a working relationship with the IRA. In the former years his confidentiality had been tested to the utmost in the halcyon days of the mid and late 70's, when the Republican Movement chose its media intermediaries with absolute caution. Tom Byrne was the only journalist who the schoolteacher had ever spoken to under the contact name 'Cara'. Over the past twenty years he had met Bob Millar on only four occasions, the secret secured under pain of a subsequent execution. It was this indefatigable quality in Byrne's character which made him the unfettered, competent journalist that he was. Many a politician or industrialist had misplaced his mild manner and low key style for weakness, naivety, much to their chagrin.

Should any Irish group or organization wish to tap the real Irish powerhouses of politics, industry, finance and the professions which existed in the United States, the first and only stop must be Tom Byrne. The words spoken over the phone by Millar, opened with a code word, were deathly arresting.

"This is Cara ... we are contemplating a permanent ceasefire. Your office 9 am, February the 25th. Repeat, your office February 25th"

The Editor knew Bobby Millar to be an obsessive disciplinarian. Byrne was no different than the rest of Millar's contacts insofar his word, his bond. A sudden shower of light rain clouded the window as the intercom crackled. Bobby Millar presented himself seconds later in heavy disguise as usual, seating himself to the front of Byrne's unencumbered desk. Newsman and Freedom Fighter shook hands briefly, the office doused to silence but for the raindrops on the window and rustle of Bob Millar shaking off his raincoat. The conversation would be simple, direct, and conclusive, that was Millar's style. Greetings dispersed with, the Editor sunk into the large swivel chair, aiming the first question in the well rounded, educated Irish accent he had never lost.

"Well Cara, what've you got?' Moving the clasped hands to rest under the nostrils.

"The Irish Caucus here in the US, may be the only force capable of averting a full blown war. We are now in a position to take the territory- and to hold it. I am ordered to direct you, within a reasonable time to effect the granting of visas for the political wing's leadership, so much as anything else a demonstration of non-intransigence on the part of both US and UK administrations. You can tell the power house here that we have the finance, the hardware, and the technology to sustain a very long war of attrition- perhaps for generations. It is important that you know that in the light of these circumstances that the Movement cares not the manner which the media behaves, one way or the other. In order your group, the United States and British Governments can move ahead, the Movement is offering the face-saving license to do a permanent ceasefire. Should the United States or London doubt us, we will act- and they will doubt us no more."

The Editor sunk both elbows on the desktop. "I always knew something like this would happen, someday-somehow. But I have a problem with credulity. Can you give me anything- anything tangible, even by word of mouth to convince them beyond doubt that they must act. If it is misused, I know you will act without notice."

"Very well! The finance; not less than, but not limited to multi millions; the hardware in place; shoulder held missiles, the technology and communication accessibility-state of the art and unlimited. I ask of you, do what needs to be done to end this. I am ordered not to make any further contact until this first step is secured. I will call in say six days. The granting of a few simple visas to the movements leaders, even for forty eight hours will, and I guarantee it change history"

Tom Byrne sat static, locked in space at the unfolding oration. The Schoolteacher rose and slid an envelope containing 3000 Dollars to cover the editor's expenses and left the office.

Byrne shook from his trance, knowing above all things that the man who had just left his office, and the movement he represented never, but never made false promises. Placing the envelope in his inside coat pocket, he summoned his editorial assistant, Michael Moran. The young assistant left the office minutes later, upbeat at the prospect of taking full charge of the entire production of that week's edition. His only attempt at inquisitiveness had been halted with a dismissive temperedness he had not witnessed in his boss before. Two hours later, Byrne, having made just three phone calls, was aboard the Washington midday shuttle.

On the fourth day, March 1, 1994, the first of the visas were granted by the Clinton Administration. A bright sunshine glazed the high risers of New York City as Bob Millar stepped from the yellow cab and entered a Blarney Stone bar on Park Avenue South for a rendezvous with Byrne. The time was 11:00 am, the long bar empty but for a few businessmen and some Mexican kitchen hands who stirred and sliced foodstuffs at the steam table in preparation of the lunchtime rush. A white-aproned bartender flicked through the channels on TV as the schoolteacher approached the lone figure of Tom Byrne squatted over a table in the rear of the dining area. He looked like a man exhausted and listless, rising to greet the Cara. Millar accepted the handshake with tiring indifference. The silence passed as the kitchen doors swung to and fro. Millar spoke.

"Do I order a ceasefire?'

"The answer is yes, but there are problems. The ceasefire cannot occur until the British have even the smallest proof of your capacity"

"OK, we would have preferred not. Some people will die" As the teacher rose to leave the editor fired a question

"Do you think it could be all over?'

The Schoolteacher replied, hands now deep in the raincoat's pockets:

"It's all over. You can shout it all over the world – it's over one way or the other," and disappeared behind the closing door into the brightness and delirium of midtown Manhattan.

On the other side of the world, in a safe house in County Wicklow, a tired old Fenian waited, his eyes fixed and dilated, the spark of his life extinguished into eternity, like with the last dying ember's flicker in the fireplace.

Over the following days, Millar had holed himself up in a fine but obscure hotel at the Oceanside in Sheepshead Bay south Brooklyn - a largely European-American middle-class community of burly upmarket detached dwellings grid ironed in fine broad roadways of expensively pampered gardens. On the final evening, he walked Coney Island's deserted boardwalk tossing bread lumps as seagulls keened and swooped above his outstretched hand. He had kept to himself save a few excursions to local Irish bars, mystified at the advances of attractive women and the rawness of their curiosities.

In the weeks to follow, there would be mortar attacks on Heathrow Airport, London, causing no appreciable damage. The British Security Forces and Government would keep their usual stiff upper lip, citing the IRA's ineptitude in firing off crudely made mortars, none of which exploded, albeit they came close enough to their intended targets.

On March 19, 1994, the IRA would take pot shots at a Royal Ulster Constabulary armoured vehicle in south Armagh Northern Ireland. There would follow the subsequent helicopter air support of Her Majesty's Parachute Regiment. An FM92 Stinger missile would blow it to pieces.

Chapter Forty Five

BOXING THE FOX

T wo months later, Detective Lieutenant Vito Liotine awoke sharply with a bolt of awareness that today was the day, and sprang from the single bed. He squinted through the threadbare curtains where the clear blue heavens draped a calm Atlantic ocean. His old Chevy sat undisturbed in the resident's car park some fifteen stories below. All round the grey corroded apartment blocks of Sheepshead Bay rose like tombstones, as a white speckle of seagulls pecked on the boardwalk, and a stray mongrel trotted askew leaving its footprints along the receding shoreline.

With well-practised deftness, Liotine manoeuvred through the clutter of the dark apartment, a testimonial to the dishevelled bachelor. Having showered and shaved, he filled the coffeemaker and rooted around inside the refrigerator, a graveyard of take-out platters and cartons and condiments - half eaten, half forgotten, and decided on the remains of last night's beef Lo Mein and an egg roll, which he would have eaten cold if not for the recent purchase of a microwave oven. His thoughts turned to the weather. His daily gambling habit, which mismanaged his life turned to The Belmont Stakes which would be run that very afternoon. This was the big day of the horse racing calendar year.

In looks and stature, Vito Liotine was very much out of the mould of Al Pacino, and not untypical of a good percentage of New York Italian cops born and raised on the manicured streets of Brooklyn's Bensonhurst. Of Catholic parents, educated by the Jesuits and more than capable of being certified three parts unstable from his tours in Vietnam, it still remained a mystery to him how he passed the psychological to become one of New York's Finest as the police are referred to in New York City. Having strapped on the Glock 9mm automatic and bullet-proof vest, he choose his favourite black button down shirt and grey double breasted charcoal suit to give some homage to this day of the racing year. As the dated elevator rumbled down past the clicking of the relays, he patrolled the events of the day before him concentrating on making the track for the first race.

From early childhood, Liotine was at battle, well...with everything. His schooldays with the Jesuits were turbulent. An undisciplined but bright child, he survived their cloistered orderliness through high school. The terror of Vietnam blooded his hounds, and as a twenty year undercover on the seething cauldrons of East New York provided a custom fit to his potency to edgework, violence and danger.

Liotine believed inerasably in his very own self-conceived doctrine that most things in life were a constituent of the same Great Lie; that the sum total of all involuntary actions, thoughts and deeds were for the benefit of profit masters seen and unseen, known and unknown. Physically small in stature but of formidable strength and fearlessness to the point of recklessness he had long been relieved of his undercover role on the streets of Brownsville and Bushwick and now headed up the outstanding warrant squad of six Detectives.

Minutes later he was bouncing the old Chevy tub down the Belt Parkway to meet his eight a.m. sign on time. Minutes later, he reeled through the open doors of the 72nd Precinct. Once inside, he stiffened, like some pony that sensed the rustle of a rattler. They were everywhere, with those snow white French cuffed banker's shirts, holstered magnum cannons and shining black submarine Mormon wingtips shoes.

Liotine knew the college educated Madonna's of the Secret Service well enough, Washington's true interpretation of all that is the 'great and the good' in American law enforcement. After all they protect the Man himself and the mighty Dollar. More of the same Great Lie!

It was of all police stations the world over with hookers, drug dealers and other sinners being shuffled to various desks for questioning. Here and there an obscenity or plea, the room hummed with the criminal banter of captor and prisoner. The rattle of aged typewriters, the clang of iron locks and sporadic drifts at humour made the place even more threatening, cheerless and hostile.

The Italian moved to the desk sergeant, an affable old Irish cop named John McNamara who got a kick out of laying on a thick affected brogue and breaking balls, particularly Liotine's.

"Ah ma man Liotine, suppose you'll be outa here like a badger out of a hole at three o'clock today, what d'ya like for The Belmont?' The Italian stared the green misty eyes and prairie of roaring red hair.

"Hey Mac, what's all these Service doin' ere?'

"Something about a forgery, your wanted in the conference room five minutes" the old cop rambled, shifting the specs from the tip to the bridge of his nose.

The Detective swaggered down along the nuthouse green disinfected corridor, to the auditorium, concentrating on the odds on the Belmont. Once turned left, the entire 72nd Precinct undercover Squad was there with yet more Secret Service.

"What the fuck's goin' on ere?" he thought, nodding his head here and there in vague morning greeting, and shouldered his path through the gaggle of theatrical under cover; everything from bespectacled accountants to bushy hairdos, rags around their foreheads, denim jackets with sleeves cut off at the armpits, chains instead of belts, moustaches, beards, sideburns and ponytails.

Minutes later, the hum of the auditorium quietened as the Secret Service agents took their places. The double doors slammed shut, and the lights dimmed as the projection TV began to view the videotape behind the line of five Dollar college haircuts. Liotine's thoughts flashed to Belmont, as he blew a faint haze of blue smoke through the open window onto the cool morning. Beyond the building, across the bay the first flecks of the June sunshine mottled the arms of the Statue of Liberty. Crossing his legs, he doused the Marlboro, and slumped into the plastic chair, pondering his chances of making the third race.

The title read:

"AN UNRESOLVED INVESTIGATION INTO A SERIOUS COUNTERFEIT OF AMERICAN CURRENCY"

The video rolled on for forty five minutes, consisting of the quality of the notes, finely calculated scientific speculation on the origin of the paper, and a pyramid of logic explaining the nature and direction of the investigation. The final topic outlined the probable psychological profile of the forger or forgers. The meeting ended with the allocation of Detectives to Secret Service team leaders.

Liotine would be working with Special Agent Stan Weiss. They sat twenty minutes later in the privacy of interview room 7. Liotine's gut told him that this would be no ordinary chit-chat. Outside the constant din of New York's car horns, screeching tires and screaming sirens filtered through the closed windows, the air conditioner hummed away, keeping the joyless naked room at comfortable temperature. Weiss introduced himself modestly, placing the pad of notes on the laminated desktop. Liotine's cop instinct shifted into gear and began its independent excursion into the character of Stanley Weiss. Middle aged, Jewish, predisposed to decades of marital torture by a cantankerous all-domineering wife, probably lives in Great Neck, Cedarhurst, or some other bastion of the great and the good.

Liotine, like most New Yorkers, had a black belt in caustic directness if not outright rudeness. Lifting his shoulders he presented both empty hands as a beggar in the street atypical of Sicilian gesticulation.

"If these forgers did such a good job, den how could you guys've found outtabout it dere?'

The Agent rose to his feet. "Okay Liotine... good question. This is all that I can tell you. It might have never been found out. It is only recently that a new scanning system caught a minute magnetic deviation in the ink of these notes that caused bells to go off. The top level brass of the Treasury take the view that there has over perhaps the past couple of years indisputable evidence of the existence of a person or persons capable of producing and laundering successfully an unlimited number of dollars. We have failed to make any headway whatsoever after over two years on this. Our criminologists have determined that there may well be more sinister and potentially dangerous motives behind this operation, like the propping up of third world economies unfriendly to us, or terrorist activity... arms... God knows what... maybe even some wayward lunatic who wants to atone for past sins and feed the starving. But we do know without doubt that this crime was not done by any back street forger... this crime was executed by high intellect, inordinate technical capacity and as much as anything else a foresightedness which is both staggering and if it must be said, admirable. What is truly remarkable is, from what our people have deduced is the crime itself is absent of the usual characteristics of greed, sloppiness, impatience and exposure. It is only in the very recent past that we have come to the opinion that we are dealing with a phantom genius who it seems has predetermined our every move, and that in the eyes of my superiors is potentially a very dangerous individual to be walking the streets of any country in the world. That's it... period."

"Liotine, the truth is that I don't know where to start on this. To the best of my knowledge and from what I am told, it is unheard of in the annals of the Service anyway, that an investigation of this magnitude has been embarked upon before, in respect of any counterfeit that is. As we sit, such briefings as you witnessed here this morning are taking place not alone all over the country but at the highest levels of investigation in every country worldwide where we have an Embassy. Before I go any further it has to be said that I am not your employer, nor your boss, nor do I sign your pay check. My solitary relationship with both of you is to direct you to what we need done. Now, we can do this the hard way or the easy way, we know what you people think about us, and maybe with some justification, but that's neither here nor there. We are all just warm bodies on this gig- mules-beating hearts in the business in our own little way of executing a massive worldwide process of elimination."

"We're on this case for too long and the powers that be are getting exceedingly impatient with the non-existence of as much as a shred of light. The international institutions are about to notify their members that an unresolved massive counterfeit of the dollar is existent and that American intelligence has failed to resolve it. What this means is that there is someone out there with the wherewithal and the ingenuity to prise every security device inherent in the US dollar. There has not been a forgery that we have not been able to solve in a very, very short time. When members of the international community get wind of this, be in no doubt that they will take steps to protect their own currencies from being infiltrated by a bogus dollar The real problem is the hysteria of reaction on the international markets to a point maybe where the question could, in time, be raised whether the dollar itself might not be acceptable as transferable currency which I know is farfetched. It is okay to say that we have pinned forty million so far, but the truth is that we don't know what's out there. For all we know, this could be just a trial run to gauge the ability of the system to deal with it. It is not the amount we are worried about at the moment; it is the quality of the forgery. That, in cold facts Lieutenant Liotine is the seriousness of the possibility that exists. We are now at the point but we have no option but to bring in you guys to assist us, we just don't have the numbers, something which has never been done in the past we are told. The ultimate test at retail level which has always protected the dollar is that of ultra violet light, and other security features which in this case have now been proved a failure."

"Over the last three years we have continued the most thorough investigation which our manpower would permit. Insofar as the actual production of these notes are concerned, we can state with certainty that the following are not involved- Cosa Nostra- the cartels of South America,-North Korea,-the Near East and the Far Eastern heroin interests. We have therefore concluded that this forgery would have been done a long time ago should the talent have been available on the global criminal marketplace. During the course of this investigation, the first shock waves paralyzed our top people when it was established that there was no watermark in the paper. This means that somebody got a sophisticated paper mill to manufacture the paper particularly for this purpose. Our chemical analysts have determined a location of manufacture probably in China, Thailand or maybe even Laos or Cambodia. But how the forgers got together, and under what circumstances they undertook such a perilous venture remains a mystery to us. It is certain that the paper must have been imported into the United States within the last five years and all of us nationwide are determined to find out when, and from where and whom, by a gigantic process of elimination. And that is all that we are gentlemen, just grains of sand in a desert of investigation. We have been assigned to Kennedy Airport to review all files of every piece of paper that came in there over the last five years from those regions. We start with Thailand which is they say is the best bet on the basis of the water analysis. So that's what we are just mules, beating hearts, but I hope together we should try ride this out and have a good time."

Twenty minutes later, the three were bounding along at high speed on the Belt Parkway in the direction of Kennedy Airport. A calm Atlantic ocean shimmered in the searing morning sunshine. By now, the rising morning mist screened the upper half of the Verrazano Bridge and the high risers of Coney Island and

Sheepshead Bay. Along the miles of shoreline promenade, the children played as grandparents drank the peace of the morning in watchfulness. Liotine surveyed the passive landscape as his years as a patrolman, then an undercover, then rocketed through his subconscious.

"How the friggin' hell did I ever come to stop off at this farmhouse,' the Detective thought as the Chevy eased over the security ramp and lurched to a halt in the Thai Airways employees parking lot. The office to which group were escorted was on the third floor of the security building 145 of US Customs was large and furnished with every piece of state of the art communication and information gadgetry the world has to offer.

Both walls which paralleled to the full landscape window were custom fitted with grey Formica worktops. The high backed office chairs sat on ball bearing wheels allowing the operator to whisk himself across the shining linoleum floor at the touch of the foot.

"Another stake out gig ... General Tso's chicken and six packs of boiling Bud under the door every few hours! A coffee peculator choked away beside the medium sized refrigerator on top of which there was a very large box of unopened bags of expensive Java guaranteed to keep men vibrating like a tuning fork for days without sleep. Goddamn stakeouts. He remembered that four week sentry duty in an arms dump in Vietnam.. For twelve hours each night he watched. Nothing ever happened. Vito Liotine was the sort of operator who needed other humans to spark him into combustion.

Two laser printers were silently churning out a continuous ream of printed matter as the battery of monitors flickered in constant observance of every square inch of the inside and the outside of the airport. Along the worktop there lay the featherweight headsets out of which there projected the long thread thin fibre optic communication cable, accompanied by lengthy lists of telephone numbers of faceless people in very high places. There were home numbers, office numbers, fax numbers, vacation numbers, beeper numbers, car phone numbers, speed dials and a myriad of instructions designed to contact any particular person within seconds from round the globe, from the Treasury, the CIA, the FBI, the Secret Service, the intelligence nerve centres of every government, embassy, police force, airport, port, customs and communication centre accessible to state of the art technology. The wall to the right of the entrance door was covered with a huge map of Burma, Thailand, Laos and Cambodia, over which there were the sixteen international digital time clocks. Outside the landscape window, the activity of Kennedy's Far Eastern section ground on to the time frame of its own agenda, huge jumbos lurching down out of the heavens, the picture quivering in the midday heat like a shimmering mirror, tiny people in strange colourful clothes alighting from the aircraft for their first glimpse of crazy town.

"Yep... all paid up for a stay at the farm," thought the Detective and sat himself in one of the high backed chairs in anticipation of the arrival of Anna Maria Gonzales, director of security, Far East Division. She arrived ten minutes later. The Detective and Weiss rose to their feet to greet her.

This was indeed a full blooded sophisticated woman out of the classic Castilian mould. The shining head of black hair swept directly away from the calm marble forehead and caressed behind the tiny earlobes in an upswept wave. The portrait face masking the light of the soul, the cream silk blouse harnessed high on the neckline above the deep veiled cleavage, the nail tips of the smooth olive hands manicured to pearls, a wafer thin platinum timepiece rested askew on the bone of the wrist. There was not a movement about this woman which did not have its grace. Liotine did not hear a word she was saying, the erotic curve on his destiny taking a life of its own. Half a minute later he managed to muster a grip on his wayward concentration.

After an hour of discussion, the task of the N.Y.P.D. was clarified to simple procedure as with all international airports throughout the USA. The intake of all paper products over the last five years was documented by Customs nationwide. The destination of such product was to be investigated in the outside hope of an absence of end user, or circumstances such as would give rise to suspicion of misappropriation. The computer nerve centre of the Department of Customs at Kennedy is interfaced with the computers of AT&T and all other telephone networks. Each end user of paper and or allied material would be dialled automatically, the contents of the discussion to be noted on the data base computer file. In the event of any end user showing to be non-existent, Andrew Weiss of the Secret Service was to be notified immediately.

Anna Maria Gonzales had determined there were 7862 files of imported paper material under section 246, subsection B, from Thailand alone to be entrusted to the labour of the 72nd Precinct. The importation of this material into New York by far outweighed all such imports throughout the USA therefore the spearhead of the investigation would be concentrated in Kennedy, Newark, and La Guardia. The most overriding weakness in this massive investment of manpower was 'paper material' could be anything from a flat cardboard box to birthday cards. By now a flaming horizon had made the greyness of the gathering dusk more prominent outside the landscape office window. The Security Director rose with poise to take her leave, the small of the spine arched to the fullness of the butt, she turned to Liotine in the presumption of his squaring the costume coat over the bladed shoulders which he did with all the dignity the Jesuits had beaten into him. The best sentiment of farewell Detective came up with were the words, "Takeireasy dere."

The bill of lading document with which Niall O'Toole had picked up the paper some four years previous was marked B178603, or cross index file number 6875 in the computer's terabyte hard drive.

Chapter Forty Six

T he man the Secret Service would be ultimately looking for lay sleeping between clean linen sheets, the tips of the woman's moist lips resting on his breast, the enclave of her knee over the spent scrotum. A slumber half-smile flecked her open mouth, through which the air of life rasped to the tempo of blissful sleep.

The tiny cottage, snuggled deep in the West Wicklow hills just 40 miles outside Dublin, where the countryside, with its meandering boreens and peaceful skies has an aura conceived out of all that is Mother Ireland. The accent is rounded and unhurried; slow clear diction, indicative of the pace of life there. The seasons change softly, where the once great drifts of winter snow would whiten the thorny countryside, heap the walkways of the villages, hush them, and suffocate many beasts in the depths of the valleys. The resurrection of Spring carpets the landscape in bountiful rich green grass. The inhabitants of this folklore blessedness are for the most part farmers, outdoor folk of singular stock, whose humility and simple wisdom spares them the entanglements of mainstream metropolitanism. The irretrievable ruins of long deserted homes and cottages pepper the landscape as reminders of past horrendous times, their tenants banished because of starvation, poverty and merciless eviction, but who still occupy with an obdurate haunting presence like tidal driftwood now resting at peace in its forgotten harbour.

A final beam of moonlight projected through the parted drapes which hued the sleepers to an alabaster white. Outside the whitewashed cottage, the cool dew of the morning had covered the lush hills as the flocks of sheep and new-born lamb ascended the mountains to the coolness of higher pastures. Across the sleeping countryside the silver of the moon would soon accede to the light of dawn. It was Sunday and soon a bleary eyed altar boy would knell the first church bell of the day to summon the dutiful to worship. Dusty Bennett was in the throngs of an uneasy slumber as he awoke in half-consciousness.

The first summoning rang out as the Sabbath-dressed families dotted the tiny village of Hollywood, past the keening hysteria of barn-shackled dogs, past the grazing cattle and sheep, and the gurgling streams and rivers to pay homage to that they believed held their destinies. The Mass would be said with the aid of two red-cassocked altar boys and the sermon would espouse the message of the parable of the day to a silent audience but for the cries of a new-born infant or an irreverent fidgeting child.

After midday, as the Forger carved his way through the late breakfast, Vito Liotine reeled into the empty Irish Circle bar just off the shoreline in Rockaway, which was a cop and fireman hangout renowned for its free poured shots and free running ice cold beer. It had been a long night jammed with a mountain of information, instructional procedure and technical data relevant to the duty to which he and his partners had been assigned.

The young Irish bartender knew the Detective well. "What's it going to be this evening, Vito?' "Gimmie the usual and lemmie get t'fuck outta ere," Liotine babbled and pulled the wad of assorted bills from the leather wallet. The bartender winced. The first 'lemmie get t'fuck outta ere' meant two to three hours and snatched the bottle of V.O. from the back bar, free-pouring the rye nutcrackers over ice, accompanied by a frosted stein mug of ice cold beer.

As the morning passed, the cops from the Brooklyn Precincts gathered in huddles to discuss the investigation. Liotine's group comprised of two Detectives from Greenpoint and one from East New York, all of whom had been assigned to the same duty in La Guardia Airport in Queens. Phone calls were made to contacts in L.A., San Francisco, and Seattle which confirmed that the investigation was both of high priority and nationwide.

Bennett's drinking had now diminished to a trickle, but for all his new found normality, there lurked along the impulses of his cerebral cortex there resided an elusive demon spitting and gouging at his every inclination to normality. The nightmares were relentless in their horror and reality. By now the ulcers were fully festered.

The daytime panic attacks churned his stomach to acid and rocks generating constant hot reflux. The blond hair had by now silvered at the temples, the gaunt pale face and sunken eyes now ravaged from lack of sleep and anguish, the protruding shoulder blades now evident from spiralling weight loss, he toyed daily with the notion of coming clean with the law. As the midday sun climbed high over the beaches of south Brooklyn, the forger was in one of his very few melancholy frames as he sat by the open cottage door drinking in the pure morning air of the Wicklow Mountains. He felt himself dozing away, his only contact with the living was the heat of the sun which pierced the closed eyelids. He drifted once again to the perfect peace, stillness, nothingness. How much must we harrow the soil of passion before the messenger in the night rears his mocking jester's head?' How much pain and gut-wrenching anguish before the Saviour of Wisdom wipes our torn brows and cradles us to sanity.

For months, Brendan Geraghty had structured a defence which he was convinced would bring in a verdict of not guilty in any country of common law, or at least 'due process' the world over. The likelihood of bringing in the verdict did not worry him too much. What did worry him were the far reaching political implications, which would overshadow and more than likely exclude the inevitable verdict of a jury. Geraghty doubted that the case would ever get near a court because of the provable absence of 'intent and the severe duress of his actions, which would be counterproductive and cause far more damage to the political establishment than to Howard Bennett. The British government would without doubt exert the most strenuous pressure on the Americans, to alter in whatever way they deemed fit the course of justice to bring the most ruthless punishment on the offender, given the 'consequences' of his actions in the north of Ireland; and to further complicate matters from the British position Bennett would indeed have a successful case of criminal compensation against the British government. With the introduction of heat-seeking missiles into the North of Ireland the territory would now come to be ungovernable, the British army tottering on defeat, the factions of Unionism and Republicans braced for civil war, the United Nations waiting in the wings for another Belgian Congo or Middle East, or perhaps even more catastrophic the inevitable and perhaps final conflict which would be played out right in their own back yard.

Chapter Forty Seven

The days and weeks had passed quickly. Each call during the twelve hour shifts not alone presented the possibility of a break, but Weiss had been astute enough to notify both Detectives of the exposure of other criminal activity which had been the direct results of their efforts. He also had time and time again, aired his absolute conviction that the document they were looking for lay in the basement filing section of Building Six which contained all original import documents from the region of concentration. The work rate had increased dramatically as the last days of Summer cooled the blistering heat. The nourishment of those days comprised of freezer cooled salads and the installation of a two gallon pail of beers submerged in all the ice they could get their hands on. Cops did their own thing in those days.

Summer had by now acceded to the rustle of New York's golden fall. The feast of Thanksgiving loomed and then soon the first sounds of sleigh bells and Christmas music would be heard over TV and radio, which always reminded Liotine it was time to hit the N.Y.P.D. Credit Union again to finance his Christmas spending spree on his battalion of nieces and nephews. Inwardly, he knew this annual loan was a payback for his gambling habits but preferred to think of it as an act of more noble intuition. It was on the morning of November 24th some ten weeks into the investigation that file number 6875 was placed on Liotine's worktop for routine investigation

Over the months, the case had ploughed on relentlessly at the Service's hysteria for a break. Word from around the country was that the overall investment in manpower had resulted in the uncovering of other cases ranging from money laundering, drugs and a whole rack of very serious importation violations mainly relating to counterfeit prescription drugs. By now, the growing intensity of the case, coupled with the sixty hour six day weeks was beginning to slump the concentration.

Most files would take just a few phone calls to establish as genuine. Others would be submerged in an octopus of grey areas ranging from changed names, changed locations, Chapter Seven, Chapter Eleven, flight from the Internal Revenue Service, flight from the country, and on and on and on. Liotine fingered the file with indifference and proceeded to make the usual calls as a wicked rainstorm began to splatter the landscape window.

Ten minutes later, the cover sheet outlined the result of the thirty minute inquiry which comprised of six calls. One each to the American Embassy in Bangkok, to the Registry of Corporations in Albany New York, to the International Typographical Association, to local 408 of the Teamsters Union and to the New Jersey Police Department in Atlantic City to check out the location of the end user. Result; blank.

"Gotta 'nuther phantom 'ere," the Detective remarked to his partner to as he photocopied two copies of the file, one of which was placed in the basket of Anna Maria Gonzales, the other for the attention of Andrew Weiss. Liotine then made a call to each of their offices to notify them of his findings.

One hour later the original document which had been used for the importation of the paper had been retrieved from the basement of the record section at Building Six and was being placed gingerly in the transparent bag with the use of the surgical tweezers. By four p.m. that afternoon, the document had been scoured for prints of which there were sixteen.

As the city of New York wafted into the misty dusk of the evening, sets of prints were dispatched to the Secret Service, the FBI, the CIA, the New York Police Department, and Interpol's 180 regional global centres.

Chapter Forty Eight

F ive days later a United States Marine, assigned to the American Embassy was escorted through the innocent green door in the tiny Rue Paul Valery in Paris which houses the headquarters of Interpol Europe. For the next three hours, he would sit hunched dutifully in the tiny waiting room just off the communications centre.

By now, the first shades of dusk began to temper the heat of a grateful Autumn Paris, as the last of the city's week enders crossed the city limits for the coolness of the coast and countryside, the city folk polished the household crystal in preparation for France's nightly ritual of many course dinners.

Inside the communications room, Marc Girard inhaled the rich blue smoke of the Gitane as the lines of fax machines punched out the reports of the world's top international crime busters. Stepping outside onto the ornate iron veranda, he searched the sprawling city and caught a glimpse of the towering Arc du Triumph, its magnificence glowing in the yellow ochre of the high pressure sodium floodlights focused with precision on its facade.

The headlights of the Ferraris, Masseratis and the odd Rolls circled The Etoile at high speed and lurched into one of the exits to disappear into the mystery of the Parisian night. The occupants of such vehicles bore no mystery to Marc Girard, a thirty year veteran of France's elite SDECE, now the DGSE, Service de Documentation de Contra-Espionage, whose activities from time to time placed him privy to the innermost modus operandi of the hedonistic rich of the Republic of France. The waistband radio crackled, requesting his presence in the basement which housed Interpol's H.Q. for International Counter-Espionage and Terrorism.

Minutes later, the agent speed read the three reports placed to the centre of the large oval desk as his eight underlings stood and sat in silence. Some sipped on black coffee laced with crude French brandy; others nursed paper containers of ice water, and sat motionless in speculation at the importance of the break in the investigation. The first report had arrived from Scotland Yard, who were the most immediate respondents, the second from the Special Branch in Dublin, and the third from Interpol's own internal resources.

The juvenile profile of Niall O'Toole etched across the fax paper accompanied by the blown up fingerprint cranked out of the fax. The personal details of the suspect filled the second and third pages of the crammed report. The rhythm of the language of France whispered, as a mist of blue smoke wafted round the ceiling along with the pop of the bubbling coffee peculator.

Half an hour later, the U.S. Marine tooled the Harley up the Champs Elyse's at high speed. In just two weeks he would be on annual vacation at his parent's house in Charlotte, North Carolina; tending honey spare ribs and molten lava 'jerk' chicken on the smoker. As he dipped the machine around The Etoile, a wayward Ferrari missed him by a hair's breadth. "Yooooooo muddafukaaaaa!! bawled into the Paris night as he straightened and threw the bike into Avenue des Champs Elysees south in the direction of the US Embassy on Avenue Gabriel.

Secret Service Agent Andrew Weiss was sitting down to his usual late dinner at 22:45 New York time, when both the telephone and beeper rang off simultaneously. The message was brief. "Call HQ now! As with most servants of the state 'on call' he had his wife pack an overnight bag.

Two hours later he sat to the front of three yawning figures in one of the conference rooms of the Secret Service New York field office at 7 World Trade Centre. He knew the director of the Service quite well, who introduced the remainder of the groggy audience comprising of one person from The CIA, one from the FBI and one from the Embassy of The Republic of Ireland. From the outset military intelligence in the form of the CIA took complete control of this meeting. John Parsons, early sixties 'matter of fact' attitude was an operative of unknown years, with a steel badger hairline, squeaky clean demeanour, hawk eyed with a marble jawline and an intimidating presence opened. The meeting was to continue for some three hours winding up with a lot more questions than answers.

"Gentlemen, let me fill you in. I have been over the last hours fully briefed by Dublin on the up to date intelligence so I have a bigger picture than you guys. Within hours of one of our FM92 Stingers was used to take down a British Army chopper in the north if Ireland we have known about it. The serial number was one of the units given to the Mujahedeen during the Soviet confrontation in Afghanistan. Despite the efforts of US, Irish and British intelligence the case is still a blank sheet of paper until this O'Toole IRA fella was tied to this forgery of yours. We don't give a rat's ass about any forgery of a few hundred million. There are half a dozen people on Wall Street ripping of that kind of money every week. We need to talk to an Englishman named Howard Bennett as it seems he is the last man standing as O'Toole and the other person we believe to be involved are both dead. The Irish special branch will be calling in half an hour and will fill you in on the background. Somebody squeezed off that godamn missile, but who is still a mystery. We need to know how many they have and whether there might be any possibility of buying 'em back. That's where we are at right now. We have been told there may well be legal obstacles between us and Bennett but we must and we will speak to him one way or the other. My instructions are to rely on you guys to make that happen. There is no way we can get involved at this stage so I leave this to your good council. That is all I have right now" and swigged a glass of water.

Weiss followed. "A near undetectable forgery of the dollar has occurred the extent of which is yet unknown. It has been confirmed that the inward customs document which imported the custom manufactured paper used in this crime bore the fingerprints of one Niall O'Toole, an active but deceased member of

The Irish Republican Army. We believe the proceeds may have been used to buy Stinger FM 92 shoulder held surface to air missiles, one of which was in the north of Ireland. Our brief is to rein in the actual forger or forgers whom we are certain are not IRA members; identify the technology employed; bolt down the possibility of a re occurrence; and if possible make the arrests, try and convict. That's it, unless someone has something to add"

To Weiss' mind, the inclusion of the IRA entangled the remedy of trial and punishment into a political morass. The fact that Irish intelligence had confirmed the deaths of both Niall O'Toole and Colm McNiff, the alleged Commander of a British-based cell of the IRA had now temporarily spiked any further progress. The group waited over coffee for the contact from the Special Branch in Dublin and British intelligence who were re-examining the reports on McNiff's movements over the previous five years. The FBI agent explained he was sent to observe, take notes and report back, the assumption being the 'job' must have been done in the somewhere within the State of New York. The Irish mid-level young diplomat was there to do likewise and to extend every assistance to the expedition of things.

The Phoenix Park on Dublin's north side bears testimony to the grandiose aspirations of 19th century British architecture. The thousands of acres have within its boundaries many public amenities. It is doubtful that a single soul of Dublin's fair city would not have crossed its parameters before taking their first steps. The elk and deer roam freely there and may be hand fed by the passing voyeur. The gardens bloom and fade with the seasons, and along the walls of Dublin's famous Zoological Gardens, the sounds of nature can be heard from the animals' captive therein. The residence of the President of the Republic of Ireland is situated almost directly across from the residence of the American Ambassador. These and other buildings in their architectural splendour, foundations of stone and gravel, their sturdiness tested through time and trial form many of the principles of structural engineering to this day. Such a building is occupied by the Special Branch, The Republic of Ireland's secret police, primarily responsible for serious crime, counter espionage and terrorism. Half a world away, in 7 World Trade Centre, another building occupied by another secret police, with its high-tech dedicated speaker phone lines brought the Phoenix Park. The Irish lilting voice hushed the room.

"Are you hearing me loud and clear?' Reply: "Yes, we're reading you."

"Colm McNiff's niece, known as a Miss Fiona Geraghty has been associating with an English citizen described as a Mister Howard Bennett, the details I'll give you later. Our background check tells us this Bennett is not alone a recognized British authority on coins, notes, and bonds; but is a lithographic printer previously employed in the security printing business before abruptly retiring. There are patches of information about a mysterious set of affairs in the south of Spain, about which he was questioned by British Police along with a friend of his, a Mister Brian Walker.

The room fell to silence as if the victim of a powerful concussion. The Irishman continued.

"Now here is the kicker, Fiona Geraghty's brother who is a very prominent barrister is the leading authority on The Prevention of Terrorism and Extradition legislation in the UK and Ireland, so it follows Bennett would have the best legal representation the State has to offer. By the way I forgot to mention he also has an Irish passport to which he is fully entitled. We have nothing on Bennett here, the British have nothing on him in the UK and off the record our Attorney General tells us the United States would need a rock solid compelling case to as much as interview this man, never mind either to coax him into the US embassy or stateside. That's all we have for now but our surveillance is on-going until this is finalised.

Weiss blasted impatiently.

"What's the status of this guy Bennett now?'

"He's in hospital here in Dublin with ulcer problems; we know his whereabouts; as I said it's all in the file. We're available here twenty four seven"

Weiss eyed each of the participants individually.

"That must be our baby folks!"

The door opened. A file was placed on the waxed table, Parsons looked to his audience. "Who bagged this Bennett initially?'

Weiss again.

"Italian guy, Liotine, Lieutenant N.Y.P.D.; Brooklyn cop; undercover specialist; real chameleon; fits right in anywhere. Good operator, real good! Maybe for this job we should use an informal touch. The last thing we want to do is scare Bennett off before we even get started. Would you like a copy of his file?'

"Yes, yes I would, clicking his fingers. All high level military have an unblemished understanding of the scope of their parameters of decision thus the power is vested in such people to be able to act immediately either on the battlefield or otherwise fortified in the immovable certainty that matters military ultimately precede all others. Parsons thumbed through the file unfazed as an idle barber and said; "This guy is perfect. Bring him in! Nobody dared question his twenty second decision.

Vito Liotine was on the fifty Dollar betting line the next day at Belmont Park, N.Y., when his beeper went off.

"I ain't leaving this fuckin' line for nobody! he hissed as he disarmed the beeper, "I'll call those fuckers when I'm good and ready!

Later, he swaggered over to the phone booth in the Bridle Bar and dialled the number of the 72nd Precinct, which half an hour before was displayed on his beeper. "Liotine eere."

"Ah, good day ya little ginzo, suppose yer out there at the Belmont bettin' winner after winner!

"What da fuck d'you want, Mac... breakin' my balls on my day off. I ain't placing no fuckin' bets for ya, so go fuck yaself"

"Well, well, well, Liotine! I have some grand news for ya... drag yer ass outta there and report to me within the hour...dares some fellas from the big house who would like to have a little chat wit'cha ..they'll be here in an hour...about that forgery thing ya were workinon !

"I don't believe this bullshit... aright... see ya when I get in, you old fart!

At 8 p.m. the Detective sat sitting faced by Andrew Weiss, Parsons; some unknown lawyer from the State department along with the Captain of the Precinct. Without as much as a murmur a three page document with the heading Official Secrets Act was pushed before him, Parson's pointed finger resting on the signature spaces. The signature was then witnessed by the Captain of the precinct and the lawyer fella from the State Department.

During the course of the lengthy orientation, the delicacy of his mission which outwardly seemed simple enough was discussed down to the finest detail. The Secret Service wished to interview one Howard Bennett in connection with the case he had inadvertently busted, and further to establish the extent of the fraud and the identities of any other persons who acted in concert. They could have sent another agent from the from any number of agencies, but this job called for not alone the 'common touch' but tact and good old fashioned street smarts. The subject must not be aroused, he must be treated with kid gloves and gently persuaded that all they wanted to know is how much was forged, how it was done and who were the participants, and if possible for what specific purpose. If necessary, but only if absolutely necessary he must be reminded of the danger he might place himself should he not co-operate.

The Detective was instructed to pick up his 'kit' at the US Embassy in Dublin which consisted of a Gloc nine millimetre pistol, a dossier containing maps, contacts, and all other pertinent information. It was decided the best first point of contact with Bennett should be in public at the rugby club near

Lansdowne Road where he was an honorary member His visiting habits as with all other information were in the dossier.

Almost a week later, Liotine and his partner Felix, sat in the near empty Irish Circle Bar in Rockaway. Being a summer spot beside the Atlantic Ocean, the place became a ghost town in Winter. Earlier that day, Liotine did some last minute Christmas shopping for his nieces and nephews, stuffing the trunk of his car to capacity. He had packed and ready to catch his Dublin flight later that night from Kennedy Airport just 8 miles up the Belt Parkway.

Liotine looked at his watch. "I gotta go. Do me a solid, Felix. Follow me out to Kennedy. I'll give you my spare keys. If I'm not back by Christmas Eve, take my car to my mudder's. Dere's a buncha stuff for the kids in the trunk for 'em dere."

Chapter Forty Nine

T en and a half hours later, the aircraft lurched to a halt at the arrivals terminal at Dublin Airport. The squat figure of Vito Liotine was met by the gaunt gangly figure from the U.S. Embassy and driven across the city to Ballsbridge for debriefing. A room had been reserved for Liotine at The Shelbourne Hotel, overlooking the charming St. Stephen's Green at the epicentre of Georgian Dublin.

He was provided with a folder containing an up-to-date surveillance report on the movements of the subject, a detailed map of Dublin City Centre, and another two maps: the area of Bennett's flat and the rugby club he frequented located near Landsdowne Road Stadium, plus his firearm of choice, a Glock 9mm, just in case. Once settled in he began scouring the file from the privacy of his hotel room. The tax returns relating to the bond business on Sloan Street in London verified that Bennett made a modestly above average living expectant of that type and scope of venture. The detail on his movements, habits and expenditure since then date of the paper importation reflected an interesting but frugal lifestyle which seemed at odds with a huge forgery. Either he was not the person Liotine needed to contact, or Bennett was the meanest millionaire on record. The details of the Spanish issue were clouded in speculation. The flight from the Spanish Police under the burden of bankruptcy and the subsequent divorce from his wife were now the focus of Liotine's attention. His New York street sense told him that Bennett must be the man, but there just too many pieces that just did not fit the profile of an arch-criminal. He was not known to the Police, an avid football player, a coach, a master printer, an collector and an authority on old currency, his wife a teacher, her family the embodiment of all that is proper in the British caste system. Liotine's focus on detail drifted into speculation.

"Dis fuckin' thing don't make no sense, maybe these IRA guys had this broad cosy up to him somehow and then scared the shit out of him. Brooklyn street logic. People like this just don't wake up in the morning and do this shit... it just don't fuckin' happen. I'm sure looking forward to gettin to the bottom of this thing. Wonder what this guy is like. I got a feelin I'm gonna like dis guy" Finally deciding the more he vacillated on the job the more difficult it would be. Later that evening, he strolled down opulent Grafton Street, stopping here and there to window shop or listen to several of numerous street musicians singing and playing instruments for their suppers. Passing open door pub after pub the banter of Dublin relaxed him. He stepped into an Eddie Rocket's where he wolfed down one of those ten ounce burgers. Then, after seeking some information from a fellow patron, he hailed a taxi to Landsdowne Road. The Detective strolled under the wrought iron entrance of the rugby club where the report had indicated Bennett had guest membership status and would make an appearance around half seven that evening. A shower of hailstones blasted the rooftops of the packed car park. To the left and right, the two playing fields were ploughed up in mud and water from the day's play.

"How could' ya play ball on that?' The Detective played with the notion in his mind. Immediately inside the main entrance, he signed the guest book and stepped into the mysterious world of Howard Dusty Bennett. A patrol of bartenders worked furiously, serving the hundred and fifty or so patrons. Dozens of team photographs covered the walls as the raucous gathering hummed along in eruptions of laughter, shameless shouts of raillery over an undercurrent of the din of merry conversation. Two wall mounted TV's vibrated the sports of the day, the only news of interest to this motley gathering.

"Geez, I wouldn't mind takin' some bettin' action in this joint," the thought as he inched his way up to the bar, which was three and four deep, but he failed to break through; instead a patron ordered his whiskey and water, negotiating the sale and passed back the change as is customary in that part of the world. And so the raillery continued. An hour passed and the premises began to clear. He easily made company with a group of club members introducing himself as a visitor from New York.

The usual battery of questions followed, the work situation, rates of pay, medical benefits, the mortgage rate and so on. As he got warmer with the company, he decided to pop the question. "By the way guys, I'm trying to contact a guy my partner knew in Spain. Blonde fella... Howard Bennett. You guys know him?' The response was in a single chorus, each man more eager than the other to assist the American. Bennett would usually be down within the hour after the crowd cleared.

The bar had almost emptied an hour later as the tall slim figure of Howard Dusty Bennett entered the bar. He seemed relaxed, taking his time to stop here and there to bid his various friends a good evening. The Forger approached the group at their beckoning, the leather soles of his shoes ringing on the parquet floor.

"How do you do mate... can't say that I remember you... understand that you got the business down in Spain also."

The Detective rose from his seat clasping the Englishman's handshake with both hands.

"Yea... me and my partner got it... got it good. Care for a drink?'

"I shouldn't - stomach problems. Thanks just the same."

"Well Howard, I'm just passin through visiting some relations. I got your name from my partner in Torremolinos. You know the way the word gets around"

"Well mate, you can kiss the money goodbye but if I can be of any help I'll be glad to tell you everything that I know I prefer not to talk about it here. Let's go to the office."

Liotine Patiently induced the Forger to unfold the whole convoluted, bizarre story, which Bennett did, in clinical detail taking particular pains to cause his willing listener an absolute understanding of the slimy methods which were employed to complete the fraud against him and Brian Walker. The Forger relented and opted for a drink. Many drinks followed as the cop related to the Englishman's experience point by point. As the clock struck midnight and last drinks were served, the Forger ventured an innocent question.

"What line of work are you in, Vito?'

The Detective looked to his prey, pausing; the ticking mantle clock the only sound in the room. Bennett awaited an answer, tension involuntarily mounting within his tightening gut. Liotine gauged his reply with all the tact any decent cop in the world could muster, sliding his badge on the table.

"Howard, right now as I talk, I'm really sorry from the bottom of my heart, real sorry to have to tell you this. This is the toughest call I had to make in my life as a cop, 72nd Precinct, Brooklyn. You've been to New York a few years ago, right?' The silence followed as both men stared each other, Bennett paralysed in shock, his Brooklyn cop, heavy and saddened at having to break the news.

"How did you nail me?' Bennett struggled, the pangs of despair choking his throat. Liotine outlined the grim details which took a full fifteen minutes as Bennett drifted to some strange ghastly space as he stood decomposed from the litany of crippling facts and winced to maintain his balance, holding himself erect with both hands on the office desk. Liotine rose from his seat, slung an arm over his shoulder and tried to him calm him down as any friend might..

"Listen Howard, listen to me, you have to listen to me...look at me...and listen to me. I'm just a two bit undercover cop from Brooklyn New York. The only reason I'm here with you at this time and place is it was me who happened to come across a file in Kennedy airport which was used to bring in the paper you used for this job but that's not the only reason. Listen...please listen. You are just a regular guy, just like me, but a better person than me. I know that. I probably know more about you than you do about yourself at this stage. So, if ever I do a good deed in my miserable life, I am going to do it here and now, for you. These are the facts, and if ever you repeat me on a word of this my life and yours won't be worth living. You can put your life on everything I am about to tell you. Neither The United States nor anyone else have a case against you. The Special Branch here has no interest in you whatsoever and your Justice Department will not extradite you anywhere simply because they cannot. We have no case to give them. These are the cold facts. All of our agencies, including Justice, The State Department, The Secret Service, the FBI, the CIA and all the rest have gone through you with a fine tooth comb, but that does not mean they would not like to have you in the US. They will not rest until they get every iota of the facts concerning this forgery, and what you know how this money was used. If you can do that under your own protection everybody is happy. And if not, who the fuck knows what they are capable of. Don't ask me to expand on that as I don't have the answers. My orders are to stay with you twenty four seven; so, my good man, call your lawyer, work with me and I guarantee in so far as I can that all will be well. Talk to me"

Bennett raised his head and gazed-eyed and shell shocked to his imprisoner.

"I will try call my lawyer right now. I will do exactly as you say. Would it help if said you have my eternal gratitude. That's all I can manage right now" He picked up the receiver, spoke for five minutes and said to Liotine.

"Ok, I suggest that you come to my flat. I'm too nervous to sleep and I do not want to be alone. We can talk through the night. My lawyer will see us in the morning."

Leaving rugby the club, they drove in Bennett's rented car for some twenty minutes through the slushy streets of Dublin and retired to his tiny flat in Clontarf on the Dublin Northside seafront. Once inside, the Forger produced a copy of the 150 page statement, one of which he had deposited in his bank safety deposit box, and one with Brendan Geraghty.

Hour after hour, Bennett unfolded the incredible litany of fairytale facts detail by detail as the Detective referred to the chronology of events outlined in the statement. Bennett reiterated the story over and over again; replying to the Liotine's probing questions time after time with absolute consistency. As the kitchen clock struck 7 a.m., they both sat exhausted, sipping tea and smoking heavily; silent. For the countless time Liotine asked the same question.

"Are you sure you haven't left anything out... no matter how small... no matter how unimportant... think; be sure."

"I've told you over and over again... that's it ... that's the whole story... let's get some sleep. I'm exhausted." Twenty minutes later both men slept, Liotine on the couch.

It was an hour later that the Detective was awoken by an hysterical Bennett.

"Wha... what... ya remember somethin?'

"Yes, I do... how could I forget the bank account! The bloody bank account in Zurich... Zurich. They put five million Dollars in a bank account for me in Zurich, under the name Rodney Anthony Lewis ... giving me the access code numbers, everything!

"How much of it have you spent Howard?'

"Nothing at all. Not a bit of it. Never could....never will!

"You're bullshittin' me, right?'

"No. Allow me to tell you something. I would not know how to take the dust from a person's pockets. I never touched that money, never will, I swear to you Vito, not a penny, and I can prove it" The Cop sprang from the couch and placed both hands on the Forger's shoulders. "You know what that is?'

"And what is that, Vito?'

"What ya just told me... this bank account in Zurich... you know what that is?'

"What?'
"That's yer ace in the hole pal.....that's yer ace in the hole!

Chapter Fifty

Hours later, Fiona and Brendan Geraghty appeared in the rented meeting room of the Shelbourne Hotel, finding an unmoved Vito Liotine and an ashen faced stoical Howard Bennett. The Barrister conducted the informal introductions,

"Mr. Liotine, how do you do?' My name is Brendan Geraghty. I represent Mister Bennett. My sister, Fiona, my client's partner. Shall we proceed?'

"What a prick," the Detective mumbled to himself. Notions of a cordial meeting in the privacy of his hotel room quickly disappeared as the barrister babbled out the conditions of any meeting with the Americans, should any take place at all. A large folder was placed into the Detective's hands. Liotine flicked through the pages, which reminded him of a past case for the indictment of the Cosa Nostra in a major bearer bond fraud in which he was involved.

Without further courtesies, the Barrister opened the first page of his writing pad and directed his attention to an apparently unprepared Vito Liotine.

"Detective Liotine, or am I correct in addressing you as such, given the fact that my client has not been the subject of any notice by any person or authority as to the specific purpose of your contact with him raises the question as to the desired outcome of your visit here. With respect I am mystified why they sent a Detective in the N.Y.P.D to contact with my client, but I am certain there must be some very good reason. It is my duty to remind you that my clients contact with you is purely voluntary and in no way recognizes any authority you may purport to represent. Furthermore, it is my duty to tell you that it is my duty to defend and protect my client to the very best of my ability and to hold responsible any person, government or authority who aspires to trespass on his rights as reflected by the letter of the law. I have been briefed on the probable circumstances surrounding the reason of your visit and in that light I ask you to refer to the document I have given you. The contents of this document, which I appreciate you have not had the time to read, outlines the conditions upon which my client would be prepared to co-operate with your Secret Service or others for the single and only purpose of enlightening your Government as to a state of affairs which occurred in 1994. Having studied the document, the following will be clear to you and the interests you represent.

That my client shall at all times enjoy full freedom of movement, including that of any destination whatsoever; that he shall be prohibited from any discussion relative to this issue without my presence and that the use of any wiretaps or any other such devices shall not be used before, during, or at any time after his assistance in this matter;

That he shall not now, or at any time in the future be the subject of any proceedings whatsoever by the United States Government, its agents or successors, and shall at all times in the future be the subject of diplomatic protection by the Government of the Republic of Ireland.

"That the time and place of any such meeting shall be at the discretion of my client. For the moment a meeting on the United States territory of The American Embassy is ruled out"

When I am in receipt of this signed agreement from your appropriate authority, I will then be in a position to further negotiate the willingness of my client to assist the interested parties. It has have long anticipated the forgery would be uncovered, and given the entirely bizarre circumstances of my clients involvement, we have prepared a contingency for this very event. I will have all the papers prepared in the next day or two. If it is the intention of your superiors to proceed with extradition could I please be informed immediately. Unless you have something to add I feel there is little more to discuss at this point Detective.

The Detective laid both hands on the shiny mahogany table. He sunk into his chair, stretched his legs and crossed them. Playing with his thumbs, he eyed the Barrister intently, with a crooked, mocking grin. He flashed a flame to a Marlboro and began to speak through the cloud of rising cigarette smoke.

"Well Mr. Geraghty, I thank you for your frankness. This enables me to contact my superiors and let them know exactly the position. Until later then, Mr. Geraghty" without any attempt at a handshake. The barrister left closing the hardwood door softly.

Liotine rose from his seat addressing the Forger.

"Wanna show me around the town pal, and you, Miss Geraghty?" The warmness of the invitation startled Bennett. The Forger turned to Fiona Geraghty and she nodded in agreement. The snowflakes began to tumble outside as the crawling traffic slowed to stop start. The group sauntered past the crowded pubs and restaurants They spoke, gestured and huddled in a group under the Dublin sky, shivering in the swirling gust. There were arguments and speculation pauses and considerations, conclusions and questions, acute pessimism and fear, fairness and weighed optimism all conducted oblivious to Brendan Geraghty's laboured advice. By now, darkness had fallen on a celebrative Dublin as they conversed subdued having with difficulty found seating in a nearby pub. Those of the more observant patrons of the pub noticed the absence of any Christmas cheer. The conversation of the strange gathering was being conducted in an ambiance more accustomed to court corridors or the waiting rooms of city hospitals. Perhaps a family crisis; a tragedy.. The publican refrained from his usual courteous introduction to new faces. These were not new locals he decided, from the odd continuance of words which he inadvertently overheard at the sporadic rises in volume.

Outside, the faint knell of Christchurch's bell chimed midnight up along a black River Liffey, as the taxis seemed more prevalent in the sparse traffic. The group hailed a cab at 12:15 and adjourned to the quietness of the Liotine's hotel where the Forger for the following three hours went over the events of the crime for the countless time. It was agreed between the group at 4:25 pm that should Brendan Geraghty feel confident with the terms of co-operation, that the Forger would answer all questions put to him at as soon as possible. The Barrister's agreement was established by phone at 5:00pm, the only outstanding matter would the location for the meeting.

Two days later, the US Embassy courier stood in the foyer of Brendan Geraghty's chambers handing the bulky packet to the Barrister. For the following 6 hours he scanned the contents with the entire devil's advocacy with which the legal mind is trained. The overriding condition upon which the agreement rested lay in the absolute cast iron insistence that Bennett be one hundred per cent truthful within the entirety of answers; standard American plea bargain procedure; otherwise all bets were off which would give rise to the certainty that Bennett would be arrested, extradited and jailed without the possibility of bail. As the dusk of the evening lit the street lanterns and car headlights, he trooped round to the local office service and had five copies made of the draft. He then placed three copies into individual padded envelopes and marked each SUB JUDICE NOT FOR INSPECTION and inserted a handwritten letter signed Brendan Geraghty, BCL. LLM.

An hour later he broached the slippery steps of the Embassy. The Barrister handed the file to a yawning secretary who signed for the contents, which were placed in the diplomatic pouch for overnight delivery to Andrew Weiss, one to the Irish Embassy in Washington and one to remain in Dublin. Before returning to his apartment for 6 hours of thankful sleep, he called Parsons to discuss the proposed venue, and the Special Branch who had pre agreed to accompany the Bennett group. On awakening the final discharges of immunity arrived on the hour by diplomatic courier. The location for this crucial meeting would be the American ambassador's residence in the Phoenix Park, Dublin for 10am the following morning, December 25th, Christmas Day.

Chapter Fifty-One

THE SETTLEMENT

At 9 a.m., December 25, Christmas Day, the convoy headed up by the American team and followed by Bennett's group with the Irish Special Branch to the rear, passed through the entrance to the Irish American Ambassador's residence in the Phoenix Park, Dublin. A dusting of snow shrouded the deserted morning of Christmas, manifesting a divine silence as if everyone had capitulated in a common communion of forgiveness and peace. The residence, built in 1776 and preserved to a pin is one of the most beautifully appointed properties in the Ireland. On this Christmas Day the residence had only a skeleton staff of twenty four hour security, general maintenance, reception and kitchen. Fifteen minutes later the Forger was seated at the head of the period conference table, a position which might ordinarily give rise to a presumption of power, but so chosen on this occasion that the interviewee face his interviewers in concert. The rooms ambiance was pacified in subdued opulence, panelled walls in ochre knotted rosewood and matching conference table and sixteen chairs upholstered in a maroon Moroccan hide leather. A baroque clock tick-tocked atop the Connemara marble and brass Georgian fireplace. The group, serious and able men, each leafed through their departmental briefs. A tan cashmere overcoat betrayed Bennett's sagging shoulders; the wool polo sleeved the neck. The ashen cropped hair completed the sinister figure which the Winter sunshine quarantined at the head of the group. He brought no papers, pens, tape or video recorders or any such paraphernalia. His truthfulness and memory would suffice their needs.

The multiple telephone calls over the last 30 hours had drained him of any inclination to conversation or pleasantry. One hand rested on his arm, the loose hand tested the growth of his stubble. As he sat wistful, prepared he believed for the wrath of his tormentors, he juggled with his drifting thoughts as he eyed the expensive leather attaches, splendid sound activated recorders, laptop computers, mobile phones, beepers, beautifully bound yearbooks with a maze of all-purpose compartments and mathematical calculators fit for any rocket scientist. Bennett had always harboured a heartfelt empathy for Americans in their desperation for self-image. An interesting observation thought Bennett, for a country which has trampled roughshod from barbarism straight to decadence without the actuality of any form of culture.

Neither time nor expense especially in times of war means anything to the US military which is why bankers, arms manufacturers and associated interests perpetuate armed conflict. Parsons had the previous evening convened a 5 hour troubleshoot briefing with his group which continued at five am this, the morning of the Bennett showdown. With the blessing of his superiors, over and over again he sandblasted his listeners with directions that this Mr. Bennett was to be treated as a friend, because, he explained that at this juncture this was the only friend the US military had on the mystery of these missing Stingers. The myriad of 'intense' interrogations immediately and after the firing of the only Stinger in the north turned up blank the conclusion being that nobody actually knew anything about the entire inexplicable enigma. Parsons, a CIA intelligence officer of some thirty years with involvement in many of the events of that period reasoned that the one and only known missing key lay in the identity of the fourth person who attended the initial 'Bennett Kidnap' meeting in the UK. Mr. Bennett was to be treated with formal protocol and a code of behaviour that would give the interrogation the best chance of some success. This mystery of missing Stingers was a sleeping mole that could become a raging monster if in the wrong hands and that meant everyone except the US military. Parsons drilled his group through unrelenting militaristic repetition to unswerving obedience and nobody as much as whispered as one word. Weiss was to conduct all the questioning to give the accused the false impression that the case was 'forgery' focussed. Parsons CIA would join in where appropriate.

The meeting opened with Stan Weiss who stood with the rest and approached the seated forger and offered his handshake saying, Hi Howard, I am Stan Weiss., New York office Secret Service, you coming here today is much appreciated, give us all the help you can! The remainder followed in much the same format. Parsons being the last described himself as military intelligence. No mention of the CIA. Formalities dispensed with Weiss spoke strictly guided by his prepared Parsons brief.

"Howard, you are here presently under protection from arrest from the agreement between you and the government of the United States of America. It is critical you be truthful with us for your sake and ours otherwise as you must know your current agreement may be null and void. We already know the main conspirators involved in this forgery: the IRA; in the persons of Colm McNiff, Niall O'Toole and Sean McCahan, all of whom are now deceased. I would ask you to bear in mind our prime objective is establish how the crime was done, to verify the extent of the forgery and the whereabouts of the cash if possible. Going forward, we need to know your whereabouts now and in the future. Which brings me to the first issue that we must resolve?' Who was the other person, the person who was present in that room on the night of your abduction?' The person you mentioned on page twenty six of the statement provided us by Detective Liotine?'

A: "I don't know - he did not speak, nor was he spoken to. I never saw him again, nor would I recognize him if I did."

Q. Are you quite certain of that statement?'

A. I am putting my life on it!

Q: "Can you recall the man who drove you, McNiff and Murphy to North Dublin to set up the Thai connection?'

A: "Yes. But I know nothing about him"

Q: "Is this the man?' An 8 by 11 black and white photo slid across the table.

A: "Yes."

Q. "Did Fiona Geraghty, know of this forgery?"

A. " No. I never spoke to her of it and she did not ask."

Q. "Was she aware of your circumstances in Spain?'

A. "She told me when I first met her she was somewhat aware of what happened in Spain. I do not know how much she knew to this day"

Q. "And you reiterate that at no time was she aware of the occurrence of the Bennett Forgery?' It was the first time that the phrase had been used.

A. "At no time Sir, I was terrified even to think about it, never mind speak of it"

Q. "You must remember this man?' Another 8 x 12 black and white photo was slid to the Forger.

A. "I'll never forget him." It was the ghostly mask of Chan Wong.

A. "I am able to let you know The Kingdom of Thailand have arrested and extradited him to us. We will be 'speaking' with him very soon. We expect to be able to inspect the paper mill and make the appropriate arrests. You are probably wondering how we got to him. Very simple, your Mr. Murphy was busted on a dealing charge while on probation, so he copped a deal with the Irish drug Squad. Both his brother in London and Chan Wong in Bangkok were busted. He in turn gave up the mill in an attempt to plea bargain. He would definitely have been able to bribe his way to freedom but for the fact that the Thai Authorities were warned that The United States wanted him so that was the end of that. He will never be a free man again"

Q. "Can you direct us to the mansion you mentioned where the notes were transferred and counted?'

A. "No Sir, I was in a blacked out van anytime I travelled anywhere and all travelling time varied greatly. I was told this was to prevent me from guessing any measure of distance or driving time to any given destination. Looking back I might mention that at all time when I might be in any potential position of security exposure, such circumstances were simply one hundred per cent neutralised. In the printing factory, or better described as two rooms there was not as much as one minute scintilla of evidence to which I could later refer when the job would be bust"

Q. "And you state that you did not at any time visit the paper mill yourself?'

A. "Absolutely not!'

Q. "How was the paper analysis procured?'

A. "The analysis was provided by some lab and given to me by Mr. McNiff. The bottom of the page had quite a few internationally recognized approval agencies, although the heading had been removed. This was a normal paper specification just the same as any other. The specification was destroyed. Anyone can have paper analysed anyway.

Q. "Can you identify these two men?'

A. "This is Mister Peter Harris and this is Jean-Claude Fernandez. So there is a God after all," the Forger mumbled. Where are they now may I ask?'

A. "There were so many cases with American citizens who were conned by this pair. Both were indicted in New York, extradited and currently on remand without bail. The investigation is quite complex and on-going. Very well Howard, these are just some very basic prelim questions. We have reams of stuff we need to go through. We are asking that you make yourself available to technicians from our technical people who wish to question you about the technical stuff, will you do that for us?'

Bennett nodded on instruction from Geraghty.

Out of nowhere the FBI agent intervened unable to hold his silence.

Q. "What payment did you negotiate for yourself?'

A. "I did not negotiate any payment. Before the job even began I was given twenty thousand pounds. Mr. McNiff said it was for the loss I incurred in Spain. I refused it but he insisted. As I had lost my house and felt so guilty about the pain and damage I had caused my wife I gave most of this to her in small sums. I told her I was working. I would ask you do not to involve her." Weiss resumed.

Q. "There is no reason for us to contact her. About your payment, do you really expect us to believe that?'

A. Yes, you can believe it and I can prove it. At the time of my very last few minutes with Mr. McNiff and the others I was handed a note with Swiss bank account details. The amount on deposit was, and I suppose is now, as we speak five million dollars. I never touched it. All of this information with the account details are in my statement I gave to Detective Liotine, actually it is a relief to have someone to give it to"

Q. "Are you sure it was in the statement?'

A. "Of course, Detective Liotine will tell you himself"

Artic silence. The room turned to the Detective, marooned for a reply but left the question hanging. Liotine knew that Weiss had just lied in his teeth and this was not the forum to call him a liar. There was no other way to put it. Weiss moved immediately to the next question.

Q. "At any time did you ever feel that you could have approached law enforcement?'

A. "No. That would have been a death warrant insofar as it would be imperative I be removed. I would have left them with no choice"

Q. "Were you beaten, or anything like that?'

A. "With the exception of my abduction and the threat to my life, absolutely not. And that is what really terrified me. I knew not the day, nor the hour"

Q. "How will they know that you have not given them up?'

A. "My instincts tell me that, now as I speak, as far as they are concerned and given the progress on the peace agreement, the object of the exercise is largely fulfilled. But one must bear in mind that they may still be in control of an awesome amount of money. Any terror perpetrated on me at this stage would be purely counterproductive. They knew as well as I did, that the job would be bust sooner or later and I am sure they must have made contingencies for that eventuality. The whereabouts of that money lies with somebody in the leadership; and I can tell you under pain of death - they will never give that up"

A. Yes indeed. We believe if we had the identity of the unidentified person at that first meeting this case would be closed"

Q. "Did you ever know that it was their intention to buy surface to air missile units?'

A. "No Sir. It was never mentioned to me. The people I was in contact with were of a high mental discipline. On looking back, and observing the continuity of events, there was not one occasion that there was the remotest of attempts to confide anything in me. You can keep pressing me and asking these same questions over and over again and that's OK. I understand that you have to do that. You will get the same answers if we are here until doomsday, because gentlemen, I have nothing to hide, absolutely nothing. I am done with this world that others must suffer and endure, including each one of you in this room. I am done, and do you know it's so fucked up, the futility of trying to change it is naive, puerile and thankless, and even if I could, I see no value in it any more. In so many ways I am a far more emancipated person that any of you gentlemen because, here and now, there is not one thought or deed within my person that is restrained. The opposite is true of you, gentlemen, think about it. Yours is a Sisyphus existence like this whole damn world of 'master and slave'. So please, do what you need to do, ask and keep asking any question you wish, tick the boxes, write the reports and then let the dice fall where they may; more than that I cannot tell you"

The darting flashes traded round the table at the ridicule of the forger's ribald impasse. A ray of Winters sunlight projected again over the forgers shoulders, forming an austere Messiah like figure at the head of the table. The rising smoke from his cigarette swirled upward and through the prism of light, the side of the blonde grey hairline glossed to chrome ochre.

Q. "Are you willing to swear that the forgery was for no more than the three to five hundred million?'

A. "I will swear to it and I will prove it Sir."

Q. "How?"

A. "Quantify the paper on the import documents and do some simple calculations."

Q. "I presume you have been made aware of the consequences of lying to us. If we find just one lie then all deals are off. Has that been made clear to you "

A. "Well, yes, but I don't need to lie. If the answer is there it is yours. For me there is no value in conceit, restrain or evasion; not to me anyway"

Q. "Are you willing to take a polygraph?'

A. "With pleasure"

The Diplomat and Geraghty objected in concert. "We will not allow it!

"The reason?"

"It would be a voluntary unreliable exercise capable of jeopardising my clients statement" Geraghty objected, shaking his head in disbelief and continuing.

"Sir, you are the applicants in this request. Let me make my position very clear lest there be any doubt about it in any quarter. It is my duty to protect Mister Bennett under the arrangement we have with the US. Let me be frank; if anything, this is a criminal matter. Mister Bennett is not guilty of any crime on Irish soil, on the soil of Great Britain and in specific legal terms, the soil of the USA, given the inarguable fact of the absence of "intent" in his actions. The USA may well try to demonstrate a degree of culpability by not opting to risk to his life and come to you, but to bring to home a successful extradition application is out of the question and everybody in this room knows that. Weiss moved to cool the mounting adversarial atmosphere

"I think that we can work something out Mister Geraghty, Your client may well have inadvertently omitted some small detail and if he did, no matter how minor, it may come back to haunt us; we really do want to close out this case. We do not doubt your clients honesty, it is just the polygraph would copper fasten things and allow us to move on"

"Gentlemen, it seems you do not understand that Mr. Bennett has a case against the British Government itself under criminal compensation, and I am not, I can assure you, using this 'fact' to sour this so called 'Special Relationship' you have with the British. Any advance of my client's compensation case will settle in his favour but will also guarantee his arrest and detention not in criminal proceedings but anti-terrorism legislation because of his closeness to the IRA regardless of the nature of that occurrence. I can say that our trust is with you; not with the British. You have demonstrated here today a determination to come to an equitable solution. What happens between these walls must never go beyond these walls. We are all to a man signed up on that" I suggest we break for lunch now before we get bogged down. We will come back with a decision on the polygraph"

The Bennett group, with the aid if the kitchen porter looted the residence's sprawling well stocked kitchen.

The door to the rear of the kitchen would open now and again, extinguishing a blast of Dublin's winter wind. It reminded Bennett of the first days of his abduction when he gazed in numbness at the international rugby match at Dublin's Landsdowne Road. The forger lurched over the table, pushing the plates and shakers to the side. "I'm taking the polygraph. I don't want any arguments from anybody. I am beginning to wonder if even you people believe me. I can say it until the cows come home, "I do not have as much as one scintilla of fact to hide from anybody including that Swiss account, which as you said the other evening, addressing Liotine, is my ace in the hole. Wild horses won't stop me from taking that polygraph"

Bennett appeared from the poly room two hours later, calm, re-assured. The result of 'truthfulness' came in just a few minutes later.

The meeting resumed. Weiss spoke first.

"Well Mr. Bennett, we see no reason to hold you any longer. Before I say this temporary farewell we must be kept informed at all times of your whereabouts so we ask you to call the US embassy each and every week, just a phone call, that's all. Reception will expect your weekly check in. As I said you will need to make yourself available to the lab people for the technical details. You also will need to sign off on our arrangements with Mr. O'Carthy and Barrister Geraghty. My driver will take you wherever you want to go. Are we done for now?' The group rose, the farewells and handshakes as cordial as the introduction.

"Yes Sir, we're done for now" and without another word Bennett, accompanied by Liotine walked to freedom with the US Embassy's driver followed by the special branch; destination: Fiona Geraghty's flat, Merrion Square.

Chapter Fifty Two

"How you feeling, pal?' Liotine asked his 'forger buddy' the following midday as they sat on a park bench in St. Stephen's Green. A light drizzle peppered the lake and foliage as the paddling of ducks skirted the water's edge. Bennett paused before making his response. "You know Vito, the truth is, I don't know how I feel. I can only tell you that I know that somewhere within my mountain of debris at this moment there is thankfulness beyond words, but I can't touch it yet. Do you know what I mean, Vito?'

Liotine nodded. "Yeah, Dusty, I think I know what you mean. It's kinda like me when I'm studying this fuckin' pony for a whole year and there's so much investment gone into it, that when the sonavabitch finally romps home it don't mean hardly nuthin"

Bennett smiled at the street simplicity. "Indeed sort of like that. Can I buy you a drink and a bite to eat before you fly out?'

Liotine rubbed his hands. "Now you're talking my language. Let's get outta 'ere!

The two went to Judge Roy Bean's on Nassau Street, a spit's distance to the foot of Grafton Street. Bennett decided to take his liberator to a place with an American Tex-Mex motif and menu. They drank at the bar for a while, then asked to be seated at a quiet table. Over bowls of chilli con carne, tortilla chips and salsa, the forger ventured. "You know what's been on my mind; did you tell Weiss about the bank account in Zurich Vito?'

"Sure, I told him, it is on my report which by the way he now has, did you tell Geraghty?' Liotine asked.

"Absolutely, clear as day, although he may have said nothing in anticipation of using 'my not touching it' as a last ditch tool. These barristers always keep the best until last, poker nosed fuckers, but they have their reasons"

A new linear of age cracked Liotine's forehead.

"Then the account was a kept secret by Weiss until you disclosed it at the meeting in front of everybody, can you believe it. But it was the FBI guy who blew the door open when he asked the question about your cut, not Weiss. It was in my report, so that means that Weiss could have omitted the detail to his boss, which means he can deny I told him about it, the fucker. My report which went direct to Weiss will soon be buried in storage somewhere" Bennett drifted to another place; indifferent.

Look this is a great day, so let's enjoy it, no more serious stuff. You know what I'm gonna do?' I'm handing in my retirement papers when I get back. I don't wanna do it no more. I'm sick and tired of all of it. You know Howard, it's only now I realize here and now, talking to you; since I got back from The Nam, I can count the days on my two hands that I didn't have a gun on me. What kinda life is that?' I gave it all up for this great big lie, to faceless people who own the planet, and now I just want to live the simple life, my simple life. I wanna be back when I was twelve or thirteen. Ever since I was a kid I loved horses. I tried out for the jockey school up in Saratoga when I was just thirteen, and you know Howard I woulda made it too, but my old man found outta bout it and put a stop to it. Sometimes, I think if kids were left to their own devices before this world gets a hold of 'em, things would be a hell of lot better for a lot of em. I'm wanna become an authority on race horses the world over. I'm gonna come to your country to see Cheltenham, back over here then to Ireland, then over to France for the Prix de L'Arc. So help me God, I'm gonna do it every year. I can get a security part time job out at Aqueduct; I got plenty of contacts out there. I'll come see you, if that's okay, and we can shoot the breeze."

Bennett could envision the Detective's dreams unravel as he observed the exited anticipation in dancing eyes. "It's time. We need to leave if you're to make your flight."

"How about you, what do you plan doing with all of this new life you have?'

"Vito, I need to heal, and I have the best help in this world. I have closed the door on all things in my past unworthy of the present. I will stay away from thoughts, people, places and things that can damage me. I will take each day, and be able to say, this day belongs to me. I am eternally humble and thankful for something very special that has come my way. Only now do I know the value of the smallest things, so let's take it one day at one time, you and I both. Please, do not loose touch with me- that would be a disappointment to me"

Forger and Detective made their goodbyes in Dublin Airport before the point of no re-entry; the Detective resisting against his will to machismo the farewell. Liotine spent the flight dwelling on Weiss's five million dollar lie, and began to tease out the nuts and bolts of how Weiss might position himself to get at that money. To shed some light on the probabilities upon which his scheme would ultimately depend, the representatives at that meeting, their specific briefs, and their parameters needed to be clearly defined. The Secret Service, in the person of Weiss was there to unearth the technical mechanics and extent of the forgery itself, full stop. The CIA was there to locate where and to whom Stinger missiles were sold to under their noses, full stop. The FBI's inclusion was on dubious grounds and entirely contingent on a successful indictment in the US, which was not now going to happen. Would the FBI guy follow up Weiss's omission? Probably not because he would assume Weiss himself being Secret Service, and the CIA would clear it up. Besides the case was now closed. There was no way one standalone FBI agent was going to buck or question the CIA who would definitely first check if the account actually existed, but in doing so they would be forced to reveal to the Swiss who they are and that in itself would open a legal can of worms which could go on for years even if Bennett was persuaded to testify in proxy. Nobody knew this more than the CIA. Any US government agency would need to declare its identity whereas any individual with the access codes could loot that account within a few minutes on a keyboard. Liotine knew that Weiss, having spent much of his career chasing hot money would be fully aware of this and on that reasoning took the well calculated plunge of silence. Weiss was the only hard copy connection to the directors of the other agencies. Everything that was agreed, acted upon, written, signed and so on was first presented to Weiss who then, for reasons of efficiency compiled everything into 'his' one overall report, minus mention of the Swiss account. All other 'hard' testimony was then subjected to the position of 'back up'. His 'all embracing' report would be scanned, and not necessarily read as the case was stamped CLOSED. Even the fact that Bennett quite innocently let the cat out of the bag on the FBI agent's 'bushwhacker' question in front of the roomful of different agencies would not mean anything, simply because other than the CIA they were in no position individually to either question, or demand to inspect Weiss's report. Another consideration was, 'they' did not have any recorded or signed written statement directly from Bennett, and to take the leap of faith in exposing the forgers remark might, in their minds be plunging them into unknown. Besides, these people were bottom feeders, and their explanations would be rock solid in the fact that the issue was not strictly within their individual briefs. Weiss knew there was absolutely no way any of the group would break rank with their individual briefs. Just consider the pre nine eleven attack, which took twice as many lives as Pearl Harbour and would, and should have been stopped but for the astonishing inertia between the NSA, CIA and the FBI. Many authors have concluded that the reasoning for this security policy lay in the potential for leaks. It was only after nine eleven that George Bush signed a secret executive order compelling the NSA to share its information with the other agencies. Believing, against his better judgement, for that moment there could be an outside chance 'the slip' could have been an oversight, the Detective had opted to stay silent when Weiss lied in his teeth placing doubt on the cold fact that he had told him in detail about the existence of that account

352

and the amount of money allegedly on deposit. The silence in the room rescued Weiss momentarily, but Liotine being trained at scoping out a liar after a lifetime on the streets, knew damn well what was going down, pinning Weiss's coy evasive demeanour and watery smiles he could not hide, at least not from Liotine. On reflection, the circumstances of the moment, the pieces on the board, the undeniable possibility of success and the vast amount of money proved too tantalising for Weiss, who clearly had decided to test the water The Detective knew there were one hundred ways for Weiss to get at that money, without leaving as much as a shred of evidence. After all, Weiss knew it was on the polygraph recording, which would at worst, the case now closed, be stored away for decades. A solved forgery of a paltry 500 million is just 'street crime material' and would never get anywhere near becoming an issue for mention within the Military, the CIA or the NSC. The sale of Stinger missiles to persons unknown is another matter entirely. As the polygraph result was 'truthful' and even if sometime in the future, Weiss was called to give some explanation, within the four corners of any question he would be one hundred per cent covered. He would blame the IRA if the account had been looted, the reason being the IRA dashed for the cash when they learned of the Bennett bust. As things stood, after all the arrests and fruitless interrogations, the identity of the schoolteacher still remained 'The Mystery' and he was the only person who had the account details other than Liotine, Bennett, and now Weiss. The spearhead of the case had now moved from the forgery itself to the absolutely crucial issue of the identity of who had gotten possession of 'Stinger' missiles, and how many, which in the wrong hands could account for unthinkable, unspeakable earth-shaking destruction. All Weiss would need would be a few weeks at most to come up with a strategy and cover his tracks. Once that account remained open the cash was there for the taking. The Detective decided Weiss would never see a dime of that money and he would first take the matter to his boss, who would take the matter further probably resulting in an expansive and costly sting operation. But these things take time and there was every possibility the funds to mount such an operation may be denied as the case was closed. At the very least he would make all the facts known to The Secret Service and the FBI. All they would need to do was to keep an eye on Mr. Weiss. It was better he did not mention this to Bennett as it would just complicate his friend's life even further. The Detective, since infancy had held steadfast to his Theory of The Same Great Lie, and this little editing of the truth came as no surprise to him whatsoever. 'To think that pink faced prick would make a liar of me in front of everybody at that meeting is not going to go unpunished" The episode compounded the undeniable fact that the higher up the chain of power or command in any given system, political or otherwise, the more outrageous the lies, the more successful the cover ups and the more contemptible the absolute disregard for human life. The Detective addressed himself. 'I need some crack in the wall, some space, where I can get to fuck away from all this shit, but not until I deal with this fucker, and deal with him I will'

Once landed at Kennedy Airport, he stepped briskly across the arrivals terminal and noticed an arrest being made on a line which had passed through customs from the Dominican Republic. Usually, the Detective would have pulled his badge and involved himself in the foray to chalk up 'the collar'. Bennett's words occurred to him. 'There's no value in it'

"Couldn't care less what's goin' on," he jabbered to himself and bellied out the automatic doors to the taxi stand. Like so many others who touched on this sordid tale, he was just one more pawn whose life would be changed forever.

THE END

P 303 ASKEW
P 123 BARCLAYS BANK